Sinful Mate

A Friends to Lovers Alien Romance

Trish Heinrich

Contents

Author's Note

Star Trek, and to some degree, science fiction in general, has been one of my great fictional loves since I was little. There were so many awe inspiring adventures among those stars. Not just for the crew of the Enterprise, but for the Rebel Alliance in Star Wars, for the rag tag group aboard Moya on Farscape, the Doctor in his Tardis, and the always one moment away from disaster crew of Firefly. More than any other genre, sci-fi has captured my imagination, it has moved me to tears, to cheer, to cringe, to gasp. It has excited my creativity, and made me forever love space.

And for as long as I've loved sci-fi, I've also loved romance.

As I got older I heard from many different places how girls weren't real sci-fi fans, especially if they liked kissing in their stories. I began to feel alienated from the genre that had meant so much to me and stopped 'fangirling' about it.

Recently, a very good friend asked me where in the world had I absorbed or heard this lesson? He's always been a supporter and outspoken advocate for women in all levels of art and fandom, and I have always felt supported by him. But he's also a man, and as such, being a fan of sci-fi, the lessons that he heard and gleaned were not the same as the ones that I'd heard and gleaned. If he were to comment on a romantic relationship in a sci-fi narrative, it would've been seen as okay because he's a guy and therefore his main motivation for being a part of the sci-fi fandom wasn't the kissing stuff (totally not true, btw, but still a preconceived notion.)

But being a woman, if I commented on liking a romantic aspect, or lamented its destruction, my fandom is suspect. Because obviously the only reason a girl would be in the sci-fi fandom was because she wanted all the characters to kiss (also not true). The fandom around Reylo is a great example of this. Putting aside whether you love or hate it, the women who are all in for that ship get TONS of hate from toxic fanboys who call their love of Star Wars into question simply because that romance captured their imagination. They have to be either a fan of the sci-fi or a fan of the romance, but they can't be both.

Well, that's bullshit.

If you can relate to this, it's time to reclaim our fandom, ladies. You can write hard core Spock-Chapel erotica on AO3 and still be the nerd who has memorized the schematics of the warp core for the original Enterprise (or in my case, every actor who has ever played the Doctor in the order in which they appeared, while also shipping Ten and Rose - fight me if you dare!)

Sci-Fi can be all about the military aspects. It can be exploration. It can be dark and grim. And it can be smutty as fuck.

Hell, it can be all of these at the same time, if we want it to be.

And just because I like smut in my sci-fi doesn't make me any less of a fan than anyone else. It took me a long time to accept and own that. Honestly, one of the things that helped was discovering the delicious, out of this world genre of SCI-FI ROMANCE!

When I found out nerdy authors were writing smutty sci-fi, I snatched up Ruby Dixons IPB faster than you can say 'nerfherder' and loved it. I went in search of more, but quickly became frustrated that so many were very light on the sci-fi aspect. Don't get me wrong, I love a good alien warrior saves the girl from slavers as much as the next girl. But I also longed for a book that had shades of Star Trek, Farscape or Firefly in there. I wanted some good old fashioned sci-fi in my Sci-Fi Romance and I wasn't finding much that fit the bill.

That was when I wondered if I should just follow Toni Morrison's advice and write the book I wanted to read.

And here's where the specter of my past rears its ugly head.

I'm not sure exactly where it came from, probably many different moments over many different years, but I had convinced myself I was not talented enough to create a sci-fi universe. I was, in fact, terrified to try writing sci-fi romance because I just wasn't sure I could pull off the kind of sci-fi that I loved and I didn't want to fail.

My husband and my best friends all told me that I could do it. They all believed in me. And, after realizing that this book was living in me so strongly that it was basically starting to over shadow every other project I was trying to write, I decided to take the plunge.

But unraveling years of imposter syndrome is not a straight line.

This has been both the most fulfilling book for me to write and, hands down, the most difficult

Fulfilling because writing it was like coming home to the genre that first captivated my imagination as a child. The one that will always be my first love. I feel that this is the genre I was always meant to write in, the one that I have been headed toward since I first published in 2016. It just took me a long time to get here.

And it was difficult for all the reasons that it was fulfilling. I put a massive amount of pressure on myself to 'get it right'. I can't remember a character giving me so much joy and so much trouble as Kier'Ahn did in this book. Of course, part of that might be that he's inspired from Spock, one of my earliest childhood crushes and, again, I put too much pressure on myself to do my love of Spock justice.

In any case, this book is in your hands now and I hope that if you're a sci-fi fan, like I am, you are swept away by that part of the book as much as the romance part. And if sci-fi is new to you, and you only picked this up because you saw it had hand necklaces and knotting (totally legit) I hope you discover something new to love right alongside the naughty.

There's room for all of us in this genre, no matter the sci-fi to kissing ratio you enjoy, and I hope I've found a good balance for as many of us as possible.

Live long and prosper and stay shiny while you're doing it!

For all my fellow Strange New Worlds Spock-Chapel shippers,
This one is for us.

Synopsis

"I wanted more. More of her blood. More of her thoughts. More of her touches that set me aflame. More of her flesh under my hands."

KIER'AHN

I have never touched anyone with desire, nor given in to the pleasures of the flesh. I am, Atavarian after all, and we cage such primal urges with logic, discipline. With one innocent brush of skin, I am overcome by a deadly rutting fever. Only Chloe can sate this burning hunger and save my life.

But when the fever passes I am not free. Instead, I am left with an insatiable craving for this fragile human and a telepathic bond that I am loathe to give up.

When a mission requires us to remain linked and pretend to be mates, our ever growing passion tempts me with something I never thought I would have: Love.

Sinful Mate is a full length Sci-Fi Romance novel with an HEA and no cheating. It features a smart, sunny human FMC, a brooding, virginal alien MMC, biting, knotting, hand necklaces, size difference, space battles, and alien societies. If you ever yearned for "Star Trek but make it SPICY" this is the series for you. It can be read as a standalone. CW's available on the authors website.

Alien Species Quick Guide

A TAVARIAN

The species that initiated first contact with Humans, Atavarians are between eight and seven feet tall with two sets of horns at their hairline and varying shades of red skin. They also have black eyes and sharp incisors that they once used to drink blood from those they conquered and subjugated. They are a touch telepathy species, able to form strong mental bonds with others. Approximately a thousand years prior, they had a cultural revolution sparked by those they now call Enlightened Ones. This caused the once blood thirsty species to reject their extremely strong emotional and primal urges in favor of logic. Strict control of emotions and their touch telepathy has formed a culture that is known for their wisdom and diplomatic skills. They are essentially vegan, consuming synthetic blood and shunning any food sourced from a living creature.

ZORESTRAN

Known as a jovial and lusty species, Zorestrans are characterized by their very tall, blue skinned bodies, white hair and large horns of varying length, curvature and color ranging from light brown to charcoal gray. They are a fairly recent addition to the Galactic Union within the last sixty years but very quickly inserted themselves into every tier of the government and the Galactic

Exploration Corps. They put a great emphasis on family and ancestor worship and have a deep spiritual connection to their home world, Zores. Mixed species marriages are welcomed and even encouraged as long as the traditions of Zores are maintained and passed on.

TALOSIAN

Tradition, love of empire, and loyalty are hallmarks of this species that prides itself on the beauty of their planet and technology. Ruled by a very old dynasty that is matrilineal, Talosians are also much taller than humans, some reaching nearly nine feet tall. They have golden skin that is accented with bronze colored scaling that runs over their backs, arms, shoulders and up the sides of their faces. One of the earliest aliens to join the Galactic Union, they are also a very proud species that has a history of conquest. They are also a strongly polyamorous society. In one family unit there can be up to eight committed adults at any given time.

BOETHELIANS

Refugees of a home world decimated by the ruthless K'Tavi, the few surviving Boethelians have preferred refugee status in the Galactic Union and are protected as citizens. Their height ranges from five feet to a towering eight feet, their skin is dark green with white hair. Those that were part of their religious orders have gold tattooing on different parts of their bodies. They were a primarily peaceful species that kept to themselves, worshiping a Triune Goddess named Amouna and her consort Tamryn.

SEAHDOHN

A very new species to the Galactic Union, Seahdohn's resemble very long, hairless ferrets that live on a planet that is not habitable to most other species. The Seahdohn are a completely telepathic species that require a host to survive off their home world. They attach to the spinal column of most sentient species, or the part of the body that is most amenable to the electric impulses that the Seahdohn gives off. They can grow or shrink to fit nearly any sized host. The relationship is symbiotic, with the Seahdohn seeing and experiencing everything that its host does, while the host receives faster reflexes, and cognitive reaction time. In addition, if the host is injured they are healed at a faster rate. This includes the ability to give functionality of limbs back to those who previously lost them. They have a trade agreement with the Galactic Union but are not charter members.

K'TAVI

Not much is known about the K'Tavi. They have mostly raided and conquered planets outside of the borders of the Galactic Union and have thus created a reputation as a violent and frightful species. They either enslave or destroy those species whose planets they conquer, stripping the planet of resources before moving on. It is unknown whether or not they have a home world.

VALTOSHAN

Valtoshans are not widely seen in the Gex-Corps, and most are trained as ships counselors or scientists. Their skin is pale, with dark gray markings along the collarbone, sides of the throat and along the top of shoulders, as well as the outside of the legs along the hips and up the side of the body ending under the arms. They have half a dozen or so very sensitive tendrils that extend from their skulls. Females have more tendrils than males. They are of a similar height to humans. Highly empathetic, this species is a more secretive culture that does not welcome many outsiders to it's central planet, Valstosh, though the pleasure moon, Lerav, is open to all. Valtoshans worship the Many Faced Goddess; a deity that rules all aspects of their lives, in particular the erotic. Valtoshans believe that sex can be transformative and a form of worship, and there are seven sacred pleasure houses on the moon of Lerav. Courtesans are trained for many years before becoming priests and priestesses and serving in the houses. The ceremonies and training is a closely held secret. Most families give one or more children to the houses to be raised and trained when they come of age, though the final decision to join a house is left up to the initiate.

Chapter One

KIER'AHN-TWO YEARS AGO.

I was surrounded.

Not by the enemy.

At least, not technically.

These were my new crewmates on the star ship Intrepid, the flagship of the Galactic Union of Planets, or GUP as most called it.

But this was also a cocktail party.

And everyone was engaging in 'small talk'. I loathed 'small talk'.

The Command crew was gathered with all the new recruits in Captain Antony Drake's quarters, which I assumed was usually quite spacious when it was not filled with bodies. There was a large bar area behind me that most were making liberal use of, which meant that the volume in the room was rising as more inhibitions were lost from alcohol consumption. A variety of foods from many planets were spread out in the kitchen area of the captain's quarters, many of which had been prepared by Drake himself, which impressed me. The lights were low but not dim enough to give me a proper view of the stars out the large windows to my right. Music filtered in from the computer, an old Earth jazz recording if I was hearing it correctly. Which was difficult with the loud chatter around me.

I was the only Atavarian on the ship, and I was not a full blooded one. Being half Human seemed to give some the impression that I would be interested in the latest sports team or Human celebrity gossip. The truth was, I was far more Atavarian than Human, having only set foot on the Earth to study at the Academy three years prior to being sent here. I arrived on the Intrepid only yesterday and had settled into my new quarters, but how to relate to the three crew mates in front of me was something no amount of study could have prepared me for.

"So that's when I said 'Come on baby, it's a Zorestran thing'," said a male by the name of Lt. Jax Vabaris.

The two others around me chuckled, slapping him on the back and I realized that I had missed the set up to his story, and was therefore incapable of understanding the final anecdote. Not that I would have understood it, even if I had heard the story in its entirety.

"So what about you?" he turned his purple eyes to me. "You get much action at the Academy? Atavarians are pretty rare there these days. I bet you had to beat them off with a stick, huh?"

There were several ways I could respond.

I could tell Lt. Vabaris that I was not interested in sexual interactions with any species and had gone to the Academy to study.

I could say that exoticising a species was insulting, as he should know since most people assumed that Zorestrans were a sex crazed species due to the fact that they had an increased libido.

Or, I could tease him in a way that would put him off and, hopefully, give me a reprieve from his inane stories.

I arched an eyebrow.

"I fail to see how hitting a potential lover with a weapon would be a good response to unwanted sexual advances," I replied.

He gave me a weak chuckle while his friends, a golden skinned Talosian non-binary person and a short Human woman, began to frown at me in confusion.

"It's an expression," Jax explained. "It means that you had a lot of interest, ya know, for..."

He twirled his hand slowly, trying to convey his meaning without using the word, which I found odd since he had no trouble using it, and several euphemisms, for sex earlier.

Even though I knew what he was trying to get at, I simply stared at him.

"You do know what I mean right?" he asked.

Now his smile faded as his blue skin darkened in embarrassment.

Perhaps it was beneath me to do this, and a more direct approach would engender friendship later. But I had been here an hour, pressed around bodies that thought nothing of touching me, though the contact was uncomfortable, and surrounded by chatter that now had resulted in a dull throb starting at the back of my eyes. More than one person had asked after my mixed species parentage, as if it were a source of study and curiosity, not my private business. And now I was, quite literally, cornered by these three who did not understand when someone did not want to take part in a conversation about sexual exploits.

Or reveal accidentally that they'd never had such experiences.

I knew enough about people, like the three in front of me, to know that they would find it amusing in a way that would make me the butt of their joking and teasing for quite some time.

"Perhaps an explanation would be helpful. Please, elucidate," I responded and stifled a smile when Jax became visibly uncomfortable.

"You know what?" the Human woman said with a forced cheer. "I think I see Commander Sonta over there and I haven't introduced myself. See you all around."

"I'll join her," the Talosian named Roarke said.

"It was...interesting talking to you," Jax said. "See you around, Kier'Ahn."

I inclined my head and breathed a sigh of relief that they had at last departed.

The drink in my hand had become warm over the course of the hour, not that it mattered. I had mostly held it to blend as much as possible, not that it helped. Even though I was half Human, I still had the domineering height of an Atavarian and, as such, was taller than most of my crewmates, with the exception of the Talosians, who were also quite tall and broad. I wondered how they would react to me if there were no physical signs that I was not fully Atavarian. If my eyes were completely black instead of green like my mother's, or if I had straight hair instead of wavy curls. If the set of double horns along my hairline were longer instead of short. At least my skin was the dark red of my father's house, and my strength was on par with most other Atavarians, even if the rest of me was not acceptable.

But this kind of thinking was childish, and never resulted in anything but feeling bad about myself. It was a waste of energy and I could ill afford such a thing on my very first assignment. I would have to find a way to handle being an anomaly here as I had been my entire life. Though I doubted I would face constant threat on the Intrepid as I had on my home planet for most of my life.

That, at least, will be a welcome change.

Raucous laughter erupted behind me and I flinched. I had managed to avoid many group settings at the Academy, and on Atavar such social events would have been quieter, more reserved. But here, I knew I would have to adapt to more lively group interactions.

The thought exhausted me.

"Lieutenant Kier'Ahn?" said a voice behind me.

I took a deep breath to stifle the spike of annoyance and turned around. I was immediately glad that I had attempted to remain calm because the man looking at me with a broad grin on his light blue face was Captain Antony Drake.

"Captain," I said, giving him a nod.

To my great relief, Captain Drake did not attempt to shake my hand as others had, he simply returned my nod and came to stand beside me. Both of us faced the windows, the stars faint dots beyond us as the Intrepid made slow progress through the quadrant.

"It's beautiful," Antony said, nodding at the view. "I never tire of it."

"You are fortunate to have such a good vantage point to see the stars in your quarters."

"The perks of the rank I suppose. I was very happy that you accepted the commission aboard the Intrepid."

"It is an honor to serve with you, sir."

Captain Drake gave me a crooked grin and he took a sip of his drink. He was shorter than other Zorestrans, and his hair was an interesting mix of black and white, instead of completely white. I knew that, like me, he had a Human mother but unlike Atavarians, Zorestrans are welcoming of mixed species unions. He'd grown up as a diplomat's son, and had traveled extensively prior to being accepted in the Academy. I had done research on him, as well as some of the other command crew so I would be well informed about their backgrounds and have some talking points for these first interactions. But now, standing here beside him, I realized how awkward such things would be to bring up and was at a loss as to how to proceed.

"I know your father," Antony said after a moment. "He was instrumental in getting me reinstated in the Gex-Corps. If not for him, I probably wouldn't be here."

The Gex-Corps stood for Galactic Exploration Corps, the pseudo military and exploration arm of the GUP. It took me a few seconds to recall my father's career as Ambassador to Earth before I placed the interaction of which the captain spoke. When I did, my spine straightened and I swallowed the lump of grief in my throat.

"I remember," I said, doing my best to keep my voice neutral. "That was one of his last trips to Earth before he retired."

"Yes, I'd heard about the attack on your family just a day after my tribunal. That was such a tragedy. I grieved for his, and your, loss."

I inclined my head but said nothing else.

"I was surprised that with your record you didn't decide to serve in the Atavarian space fleet," he continued.

"I was offered a commission, as well as entry into the Science Institute but it would not have offered me what I was looking for," I answered, the rehearsed response rolled off my tongue.

"Ah, I see."

My gaze slid sideways toward him, and I saw a knowing look on his face to match the tone in his voice. Was he perhaps more familiar with the difficulties of being of mixed species parentage than I thought? Or was he simply making an assumption based on gossip?

"Well, in any case, I am happy to have you here. I have a small officers brunch once a month, I hope you can join us. It is much quieter than this," he said with a chuckle. "And I make a very good blood infused vakla egg omelet if that helps entice you."

All Atavarians need blood to survive. Before our Enlightened Ones pulled us from the dark, primal ways in which we'd been living, we would drink from those we conquered, or those weaker members of society. But since our Enlightenment, we consumed synthetic varietals that took care of our needs.

"That is most kind of you, sir, I would be happy to attend."

Captain Drake gave me one last grin and turned to speak with some of the other new crewmembers. I closed my eyes for a moment and took several deep breaths. The gathering was becoming louder, I was sure of it, and my senses were quickly becoming over saturated. I needed quiet, a reprieve from the required discourse with strangers.

I have spent enough time here I think. No one will miss me if I leave now and I could use the rest before my first day tomorrow.

I turned abruptly, excited to leave, and collided with a short Human woman, causing her drink to spill down the front of her white and green dress.

"Oh shit, that's cold!" she gasped.

"My apologies!" I said at the same time.

I was about to try and wipe up the spill of purple liquid across her exposed cleavage with the small napkin I'd been holding with my drink, when I realized that would likely not be a welcome touch and stopped. She plucked the napkin out of my hand and dabbed it up herself.

"Well, that's one way to end the evening," she said with a chuckle.

"I must sincerely apologize, I was not paying attention to my surroundings."

"It's alright, if you hadn't done it, I would have at some point. I'm Chloe Carter by the way, civilian nurse and the only one that can corral doctor Mc-Grumpy over there."

She said the last part louder and directly to her right.

"Goodnight, Nurse Carter!" said a man who had the small stature of Dwarfism and was giving Nurse Carter a very rude hand gesture.

But she was not insulted. Instead, she threw her head back and laughed; a soft, melodic sound that was the first laugh I did not find grating all night.

It was then I noticed that she had two slightly crooked front teeth, and that she barely came up to my shoulder. Her blond hair was tied back and when she looked back at me, I stared into a pair of bright green eyes that did not size me up or analyze me. She simply looked at me.

It gave me the most curious sensation that I wanted to explore further but Nurse Carter was speaking to me again and, unlike everyone else here, I did not want to miss what she was saying.

"So I'm guessing that, since you've been in that corner for most of the night, your drink is warm and you ran into me like a man desperate to get out of dodge, you're not enjoying yourself."

My mouth opened and nothing came out. All I could do was stare at her as she gave me a broad grin that had an edge of teasing about it that I did not find annoying.

"I was, well this is…I am not used to such…boisterous company," I managed to say.

"Yeah, I tried to talk the captain into a sit down dinner but it turns out I was over ruled by Commander Sonta Velheim," she gestured at the Talosian woman with dark gold skin and long black hair that was tied up in an intricate set of braids. "She loves a good party, though she'll deny it if you ask her. Now, where were you headed?"

"I thought I'd get some rest before my first shift tomorrow."

Nurse Carter nodded and her grin turned conspiratorial.

"Or, I can show you the one place on the ship that's great when you want to hide from everyone. Well, except me because I would know, but I promise to never find you unless you want me to."

A moment ago, such an offer would not have enticed me in the least. But something had shifted since I bumped into this woman, and I found myself very much intrigued.

I gestured ahead of us and her eyes snagged on the gloves I wore that prevented me from accidentally using my touch telepathy.

I braced for the questions I was used to fielding about it, but they never came. Instead, she glanced at the gloves, up at me and nodded as if she understood and accepted this as part of me.

"I'll clear the way for us," she said, dumping the soaked napkin and empty glass onto a nearby table. "And if anyone asks, you're going to sick bay with me because you missed one of your inoculations. Don't need the gossips thinking anything is going on."

"Do you wish to change your attire before we go wherever it is you are taking me?"

She glanced down at her dress and waved the suggestion away.

"Nah, it's almost dry and we're nearing the Selestine system, I don't want to miss the purple nebula."

I was about to ask what she could mean but did not want to fall too far behind.

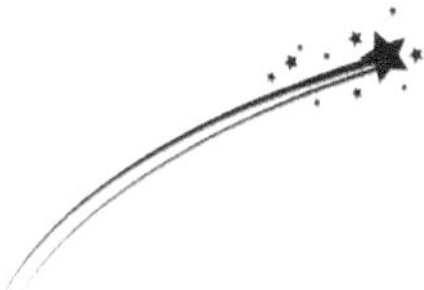

"Come on, it's just up here," Nurse Carter gave me a wide grin as I followed her up a small ladder.

I was doing my best not to stare up her skirt, but the flashes of thigh were quite distracting.

Once we'd exited the captain's quarters, Nurse Carter had led me to a nearby lift which took us to the top most deck. From there, I followed her down the hall to a maintenance shaft, and now the ladder.

She popped a hatch and hoisted herself up through the hole in the ceiling. It then occurred to me that this may be an off limits space, and that if anyone ever found out we were here, it could cause repercussions. But it was far too late now for such worries and my curiosity far outweighed my concern.

Once I hoisted myself up through the hole, I was struck speechless by my surroundings.

The room was enormous. In the center was an antique telescope, the kind my mother had loved to use on Atavar. Along the walls to my right and at my back were stellar cartography equipment and computers. The telescope was obviously ceremonial, though I wondered if it was functional and if I could use it.

My attention was quickly diverted from the device when I glanced up.

Above us stretched a clear dome that exposed the vast symphony of space. There were no beams, no obvious structural obstructions of any kind. Indeed, it looked as if it were one half of a giant globe that someone had mounted on the top of the ship. And as such, my senses were tricked into feeling as if I could simply reach up and touch the stars and planets we drifted around. Some were small, blurred dots as we sailed through space. I saw what Nurse Carter may have erroneously referred to as a nebula as we began to drift through a glittering purple dust field.

"This is actually not a nebula," I said as I continued to stare up. "A common misconception when it comes to a micro debris field of this kind that is mixed with—."

"I know," she said with a lopsided grin. "But right now I just want to enjoy it. Like floating through sparkly clouds and not think of the science."

I considered this and realized that it would be relaxing to not analyze and simply let myself experience this. I gazed up, turned off that part of my mind that was constantly taking in data and observed.

"Remarkable," I said after a few minutes.

"Isn't it breathtaking?" she whispered.

"It is indeed a rare sight."

"Come on, I'll show you the best place to see it all."

She did not take my hand and yet, I still felt pulled after her. She ran to what I assumed was the front of the room from the way the stars and planets were flying by us. Then she laid down on the floor, on her back, and patted the space next to her.

I hesitated for a moment, worried that she might expect...well, I didn't know. But if her behavior thus far had been any indication, Nurse Carter was kind, observant and respectful of my boundaries in a way few had been tonight.

I will trust her.

So I laid down next to her, leaving several inches of space. If she noticed, Nurse Carter did not comment. Instead, she folded her hands across her stomach and smiled up at the lazily drifting planets and moons above us.

All night, I had felt the pressure to talk, to listen, to try and be aware of social rules that never seemed consistent from one event to the next. I hadn't been truly relaxed from the moment I'd stepped into the party.

Until now.

There were no expectations of me, only the pure enjoyment of the moment and the beauty of space. It was meditative, peaceful. My shoulders relaxed and I took my first deep breath of the night.

We passed through this part of the system slowly enough to take in the way the cosmic debris swirled like oil on the surface of water, and received a glimpse of far off planets through the fog of it, the brush of its cloud like texture against the dome. Not since I was a child had I felt so free to let go of all the things weighing me down. I almost forgot I was with someone, when Nurse Carter let out a giggle of delight.

I looked over and was transfixed by her face.

She glowed with joy, her mouth opened wide in a smile that lit her from within. As completely carefree as I felt, that is how she looked. Again that strange sensation from before struck me, and I realized that it was affection, a desire for friendship. It had been a long time since I had anyone to call a friend.

Possibly not since Zephyr left Atavar all those years ago.

I shoved the memory of my half-sister's departure aside; I did not want it to ruin this time. It was too precious.

She must have felt me watching her because Nurse Carter turned. I worried for a moment that she would find my staring uncomfortable and close herself off. Instead she studied me right back, her head tilting just a little. I was used to being examined by others. On Atavar I was an anomaly, I was 'other'. It used to hurt, but as I grew, my ability to partition off my emotions with discipline and the meditative arts helped me weather such things.

But here, with this intriguing Human, I found myself willing to be slightly affected by her interest. I turned back to watching the wonders above us and was unexpectedly moved to share my thoughts with her.

"This reminds me of my mother," I whispered.

"How so?"

"She was a stellar cartographer before she mated my father. It was how they met."

"It sounds like she gave it up after?"

I nodded, a stab sadness hitting me in the chest.

"She attempted to do her work on Atavar but she was not accepted in the scientific circles. That did not stop her from teaching me about the stars, how to map them, how to find my way as the old Earth explorers used to. My father built her a small observatory on our property in the country and there were many nights she would be there until the sunrise. It was her most treasured retreat."

"And yours."

I glanced at her quickly, startled by the astute observation. I was very good at masking my emotions, ensuring that they were controlled, harnessed behind my cognitive barriers. While the memories I had just shared were bittersweet on my tongue, I knew that I had not been demonstrative in my telling. Yet, this woman had seen past all that to the pain I kept locked tight within me.

Her face was pinched with compassion, with understanding. I did not know why, but I knew that I could be honest and, therefore, vulnerable with her.

"Yes," I whispered.

Our eyes held each other for a moment that stretched between us, infused with something I could not name but knew was vastly important. That was why I did not look away, why I allowed her to stare openly into my eyes without attempting to hide. When she finally broke the stare, I felt the loss, small and unnerving in my mind.

"My father loved the stars too," she said after a moment. "He was a doctor in the Galactic Relief Organization, so I've seen hundreds, thousands of different stars over so many different planets with him. I think I could read a star map before I could read most words."

She chuckled at that and I gave a small huff in return.

"I look up," she continued after a moment, her voice tinged with sadness, "and I can almost hear him asking me about what I see. What constellations do

I see in the stars? What looks like a planet, what makes up that borealis or that streak of blue? He was the most curious person I'd ever known."

"And he passed that on to you."

Now it was her turn to look at me with surprise and she nodded.

"He never let me believe in limits, not with science, or with compassion. I'm here because of him."

"He sounds intriguing."

"He was."

The statement was so quiet, and yet so filled with grief that I understood intimately. For the first time in years, I longed to touch another being. If only for a moment to bring her comfort. But I could not risk seeing into her mind; even with the gloves on my hands keeping me from skin to skin contact. So instead, I was present with her in this shared grief, allowing the silence to wrap around us both as we looked at the vast beauty of space.

"I am humbled that you would share this place with me," I said after a moment.

She grinned at me.

"Well, how else was I supposed to get the hot Atavarian alone and seduce him?"

There was a playfulness in her tone that told me she was not serious, still her words caused a stirring in a part of me that had not felt anything in a very long time. I closed it off, controlled it, but decided to tease her back.

"Well then," I said, sitting up. "I suppose we should get to it. I have an early shift tomorrow."

She stared at me, open mouthed for a moment, before I arched an eyebrow at her and she let out a long, loud laugh.

"An Atavarian with a sense of humor?" she asked, sitting up next to me.

"Many of us do, but not many are able to see it."

"Well, bravo. You got me."

I could not resist a slight upturn of my mouth.

"The first of many times, perhaps."

Her smile softened, as did the look in her eyes just before something caught her attention and she gasped, pointing up at the ceiling. We were passing through another part of the debris field, and her eyes lit up with excitement.

"I love the way it swirls like that. Reminds me of sherbet ice cream from when my father used to take me to Earth," she said.

I nodded.

"There is a treat on Atavar similar to ice cream. When my mother would make it for me she somehow created that same effect. I've never been able to duplicate it."

"Is that frozen blood cake?"

"A rough translation but yes, essentially."

"If there's a particular blood recipe you'd like just let me know. Blood synthesizing is done as part of the medical department so the food banks won't have any for you."

"I do have a special blend," I admitted slowly, focusing on the stars above us instead of her face. "Due to my Human physiology, my body does not naturally produce enzymes to break down the blood for sufficient nutrients. It can be quite...inconvenient at times."

"Do you have the recipe on a data stick? I can program something just for you by tomorrow afternoon, if you'd like."

The judgment I had received from my fellow Atavarians all my life was completely absent. There was not even mild curiosity about my condition. Just acceptance.

I let out a breath and the corners of my mouth tilted up ever so slightly.

"Thank you, Nurse Carter, that is most kind of you."

"Chloe," she said. "Call me Chloe."

"If you wish. How long have you served on the Intrepid?" I asked.

"Six months, most I've been anywhere for one time. I like it here so maybe I'll stay even longer."

"Do you have plans to be a doctor someday?"

She shrugged.

"I don't know. I like nursing, but I do keep collecting doctorates so who knows. Of course, they're all 'honorary' or 'commission certified' so some people might not accept them with as much seriousness as if I'd ever gone to college."

My interest was piqued at hearing that.

"How many do you have?"

"Three. One in Xenobiology, one in Infectious Diseases with an emphasis on viruses, and one in Vascular Medicine. Of course I've got my Aerospace Medicine degree, but that's basic, I've had that since I was seventeen. I'm working on getting certified as a physician for six GUP species, but I only have three so far."

I stared at her for a moment before I realized what I was doing and turned away. My mind was spinning with excitement as I thought of all the interesting conversations we could have. I had not explored nearly enough of the medical courses at both the Atavarian Science Institute or the Academy. To have achieved all of that while still so young spoke to a mind that I very much wanted to know better. Perhaps she would like to learn tri-level chess? Or maybe one of the many Atavarian logic puzzles?

"You just got really excited by all that, didn't you?" she asked me with a playful grin.

I stiffened and cleared my throat.

"I am quite intrigued by your knowledge."

She chuckled.

"I'll take that as a compliment. I'd bet there aren't many who could elicit a response like that from you."

I observed her for a moment, and relaxed. She was not making fun, or uncomfortable by my admiration. In fact, she seemed pleased.

"No," I finally answered her, "there are not."

Her smile changed ever so subtly, but in a way I could not decipher. All I knew was that it sent a warmth coursing through my body I had not felt before.

"Good," was all she said before turning back to stare up at the stars.

"If you do not mind me asking, how old are you?"

"I don't mind, but be careful asking females that question in the future."

"Noted."

"I am twenty-eight."

"You seem quite young to have accomplished so much."

"And I'm only getting started."

"I believe that."

She gave me a sidelong grin and then turned her attention back to the stars.

We sat there a bit longer, now past the purple clouds of micro debris, and the sky was filled with more stars, with a few distant planets and moons from the system. I knew I would return here often to find quiet.

"Thank you for sharing this with me, Chloe."

"Thank you for being someone I thought I could share it with."

Chapter Two

CHLOE-NOW

I'd never been more grateful for environmental controls in my life.

This planet, Jahnus Five, had a near constant seventy percent humidity. Most of the crew were in more casual, lightweight uniforms such as tank tops and shorts to help stay cool but I'd still treated three cases of dehydration and overheating today, and it was just past lunch.

I was one of the lucky ones, working in the clinic where we'd been able to rig up an environmental regulator that kept the prefabricated structure cool and dry compared to everywhere else in the colony.

The Intrepid had been following a strange energy signature when we'd happened upon this struggling colony on the edges of GUP space. Their distress call would have overridden our pursuit even if the energy hadn't disappeared right before reaching the planet. It turned out that this colony hadn't received their shipment of food or supplies in over six months. In addition, their buildings were rotting away in the humid atmosphere, having not been properly sealed against such an environment. For the last two weeks, the entire crew had worked in shifts to repair what we could, and replace what we couldn't, hence the nice environmentally controlled prefab clinic.

Engineers had gotten the tech fixed and proofed against the weather, and our galley had supplied many fresh foods to the malnourished colonists. It had been a full ship effort and exhausting work. But today the colony was back up to GUP standards and set up with supplies for the next few months while they waited for the ship that Captain Drake had ensured was on its way.

Dr. Eddie Goodman and I had been working nonstop at the clinic, helping the injured and sick. This was a multi-species colony, so we were treating Zorestrans, Talosians, Humans and a few Boethelians too, which were rare this far out in space. Most of them preferred interior planets, and since they were considered endangered refugees, they were given clearance to settle wherever they wanted.

Still, we couldn't help everyone, and it didn't take long before we had our first casualty. Which necessitated digging out an appropriate sized graveyard just a half mile away from the clinic. We'd buried about a dozen colonists by now, several of them Boethelian, which broke my heart.

I stopped at the bedside of a Talosian woman who'd had a broken leg that had become infected. We'd been worried that we'd have to amputate but the antibiotics worked just in time.

"How's your pain level this morning?" I asked.

"Hardly anything at all," she smiled up at me, her skin a bright gold now instead of the dull color it had been. "Do you think I'll be able to join the celebration tonight? My son has been wanting to show me the target area your crew made for him and some of the other kids."

"I think so, but I want to check your levels to make sure."

I took a small blood sample and put a dot on the medic stick on my holo tablet. As I waited for the sensors in the med stick to do their work, I examined her leg, which had been in a mending sleeve for the past two weeks.

"The bone looks pretty good," I said, "but you'll still have to wear a brace to support it. And use a set of crutches too for at least the next two weeks."

"I can do that."

My holo tablet beeped and I looked over her blood results with a grin.

"There is no sign of infection. So I think as long as you promise to take it easy, and sit at the town square, you can go home this afternoon."

Her bright blue eyes teared up and her smile warmed me through and through. She gripped my hand and squeezed.

"Thank you, Nurse Carter, you don't know…we had given up and your crew has given us a second chance. Thank you so much."

"You're more than welcome, I'm just so glad we were able to help."

I motioned for one of the ensigns to come over and gave them instructions for her discharge, including a small dosage of pain meds. I moved on to the bed next to her, a Human child that was healing from burns. The skin grafts were taking and they had just come out of the isolation pod yesterday after the threat of infection was gone.

"There's a party tonight," he said, his voice still a little drowsy from the sedation.

"That's right. But I think you still need to stay in bed."

"But I wanna go."

I knelt down so I could look him in the eye.

"How about this, I'll have someone bring you a treat. I hear there's going to be cake."

His eyes lit up.

"Can I have an end piece?"

"Ooh, extra frosting, huh?"

He nodded emphatically.

"Kid after my own heart. Absolutely, I'll save you the most frosting end piece. But you have to do something for me."

"What?"

"Rest and get better, can you do that?"

"Yeah, I think so."

I checked his blood and saw a small spike in his white blood cells.

"Get him a hypospray of antibiotics and check his bandages in a few hours," I said to a cadet nearby.

I was looking down at my tablet and reading over the little boys test results from yesterday, not looking where I was going and nearly crashed right into a hover cart full of small pots of blue flowers.

"What the—?"

"I am sorry, Nurse Carter," Kier said as he held the cart steady. "I did not see you there."

His deep, resonant tone was so familiar that it was soothing in some ways. Kier's green eyes roamed my face and a tiny wrinkle appeared between his eye brows. I knew what he saw: a tired, over worked woman who was in desperate need of a nap. But I really didn't need to hear from him that I needed to take care of myself, not when there was so much to do.

So to distract him from the lecture I was sure he was composing at this moment, I crossed my arms and gave Kier a playful grin.

"I've seen quite a few crew make up wild excuses to get out of the humidity but yours might be the most creative. Flower delivery, really?"

He arched an eyebrow and crossed his own arms as he turned to face me across the cart.

"I am not one for such subterfuge."

"Which is why no one would suspect you," I replied.

"But you know me too well?"

"Why thank you, yes I do. Glad you finally admit it."

I was rewarded by the almost imperceptible up tick of Kier's lips. A light kind of heat radiated through my chest knowing that I was one of the rare few who could do that to him.

"In order to soothe your suspicion and potential disappointment in me," he said, plucking a small potted plant from the cart, "these are Tears of Amouna, a sacred plant to the Boethelians. Lieutenant Commander Kavat thought they would bring comfort to them but she had to return to the ship. So I volunteered to deliver them on her behalf."

I narrowed my eyes playfully at him.

"A likely story but I'll give you the benefit of the doubt."

"How very generous of you."

"I do try."

He inclined his head and I moved to my next patient, who just happened to be Boethelian. Her green skin was still dotted in sweat and her temperature was elevated so I ordered another round of meds to bring her fever down. The playful mood that Kier had created in me faded quickly as I looked over her chart.

This woman wouldn't last the day. She'd been fighting a severe infection in her lungs which I had treated with the best meds I could. But Boethelian biology was still new to our medicine and, while some of their doctors had survived the purge by the K'Tavi, we hadn't been able to create enough meds to combat some of the more complex illnesses that plagued Boethelians.

My mind furiously ran through potential treatments that may extend her life long enough for us to work out a better antibiotic treatment. But the ones I typed into my tablet were contra indicated for her species and the others were too rare to be stocked on the Intrepid.

As the realization that the only treatment available would be to make her as comfortable as possible until she passed, Kier placed a plant on her bedside table and her eyes lit up.

"Amouna...Amouna..."

I glanced at Kier, and his eyebrows drew sharply down as he discerned the situation.

"Can you distract her while I take her blood?" I asked Kier. "She gets very nervous when I try and I need to see where she's at."

It might've been pointless, but I had to make sure that there was really nothing else to do.

Kier inclined his head. I expected him to stand over her, perhaps not get so near since he didn't like risking touch. But instead he sat gently on the side of her bed and took the plant from the table, holding it out to her. The woman grazed her trembling fingers against the shimmering petals and was calm as I took her blood sample.

"Amouna...your tears are here for me," she whispered. "I am content."

"Amouna waits by the river," he murmured to her.

The woman let out a long sigh and nodded.

"Thank you...thank you..."

I bit the inside of my cheeks as I looked the data from her blood sample. I was right. The infection was just too aggressive.

I swallowed back the disappointment and frustration of not being able to do more. But when I looked down at the woman, she was happier than I'd seen her since she'd come to the clinic two weeks ago.

"Amouna is here," she whispered.

"Yes, she is," I said, even though I had no idea who or what that was. "Rest now."

She nodded and watched as Kier replaced the plant on the table, her eyes fixed on it as we both walked toward the makeshift front desk.

I stowed my holo tablet, connecting it to their now working network. It helped to do this simple thing, but once it was done, the emotions I'd been caging for the past two days came crashing in on me. Two people had already died this morning, and I was going to lose a third before sun down. Yesterday, I'd had to amputate the arm of a young Human woman and while prosthetics were a possibility, it wasn't a guarantee she'd get one this far out in space. Eddie and I had done a lot of good here, but the loss, the patients I couldn't fully help, that had been steadily weighing on me and this morning, I felt it all start to spill out. I covered my mouth with my hand to hold in the sob. There was a lot to do, I didn't have the time to break down.

"Chloe," Kier's voice was gentle behind me.

"Yeah?" I asked, wiping my eyes and turning to him.

"Are you alright?"

"No," I admitted, more tears spilling. "I just...it's a hard day today."

He nodded.

"I understand. Or...no, I do not, but I would like to."

That made my chest squeeze and the tears fall harder.

"I have said the wrong thing?"

"No," I said with a brittle laugh. "You said the right thing but I can't explain it. I guess...I want to save them all, and I understand I can't. But that doesn't make it any easier."

I wished he could hold me, that I could bury my face in his chest and cry all of this out. But I would never breach his boundaries like that, not even for my own comfort.

As I watched him, his hands tightened and there was the barest hint of tension in his face, as if he were having a terrible struggle inside of himself.

Finally, he spoke, "Have you eaten the afternoon meal? It may help you to get outside, into the sunlight. Take a break perhaps?"

I nodded, really not wanting to talk about whether or not I was taking care of myself. I would be fine once I'd done what I could for everyone here. Still, Kier might have a point. A little fresh air and a sandwich might help me think better.

"Yeah, that's a good idea" I said, only a little disappointed that he hadn't done more. "I haven't eaten much today."

"You need to keep your strength up. There is a shuttle returning to the Intrepid within the hour. Perhaps it would be good for you to go, get some rest and food."

His concern for me made that warmth return and spread through me and I smiled at him.

"Worrying about me?"

"Yes."

He said it so simply, as if it were obvious, but I heard the small rumble in his voice, the way his eyes studied me. And I liked it. A lot.

"You don't need to," I said, making my way to the small decontamination unit toward the front of the clinic. "Eddie is already barking at me to come back to the ship."

Kier walked in to the unit behind me, which surprised me. It was a two-person unit to cleanse us of anything that could be transmitted onto the ship. And while the first cycle through was clothed, the last was not. I gave him a curious frown as the door shut behind him.

"I have recently read a study about medical personnel during crisis and their tendency to over work," he said as the unit door locked. "It is not only dangerous for your patients, but for you as well."

"Yeah, I know that, but Kier—"

"You have dark circles under your eyes and I distinctly heard your stomach growl while you were doing your rounds. I must insist that you take a longer than normal break on the Intrepid."

I tilted my head and smirked.

"Is that so?"

"It is. I outrank you. I do not want to have to pull rank but I will."

"Why Lieutenant, someone might think that you care about me."

"I do."

It was a simple statement, and could be said by friends, which was what we were. But there was heat under it, a moment of intensity that made my grin wobble. It might've even made me bold enough to ask him about it if the computer hadn't chosen that time to interrupt.

"Cycle one of decontamination to commence in thirty seconds. Please stand on the indicated markers and stand by."

Kier's eyes widened and he glanced around quickly. If I didn't know better, I'd say he was panicked.

"I did not realize...that is, I was not aware that I had followed you in here," he said.

"I tried to tell you but you were kinda on a roll."

"Yes, I can see that."

"Please stand on the markers indicated."

I moved to the markers nearest me and shook my head.

"You better do what she says, this computer can get testy."

I had to admit that the thought of seeing Kier naked and soaked in slick, soapy decontamination solution was more than a little appealing. But what was almost as good was giving him a hard time about being in here with me at all.

I was pretty comfortable with nudity, but I wasn't sure he was.

"I won't look," I said, as I saw the small flare of panic on his face, "if that would make you more comfortable. I'll keep my eyes down."

He swallowed and walked over to the markers.

"I am not frightened of nudity, and we are friends," he said.

"That's true. But it's up to you."

"It does not matter to me."

Was I imagining it or was that a little bit of a dare?

I grinned at him.

"Okay then, I'm fine with it too."

He inclined his head, right before the cold spray of the unit washed over us. It was impossible to keep my eyes open once it started and I missed the sight of Kier's lightweight long sleeve shirt and pants clinging to his body until the sprays stopped.

It was obvious that he was built, the uniform only hid so much. But that was nothing compared to what I was seeing.

Black fabric clung to his torso, showing every dip and curve of his body up to his rounded biceps and shoulders. I was so distracted by him that I almost missed the way his eyes raked over me as well.

"Remove clothing and place in sonic dryers. Then prepare for the second cycle by stepping on the markers."

Kier and I turned our backs to one another and began to peel the uniforms off. This next part had to be done with absolutely nothing on. While I'd done this decontamination with every member of the medical team and a few of the other crew, none of them were a source of intense curiosity and, dare I say, attraction like Kier was.

The man was covered twenty-four, seven from his neck down. The only reason I knew what the column of his throat looked like was because of the very narrow slit in his high collar. And I'd thought about that sliver of flesh for far too many hours of late.

Not appropriate! This is a professional environment, Kier is my friend. I need to keep this in the friend zone and not make this voyeuristic.

Still, the skin at the back of my neck flushed, spreading to my face and chest. I was intensely aware, as I peeled my pants and tank top off and waited for the second set of sprays and scans, that I was stripped down to nothing with the man who had lately invaded my sleeping and waking fantasies.

Suddenly the playfulness from before was souring as I realized that here was a man who was too private for touch. It didn't feel right to joke and push him to show me his body.

"Kier, if you're not comfortable with this—" I said before returning to my spot.

"It is fine, Chloe," his voice rougher, lower.

It sent tingles all the way down my spine and I glanced over my shoulder to see his glittering gaze skating slowly down my body before returning to my eyes.

I was hot all over, and I swore my legs shook as I stepped into place, with my back to the wall. These sprays were from the sides and behind instead of directly overhead so after the initial burst of fluid, I opened my eyes and met his gaze.

We didn't look away from one another the entire time the decontamination was happening, all ninety seconds of it. But oh my goodness, did it feel so much longer.

I didn't dare look lower than his pectorals because I was scared that if he had an erection, I might just die on the spot. I was already feeling hot and aroused, barely resisting the urge to rub my thighs together at the sight of Kier's red, muscular body shining and wet. His dark hair curled more than usual, and a couple strands hugged his small horns. I wondered what his hair felt like. Was it soft and feathery? Were his horns hard and ridged like they looked? Or were they smooth? Would his arms be velvet wrapped steel under my hands?

I hoped I was hiding all of this, because Kier sure as hell was. Or at least, for the most part. His jaw clenched the longer he looked at me, and his green eyes became hard, determined. I wished I knew what was going on behind those eyes. Maybe if I stared long enough...

"Please prepare for sonic drying to commence in five...four...three...two...one."

The sonic waves hit me fast, startling me and I closed my eyes, breaking the contact with him.

"Rotate to fully dry."

I turned around slowly, my entire body buzzed with emotions that moved far too fast for me to pin down. I recognized nerves, a bit of self-consciousness and a large helping of lust. But there were other things there too, feelings that had been lurking on the edges of my mind lately. Feelings that I was afraid to admit to.

Next came the blue lights of the scanners, which ran over me three different times before the indicator light shone green, letting me know that I could get dressed. I moved fast, efficiently and pulled on the freshly dried pants and tank top, along with my boots. I turned just in time to see Kier with his back to me. He was just pulling his shirt over his head, and his hands, which I'd never seen before, looked strong, with thick veins running over the top. His forearms flexed as he pulled the shirt over his head and I swear my mouth watered at the sight.

"I'll see you at the party tonight?" I asked, forcing cheerfulness into my voice as I bolted past him to the door.

He turned and gave me a brief nod, the skin around his mouth and eyes was tense.

Oh god, does he know that I'm lusting after him?

It was a silly worry. I mean, I wasn't obvious about it, and it wasn't like I ogled him, for crying out loud. But it stuck anyway and I wasn't watching where I was going. Some of the sanitation solution was still lingering on the ground, slippery and thick where the sonic waves had pushed it into a small puddle. I'd cautioned others to be careful about the solution just this morning, but my mind wasn't on my surroundings; it was on the way my heart was pounding behind my chest, the way I wanted to know what those shoulders would feel like under my hands.

That's why I stepped full onto that sludge of a puddle and my feet went out from under me.

I expected to fall flat on my ass, but instead, I was caught by strong hands. One clutching my upper arm, the other clasped around my hand. I looked down because the sensation was so different, not fabric but skin.

Soft, firm, warm skin.

When it penetrated my foggy brain that we were actually touching skin to skin, my gaze shot up to Kier's, and for once, his expression was unguarded. His eyes widened, mouth gaped at me, pupils blown as he held me steady. It was almost exactly like what he'd done three months ago when we'd been shore leave and I'd nearly fallen over the edge of a platform. Only then he had been wearing his gloves, and right now, he most certainly was not.

I expected him to let me go, to run, to do anything except what he did.

He held on.

His body inched toward mine.

And everything around us contracted and stood still as I held his shocked gaze. Seconds stretched, and there was a sensation in my mind, like a feather slowly dragged against flesh. Soft, ticklish and inquisitive. I chased it, grabbed ahold and was shocked to find that there was another consciousness attached to it. Someone familiar—

"Kier," I gasped.

He released me with cry of shock, as if I'd burned him. Without another word or look, he snatched his gloves and ran out of the decontamination room. All I could do was stand there, panting like I'd been running. The phantom pressure of his hand on mine and the soft memory of his mind touching mine seared me like a brand.

Chapter Three

CHLOE

I hadn't been able to shake off what had happened in the decontamination unit all day. I'd tried to keep busy on the ship but even the new nanite tech that we'd received a few weeks back hadn't been enough to hold my attention. So in spite of Eddie's protests, I took an extra shift in the clinic down here on the planet. But the moment I entered the decontamination unit again, all I could think about was Kier's hot gaze on me, his hands on my flesh.

Helping set up the tables and food for the celebration tonight did little to stop my spinning mind and I finally gave up trying to engage with anyone; I was only half present in most of the conversations anyway. The party had started an hour ago, and Kier had yet to make an appearance, though I'd seen him helping Lieutenant Commander Althea Kavat transport some of her plants up the hill to the graveyard.

After arranging for food to be brought to some of the patients in the clinic, and making a special request for the corner piece of cake for the Human child, I leaned against one of the buildings that surrounded what the colonists had dubbed a 'town square' and watched them set up an area for live music. I nursed the metal cup of wine in my hand, and tried to focus on the soft breeze that was starting to flow over us as the day faded into night. It was still humid and my skin felt sticky, but the growing twilight was lovely.

Tall trees of red and orange leaves towered on the edges of the small colony, making it feel enclosed, safe. Bright flowers of purple and pink hung from some of the boughs, while on the ground, round red and blue berries grew on bushes. The breeze brought with it the sweet scent of flowers, followed by the smell of the roasted meats our ship's chefs were teaching some of the colonists to prepare over cook pits. The faint blue glow of this planet's version of fireflies danced in the distance, adding to the festive feeling on the air.

As I continued to watch the celebration, I was finally able to shake a bit of my distraction over Kier.

Someone nudged my shoulder and I turned to see Lt. Jax Vabaris' dark blue face smiling down at me.

He was a full blooded Zorestran and towered above me at seven feet, his thick horns adding about a half a foot to that. Brilliant and built like a bull, Jax was a security officer and copilot on the Intrepid. He leaned next to me, arms crossed.

"You're thinking about medical stuff again, aren't you?" he teased. "That's why you're over here, instead of where the fun is. You can't wait to get back to your toys."

That wasn't it at all, but I was absolutely not going to tell Jax, of all people, about what had happened with Kier. The man was an awful gossip. So instead, I leaned into his assumption. Honestly, it didn't take much pretending to be excited about the new toys in my lab.

"They're just so interesting," I gushed. "You have no idea what I could do with those little nanites."

"Unless it has to do with increasing my already impressive stamina in bed, I'm not interested," he said with an eyebrow waggle.

I snorted.

"If you weren't so good at your job, I'd say you missed your calling."

"Oh, I already break hearts."

"No, I was thinking high paid courtesan at a Valtoshan pleasure house."

He tapped his chin with a finger, looking up.

"Tempting, but no thanks."

"A little too much putting the other person first?"

"Ouch! You're getting as bad as Thanh. And speak of the she-devil..."

Jax tensed behind me as Lt. Thanh Nguyen walked up to us, her gait a little uneven.

"Everything okay?" I asked. "You're limping."

"Oh, yeah, I lost a bet," she said waving away my concern.

Jax opened his mouth and she stuck her finger in his face, no mean feat since she was a good foot and half shorter than him.

"I swear, Jax, you say it and I will punch you right in the balls."

"Damn," he put a hand over his dick and shied away, "always going for the boys. If you weren't constantly threatening them, I'd think you were obsessed."

Her face flushed and she crossed her arms. Her dark brown faux hawk was frizzy from the humidity and there was a sheen on her face. I wondered if she'd been properly hydrating and made a mental note to make sure everyone on the crew was drinking water along with their alcohol tonight.

"The only thing I'm obsessed about when it comes to your junk," Thanh spat out at him, "is wondering why it hasn't fallen off yet."

Usually Thanh was much better about controlling her obvious dislike for Jax. Whether it was the humidity or whatever had caused her to limp, Thanh was obviously at the end of her rope.

"You know, I could use a little water," I said, looping my arm through Thanh's. "See ya, Jax."

He gave us a wave, staring too long at Thanh before marching off toward the bar. I had no idea what had ever happened between the two of them. Thanh swears she barely knew Jax at the Academy, but her dislike for him bordered on hatred. Considering Thanh was one of the sweetest, most even tempered people I'd ever met, I knew there had to be a story there, though I'd never pushed her to tell me.

We took a stroll around the edges of the town square, which was looking much better than when we first got here. With the warm lighting that the engineers had helped them fix and the laughter accenting the slightly off key music that was playing, my spirits were starting to lift. After a few minutes, Thanh's body started to relax and her limp disappeared. The yellow shifting lights on the small disc at the base of her skull told me that the symbiote attached to her spinal column, called a Seahdohn, had healed whatever injury she'd gotten, though that was a side benefit to what the Seahdohn was really there for, which was helping Thanh walk.

With a hiss, Thanh winced and reached back to touch a spot along the raised ridge of her back where the Seahdohn's body protruded under her skin.

"Everything okay back there?" I asked.

"No, I think the humidity is irritating my skin where it meets the metal. Can you take a look?"

"Sure, let's go to the clinic."

The symbiote was delicate so most beings who had one of the Seahdohn opted for a narrow casing of steel and adomite along their spine to protect it.

We walked up the short hill where the clinic sat, in silence. The warm lights illuminated the inside and I wondered how the patients were doing.

"Can you just take a look out here, I hate that decontamination unit," Thanh said.

I nodded and led her around to the side of the building, pulling up her tank top. I sucked in a breath when I saw the bright red rash on either side of the armor.

"Good grief, why didn't you come to me sooner?" I exclaimed. "This looks awful!"

"I was trying to just deal with it," Thanh replied. "How bad is it?"

"Pretty bad, you're bleeding in a few spots."

"Shit. Tohm-Tohm was worried about that. He's having difficulty healing around the armor lately."

Tohm-Tohm was the Seahdohns name, and from what I could gather from Thanh, the two of them shared a consciousness.

"I can do a diagnostic on the ship," I offered, " but for right now I have some salve I can use."

She groaned.

"Calm down," I said, grabbing one of the first aid kits we had outside for emergencies. "I've got it right here. I don't know why we're friends if you hate doctors so much."

"I don't hate doctors," she flinched as I began to apply the salve. "I just have bad memories of them, that's all."

I didn't press for details as I continued to apply the cream to her rash.

"Getting Tohm-Tohm wasn't an easy experience," she whispered, "for either of us. The exchange program wasn't what it is now and the procedure...well let's just say that being one of the first Humans was less exciting and more terror inducing. Being a lab rat isn't fun."

"I'm sorry," I whispered, putting some clear bandages over the top of the rash. "I had no idea."

"No one does. But it's over now, and Tohm-Tohm and I are good," she chuckled. "He says thanks for the assist."

"How's he doing?"

"Fine, a little itchy from the rash but okay."

"I wish I knew what that was like. A whole other consciousness in your mind."

And I stopped short, realizing that I did know, just for a moment.

Kier...that had been...

"It's wild," Thanh said, interrupting my thoughts. "And hard to get used to, he's chatty...I like it buddy, but you are chatty."

It still took me by surprise when Thanh just burst out talking to her symbiote.

"Tohm-Tohm wants to know who's in the graveyard," she said, pointing to where we could just see candles through the thin foliage between the clinic and the new plot.

"I saw Kier and Althea go up there a while ago. She's probably doing some rituals at the graves."

"Kind of a freaky place for a hook up."

"What? No! He's just helping her. Althea is super stand offish about relationships of any kind. I once heard her say that she'd rather live in celibacy than sleep with anyone she served with."

"Can't fault her wisdom there," Thanh said with more than a little bitterness.

"And what does that mean?" I asked, as we made our way around the clinic. "Who have you been cavorting with?"

"Cavorting? What are you an old nun?"

"Answer the question."

"You first."

"What question?" I asked with trepidation.

"Would you fuck Kier if you had the chance?"

I choked, my face turning three shades of red, while Thanh laughed.

"I'll take that as a yes," she teased.

"No," I coughed, "no, you won't," and coughed again.

"Seriously? The way you look at him, the way he looks at you?"

"You're seeing things."

She gave me an incredulous look and raised her eyebrows.

"You are!" I insisted.

"Okay, if you say so."

"I do."

"Mind if I give him a go?"

"Be my guest."

"You said that too fast," Thanh said.

"Because I know you won't."

"How do you know that?"

I turned to meet her eye because this situation needed some quid pro quo.

"Because you are hung up on someone else on the ship, and I know who."

Her smile faded, and while I had been mostly joking, her reaction made me practically salivating with curiosity.

I didn't get the chance to follow up, however, because Kier and Althea were coming straight toward us from the graveyard.

The second his eyes met mine, a zing of energy flowed between us and all I could think about was the sensation of his mind brushing against mine. I was struck speechless and knew that Thanh was going to give me monumental amounts of shit for this later. A flush rose up on my cheeks and I gave him a tight smile in greeting.

"Chloe, Thanh," he said, nodding to each of us.

Althea nodded at us, her purple eyes wet with tears. Dirt smudged her face and the front of her casual uniform. Her dark green skin was covered in swirling gold tattoos that ran from the tips of her fingers all the way up her arms, across her chest, up her neck and the sides of her face, ending on the shaved sides of her head. Her white hair was long down the center and kept in a tight bun at the nape of her neck.

"I would ask how it went but…" Thanh said.

Althea gave her a sad smile.

"She is with Amouna now, that's all that matters"

"Have you always performed burial rites?" I asked.

"No, I was not a Mistress of the River, as we called that aspect of Amouna."

"What did you do, if you don't mind me asking?" Thanh said.

"Not at all," Althea's eyes hardened a bit. "I was a Mistress of the Cleave, I served Amouna's warrior aspect. Now…well, there are too few of us to worry about what roles we were sanctified for."

She gave us all a sad smile and shook her head.

"This topic is far too gloomy. Aren't we supposed to be celebrating?"

"Yes," Thanh said, "and I could really use a drink."

"I'll go with you," Althea said, glancing back and Kier and me. "You two coming?"

Thanh gave me a knowing grin that I tried very hard to ignore.

"Yep, right behind you!"

I glanced at Kier, who was standing in his usual straight, reserved posture with his hands behind his back. But it was his eyes that were different. It was just a glimpse, but I swore he was looking at me like I was dinner and he was starving.

We both looked away and my cheeks turned hot.

"Do you want to…?" I gestured to the path.

"Of course."

I nodded and we started to walk. The planet's green and blue moons were hanging above us, one nearing full while the other sat above it, a sliver. It was beautiful, romantic even. But I was so nervous and ill at ease that I couldn't really enjoy it. I hated feeling this way around Kier, one of my best friends.

"Can we—"

"Chloe, I must—"

We both started at the same time and I burst into laughter.

"Why don't you go?" I asked.

"No, please," he said, the tiniest uptick at the corner of his mouth.

"I don't want this afternoon to affect our friendship," I said. "You're too important to me."

His shoulders relaxed as he exhaled long through his nose.

"I was thinking the same," he admitted, "and wanted to offer an apology for touching your mind without your permission. The moment came upon me suddenly and I did not have the chance to raise my usual defenses against breaching another's thoughts. It was a terrible intrusion and will not happen again."

So that's why he was being weird; not because he'd seen something he liked while I was naked, but because he'd accidentally gone into my thoughts. I wasn't exactly sure why, but I was slightly disappointed that was all that bothered him.

"It's okay," I said. "As long as we've known each other I'm surprised it hasn't happened before. And besides, I trust you."

"For an Atavarian, what I did is one of the worst sins. It is..." he looked away, a deep frown creasing his forehead. "It is why I have to wear gloves. I have never been skilled at control."

A spike of anger hit me square in the chest. From what little Kier had told me of his upbringing on Atavar, he'd been made to feel like a failure and not a 'real' Atavarian at every turn. I had an image of finding whoever did this to him and smacking them across the face.

Kier was the kindest, most incredible man I'd ever met. I trusted him implicitly, and I could count on one hand the men I'd felt that way about in my life. He was honest and compassionate, smart and funny, though maybe not in a way that everyone saw. I wished he could see himself as I did. Maybe that's why I stepped closer to him, and caught his eye.

"There's nothing wrong with you," I whispered. "What happened was an accident. And, in fact, if you hadn't caught me, I might be down with a nasty concussion."

His eyes flared, as if the thought of that was deeply troubling to him.

"You're not on Atavar anymore," I continued. "You don't have to worry about their rules unless you want to. So if the gloves make you feel better, okay. But if you're only doing it because you feel like this part of you is wrong, well, maybe question that premise."

He tilted his head to the side, his gaze far away as he considered my words. Eventually, he gave me a slow nod.

"That is wise," he admitted. "But I do not like the sensation of being touched casually, nor do I like knowing what others are thinking. It is...loud and overwhelming."

"Well then, there you go. The gloves are for you, not whoever told you that you weren't good enough."

The words came out a bit more fiery than I'd intended, getting Kier's attention. He studied me and the curiosity in his gaze made me realize just how close we'd gotten. There were only a few inches between us, the rise and fall of our chests nearly closing that distance. And if I hadn't known better, I would've sworn he leaned toward me.

"Thank you, Chloe."

"You're welcome."

Our words were soft, barely more than a whisper between us. His breath fanned across my cheek and I noticed the way his lips parted, the sight of his sharp incisors. Had they always been that long?

I had the insane urge to reach out and trace his full bottom lip with my index finger when he took a step back, breaking the mesmerizing spell.

"We should attend the party," he said.

"Yes," I agreed, following him the rest of the way down the path.

We had just reached the outskirts of the town square when our wrist coms buzzed.

"All crew return to the ship immediately. Energy signature detected."

In the town square, the music stopped and our crewmates scrambled to gather their things and say good-bye.

"I should check in with Eddie in the clinic," I said, "see if he needs any help wrapping anything up."

"I shall accompany you."

"No, you'll be needed on the bridge. We'll be right behind you."

Kier hesitated, and then gave me a nod before taking off toward our shuttles.

Chapter Four

KIER'AHN

For all that the crew had been celebrating quite vigorously moments before, they were efficient in their efforts to leave the planet. I was grateful for the distraction provided by my duties as it made me less likely to become lost in memories of this afternoon.

It had been a shock to discover that I'd been locked in the decontamination chamber with Chloe. I was not shy concerning nudity, it was a natural state after all. Everyone was just a body that housed a soul, nothing more or less.

However, Chloe was different. She had become something more to me, over the years. A confidant, a best friend.

I was relieved that there would be no lasting damage to our relationship from what had occurred in the unit today. But that did not seem to help the sense that something had shifted in me.

As we docked in the Intrepid, the bustle of activity redirected my focus. There were far more pressing matters than the pleasurable softness of her skin, the flush of her cheeks...

Yes, far more important things.

Unfortunately, when everyone was safely aboard, the captain had retracted the call since the energy signature was going in and out of our sensors once again; we could not get a proper lock on it. Beta crew would continue to monitor the signal and, if necessary, Alpha crew would be recalled to stations. So, for the moment, we were all on standby. Not an ideal situation when I desperately required distraction.

It was too early to go to bed, and I was afraid that such a thing would give my mind too much freedom to wander back to this afternoon. So I took a cold, bracing shower and decided to meditate.

An hour later, I stood from my meditation cushion, still struggling with these thoughts and desires.

It was not merely the physical sensation of touch, something that I had not expected to enjoy so much when my hands had gripped Chloe's skin. No, it was also the mental touch that had happened by accident.

My touch telepathy was not as chaotic as it once had been; I was much better at controlling it. But when touch happened in an emotional situation, and I did not have a moment to prepare myself for it, my mental abilities sometimes took advantage of others' openness. And that was what had happened this afternoon.

Chloe's mind had been open to me, and I had seen, just for a moment, a golden, beautiful landscape full of complex emotions. There had been shock, worry, sadness, and desire.

So much desire!

And most shocking of all it had been directed at me.

She had wanted me to touch her more. She had also wanted to touch me back.

And instead of being repulsed or frightened by the prospect, it had awakened something in me that I had thought long dormant – an ache for my body to be explored, and to explore another in turn. To be touched, and to touch, without fear or recrimination.

No one else on the ship elicited such longing; only her and I did not understand it.

Perhaps it was merely that I trusted her. But that did not explain the bone deep longing that, even now, haunted me. That was different, special, and potentially destructive. If I let it out, if I indulged in such a thing, I could harm

Chloe's mind by accident. I could cross a boundary that our friendship would never recover from.

I shivered in fear and took a breath, placing the emotion behind the appropriate cognitive barrier.

Clearly meditation is not enough. I must engage my mind in another way and I will not find that by staying in my quarters.

I slipped into my uniform jacket and pulled my gloves on before heading toward the lift. It might've been futile to try and forget Chloe by going to the stellar cartography room, but I was drawn there in moments like this. The utter peace, the distraction of the stars all around me. And, the feeling of being close to my mother.

After her murder, I'd been so badly injured that I could not attend her funeral. My body was in a healing chamber for weeks as the healers attempted to make the skin grafts take on my back and left arm. My Human physiology made this extremely difficult and as a result, I still had scars. When I was, at last, released from the healing chamber, I stumbled to the small observatory that my father had built for my mother and hid there. One of the staff on the estate would find me tucked away at the base of the telescope every morning for months. My father was absent from the situation. In fact, after putting my half-sister on a diplomatic shuttle back to Earth, I did not see him for three months. I was left alone to process the loss of my mother, and the frightening intensity of Atavarian emotions often made it impossible to sleep or eat.

The only place I ever found peace, was the observatory.

Then, one day, I woke to see builders dismantling it, piece by piece.

It was like watching her die all over again.

I ran screaming up the hill, enraged as I snarled and tried to bite the males tearing it down.

It was not my father that stopped me, but another voice. One I would grow to both fear and love in equal measure.

"Kier of House Ahn, control yourself."

I looked up to see my aunt Prem'Ahn looking down her nose at me, a tense frown on her face. Her voice had not been loud, just firm and filled with the disapproval I was growing familiar with.

"You are Atavarian," she continued, "and as such, you will conduct yourself in keeping with the Enlightened house of your forebears."

She made me watch them destroy my mother's favorite place, and I felt each rip and tear of the metal in my soul. I cried the entire time and when it was done, I wiped my eyes and turned to my aunt.

"Now," she had said, "that is done. Tomorrow, your tears will be dried, your mind focused. It is time we begin to make you the male you are supposed to be."

That was the last day I wept for my mother. I had not looked up at the stars in the same way again until Chloe showed me the cartography room. It comforted me, and reminded me of being loved, of simpler days of safety. And I found that I needed that tonight.

When I finally ascended to the room, I was terribly warm, so I shed the jacket and relished the cool air as it hit my bare arms. Lately I had been incredibly hot even on the ship and had taken to wearing a tank top under my uniform jacket to prevent myself from sweating through. Since I was alone, I also shed my gloves and folded my discarded clothes neatly in a corner of the room.

There was a console near the end of the cartography equipment where I could check in on the status of the energy signature and I went there first. So far, all we had were theories, one of which was that it was some kind of rogue Pirate Federation ship since the energy was distorted in a very distinct way.

I wondered briefly what Lieutenant Vabaris would think since he had grown up in the Titus Pirate Federation. But he was quite close lipped about his time there and we were not friends. Though, he was friends with Chloe.

Very good friends with Chloe...he's always around her, making her smile with his easy jokes.

My hands curled into fists, an uncomfortable spike of heat flared in my chest.

He touches her all the time, he can because for him it is nothing...he knows how her skin feels, what it feels like to hug her. Does he know how her mouth tastes? Have they...?

I cringed as a low growl rolled up my throat.

This was not good. I should not be having such a response to these thoughts.

I let out a long breath and forced my hands to relax. After a few minutes, the anger had faded to a mere aggravation, which seemed to be my base line when it came to Lieutenant Vabaris.

I turned to the large telescope and cartography equipment and ran my hand over the cool metal. It may have been a decoration, but it was also functional. The cartographers did not use it to track the stars, that was what the sophisticated computers were for. But they still kept the telescope maintained and clean, for which I was very grateful since I was one of the few who actually used it. Tonight, I was not sure what I would be able to see, and that was fine. Just having my hands on it, just gazing up at the dark expanse above me was enough to soothe the restless ache in my chest.

I brought up the star chart on the computer next to the telescope when I heard the hatch at the other end of the room pop open. My head snapped up from the relay I was reading and my palms immediately began to sweat. There was only one other person who would be here at this time.

I glanced at where my jacket and gloves sat across the room and began to move toward them when Chloe came around the corner of the telescope. She stopped short when she saw me, eyes wide as she clutched a small blanket, a box of food and her tablet to her chest. Her hair was up in a haphazard fashion on the top of her head, and there was a flush to her cheeks much like there had been when I had prevented her from falling earlier. The memory brought a burning sensation to my palms and I quickly thrust my hands behind me. The sudden temptation to touch those pink cheeks, to run my finger across the plump lips that were parted just enough for me to see her adorably crooked teeth, was sudden and painful.

I took a step back and straightened my shoulders, desperate to gain some control over myself.

"Kier," she gasped. "I, uh, I didn't…Eddie kicked me out of sick bay and I can't seem to rest in my quarters so I thought maybe a change of scenery would help me think."

"So I see."

She glanced down at the bundle in her arms and laughed. It was not the first time I found her up here with such items, but it was the first time that I was tempted to lay her down on the blanket and find out what her skin felt like under the loose shirt she currently wore.

The image was startling, visceral, and I shut it down with brutal efficiency.

"If you want to be alone I can go," she offered.

"Not at all."

I should have left, should have told her that I needed space, or sleep. But I was weak. I wanted to stay with her, in our own special corner of the universe where everything was simple, safe.

Her smile disarmed me utterly and my chest gave a strange flutter that I refused to examine too closely for fear of what I would see. I cleared my throat and gestured for her to lay her blanket down.

"Would you mind holding these?" she asked.

I took the snacks and tablet from her carefully since I had not retrieved my gloves yet. As she spread out the blanket, something on the tablet caught my eye and I forgot about my gloves and jacket.

"What's this?" I asked as my eyes ran over the data.

Chloe bounced on her toes and gave a little squeal.

"Okay, so that new nanite technology? Well, one of the newer GUP planets called Shankar used these to create a universal anti-viral medication. The GUP hasn't approved it for living trials yet *but* I got my hands on some of the test results from Shankar and I'm running models to see if I can apply it to a more complex virus. I don't have living samples, of course, just 3D models but I'm calibrating the nanites to run a theoretical model to see if maybe I could create a universal vaccine to this virus like the Shankar did with their virus, which was much simpler as it only affected their species but..." her voice trailed off. "Why are you looking at me like that?"

I blinked, cleared my throat and attempted to check that my feelings were firmly behind the correct barriers. Recently I had found myself becoming lost in the way Chloe's cheeks flushed when she spoke of her scientific interests. The light in her eyes made me want to keep her talking so I could be carried away with her enthusiasm. She was a dreamer, something I usually did not connect with, but somehow she drew me in, made me want to ride along with her as she imagined a galaxy that could be healed of the diseases that plagued it. Her mind was truly remarkable. I never tired of hearing about all the theories and discoveries that she was making.

"I am fascinated by what you are uncovering. It is truly incredible," I said quickly as we sat on the blanket. "The applications of a universal anti-viral..."

"I *know*, and if the nanites could be programed correctly and we could overcome the issue with accelerated degradation of the nanites themselves, it could eradicate deadly viruses across species, something that has been impossible until now. I mean, at the moment it's all theoretical. I would need to test this on live samples, but if I can get these models right, then I could present this to the GUP Medical Council."

"You are extremely talented, Chloe, an asset to this kind of research. Your contribution will surely speed the process."

She ducked her head, a shy smile spread on her face.

"Aw, I bet you say that to all the nurses."

"No, I do not."

She looked up at me and I was surprised to find that I was leaning toward her. Our hands were close where they rested on the blanket, too close. I should have leaned back, should have put distance between us. But once again, I was reckless and could not bear to listen to reason.

Chloe looked away and began to fidget with a loose string on the blanket, winding and unwinding it around her finger until her skin was crisscrossed with red marks from it.

"You know, sometimes," she said, her voice quiet, "I wonder what it would be like to be able to go into a situation like this colony, and know for certain that you had the answers to every disease, every infection. That you knew you wouldn't lose anyone."

"You feel the loss of them deeply."

"Yes. I suppose it's good that I never got used to death, that I've got compassion still after seeing so much of it traveling with my father during his work. But...it's still just as terrible as the first time I saw it. Maybe more, in some ways, because now I see all the possibilities for curing illness if only we knew just a little more about a few things."

"You will get there."

She gave me shallow chuckle.

"And how do you know that?"

"Because you are the most tenacious person I have ever met, Chloe Carter. And if anyone could do it, it would be you."

She gave me a wobbly smile.

"I would say that you're just being nice, but I know better. You don't say things like that unless you mean them."

"I do, very much."

"Thank you, Kier. You don't know what that means to me."

A warmth spread through me, followed by a lightness in my limbs. I had made her feel better. I had encouraged her, and my words meant something precious to her. I may not have been able to touch her like Lieutenant Vabaris, but I still managed to be a good friend. It made me want to do more.

"What is your first step with this new research?" I asked.

She took a pink sugar-encrusted cookie out of the small container next to her and bit into it. Some of the pink sugar fell onto her bottom lip and remained there as she chewed. It made the fullness of her mouth more pronounced, and tempting in an unexpected way. A sudden urge to lean forward and lick the sugar off her lips took hold of me and I had to tense my body to keep from lunging at her. I was very grateful that she began to speak, giving me something to focus on besides the way her tongue had darted out to lick up the sugar.

"I have to calibrate the nanites to a virus. I'm going to use one I'm familiar with so I chose the Lavat virus."

My eyebrows raised at that.

"I know it well. It has been a scourge to Atavarians for centuries."

She nodded.

"I, um, well I did my thesis for my Xenobiology degree on the virus, and put forth a possible solution to the problem of a vaccine. It was used as the basis of the research that led to the creation of the vaccine, actually."

"I did not know that. You are not mentioned in any of the research for it."

"Yeah, I was pretty young at the time, and naïve, honestly. I thought that they'd just give me the credit. But it turns out that's not how these things work and the Atavarian and Zorestran scientists took my theories and never mentioned my name."

Chloe shrugged but I saw the frustration and hurt on her face. I shared it quite acutely and a sharp desire to correct this began to course through me.

"I am sorry," I said. "That is not fair."

"It still bothers me," she admitted, "but ultimately, I'm just happy a vaccine was discovered. It's a horrible virus. I've heard there's a mutated strain that's popped up recently but I can't find any news about it or models of the mutation. So, I'm going to use a model of the original one and see what the nanites can do with that, just to get a feel for it."

"The Atavarian Science Institute may have a model of the mutation. Perhaps I could inquire if anyone there would be willing to send you more extensive information. If you send me the specifics of what you need I can pass them along."

"That would be amazing! I'll send them to you right away."

I reached down to hand her the tablet at the same time Chloe went to take it off the blanket. My fingertips, devoid of the gloves I usually wore, lightly brushed against hers, but it was enough to set my skin on fire. The exact moment I'd been resisting all night had suddenly occurred and I was held immobile by this sliver of contact between us.

My eyes locked on the sight of her small, slender fingers lingering against mine. The contrast of her pale skin and my deep red, the insanity of how *good* this felt.

I expected her to withdraw, to put distance between us.

She did not move.

In the decontamination unit, the shock of my mind and hers connecting had pulled me away from the temptation for more.

But that was not the case this time. The warnings of all my teachers, the lessons drilled into my mind that told me this was more dangerous than anything that I had ever done, all of it faded to nothing as a yearning so strong took hold of me that it rendered all else inside of me powerless.

My heart thundered in my chest. This felt so illicit, but also undeniably *right*. I slipped my fingers toward her, the tiniest of motion that had the pads of my fingers covering her delicate, pink fingernails. I trembled as the sensations flooded my system. Slowly, I looked up at her, afraid of what I might see. Would she be angry? Afraid?

Chloe met my gaze, hers so wide and shocked, the rise and fall of her chest quick. I dared to reach out mentally, to reassure myself that she wanted my touch as much as I longed to give it to her.

The contact with her mind was brief, a small crack of a door opening. And it took my breath away.

She was fascinated, enthralled by what I was doing. It gave me the boldness to skate my hand further down her fingers until my large ones were dwarfing hers. A protective desire shot through me as she turned her hand over, palm up. This was so *much*. The physical sensations shot through me while my mind was held in the gentle warmth of hers. Both my hand and my mind were barely connected with Chloe, yet, what I felt was so strong it threatened to overwhelm me.

"Chloe," I rasped.

"It's okay," she whispered. "Don't be afraid."

It wasn't okay.

It was bliss.

It was indescribable.

It was fire and ice.

The softness of her skin, the tremble in her breathing, the beauty of the fragile veins of her wrist, I drank it all in with a thirsty intensity that shocked me. I was compelled to trace the lines of her veins with my index finger. She shivered and I glanced up to see that we had leaned toward one another, so close that her breath feathered across my cheek.

Her eyes flitted down to my mouth and I was drawn to the plump pillows of her lips. But I had never kissed anyone before, and while I knew that Chloe wanted me to, I was scared of what door it would open if I did, so I pulled back. I was already flooded with emotions that had been caged and forgotten for so long. I had no idea what would happen if I let them out, if I allowed myself to simply give in to such things.

So I focused on her small hand and the thin lines on her palm. I let my touch dance along those lines, memorizing what they looked and felt like.

"What do these lines mean?" I whispered, looking back down at her palm.

"Some think they are a story," her voice was breathy, thick with something I could not interpret. "Our past and our future."

"Hmmm," I said, continuing to touch each of them in slow succession. "Curious, and inexact I would think."

Her laugh was soft, familiar.

"Depends on who you ask."

Threads of heat wound around my body the longer I touched her, and my incisors began to ache. The sweet tang of venom from my fangs hit my tongue and I froze. I had been educated in what the beginning of a rut fever entailed, even if I had never experienced one. I'd been on rut suppressors since I was thirteen, having never passed the trials necessary to qualify for a mate. It had been a relief at the time, one less thing to disappoint my family with. But now I found myself hurtling toward something that I had been told was too dangerous for someone with my lack of mental control to participate in.

I had my dose last month. This cannot be happening.

A sudden impulse to open the doors of my mind and bring her in was overwhelming. Followed closely by the need to taste her, to mark her.

"Kier, are you alright?" Chloe asked. "Your skin just got incredibly hot."

I yanked my hand away just as both our wrist coms beeped and a message came through.

"Yellow alert, Alpha crew to stations."

I rushed to my uniform and gloves, my entire body vibrating with heat and instincts that I had never experienced.

Until now.

"Kier, seriously, if you're running a fever—"

"I am fine," I ground out, not looking at her as I passed.

"You could've caught something down on the colony. I need to get you to sick bay and—"

"Chloe, you need to leave me alone," my voice was steady but I rushed to the hatch that would take me to the hallway.

"Kier, stop!"

She seized my upper arm and I turned fast, gripping her wrist and pulling her hand off me. Instead of pushing her away, I yanked her to me until I held of both her wrists, her body an inch from mine.

"I am not sick but I am dangerous to you," I growled, my fangs starting to lower. It took all of my willpower not to press them to her throat. "You need to leave me alone. Do you understand?"

Chloe's eyes widened and I felt her fear, an oily sensation in my mind that sickened me.

She nodded, mouth opening and closing several times before she croaked out, "Y-yes, I understand."

I let her go and ran out of the observatory, having no doubt that my friendship with her was likely now at an end. A throbbing ache erupted in the center of my chest as I ran into the lift and directed the computer to take me to the bridge.

I closed my eyes tightly, forcing all of these things back behind the barriers in my mind. In the few minutes it took me to pull my jacket and gloves back on and reach the bridge, I drew on every single ounce of strength I had to find my calm. The captain, and the crew, needed me to be focused.

"I am Atavarian, of the House of 'Ahn and I will not shame my species or my house."

I repeated it, breathing in and out until the doors to the bridge opened.

Chapter Five

KIER'AHN

The doors to the lift slid opened and I straightened my shoulders before stepping out onto the bridge.

It was a wide open space with weapons and security systems to my left where Lt-Cmdr Althea Kavat was currently stationed, coms was currently being manned by an Ensign I did not recognize, scanning and science station to my right, was my station. A few steps down was where Cmdr Sonta Velheim was sitting beside Captain Drake, assessing the situation. And then out front was here Lt. Jax Vabaris was at navigation and Lt. Thanh Nguyen was in the pilot's station. The holo screen, which was usually filled with the readouts of navigation and scanning was currently showing a small vessel in front of us. We were at yellow alert, with shields up and our secondary weapon systems warming up.

I took my place at the science and scanning station, quickly looking over the information from the last few minutes. The vessel was the source of the mysterious energy but the ship did not appear to be a known Pirate Federation vessel, nor did it belong to the Gex-Corps. I had been running complex algorithms and data equations for the last few days on the energy signature, attempting to dissect it to determine its origins. Those results were finally ready and I brought them up on my screen, only to have fear attempt to distract me as I quickly read through them.

"Sir," I said, "I have been able to determine that the energy signature contains K'Tavi radiation. As such, I believe we are facing a new type of K'Tavi vessel."

The moment the name of the aggressive species was out of my mouth, tension rose around me. The K'Tavi were ruthless conquerors and most did not dare stand up to them for fear of being destroyed. Only one other Gex-Corps vessel had ever faced a K'Tavi ship and lived, and that crew had still been decimated. That had been a year ago, and no one had seen them since.

Everyone sat up straighter, and Lt. Cmdr Kavat swore under her breath as her fingers flew over the keys.

"Has the ship changed course or powered up their weapons?" Captain Drake asked.

"Negative, sir," Althea said, "but I think we need to ready our primary weapons systems at the very least."

"If we do that, they might see it as a sign of aggression. Are we certain that this is a K'Tavi vessel? It doesn't match any of the known designs."

"The radiation is consistent with other K'Tavi vessels," I said. "According to the data from the scans, it would appear that the reason we did not recognize it before was that the K'Tavi are likely using a sophisticated cloaking system."

The crew was nervous before, but the mention of a K'Tavi ship with cloaking capabilities made the atmosphere around me nearly unbearable with the weight of emotions.

I wiped sweat from my brow and paused in shock. I did not normally sweat. In fact, I was usually more prone to being colder than the rest of the crew. Yet sweat was trickling down my back. My hands shook as I typed in the request for more data on the ship in front of us.

Though I had managed to force my incisors back to their shortened length, my body was still progressing through the beginning of a rut fever.

Sweats are usually several days after incisors drop...this is accelerated somehow. However, I must control this through the current crisis and then I will request medical leave to my quarters.

It was a sound plan, though having never experienced a rutting fever, and the fact that I was not progressing in the way a full blooded Atavarian would, I had no idea exactly how long I had before I was incapable of performing my duties.

A flare appeared on my screen, an energy spike from the ship that I nearly missed due to my physical condition.

"Captain," I said, forcing my voice into a calm tone, "the ship appears to be powering up systems. It is unclear whether it is a weapon or not."

"Red alert, arm torpedoes and have ion cannon at the ready," Drake ordered.

"Ship is firing!" Althea shouted.

A bright green bolt hit us and the Intrepid shook.

"Shields holding at eighty percent," I announced as I examined the report on the weapon blast.

"Fire torpedoes," Sonta ordered.

Just as the torpedoes fired, the offending ship accelerated away from the planet, dodging the damage.

"Follow that ship, Lieutenant Nguyen," Captain Drake ordered, "don't let it get far enough to disappear on us again."

"Aye, sir," she answered.

The Intrepid turned to the right and dipped down toward the K'Tavi vessel, which was headed for a nearby asteroid belt. It would be harder to track the vessel in there, even for Lieutenant Nguyen, and I scanned for any indication that they were about to use their cloaking device.

It is odd that they would not if they wanted to escape us.

"Vessel within firing range," Althea said.

"Fire a warning shot," Captain Drake responded. "I want to try and take them alive if we can. We need to know why they're inside GUP space."

Althea's lips pinched together but she followed orders. The torpedo sailed near to the vessel, which veered away in the opposite direction.

"Vessel coming about," I announced, "and powering up their weapon."

"Evasive maneuvers," Sonta ordered.

We veered sharply to the left as another blast came at us. It sailed just past us, but was closely followed by three smaller blasts that hit us square. Sweat poured down my back and my fangs were aching horribly as they flooded my mouth with sweet tasting venom. I was thirsty and my mouth was suddenly filled with fluid.

"Lieutenant Kier'Ahn," Sonta barked, "status of the shields."

Her tone indicated that she had just repeated herself. In a combat situation, that was less than ideal, to say the least.

"Apologies. Shields down to sixty-five percent," I answered.

"Captain, they're heading for the asteroid field again," Althea said. "I recommend we pursue."

A blip on the screen drew my attention and I directed the computer to focus scans on the strange signal. It flickered in and out, much like the ship in front of us had when we had been pursuing several days earlier. My eyes widened and before I could alert anyone, the ship shook violently.

"Another K'Tavi vessel decloaking behind us," I reported. "The first ship is powering up weapons."

The Intrepid shuddered and an alarm went off indicating a chemical leak.

"Deck twelve is evacuating sector B," I said. "And there are reports of injuries starting to come in."

"Nguyen," Drake said, "did you study Vickram's Gamble at the Academy?"

Lt. Nguyen took in a sharp breath and clapped her hands.

"Yes I did!"

"Do it."

"Yes!" she pumped her fist excitedly into the air as if we weren't in a fight for our lives.

I would never understand Human emotions under stress.

The Intrepid shook again as the vessel behind us fired.

"Shields down to fifty percent," I said.

"Lieutenant Kier'Ahn," Lt. Nguyen said, "tell me when the power of the forward vessel is almost to firing capacity."

My eyes clouded and burned, and I rubbed away the discomfort. Just a few more minutes, I could hold on that long. I had to. I stared at the screen, tracking the incremental rise of power until it was the level I thought Lieutenant Nguyen would need.

"Now, Lieutenant Nguyen," I said and rubbed my eyes again.

"Hang on!"

The Intrepid took a steep, fast dive that sent my stomach dipping. The ship trembled around me from the proximity of the bolt as it flew above us and struck the second K'Tavi ship, which began to list, power quickly decreasing. The burning in my eyes dissipated, replaced by a sharp pain through my temples that I breathed through so that I could focus on the read out in front of me.

"First ship is headed toward the second," I said, my voice strained. "They're firing the secondary weapon at their own ship."

The second vessel exploded on my sensors just before the remaining K'Tavi ship put on speed and attempted to escape.

"Don't let them get away," Captain Drake said. "Fire torpedoes to cripple, not destroy."

Two torpedoes sailed through space toward the K'Tavi ship. One made impact and the engine flickered as the ship slowed.

"Tractor beam, and open a channel."

I typed in the command just as another sharp pain hit me. This time I gasped as my vision went white for a moment.

The tractor beam had not fully locked on when my sensors beeped out an alarm and I canceled the order.

"The ship's engine is reaching critical. I believe they are attempting to self-destruct."

"Get us minimum safe distance, Lieutenant Nguyen," Sonta ordered.

We had just begun to move when the sensors sent another alarm. Before I could warn the captain, the K'Tavi vessel exploded, sending a small shockwave toward us.

The Intrepid shook violently this time and several alarms blared. Before I could check the damage report, another blast of pain hit me, this one worse than before. I did not remember learning about such intense discomfort during rut fever, but I did know that my mind was releasing intense hormones that would cause my telepathy to seek out a connection to a partner. Without that connection to help relieve the flood of hormones, they would build up in my system, causing intense pain, hallucinations and mental decline.

For a full blooded Atavarian it takes two weeks, but for me...

I could not make the calculations, the pain was too intense for me to focus.

"Lieutenant Kier'Ahn?" Captain Drake's voice cut through the pain.

"Yes...sir?"

I opened my eyes to find him standing in front of me, eyes wide with concern.

"Are you injured?"

"No, sir."

"You looked like you were in pain."

"I...I am capable of discharging my duties until the Intrepid is out of harm."

"You're sure?"

I nodded.

"Very well. Damage report, Lieutenant Kier'Ahn?"

I switched screens to the internal reports and forced my expression to remain neutral, even as my emotions tried to send me into a panic.

"Three decks report damage, the chemical leak on deck twelve section B is being contained," I said, as a dull, throbbing pain settled behind my eyes. "Minor injuries and no casualties. There is a coolant leak in sick bay and all injured personnel are being diverted to the secondary bay while engineering attempts to repair it."

Chloe...was Chloe caught in the coolant leak? Was she hurt?

I managed to stop my mind from spinning with these worries, but could not cease the constant repetition of them. I had to stay away from her, that was clear. If she triggered this rut fever somehow, then being near her would make it worse. I might act on the primal instincts to bite and rut her, I might force a mental bond with her as my forebears used to do before the Enlightenment. I would never forgive myself if I hurt her in this way.

I will have to quarantine myself until Dr. Goodman can administer an additional suppressant. Then request leave to go home to Atavar for a time and purge whatever connection I have made with Chloe.

A jolt of pain hit me across the chest and it had nothing to do with the fever. This was purely a reaction to my desire to hold onto my relationship with Chloe. It was only natural to mourn, to resist even. But these feelings would not dictate my course of action. They could not.

"See if the repair crews need any assistance, and if Doctor Goodman needs any help moving injured to the secondary sick bay. Any sign of other ships?" Captain Drake asked.

"No, sir."

He nodded and returned to his seat.

"Give me a ship wide channel."

The ensign in charge of the communications opened the channel and Captain Drake swallowed hard before making his announcement.

"This is the captain speaking. We have just made contact with the K'Tavi. All crews to remain on red alert until we are sure there are no more ships in this sector. Drake out."

I glanced at Althea, who was staring at the holo screen with a grim set to her face, back straight.

"Assessment, Lieutenant Commander Kavat?" Sonta asked.

"Those were likely scouting ships," she said, her voice hard. "K'Tavi see capture as a great shame, which was why they would rather die than have us take them. They are also quite secretive about their technology. So if they have managed a new kind of cloaking, that's likely why they destroyed their own ship as well, so we wouldn't get our hands on it."

"Will they be back?" Captain Drake asked.

"I'm not sure. This planet isn't densely populated and there's no advanced infrastructure or resources. If they were scouting this area on purpose it could be because they are looking for weaknesses within the GUP."

"It might also explain why the colonists have not received supplies," I responded, "if the K'Tavi attacked the supply ship to keep its presence here a secret."

Captain Drake nodded.

"I'll make a report to Command. Lieutenant Commander Kavat, you're with me, Commander Sonta you have the bridge. And Lieutenant Kier'Ahn, you're relieved of duty until Doctor Goodman clears you, go take care of yourself."

"My apologies, Captain," I said, getting to my feet.

I swayed briefly and gripped the back of my chair for support.

"Do you need help getting to sick bay?" he asked.

I shook my head.

"I believe it would be better if I retired to my quarters. I will call for Doctor Goodman once the injured have been seen to."

"Very well, but please take care of yourself. I have a feeling this is bigger than we can tell right now, so I'm going to need you at the top of your game."

"Understood."

I forced my legs to hold steady, and to walk with my back straight, as I rushed to the lift. Once the doors closed I slid against the wall and held my head in my hands. The back and under arms of my jacket were soaked and my legs shook. This was far more severe than it should have been, either because I had never let my body go through a rutting fever or perhaps another reason that was not obvious. Whatever the cause, I suspected that I may be too far along for anything to be done.

Except...no. That is not an option. I will either recover from this or I will die. But I will not give in to it.

Chapter Six

CHLOE

It had been two days since the attack on the ship.

And two days since one of the most erotic, and confusing moments of my life.

We were still in orbit around Jahnus Five, letting the engineering team finish repairs and awaiting further orders from Gex-Corps High Command. It turned out that one of the K'Tavi ships had actually fired on the colony, something we hadn't known until we'd received a very garbled distress call.

The shot was wide, hitting the backup power station we'd constructed for them and several civilians were injured with burns from the explosion. No one was killed, though everyone was understandably shaken. With the exception of a very small engineering and medical team, the captain wasn't letting many of us down on the surface, in case we encountered any more K'Tavi. So far, none had shown up but being kept on yellow alert and the possibility that there were more of the aggressive species out there, lurking and waiting had us all on edge.

Althea perhaps most of all. She'd been in meetings with the GUP, along with the captain, since the attack. I'd seen her once in the officer's mess and sat with her as she stared out at the planet, not saying a word. When my break was over and I got to my feet, she had grabbed my hand and squeezed it tight before letting go. I hoped she was alright, that she was talking to someone about how she was feeling. Though I'd heard she spent most of her free time in the training room beating the crap out of anyone who dared spar with her.

We all have our ways of dealing with grief.

But that wasn't *really* what was bothering me. At least, not entirely.

It was good that I was kept busy between the colony and the crew. Otherwise I'd be obsessing more than I already was about that moment in the observatory.

Two days and no one has seen him since his mysterious illness on the bridge.

I closed a lid on an antibiotic case a little harder than needed in my frustration. No one could tell me exactly what happened and I got the distinct impression that the questions were annoying everyone. They all saw much bigger and more serious issues at hand than why the mysterious Atavarian left the bridge with a fever and dizziness.

While they had a point, it didn't mean I would stop trying to figure it out. I'd run every simulation I could think of, trying to figure out what illness could have affected him in this way. So far, nothing matched with what little I knew of his symptoms.

That doesn't mean it's not one of those things though. His Human physiology could have all of these illnesses presenting differently in him and I wouldn't know it because Atavarians don't account for hybrids.

I slammed the case down on the hover cart and growled out a grunt as I picked up another one filled with plasma for the colony. All the usual things I'd do to distract myself weren't working anymore and I was five minutes away from marching up to Kier's quarters.

I'd heard rumors that he'd been foaming at the mouth, that he was sweating so much that he left a puddle at his station, even that he'd snarled at the captain. All of it was false, I was sure, but what I did know as that the last time I saw him he'd been burning up with fever and not at all himself.

And that he'd touched me in a way that I'll never forget.

My palm still tingled at the memory, and I blushed remembering the wonder in his eyes. I'd been with dozens of men, women and non-binary people. I'd done things in private, and public, that were wild by anyone's standards. But sitting in that observatory, fully clothed with Kier caressing my palm was hands down the most intimate, sensual experience of my life.

I stared down at my hand, at the veins in my wrist that he'd seemed so taken with. Had he wanted to bite me there? When he'd snapped at me just before fleeing the observatory, he'd looked at my throat like he wanted to sink his teeth into me. And for the first time in my life, I wanted to know what something like that would feel like.

No, I wanted to know what it would feel like from him. I want things I shouldn't want from my friend and I don't know how to turn it off.

I'd awoken in a cold sweat the past two mornings, and I swore that every once in a while I could feel Kier in my head. He was in pain, scared; that's what came through. But it was a flash so brief that I couldn't at all be sure if I was feeling him or just my own worries.

Eddie had assured me that Kier was not technically 'sick' but that was all he'd tell me. He went to Kier's quarters three times a day and every time he came back looking more worried than the last time. But when I asked him what was wrong, he clammed up. Finally, I tried to hack into Kier's records, something I had never done before, and couldn't get past Eddie's special fire walls. When Eddie had found out what I'd done, he'd threatened to report me.

"He's my friend, I need to know what's going on!" I'd shouted at him last night.

Instead of fighting back like Eddie always did, he'd slammed his hand on the counter and stormed off.

We didn't say a word to each other this morning, outside of whatever was necessary for our duties, and now he was off on his second house call to Kier.

I rubbed my temple where an odd headache had been simmering since yesterday and tried to focus on the results from my latest nanite test. My mind kept wandering to Kier, to the way his skin was scorching hot to the touch, and the fear that he'd fled that room with.

Was he really sick, and he and Eddie were just trying to protect me? The thought that Kier was dying and I wasn't at his side kicked me in the gut and I plopped down in my chair. They wouldn't do that to me, would they?

"I'll kill him if that's the case," I muttered, my hands curling into fists.

Eddie was like an uncle to me; he'd been my guardian after my father's death and had sponsored me into the Gex-Corps Medical Academy when I turned seventeen. I trusted him with my life. And he'd never, ever lied to me before. So if he was keeping something like that from me, the betrayal would be even more acute.

But he'd also have to tell the captain if there was a serious illness on board and there would be quarantine protocols in place. That wasn't the case, which meant something else was going on.

The doors to sick bay opened and Eddie walked in. He was a person of small stature, and the sensors in his shoes reacted to the flooring on the ship creating a shifting platform that enabled him to reach anything in any room on the ship, no matter how high up it was. His curly hair was graying at the temples and his beard was in serious need of a trim, or maybe it was just extra full because he'd been fidgeting with it ever since the attack.

I leapt out of my chair and marched toward him. The way the floor was raised up meant that I could face him, but not get *in* his face, though I did jab my finger at him as I spoke.

"He's sick, and as his best friend, I have a right know."

"No, you don't."

He turned away from me and I spun him around.

"I need to know if he's okay!"

Instead of lashing out or bellowing at me that it was none of my business like he did yesterday, Eddie's face softened and he patted my hand.

"Chloe, you need to prepare yourself."

The air left my lungs and I stumbled away from him. It was what I'd feared, but I still hadn't really been prepared to hear it.

"What is it?" I whispered. "Did he catch something on the planet? I've been running models on every Atavarian virus and—"

"No, it's nothing like that. Is that why you've hardly slept the last two days? You've been in here thinking Kier was dying from an illness?"

I nodded my throat so tight I didn't think I could get words out.

"Why would you think that?" he asked.

"He had a fever when I saw him last, he was being emotional, at least for him. I thought…I don't know. But if it's not that, then what is it? Is it communicable?"

"No."

I frowned as I blinked away tears.

"Then why can't I see him? Why is he all alone in his quarters?"

"Because it's safer for everyone, including Kier."

Confusion and anger beat against my brain, replacing the bone deep grief I'd nearly been lost in a moment ago.

"You're not making any sense. If it's not contagious, then why is he suffering alone?"

He opened and closed his mouth several times before letting out a grunt of frustration.

"Fucking Atavarians and their puritan levels of privacy."

"Elaborate, please!" I snapped.

He grunted another expletive and shoved the data pad at me. I grabbed it with shaking hands and read the report.

Then I read it again.

"He…he's in an Atavarian rut?" I asked in disbelief. "I thought he was on suppressors?"

"Yes, and he started having issues with the efficacy about three months ago. I've been adjusting the dose ever since and I thought we'd worked it out but something triggered it strong enough to push past the drugs."

I had a moment to wonder if our encounter in the decontamination unit, brief though it was, had been enough to do that before returning to the data pad. The lab results showed abnormally high levels of Veltine, the hormone that enables Atavarians to have telepathy.

"This isn't right," I murmured, and scrolled through to see the lab levels for the last three days. "They're increasing. Why are his Veltine levels increasing? If they get much higher, he's going to become comatose."

"It's part of the rut fever. Apparently it's not just about the physical act of mating with a partner, they have to share minds as well to siphon off the extra Veltine that's produced. Which is why male Atavarians have to prove that they can exercise complete control over their telepathy before they are allowed physical mating. The risk of creating a permanent bond is high, and during a rutting fever, the primal instincts of Atavarians are on a hair trigger. So the ability to control the telepathic connection and not let it get too deep is especially important. Some opt not to even try, and a very rare few, like Kier, are never given permission to do it all."

My mind stuttered to a halt while my heart sped up at that revelation. I'd always suspected that Kier might have been inexperienced when it came to sex, but to hear confirmation gave me thoughts I didn't need at the moment.

"His system is overloading with hormones and chemicals that a full blooded Atavarian would have a hard time managing," Eddie continued. "His Human physiology makes it more difficult on his body than what is normal and therefore it's putting tremendous strain on him. Atavarian males, if they are in this state too long they can experience hallucinations, bouts of extreme rage and finally—"

"Death."

"Yeah."

I swallowed, forcing my mind not to spiral. That wouldn't help Kier right now. I had been determined to cure whatever was happening to him for the past two days. Now that I knew it was something else, I wasn't going to let my mind give in to panic and fail him.

"Okay, so what's the treatment?" I asked.

Eddie tilted his head and raised his eyebrows at me.

"I mean, besides the obvious of him...ya know...having sex."

"There isn't one," Eddie admitted.

"Then we need to tell the captain to get us to Atavar. Don't they have rut partners there, kind of a sacred courtesan situation?"

Even as I asked it the thought made my insides tense with jealousy. The mere mention of someone else touching him had me wanting to throttle the person, but if it would save his life then I'd deal.

"Usually, yes. But we won't be able to get to Atavar in time."

"It's not that far, three, maybe four days with a jump gate."

"I know but we're being diverted to jump gate Alpha—"

"Which is one of the quickest jumps to Atavar!"

"Let me finish please!" Eddie ran a hand over his face and I saw the exhaustion hit him hard. "We have a meeting with the top brass at the station to discuss the situation here, we will be there for at least two days. And even if I could send a medical override for a transport, there is no guarantee that Kier will survive until then. At the rate the Veltine is increasing in his system he could be comatose by this time tomorrow."

I stared at him as my mind processed those words and quickly came to a conclusion.

Kier needed help.

I was his friend, someone he trusted.

I could help him.

I could save him.

The fact that saving him meant sharing an intimacy that made nerves flutter like drunk butterflies in my chest was something I would have to get over.

I handed the data pad back to Eddie and headed for the door.

"Chloe, no!"

Eddie ran and caught me just before I got out into the hallway.

"You know as well as I do that there's only one way to save him, and as stupid as it sounds, I am the only one he'll trust to do it."

Eddie lowered his voice and speared me with a look.

"This is *not* your normal one-night stand crap. He's feral, damn near out of control! He wouldn't realize he was hurting you until it was too late. Especially since he's never..."

Kier would be mortified to know we were discussing his rut fever and virginity, but we were medical professionals and it wasn't gossip or crude. Although, if I was honest with myself, I was only calm and professional on the surface.

Underneath, in the parts of me that had been unnerved and aroused since he'd touched my hand in the observatory, I was a confused mess. I wanted this, more than I cared to admit. And that felt deeply problematic. Was I about to march off and punch Kier's 'V card' because it was the right thing to do clinically, or because I wanted him more than I'd ever wanted anyone in my life?

I have to approach this professionally. It's no different than giving a dying patient some of my blood or a tissue sample for an artificial organ. Sure, this is ten times more intimate, but Kier is too important for me to let him suffer and die just because I'm having a question of conscience.

"I trust him," I said, my voice breaking on my next words, "and I can't lose him."

Eddie's face softened and he let out a long breath.

"Hold on, let me give you this since I can see that I won't be able to talk you of it."

I let loose a tiny smile as he went to a cabinet and came back with a hypo spray and a portable plasma regenerator.

"The hypo is filled with an exceptionally strong sedative. It should knock him out but if he's really feral it might only slow him down. And the PPR is in case he bites you."

"Bites me?"

"Yeah, apparently that's a possibility."

I liked that far more than I ever thought I would, and felt my cheeks turn red. Instead of saying anything, because I didn't trust my voice, I just nodded and took the two devices from him.

"If I don't hear from you by morning I'm getting a security team and breaking down the door, you understand? So keep that in mind, and make sure to let me know you're alright."

"I will."

He nodded and then gave me a gruff chuckle.

"It feels weird to say good luck but...well, good luck."

I managed a wobbly smile before making my way out the door and to the lift. It was the longest walk of my life as I tried to think of how to approach this, tried to prepare myself for what might happen.

With the exception of the observatory, I had never seen Kier come close to losing control of his emotions. If that had been just a mere taste, if he was truly feral as Eddie had just warned me, what would I see?

Atavarians were stronger than Humans, would I be able to fight back if I needed to?

Stop, this is Kier. He's my friend, he would never hurt me.

I repeated the mantra in the lift; kept telling myself this wouldn't change anything between us. Because the thought that what I was about to do might cause a rift between us was devastating. I had to keep him in this galaxy, that was all that mattered. The rest we would figure out together. Maybe this would be a good thing in the long run, get those weird emotions that had been stirred up by our recent touching out of our way so there was no more tension.

Deep down, I knew I was grasping at straws, but that didn't really matter, not where Kier's life was concerned. He was worth every risk, every moment of discomfort. It was shocking to realize just how much I was willing to do for him, how much I was truly willing to give for him.

I glanced down at my wrist, at the veins carrying my blood through my body. I felt the pulse in my throat, remembering the hungry way he'd stared at it, and something profound clicked into place.

If he wanted my life's blood, it was his.

If he wanted my body, it was his.

If he wanted my mind, my thoughts, the depths of my soul, they were all his.

And when I realized that, I was terrified that I was so willing to give him all of me; far more so than anything he could actually *do* to me.

Before I was quite ready for it, I was out of the lift and standing in front of Kier's door. I had the medical override code and something told me that pushing the com button wasn't going to cut it today.

I took a deep breath, ignoring the way my hand shook as I typed in the code and stepped inside.

Chapter Seven

CHLOE

His quarters, which were usually so neat and pristine, were a wreck. Furniture was upended, the collection of Atavarian ceremonial masks were scattered all over one side of his room, the contents of his desk were tossed, the holo tablet was a busted mess of wires and bent metal on the floor. There were actual dents in his walls, and the temperature in the room was much cooler than usual. The lights were dim and it took a few seconds for my eyes to adjust properly. When I did, I saw even more of his belongings on the floor, along with his uniform and gloves. I had to walk further into the room, maneuvering around the upside down couch, to find him.

He was huddled on the floor, bent over with his legs tucked under him, his arms over his head as he moaned and shivered. It was such a vulnerable pose, like a child trying to hide from a monster. I wanted to hold him, to rock him in my arms and tell him it was going to be okay, that I would make it all better. But I was frozen to the spot, unsure how to proceed. I was here for a lot more than hugging, but how the hell did I take us from two illicit skin to skin touches to full on sex?

I took a moment to breathe and let myself indulge in just looking at him. I'd never really let myself do that before and the restrained power in every line of muscle on his arms and back was truly beautiful. His skin was a rich red color, smooth everywhere except for a patch on his back, along the left shoulder blade and down the back of his arm. It looked like a burn and I wondered what could've happened to cause a wound to scar when there were many ways on Atavar to ensure against that.

As I watched his body rock back and forth, I couldn't help but admire the utter perfection of his body. The trim line of his waist, the round temptation of his butt under those tight black boxer-briefs, the breadth of his thighs.

But what made his body truly magnificent, more than his strong hands, and arms, was that it housed the soul of one of the best men I'd ever known.

I felt bad standing there and taking him in; this wasn't supposed to be about titillation, this was to save his life. But never had I been so mesmerized by the sight of a male's body as I was by Kier's in that moment.

Then something changed.

He stopped rocking forward, his body went utterly still and his moans ceased. My heart hammered behind my ribs and I suddenly felt like a rabbit caught in an unexpected trap as he lowered his arms. When Kier turned his head to me it was unnaturally fast. Those green eyes I knew so well narrowed and he bared his teeth at me.

This wasn't the Kier I knew – the calm, controlled male. Eddie had warned me but seeing it struck me dumb. I couldn't move in the midst of that gaze.

"What...are you doing...here?" his voice was deeper, his incisors longer so that they showed more when he spoke.

I swallowed and tried to get words out, though nothing but a squeak made it past my lips.

Kier unfolded himself from his crouched position, graceful in spite of his size and stood before me, his chest heaving like he'd been running, drops of sweat tracing his pectorals like a lover. Every muscle in his body was drawn so tight that I could see the definition of them. His hands were curled and even his toes were digging into his carpet, which I could now see was shredded in places.

As if drawn to it, I glanced down at his phallus and my eyes bugged out.

It was the biggest dick outline I'd ever seen. In fact, the waist band of his boxer briefs wasn't even flush with his skin. As I stared at it, small bulges along the sides pulsed and then a ring around the base started to enlarge.

His knot, how had I forgotten about that?

I'd been with plenty of males with knots, it was hard to have interspecies sex with a male that didn't have one. Still, I'd never let one of them slip it in. I had always been very clear about that and lucky that they'd all listened.

Something told me, however, that Kier needed to knot in order to get this rut under control.

Okay, no reason to panic. It's a new experience and it's with my best friend…who is currently looking at me like I'm the main course.

The powerful hunger in his gaze was overwhelming. A wild thing stared at me from those green depths, just barely restrained by Kier's sheer force of will. Though he was disheveled, mostly naked, and now shaking from the effort of holding back, the more I looked at him, the more I realized that this was still Kier. And no matter what was going on right now, I could trust him.

It didn't dislodge the nerves ricocheting inside of me, but it calmed me enough to think straight.

"I know what's going on, and I'm here to help," I said slowly.

His eyes widened and he stumbled back into the torn remnants of one of his chairs. Kier fell onto his side and I ran to help him, stopping just before my hands touched his bare skin. It was habit, but if I was really going to save his life, we were going to have to do a lot more than simply touch. So I might as well cross the line now.

My hand closed around his bare forearm and he groaned as if it were the most exquisite thing he'd ever felt. I had to bite back a gasp at just how warm he was. His body was hairless, smooth and firm under my hand, and it felt special to be able to touch him like this. I reached down with my other hand to take his and try to pull him into a sitting position but I never got the chance. With one smooth motion, Kier pulled me instead and I found myself with my back pressed against the underside of his tipped couch as he held my upper arms in a tight grip and loomed over me.

Kier's eyes locked onto my lips and he surged forward only to stop himself inches away from my mouth. I strained to sit up and meet him, but he held me too tight. He was shaking again, jaw tight as he stared into my eyes with such naked fear that my heart ached for him.

"You...need...to...leave," he growled through gritted teeth.

"No."

"*Leave!*" he screamed in my face.

Kier scrambled to get away from me, flinging his body through broken belongings and strips of torn fabric, as if he were fighting himself to stay away from me. I stared, open mouthed at how powerful those emotions were, how raw. When he glanced back, he gave a whining cry and shook his head.

"Look, it's okay," I said, my voice calm, soft. "I know what's going on. I know you haven't had sex before and that's okay too. If you're nervous—"

"It's not...that," he breathed. "I am embarrassed...nervous is secondary...to the urges..."

He let out a groan that ended on a rattling growl. The sound cascaded down my spine, arousing me as much as frightening me.

"I will not be a shy virgin," he said after a moment. "I will be an animal. I will be driven by instincts...I will hurt you...I won't be myself. You have to leave, Chloe, please."

"I'm not leaving you here to die."

"You don't know what...what...I could do to you!"

I decided a gentle approach wasn't going to cut through the terror and obvious unmoored panic that was raging through him. I'd have to get firm, blunt. I'd have to shock him out of this.

So I got to my feet and strode over to him fast before he could move away. I knelt down to him, forcing him to look me in the eye.

"I know you're going primal, that you could bite me and that you might get a little rough. Not my first experience with all of that, by the way."

He bared his teeth and growled.

"I don't want to hear about your past lovers."

"And I'm not going to tell you. What I *am* going to do is tell you that you're being an idiot and that we can be grown-ups about this. It's just mating, right?

Just some down and dirty fucking. We do it, and you're better and that's that. We go back to not touching and being just friends."

Of all the reactions, Kier giving me a low, hollow chuckle wasn't one of them. "You think it's that simple?"

In the blink of an eye, he leaned toward me until I was sitting back on my elbows and he'd caged me in with his hands on either side of my body, pressed into the floor, and so careful to be near me but not touching me. I'd seen him in a hand to hand fight, seen him angry at Jax Vabaris for being an asshole. But this was the first time I'd ever seen him truly aggressive.

I saw the ferocity of his ancestors, the terrifying beauty that had once made them the most feared and also most desired species in the galaxy. This side of him had me speechless and turned on beyond belief.

What would it be like to have him unleash this on me? To be the sole object of so much feral passion?

"Do you want to know what I would do to you?" His deep voice rumbled through me. "Should I show you?"

I didn't have the chance to ask how he'd show me, because Kier looped one arm around my back, stood and picked me up like I weighed nothing. I was pressed tight to him, my legs wrapped around his waist. I clung to those broad, strong shoulders and for a moment, we just held each other. He nuzzled my throat, up to my jaw and I felt the scrape of his incisors along my skin. My eyes fluttered shut as a sensation like warm honey flooded my body.

"Do you...want to see...what I *want* to do...to you, Chloe?" he rasped against my ear.

The word slipped out on a gust of breath. "Yes."

Before I could fully grasp what was happening, Kier spun us around and slammed my back against a wall. The arm around my waist disappeared and his hand clutched my throat while his body pinned me in place. I looked up into green eyes rimmed in red now, full of fire that wanted to consume. He towered over me, all raw primal energy, a beast that had been caged for too long and was now free to unleash everything.

On me.

For a split second, I knew fear.

He was over seven feet tall, stronger than a Human and right now, that legendary Atavarian primal ancestry was at the fore. He could snap my neck without any effort in this state. But there were other things he could to too. He could hold me down and rip my clothes to shreds right before he tore me in half with what I was sure was a very impressive cock.

His thumb stretched up and caressed the underside of my chin right before he pushed into it, tilting my head up until his lips hovered above mine.

"I won't tear you in half...I want to rut you until you can't stand. I will fill you until it runs down your thighs and then I will do it again."

It should've been frightening to have someone else's voice in my head and there was definitely a little of that. But there was also *Kier*, and I recognized his presence. Warm and inquisitive, and this time, there was a sharpness to it, a hunger that was bone deep. His instincts were brutal, wild things beating at the doors of my mind, tearing down any barriers between us. I took comfort in knowing that Kier was still in there. This was just the side of him that he never let anyone else see, the side that he'd learned to fear and control at all costs. And now here I was, seeing it with him – the one he trusted to experience the parts of him that he feared most.

My breath caught as his emotions were poured into me through this strange connection of ours. I felt his terror at the instincts rushing through him. He needed me, but he also feared that, at the end of this, I wouldn't look at him the same way. That he'd hurt me deeply, physically, mentally and that would be end of our friendship. He feared losing me more than he feared a terrible death.

That was how I knew that Kier would never, ever hurt me.

He ran his nose along my jaw and cheek again, taking a deep breath that ended on a groan.

"You smell so good...devour...rut...I will not be able to control it. Decide now...are you sure? Because I do not know... if I can stop."

His voice in my head was getting deeper, more like a growling beast than the way Kier normally spoke. All of his intellect would soon be drowning in the feral parts of him. That was the risk, that my words might not penetrate all of that beastly power.

I'm not afraid of him. I trust him.

As if he'd heard me, Kier whimpered, a sound that shot straight to my heart.

I pushed on his chest with my free hand; I wanted him to look me in the eye as I said this. I wanted there to be no recriminations in the morning, no doubt about my choice.

He pulled back just enough to look at me and I felt something shift deep in my chest as I stared at him. I didn't know what it was, and I didn't need to. I'd find out later. Right now there was just the pulsing, feral need between us that wanted to possess me utterly.

"I want whatever you give me. I want *you*, Kier. Show me all the things you're afraid of, and trust me to be your anchor when things get scary. Trust me to ground you, to keep you in touch with the man I know you are. The man I trust with my life."

The world around us stood still as his feral gaze softened and raked over my face to his hand around my throat and back up. I didn't understand the mental sharing that was happening between us, and I didn't need to. All I needed to know was that Kier saw what I felt, what I knew in the marrow of bones: that I was his, without hesitation.

"Chloe...mine."

"Yes, Kier."

With a cry, Kier crushed his mouth to mine in a devouring, brutal kiss. Everything crashed into me at that moment. All the longing between us burst in an explosion of fire that was consuming us and I could not bring myself to care that there wouldn't be anything left of me at the end of it.

Yes...yes...yes...

In time with my heart, with every whimper, with every sweep of our tongues against one another.

Yes...

Was I saying it, or was he?

Was that my blood pumping with molten heat, or was it his?

When his fangs pricked my lips, causing blood to well up, Kier took in a deep, sharp breath before snarling against my lips. He sucked on my bottom lip, drawing the blood into his mouth.

I was here, pinned against the wall by Kier's huge body, his hand at my throat, but suddenly, in my mind, there was a completely different experience happening.

I was bent over his bed, completely naked, my pale skin a startling contrast to his red. Kier's mouth trailed burning kisses down my back to my bare ass and back up again. His heavy cock was pressed to my nethers, the tip breaching me as his hand snaked around and clutched my throat.

What...?

Kier snarled, in my mind and against my mouth. He wanted to devour me as he stared down at my naked body, he wanted to drag his teeth over every inch, to mark me with his mouth and his seed. He wanted me a mess under him, screaming, coming around his phallus. The desire pulsed between our physical bodies, causing me grind down on him as he speared me to his knot in my mind.

"Kier!"

Our physical bodies dry humped one another against the wall, and I was fully aware of two realities crashing against my mind and body, both visceral and explosive.

Psychically, he was fucking me hard enough to shove me across his bed; the sensation of his sheets against my hands as I grabbed handfuls to steady myself was just as real as the way I clutched his shoulders while we writhed against one another.

In my mind, Kier held me in place by the throat and the hip, as his body slapped against mine. His breath was hot on my shoulder where his mouth was pressed, his sharp teeth starting to break the skin.

"Mine...Mine...Mine!"

I didn't recognize the voice in my head, the impossibly low and animal growl that was spilling from him. I suddenly didn't even know for sure where I was.

Was I still against the wall or was I on his bed?

Was he thrusting inside of me, or were we still clothed and desperately gyrating against one another?

Heat built in a crashing wave inside of me until I couldn't take it anymore. In my mind, Kier was filling me as I came around him, and against the wall I was screaming as the dual orgasm hit me, my toes curling in my shoes.

I whimpered, and trembled as the images receded, and I was left wet and breathless.

Kier looked down at me as we panted, his entire body rigid and shaking. He was holding himself back from doing those things to me by the slimmest of margins. I could feel it in my mind as much as I felt it in every line of his body against mine.

"Run...now...if...you...don't...want –"

I stopped him with my mouth against his.

"Shut up and fuck me," I breathed.

He let out a groan before pulling me against him and stalking to his bed where he set me on my feet. I started to unzip my uniform jacket when the batted my hands away and ripped it down the middle. I stared in aroused shock at the shredded mess he proceeded to make of my pants as well. With a hot hand on my chest he shoved me back onto the bed and pulled my shoes and the remnants of fabric off my legs. I was about to pull my underwear off when he beat me to it and ripped them at the seams, tossing them to the side as if they offended him.

I was now stretched out before him, every part of me on display. Kier's hot gaze drank me in like a starved man seeing food for the first time in ages. With a savage growl, he lunged at my body, his mouth latching onto one of my stiff nipples and he drew it deep into his mouth. It was sudden and a bit too hard but I didn't care. What he'd done to me against that wall brought on the strongest orgasm I'd ever had, and yet it had seemed to only wet my appetite.

I wanted to be used and filled.

I wanted his beautiful brutality.

I wanted to be the object of the ferocious passion he caged for everyone else.

But not me...I want it...I want it all.

"Yes," he groaned out against my skin.

I couldn't think clearly, as his fangs scraped along the sensitive skin, while his hand kneaded my other breast so I had no idea if I'd spoken those words or not, and I didn't care. My back arched as his touch became more possessive, more demanding.

His mouth burned a trail all over my torso and up to my throat, leaving red scrapes from his teeth in his wake, just like he'd imagined.

The jarring lack of his touch brought me back from the blissful fog and I looked up to see him tossing his ripped boxer briefs aside and taking himself roughly in hand.

His phallus had six nodes on each side. They looked a little like the bumps on the tentacles of an octopus but without suckers. The head of his cock was thick and had a Human foreskin but the base had a round protrusion all around.

His knot.

A bolt of heat shot straight through me at the thought of taking a knot for the first time. But not just anyone's knot. Kier's knot.

He looked into my eyes as he stroked himself; a silent question, one more chance to run. And I shook my head.

"Not a chance."

With a fierce growl he fell on me, his arms holding him up so I didn't take all of his weight. I opened my legs wide and wrapped them around his waist, wanting him as deep as I could possibly take him. When the thick head of his phallus finally breached my opening we both let out a guttural moan.

Kier's eyes held mine as his hand once again came around my throat, his thumb running hard along my bottom lip, opening up the bite marks. He lapped up the bloom of blood as he pushed himself into me.

My back arched as the pressure of his girth brought me to the point of pain. Every single one of his nodes pulsed against my inner walls as he began to rut me, hard. I met his body with an undulation of my hips, welcoming the stretch of him, the strange ripple of those nodes that pressed on nerve endings I didn't even know were there.

I clung to his hard biceps as I began to feel unmoored, cast out to sea with nothing to save me. Everything was suddenly so *much*. I was penetrated, and penetrating. I was under him, but also above myself.

I felt the raging storm inside of him as it beat against all of his senses, even as I knew that I was not the one in a rut. The need to bite and claim me was burning him from the inside out, a hellish white hot burden that he was struggling to hold onto.

"Kier...I..."

Tears fell from my eyes, everything hurt so damn good, but was also so frightening as my mind struggled to grasp everything.

Kier released my throat and slipped his arm under me, holding me close even as he continued to fuck me harder.

"Ky priash...priash vel daqsh...ky priash"

His Atavarian words exploded in my mind in a swirl of color and I was spellbound. I had no idea what it all meant, but I knew I was cherished, I was safe, I was *everything*. And Kier was not going to let me float away. He was experiencing this with me, not apart from me.

It soothed the panic, and I was able to just let go and feel all of this. I tightened my arms and legs around him. The colors continued to spin in my mind as that delicious agony built higher and higher in my body.

"Priash...vel daqsh..."

Higher.

Faster.

And when his mouth latched onto the place where my shoulder met my throat and his fangs sank into my flesh, instead of terror at being fed from, I came with a shuddering scream that pulled me apart as much as it put me back together.

The colors danced and sang inside of us, and when his knot slipped into me, the burst of pain was swallowed up by another rush of pleasure that was almost too much for me to bear. I didn't know who was crying, me or him. Warmth filled my body and my soul as he emptied himself into me with shuddering, shallow thrusts. There was no darkness between our minds, only a spinning ribbon of color that tied us together.

Chapter Eight

KIER'AHN

The rampaging beast that I had caged so carefully my entire life was at last receding. As if the very act of connecting telepathically and emptying myself into Chloe had soothed its raging urges for the moment.

The taking of her flesh, the drinking of her blood, it was all I had been able to the think about. But now, I was at last coming back to myself, back in control. Even if I was not sure I would ever be satisfied with synthetic blood again after tasting her sweetness.

"Kier...stop...you're taking too much."

Her fingers stroked my horns, down to my cheek.

"Kier...listen to me...stop drinking."

I'm still drinking...I have to stop!

I withdrew my fangs, glad that the sweet venom had given her pleasure and not pain, and licked the wounds to close them. When I pushed myself up to see her, Chloe's eyes were closed and for a moment I feared that I had taken too much.

"Chloe?" I whispered, smoothing some of her hair from her face. "Are you alright?"

She opened dazed eyes and gave me an almost drunken smile.

"I'm absolutely wonderful."

She let out a breathy moan and pulled me close for a soft kiss. It shocked me at first, even after what we had just done. The blind urge to rut was passing, leaving in its wake an odd state; I was definitely still aroused, but I was no longer driven in the same way. I wanted to keep kissing her, but it was also very much something new.

"No more thinking," she murmured against my mouth. "Post coitus is for kissing and holding."

"I defer to your expertise," I said and let myself kiss her with slow, thorough strokes of my tongue.

I rolled her so we were on our sides, my knot still firmly locking us together. She was so sweet, so soft in my arms. I had no idea touching could be like this, filled with wonder and passion instead of fear.

And the taste of her blood.

It was unlike anything I had ever imagined, tinged with arousal and something else, something meant just for me.

When Chloe had come into the room earlier, and her scent had hit me, it focused the raging in my veins. I wanted her with a hunger I had never known before. It was beyond food, beyond blood. It was in my very soul. And she was the only thing that would satisfy me. That had terrified me because what I wanted to do to her was uncontrollable, it was the animal in me, goaded by the Human weakness that infected my blood.

Now here I was, having rutted her savagely and drank from her, but Chloe was not afraid of me. She was not pushing me away. Instead, she curled against me, her fingertips running in lazy lines up and down my back and side. As I relaxed, I noticed that the rutting instinct was still there, though not as blindingly fierce as before. It had muted the nerves that would have likely accompanied my first time with a partner. Perhaps later, when I was alone, I could confront the unhinged way I had used her, I could look at my embarrassment and purge it. But not now.

Now, I found myself at once sated, and hungry for her, all over again.

Once would not be enough.

I wanted more.

More of her blood.

More of her thoughts.

More of her touches that set me aflame.

More of her flesh under my hands.

As if sensing this, Chloe chuckled against me.

"You're going to have to give me a little bit of time before round two."

"I...do you...I mean, I was not expecting..."

She cupped my cheek and shook her head. The smile she gave me was so warm, so beautiful. I traced the line of her mouth with my finger, in awe of it.

"I didn't think one round would be enough to quell rutting fever," Chloe said when I stopped touching her lips.

"Are you sure that you are alright?" I asked, holding her closer to me.

"Stop worrying, I wouldn't lie about that."

I pressed my forehead to hers, and let out a breath, needing a moment. It was so odd how that release could lift the fog off my mind so quickly. But this bliss, this peace that wrapped around my soul and body, that was the true shock. I never wanted to leave this simplicity.

"Are *you* alright?" Chloe asked.

I nodded against her.

"I just...I did not expect it to be so..."

"Good?" she asked with a hint of worry.

I huffed a laugh and indulged in a brush of my lips across hers. They were so soft, so sweet. I could kiss them all night.

"I have nothing to compare it to," I said once I stopped kissing her. "But I would imagine if I had, this would have been the best."

Her cheeks flushed deeper than they already were, warmth brushed up against my awareness. She was happy.

"You're quite the charmer after a good orgasm."

"I had thought I was charming in general."

"Okay, *more* charming then."

"That is acceptable," I glanced down at the bite marks on her shoulder, scabbing over now.

I brushed a fingertip over them and she shivered beneath me.

"Did you mind that I drank from you?"

I was afraid of the answer but I had to know, had to hear it from her lips.

"No," she said. "I...I liked it. And believe me, I never thought I'd be in the fang fan club, but it made things more... intense."

"In a good way?"

"Yes. Kier," she cupped my cheek and turned my face so I would look at her, "I had a good time. I liked this, a lot. You don't have to worry."

Her words soothed my fear that if I ever let down my guard, I would become a monster. It had been the point in every lesson. The recrimination every single time I let my feelings take control, when I'd failed to keep my telepathy in check. Emotions were dangerous, mine especially because my humanity meant they were more difficult to control. Emotional Atavarians were cruel, thoughtless, dangerous. That was what I had been taught, that was the warning I had lived my life by.

But Chloe had anchored me when I had nearly lost myself tonight. She had been the one constant I had clung to and wrapped my consciousness around during all of it.

"Thank you," I rasped.

It was for so much more than simply being the focus of my rutting fever, so much more than I would ever be able to tell her, even though I wanted.

"Hey," she said with a small shrug, "what are friends for?"

Chloe said it as if it were nothing, but there was something unsettled beneath the words that I could not pin point. Perhaps because the word 'friend' grated on me, and I could not understand why. It was what we were after all.

Friends.

But now, it did not seem to fit in the same way.

"While we have some down time, I might need to replenish my plasma," she continued. "Eddie sent a PPR with me, but I dropped it over by the couch."

"Yes, of course."

I sat up and we both gasped at the tug on our nether regions.

"Um, I...I apologize, this is the first time I have knotted anyone. We may be like this for a period of time."

"How much time?"

I swallowed.

"The first few times knotting can be...prolonged."

She smirked at me.

"So what you're saying is that I'm spending the night."

Warmth bloomed in my chest and my hand idly caressed her hip.

"I doubt it will last all night, but I would very much like you in my bed tonight."

Her eyes widened and she bit her bottom lip. This delighted her, the thought of being with me tonight.

"I would like that too," she said.

I pressed a tender kiss to her mouth, wondering how I would give this up tomorrow when there was no longer an excuse to touch her in this way.

"We should get you that PPR," I said after I was able to tear myself away.

"And how do you propose we do – ah!"

In a swift motion, I grasped her under her nicely rounded bottom and picked her up. The change in position rubbed against my sensitive knot and nodes, and a jolt of heat shot up my spine. Before I could stop it, I was pulsing up into her while Chloe whimpered and ground down onto me. Within seconds, I was once again spilling inside of her while her channel tightened around me and she let out sharp cry. The colors I'd seen in my mind when we'd been together before curled up and spun, twining around one another. There was something about that, something I felt I should know, but I could not focus beyond the catastrophic pleasure of being joined with Chloe.

"Is that...normal?" she gasped.

"I do not know," I admitted. "My apologies, this may be a longer evening than either of us had planned."

"First of all, don't apologize again. And second," she gripped the back of my neck and slammed her lips to mine, "those were the best orgasms I've had maybe ever, so it's really okay."

I could not contain a tiny smile.

"Best ever, really?"

"Pride? I thought that was 'illogical'."

"Unless it is warranted, which in this case, it sounds like it is."

She chuckled and shook her head.

"Shut up and get me the PPR."

"You are very demanding post coitus."

"And you like it."

My lips widened into an actual grin, though a much more subtle one than a Human's.

"Yes, I do."

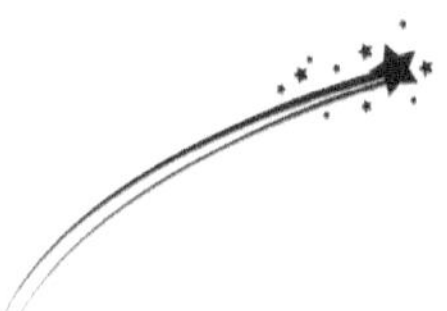

Four more times.

Four more times I spilled myself within her.

Four more times of feeling our conjoined passion in a riot of color and sensation.

Four more times of being closer with Chloe than I'd ever dreamed of being with anyone.

One of her legs was now slung over my hip, her other leg tangled with mine as I held her close, the two of us facing one another on our sides. I could not help running my hand over her skin, my thumb grazing the sensuous curve of one breast. I had heard many a male speak of breasts and I could never understand the appeal.

They were globes of fatty tissue meant to give nourishment to babies, they were not alluring. And then I had seen Chloe's.

A lot of the rut might have been a vague fever dream, but I remembered her breasts. A perfect handful, firm and pliant. Her light pink nipples had tightened to hardened points that made her writhe and tremble in my arms when I sucked them into my mouth. I had marked them over and over with the drag of my incisors. Even now, hours later, I could detect the faint red lines from where I had bit and kissed them.

It gave me an illogical sense of pride, ownership.

The lights were lowered to a faint glow, lending just enough illumination so that if I woke up in the middle of the night, I would not have flashbacks to being buried alive in the explosion that had killed my mother. It was more than enough light to watch Chloe sleeping, her head resting on my bicep and her small hands curled between us.

Chloe's personality was quite large, and I sometimes forgot that she was small compared to me. Now, as I held her in the vulnerable web of sleep, I was acutely aware of our size difference. Her bones were so much more fragile than mine, her breaths soft and punctuated by tiny snores that I found oddly endearing.

I would have never thought that watching someone else sleep could be a pleasurable experience, yet I was mesmerized by her. The gentle fall and rise of her chest, the way she curled into me as if she were searching for warmth.

I pulled the blanket over her and tucked her close to me, my arms surrounding her. She let out a little sigh. Trusting me completely in spite of the primal side I'd shown her tonight. She never shrank away, never cowered or proceeded with fear in her mind.

Whenever things became too much, she told me, gently, firmly. And somehow, her voice would always cut through the fog of the rut. As if the beast inside of me knew her too, and needed to keep her safe even as we ravaged her.

Chloe trusted me then and she trusted me now. It made me feel...happy, protective, possessive. I could keep her warm, I could keep her safe, and I could give her pleasure. Such small, silly things but it all felt significant.

It felt *right* in a way that unsettled me.

Suddenly images of flowers tickled the corners of my mind, the scent of a garden, but not one I'd ever seen.

I frowned, unsure where this was coming from and chose to examine it to determine the source. I only had to touch the picture of the flowers in my mind to be transported to a beautiful, sun drenched garden somewhere on Earth.

The grass was green and soft under my feet, and bees buzzed around the bright flowers to my right. And to my left, smiling up at me, was Chloe.

"There you are," she said. "I was wondering where you went off to."

I stared at her in my mind, shock rooting me there for a moment, before I tore myself out of that place.

Chloe stirred in my arms, whimpering, and whispered, "Kier."

"It is alright, you were dreaming. All is well," I said, soothing her.

When Chloe had drifted back to sleep, I eased myself out of bed and rushed to my bathroom. The lights went up automatically and I stared at myself in the mirror.

"What have you done?" I demanded of myself.

I went through every moment I could remember of my mind touching Chloe's. It was difficult to remember everything. The rut used a different part of myself, and so much of the experience was shrouded in a dream like state, fluid and changeable.

I knew that I had given her pleasure mentally several times, that is part of the very basic instruction on mating that all Atavarians are given.

She had spoken to me mentally a few times, especially toward the end. It had been the most intimate part of it all, at least for me. Sharing my mind, my soul with another and not fearing rejection but instead experiencing complete acceptance. It was everything I had ever wanted and had believed I would never have.

But what if that had consequences now? What if the strength of my need for connection forged a bond with her?

One more memory surfaced, a word I had spoken in the heat of passion, so gone in my rut that I had mentally turned off my subdermal translator.

Priash...I called her priash...soul mate.

Ripples of gold teased the back of my mind just moments before Chloe knocked on the bathroom door.

"Kier, are you alright?" she asked.

"Yes, nothing to worry about. Please, return to your rest."

"Alright," she yawned and I *felt* her fatigue.

I felt the soreness in her lower muscles, I felt the warm delight that still coursed through her after so much pleasure.

This was the beginning of a mating bond, the sensing of emotion and some physical sensation. Next would come flashes of thought. And lastly, the ability to communicate mentally, well beyond the simple things she and I had communicated during my rut.

Anger boiled up inside of me, eating away at the bliss and peace I'd felt only moments before.

I had done something unforgivable, the exact thing that I had been warned against. I had forged a mating bond with Chloe without her consent and put her mind in danger. If I mishandled this, I could drive her into a depression, or worse. I could cause her to go insane.

Bile rose in the back of my throat and I could not stand to look at myself for a moment.

But these were all *emotions*, and would do neither of us any good in this situation. I had to think logically if I was to discover a solution. So I concentrated, used my mental exercises to sequester and block off these emotions. Soon, the spiraling panic stopped, the rush of fear was gone. I could think clearly again and I began to sequester the bond behind new barriers. It was clumsy work, hindered by my proximity to her.

I waited until I was sure she was once again asleep before dressing and leaving the bathroom. The more distance I put between us, the better and I must begin now.

The sparring room would be empty, but perhaps I could offer to help the night crew in the hydroponics lab. Or perhaps I would simply go to the officers lounge and stare at the stars. Something, anything that would keep me from strengthening this bond.

I was about to leave when the faint rattle of Chloe's snore pulled my attention back to where she slept in my bed. Her hand was above the covers, resting on the exact spot I vacated, as if she were waiting for my return.

A sensation like the pull of a magnet burst in my chest and I took one step toward her before I could stop myself. She had always been my preferred orbit, the sun I would always seek out. But now, it was worse than a simple preference. This was *need* and it made me moan as I refused myself and stepped back.

If I truly cared for her, I would protect her from me and this bond I had forced upon her.

And that was the final deciding factor. I did care, more than I wanted to examine right now, and while I would not normally allow such feelings to drive me, in this matter, it was a vital compromise.

My body ached as I turned away from her and fled my quarters.

Chapter Nine

CHLOE

I woke gradually in a bed with covers so comfy it was like sleeping on a cloud. I knew before I'd even opened my eyes that this wasn't my bed and had a moment of confusion before last night came back to me.

Oh, yes.

Kier...

Kier in a rut.

Kier...naked.

My breath hitched at the memory of that man's body.

And by 'body' I mostly meant his dick.

I knew Atavarian biology, what their genitalia looked like and yet nothing could've prepared me for taking that thick cock with its magic nodes. I still felt the phantom sensation of him sliding in and out of me, the way he hit every nerve ending, how his knot had pressed against my clit just right with every thrust. I wondered if he would like me licking around where the head just barely peeked out from his foreskin.

One time thing, remember? One time.

Still, my mind was obsessed with his cock. He'd been so hard and hot, the nodes had pulsed just right inside of me and his knot was the most erotic thing I'd ever seen.

Oh my god, his knot! I finally get the appeal.

My hand traveled to my clit before I could think better of it. I was still sticky and wet down there and not from my morning arousal. He'd filled me up, until I was overflowing, and even as I drifted off to sleep, I had wanted more. It begged the question of who was in rut, him or me?

If that was what an Atavarian rut looked like, why in the world would they want to refuse themselves or their partner that kind of pleasure? I knew that Atavarians considered the time before their Enlightened Ones came as a dark age, full of mindless actions that were beneath them now. And, for the most part, I think I agreed. If the legends were true, they were the most feared and brutal warriors in the galaxy.

But what I'd experienced last night was nothing short of a religious experience, and I'd had plenty of good orgasms in my life. Several that yes, I swore I saw the face of *some* deity while lost in it. Last night was different. And as I dragged Kier's cum from my opening to my clit and coaxed it to life, what came to my mind wasn't his hands, which were huge on my body, or his supernaturally amazing knot. It wasn't how strangely good it felt when he bit me or the rasping words he'd spilled onto my skin.

It was knowing him in a way no one ever had. His mind was a beautiful, tortured landscape and I was the one he'd shared it with. I'd never been so connected to another living soul, never felt so known as I did when I opened my mind to him, or believed I was so adored as when Kier trusted me with his thoughts.

And that's what I thought of as I wound myself tighter and tighter. The memory of what we'd done was a good distraction from the niggling worry that I had opened a door last night that I wouldn't be able to close.

I want him...I want him again and again.

With my eyes closed, I remembered his voice in my head.

"Good morning, Nurse Carter," the computer said, *"it is zero seven hundred, time to rise and begin the day."*

"Ah!"

"Are you in distress? Shall I call for the doctor?"

"No, thank you, computer, I'm fine. Clit blocked, but fine," I said, tossing the covers back with a sigh. "Where is Lieutenant Kier'Ahn?"

"Lieutenant Kier'Ahn is in the officer's mess. Shall I page him for you?"

"No! I'll just get dressed and—"

"I've been instructed to offer you a warm shower or a bath if you wish. I have printed your preferred soap and shampoo, as well as a freshly printed uniform waiting in the en suite. Shall I warm the water for you?"

I smiled at Kier's thoughtfulness. Of course he would've programed the computer for me.

Never had sex and is still ten times more thoughtful than most of my previous lovers.

"That would be wonderful, thank you."

The computer chimed in affirmation and I swung my legs over the edge of the bed with a wince. There was a *very* well used feeling between my thighs and an ache on my shoulder where not one but *two* bite marks were still healing.

Kier hadn't been gentle that last time, but we'd both been too far gone to care about that. Heat rushed to my face remembering how I'd completely let my guard down with him. I'd done some wild things with partners before, I wasn't shy about that. But with Kier, it had been different, more free, more vulnerable. I'd held nothing back from him. Not with my body and not with my mind.

And for the first time, Kier had been vulnerable with me too. He'd pulled back the curtain on his logical side and let me see a side of him no one else did. It was so tempting to take every one of those moments and see them as proof that Kier wanted more with me. But I knew he never would have shown me that if not for the rutting fever. It hurt, but it was also the truth.

There was nothing more between us than friendship. Anything more that I'd glimpsed, anything more that I felt from him, was the rut. Period.

Now *my* feelings on the other hand, were an entirely different story. And there was the problem.

By the time I'd drifted off to sleep last night, I'd been starting to realize that something significant had changed for me. The moment my lips had found his, I *felt* the shift inside of me, even if I didn't acknowledge it. And now this morning, there was no way to hide from the fact that I might have feelings for Kier that were well beyond the scope of friendship.

I'd done a pretty damn good job of hiding them from myself the last two years, believing that Kier was not capable or interested in showing me anything other than friendship. But no matter how much I tried to repeat to myself that everything I saw was from the rut, that it wasn't real like the last two years had been, I still wanted there to be something more.

The place in my mind where he had been last night still resonated with a little bit of him, but it wasn't as strong as it had been. And I missed it. I missed seeing, and being seen, by him.

I wondered what he'd be like this morning, or if he would make himself scarce. Maybe he just went on to breakfast and would go about his day as if we hadn't fucked like horny bunnies last night. And I'd go right along with it, because that was safer than the alternative.

It was just a casual, lifesaving marathon session of sex and now we'd return to being friends.

Yeah right. What was I thinking? That was never going to work.

I knew me. The second I saw him, I'd start remembering everything we'd done and then I'd be aroused and then I'd be weird about it because he didn't sign up for a girlfriend last night.

I took a deep breath as I toweled off and started to comb my hair.

"Okay, Chloe, you've done awkward morning afters before. No big deal. You've got this just act normal, make a joke to diffuse and whatever you do," I pointed at myself in the mirror, "do not let him know that you are obsessed with his dick... And his mind...and every single thing about him."

I whimpered as I buried my face in my hands.

"No," I said, shaking it off, "get a grip. You want to lose a friend? Cause this is how you do that. Now, I just need to shut down any thoughts about him and last night, distract myself with something else. Everything will be fine. Friends...we are friends."

It wasn't until I was done that I noticed that the comb was a printed version of one from my quarters. Kier had been inside a few times for small get togethers, he'd probably seen it. But it was the thoughtfulness of such a small detail that touched me, had me starting to feel things that were dangerous.

He's always been thoughtful, it's just this is the first time it was after having sex with him. Four times...four of the best times of my life.

I dropped the comb and groaned as I buried my face in my hands again.

This would all work itself out. I just had to wait for us to get through the understandable weirdness of this new knowledge of one another.

I got dressed in the still warm uniform and stepped out of the bathroom, but stopped cold when I saw Kier standing with his back to me across the room, his focus on something on the table. He was dressed in his uniform, hair perfectly combed. He turned, sensing me, and gave me that sweet little smile of his, the one so subtle Jax and Thanh hardly ever noticed it.

"Good morning," I said with a shy smile of my own.

He clasped his hands behind his back, straightened his spine and nodded.

"Good morning," he said, the only sign that he was at all affected was the slight roughness of his voice. "I expected that you would be hungry after last night so I brought you some breakfast."

That made me smile even more and warmth once again spread along my chest like a hug, as I moved toward him.

"That was sweet of you, thank you."

He nodded at that.

"I am not familiar with the expectations of a 'morning after', but I thought this was logical."

I bit my bottom lip at how damn cute he was. The careful way he spoke and moved may have seemed stiff to others, even emotionally cut off, but I knew better. Kier was nervous, unsure and it was because he wanted to do this right, for me.

"You're doing great," I said, and squeezed his upper arm before I could stop myself.

His eyes drifted down to my hand and I let him go quickly.

"Sorry. Not doing that is going to take some getting used to after...well, after everything."

He seized it before I could retreat very far. My breath caught in my throat as he held my gaze and brought my hand up to his mouth, pressing a soft kiss to my palm. Shivers ran in hot and cold waves down my spine and I could only stare at him.

"It was pleasant to have you touching me last night," his voice was soft, rough. He gazed at my palm, a look of longing crossed his stern features so fast I almost missed it. When he released my hand, his usual, stoic expression was firmly back in place and he said, "But it is not what people in friendships do. At least, not our friendship. And in the spirit of returning to that, perhaps we should refrain."

My mouth opened, but no sound came out for a moment as my mind attempted to figure out what to say. I felt like someone had punched me in the diaphragm with a smile on their face. A brief frown crossed his face before disappearing and I quickly spoke to cover any confusion as to why I hadn't answered him.

"I...that is logical," I admitted.

He gave me a short nod.

"Good. I hope you do not mind, but I brought my breakfast up as well," he said as he gestured to the table.

I hadn't noticed it before, but he'd cleaned up this corner of the room so that we could sit at a table and eat together. Not only that, the table he'd set was thoughtfully put together with my favorite croissant, a plate of crispy bacon and a small pot of coffee, and the sugar cubes I loved. He had his usual synthetic blood, porridge and the bowl of fruit he never ate but always let me steal. Between my food and his was a single, beautiful white rose. I leaned down to smell it, the sweet perfume exquisite and not at all from the printer.

I turned to thank him, when the look he was giving made the words die on my tongue. His hungry gaze was intense, taking in every inch of my face right before it flitted to the bite marks that were just visible with the way my uniform jacket was open. I got the distinct feeling that he wanted to throw me down and feast on *me* instead of our breakfast. And for a moment, there was a growl in my mind, an image of him running the soft petals of that rose down my body, teasing the stiff peaks of my nipples.

And then it was gone.

I really need to get my libido under control. He just said he didn't want us touching anymore and I'm imagining that?

I swallowed and tore my eyes away, desperate to get some control of these thoughts, which was definitely a reversal for us. But if I didn't, I was going to have a very hard time letting this go and getting our friendship back on track.

"Where did you get a rose?" I asked as I sat down at the place he'd set for me.

Kier took a moment to answer, clearing his throat before joining me at the table and sitting across from me.

" Althea gave me a clipping from one of her plants as a thank you for helping her with the colonists."

I poured my coffee and plopped two sugar cubes in the cup.

"I had no idea Althea grew any Earth plants."

Kier poured his synthetic blood into his usual breakfast and stirred it.

"Neither did I, but it seems that her gardening skills are quite extensive."

"I wonder how she's doing with all of this. I should check on her later."

We chatted about the attack since I hadn't had the chance to talk to him before. In between me filling him in on what he'd missed, I stole handfuls of fruit from the bowl beside his breakfast. This was so very normal for us that I could almost forget what had started to make all of this weird.

I was just about to tell him how glad I was that we were okay after last night, when I got a strange feeling in my mind. A sense that Kier *liked* it when I took the fruit from his bowl because it meant that I was comfortable enough to allow him to take care of me, even with something so small as a little sweet fruit in the morning.

I glanced up at him, and caught a glint of delight in his gaze as I plucked a grape from the bowl and popped it into my mouth. When he caught me looking at him, the spark was gone and he turned back to his breakfast with a determination that had my head spinning.

Had I imagined that? Where had that come from?

Pure wishful thinking on my part, that's what. I'm making up what I want to see because orgasms. Really, really good orgasms.

I chose to believe that, even though none of it felt right. I also wasn't sure I wanted to possibly up end our friendship by asking "So what does this all mean now?"

Kier was uncomfortable enough when it came to emotions and being vulnerable. And he'd been all of those things and more with me last night. I was sure he needed time to process, and me making things weird wasn't going to help.

No, what Kier needed was stability, the sense that everything was okay. And I could give him that by not turning this into some romantic fantasy.

The silence stretched between us, poisoning the nice breakfast we were having like a horrible smell. I could tell that Kier wanted to say something but he was deeply unsure about it. He liked to get things just right and it could be really charming. But in a moment like this, I just wanted him to say *something*, even if it wasn't perfect.

When it became apparent that he wasn't going to, however, I scrambled to figure out how to diffuse this tension.

I glanced up at him and caught him looking at me with an intense stare that made my stomach flip. He dropped his gaze back to his breakfast in an instant and I knew that yeah, there was no way in hell I could admit to any of what I was feeling if I wanted to keep Kier as a friend. He was way too skittish this morning.

But this silence between us, the tension where there was usually an ease? That had to be resolved, and right away. So I drained my coffee, took a deep breath and decided to dive in with something half way between two truths.

"I had a good time last night," I said, my voice soft but still a little too bright. "I want you to know that I'm alright this morning and that I'm glad I could be there for you."

His shoulders relaxed inch by inch, and he sat back, finally meeting my eye for longer than a second.

"I am relieved to hear that you are unharmed and that you enjoyed it. I too liked the experience and I...I am unsure if this is alright to say."

My heart hammered with hope and I smiled at him.

"Whatever you need to say, I want to hear," I assured him.

"I am glad that my first time experiencing a rut was with a good friend like you. Thank you for saving my life."

Good...friend. Friend...right.

The words were earnest, said without any malice or dismissal. Yet, they hit me hard.

I needed that though. It's a good reminder. We are friends, nothing more. I'll get over whatever these feelings are and then we can just keep on.

It hurt, but I hid it behind a wide smile and a nod.

"Any time," I said with a chuckle that sounded hollow to my ears.

"Do you have a busy schedule today?" he asked.

I attempted to play along as if my heart wasn't being shredded by his nonchalance. He'd acknowledged the elephant in the room, reminded me of the boundaries of our relationship, and reinforced that he was just fine with them. And now we were moving on to small talk.

I hated small talk.

And so does he...so why the hell is he doing it? Is he actually uncomfortable and unsure how to talk to me about it? Am I projecting something to him?

Still, I decided to go with it since that was what he wanted at the moment.

I rattled on about the tests I was running on the nanites and a new article that had been published by an Atavarian scientist regarding a new technique to replace organs faster. Usually, this kind of talk would get me beyond excited, and I'd go for however long it took for me to run out of oxygen. But this morning it lacked the usual joy I felt when gushing about my job.

"What about you?" I asked, wanting to get the focus off me.

"I am uncertain. Since I left the bridge soon after the attack and haven't been back for several days, I do not know what awaits me but I am sure it will be extensive. I may be quite busy for the next several days."

I frowned at the way he'd said it, like he was giving me a brush off. But Kier was usually more direct than that so I tried not to let it get to me.

"Well, we're on our way to Alpha Gate Jump Station," I said, "so it's probably going to be a little boring."

"Possibly."

My wrist com chimed and I tapped on it.

"Nurse Carter, you are to report for duty to sick bay in ten minutes."

"Acknowledged," I tapped on the com to put it sleep and let out a frustrated breath. "Eddie moved my time up by an hour. He's probably worried about me."

"It is understandable."

"You would never hurt me, I just wish he believed me when I told him that."

Kier's eyes flicked toward the bite mark on my neck and back to my eyes.

"That wasn't you hurting me," I said.

"It was not usual. I could have easily taken too much. I should not have—"

"Stop. I don't want you to regret anything we did. I would have said 'no' if I didn't want it. I trusted you then as I do now. Please, no regrets. Remember what we did better than that, okay?"

"Yes, Chloe," his voice was rough, low.

I could melt in that sound and the longer he looked at me, the more I wanted to.

But my wrist com beeped again, breaking the moment.

Kier turned away from me and I let out a grunt of frustration when I saw that it was a message from Eddie informing me that if I didn't report on time he was sending a security team to Kier's quarters.

"I have to go," I said. "Eddie is all worked up."

"I understand."

"Are we still meeting at the observatory tonight? It's our usual junk food and star watching night."

He got to his feet, hands clasped behind him and opened his mouth with hesitation.

"Considering how intense last night was, I believe that could create a situation that would make it tempting to indulge in the kind of behavior in which friends usually do not indulge. Perhaps we should wait a while before we are alone together again, in order to re-establish our boundaries."

That stopped me mid step. He'd said it simply enough, like a statement of fact that he had no feeling about. But it still managed to feel like a rejection. Was he seeing the feelings I was just starting to be aware of and was it making him nervous? Was he trying to put distance between us because of them, or some other reason?

I wasn't about to act like it had hurt though, even though my heart was burning like someone had ripped it out of my chest and stomped on it. Instead, I gave him a playful smirk and resorted to my old standby: flirtatious humor that I could pass off as nothing.

"Kier, are you saying that I'm so irresistible, that if we were in private you'd fuck my brains out again?"

He cleared his throat, looked down, back up, down again before meeting my eyes. The whole time his emotions were practically being shouted in my mind. He was embarrassed, amused, turned on and a little confused, like he was when I'd flirted with him in the past.

There was no way I could possibly know all of that, however, and I chalked it up to yet another example of how much I was projecting what I wanted onto everything he was doing. So of course I went for another joke to try and lighten the situation.

"It's okay that you're tempted. I mean," I gestured with my hand down my body, "look at me."

"I am...did...have...I...am not sure the best response."

I bit my lip and failed to stop a laugh from escaping.

"That was a perfectly fine response. And I'm giving you a hard time, by the way. You know, like I usually do?"

His lips relaxed.

"Yes, that is true. I see. I am glad you are still comfortable with our friendship."

I was getting really tired of that word and his insistence on using it so much. I got it, we're *just friends*.

"Have a good day, Kier," I said, unable to hide the hurt this time.

I thought he was about to speak, but I just couldn't take any more and walked out.

Chapter Ten

KIER'AHN

I attacked Althea with the Leigth blade, a traditional sword from Atavar, as she deflected with a very heavy-looking weapon with a curved, flat blade at one end and a blunt on the other. It was, apparently, a replica of a K'Tavi weapon, one of three that she owned and liked to train with.

Usually I enjoyed my sparring sessions with the Lieutenant-Commander. She did not hold back with me, and liked that I did not with her either. The sessions usually helped to center me.

But today, I was not finding that peaceful moment of detachment.

It had been four days since I had last seen Chloe for breakfast. That first day, I had managed to avoid her the rest of that day, deflecting her suggestion of dinner with the excuse that I had many scans from the attack to analyze. I felt her disappointment from across the ship, which was not good. The distance between our stations should have minimized the psychic link so that I only received impressions. Instead, I was getting her feelings with an intensity that shocked me.

When I realized that, I doubled my efforts to stay away. I avoided our daily breakfasts by not getting my meal at the usual time. I took a different lift to my quarters and have not gone to the observatory. The sparring room was the only place I allowed myself to go where I may run in to her because of the potential benefit to my mental state.

Yesterday, it had worked. Today, it's efficacy was wearing off.

Althea slid down and around me, jabbing me in the back with the blunt end of her weapon. I let out a hiss of discomfort and pivoted around feigning an overhead strike to land a blow with the Leigth to her side. The sparring armor we wore protected us from the blades, though it did little to minimize the pain from the impact of a blunt weapon.

"That's better," the Lt.-Cmdr panted as she got to her feet and took a swig from her water bottle. "You've been off today. Care to talk about it?"

"I do not."

She nodded, and I appreciated that unlike so many others, Althea did not feel the need to interrogate and find out what was wrong.

"You done or do you want to go another round?"

"Another," I said, checking the clasps of my chest armor.

Althea eyed me.

"Are you sure? You were already finishing a spar with Commander Velheim when I got here. Tired partners tend to get hurt."

"I am quite positive."

"Then get to your position," she ordered.

We sparred until my arms were too tired to lift the Leigth, and she had left more than a few bruises on my body. It was only then, to the point of pain and exhaustion, that I did not sense Chloe's presence in my mind as more than a mere glimmer, there and gone again. I let out a long breath, as a bit of sweat dripped off me, not unusual after two hours of exertion.

I took the time to rub oil on the blade of my weapon and then sheath it, the action meditative and soothing.

"Whatever it is," Althea said, after having done the same with her own weapon, "deal with it before it eats you alive or you do something stupid. I'd hate to lose a good officer and friend like you, Kier'Ahn."

Her words shocked me and I stared at her for a moment before giving her a short nod as she left.

My body was sore enough that I reasoned that meditative stretching was in order. I began slow, my movements matched to my breath, the stretches gentle. For a while, it worked, but then I had a flash of sadness, loss. I pushed them aside with my breath as I moved.

Then came the echo of words, faint at first. But then they were becoming stronger, clearer.

I forced myself to concentrate on the movements, on the pain in my muscles that was getting stretched, the breath in and out. I focused all of my mental strength denying the mating bond's need to strengthen between us.

When I was done, I was not restored. Instead, I was even more exhausted, and the day was not done. I still had a duty on the bridge to fulfill. I collected my things and grit my teeth against the urge to grab ahold of Chloe's presence in my mind. I missed her deeply, though I tried to refrain from admitting such things to myself too often. But the exhaustion of my body, which was supposed to free my mind from these burdens, only made me more susceptible to them and I closed my eyes, unable to stop myself from thinking of her laugh, her voice.

I pictured the way her eyes lit up when she spoke of her research, the determined set to her jaw when she was pushing through a problem. The way the light glinted off her hair in my quarters, how shockingly responsive her body had been under my hands.

I groaned as longing and arousal hit me like a physical blow.

I found myself wanting more than her mind. I wanted her body too. I wanted to sheath myself inside of her and, this time, commit it all to memory. I had flashes of what it had felt like during the rut, but nothing substantial. It was frustrating to know the sensation, but not have the image in my mind. But even as I longed to touch her more, I knew that it would be overwhelming without the rut to turn off my more logical mind. It had been so long since I'd regularly touched, or been touched, that to do all I wanted would overload my senses. I would need to ease into it, small touches...

That golden glimmer was stronger in my mind, warmer, and I heard her voice, something about nanites and how she couldn't concentrate.

I took in a sharp breath, realizing how far I had allowed myself to go and punched the wall before I could stop myself. Had it not been padded, I would have likely broken my hand. But the pain felt bracing and I took a deep breath. This could not go on. I would insist that Dr. Goodman find a psychic healer at the jump gate station, or I would ask permission to leave. Distance across the galaxy was sure to weaken and eventually break the bond. And then, the desire I felt for her would fade. I would return to how I had been before.

Before Chloe had shown me a glimpse of something I can never have.

I stalked from the room, now determined.

"I will conquer this."

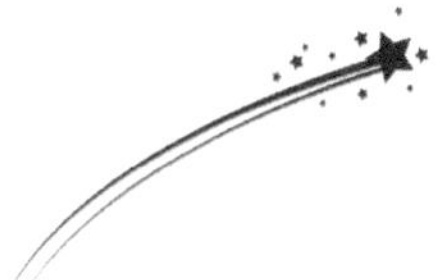

I'd been at my station on the bridge for the past two hours. The scans I was now conducting were standard; the only thing I needed to monitor was if we came across any more of the strange energy fluctuations or K'Tavi radiation.

I was also attempting my own analysis on the cloaking signature, hoping to create a tracking algorithm. This should have been a simple task, yet I still had not completed it. My mind was distracted by the occasional whisper of words from her. She was not intending to send them to me, this I knew, but I was getting them all the same. Just when I tried to defend my mind against one thing, another would come up. A feeling, an image.

"Anything, Lieutenant Kier'Ahn?" the captain asked.

I realized that I had been distracted by these thoughts, and Captain Drake was looking at me with concern and bit of impatience. I refocused on my console and surveyed the information in front of me.

"No sir, there is nothing out of the ordinary."

"Keep a close eye out, we don't want to be taken by surprise."

"Aye, sir."

After a few minutes I finally got my body and mind under control once again and I breathed a quiet sigh of relief.

Captain Drake let out a long breath through his nose, his brows furrowed. I'd served alongside him long enough to know that he was concerned. The attack on us had set everyone on edge. We had no proof that the K'Tavi had never ventured this far into GUP space before, and to attack a Gex-Corps ship was a bold move. One that could signal a shift toward hostilities.

From what I understood the Gex-Corp and the GUP were holding a decision about how to respond until we arrived at Jump Station Alpha. A war would be devastating, and depending on whether or not other attacks had happened in other quadrants, it may be unavoidable.

I had to admit that the K'Tavi attack did not seem logical. They could have stayed cloaked and we would never have been the wiser. Why lure us to the edge of GUP space? Why come here at all? What did they have to gain by war with a superior foe?

My scanner beeped to indicate that it had picked up something. I took a closer look at the energy, and what the scans were revealing, and frowned.

"Sir," said the ensign at communications next to me, "we are being hailed."

"A vessel is pursuing us," I said as the image of the ship stabilized behind us. "A GUP Viper class ship with a classified transponder signal."

Captain Drake's eyebrows went up.

"We aren't due at the station for several hours," said Lieutenant Commander Kavat. "Why is a classified ship following us?"

"That's a very good question, let's find out," the captain replied. "Up on screen, Ensign."

The holo screen went from a view of the space field in front of us, to the image of a woman I knew quite well. With a crooked grin that pulled at the cybernetics comprising her left eye and cheekbone, my half-sister, Zephyr, stared out from the screen.

"Captain Drake, apologies for startling you. I need you to divert to the following coordinates and open an airlock bridge between our ships."

"Not until you tell me who you are and what this is about."

Her grin widened, eyes slid to me for half a second before going back to the captain. The coordinates beeped at navigation and a coded message appeared on my private wrist com.

"Brother, this is serious. I understand your captain's hesitation, but I need the way eased."

No one knew that Zephyr was my sister. Her real name wasn't even Zephyr, that had died the day she supposedly had with our mother. I usually found Zephyr in my quarters as if by magic whenever we were in the same vicinity. Her work with the Disavowed, the part of GUP Intelligence that most thought were a myth, meant that she always knew where I was, but I never knew where she might be.

Seeing her now, I could not help but feel hopeful that I might speak privately with her. My sister always had a way of putting things into a perspective that I could not. Perhaps she would have some insight on how best to navigate things with Chloe.

Although, if she is here requesting assistance, it is not the time for such frivolities.

My fingers flew over the keys at my station as I attempted to bring up something that might soothe the captain's worries.

"Captain, my identity is classified," Zephyr said. "I can't just say it over coms. But your lieutenant at science and ops should have something that will convince you."

She did not give me much time to find it, but luckily, I knew where to look for the proof she offered.

"Kier'Ahn?" Captain Drake asked.

"I ran the transponder code through a GUP software and received confirmation that the vessel is ours, used by the Intelligence branch of the GUP. As such, I believe she is telling the truth."

"How many of you are there?" Drake asked.

"I will have an associate with me, an Atavarian," she replied.

"Just the two of you then?"

"Yes, Captain."

"Give me a moment," Captain Drake said.

The ensign next to me ended the transmission.

"We have the coordinates," Jax said. "It's a stable asteroid field nearby that's a known dead spot due to the type of metallic residue in the asteroids. It will make it impossible for us to be detected by other ships, or for us to detect ships."

"Sir, this could be a trap," Althea said. "There could be another vessel there, waiting for us."

"Why would the GUP ask us to meet at the Jump Station and then divert us to a secret location?" Jax asked.

"You have answered your own question," I said, keeping my irritation in check. "The call to Jump Station Alpha could have been a ruse to get us into a place where the GUP Intelligence branch could meet with us without anyone knowing."

"Velheim, your thoughts?" Drake asked.

"The Intelligence branch has been known to divert ships in time of crisis," she glanced at me and then back at the captain. "I agree with Lieutenant Kier'Ahn, this makes sense to me, though I think we approach with caution."

"Agreed," Antony nodded at the ensign, who re-opened the channel. "We'll meet you at the coordinates. You'll understand if we request that you bring no weapons aboard."

Zephyr tilted her head in acceptance.

"We will see you soon."

The screen went back to the star field, which slowed as the pilot began to divert us to the asteroid field. I kept my eyes on the scanners, watching Zephyr's ship follow us to the rendezvous. This had to be about the attack by the K'Tavi. And if the GUP brought Zephyr in then this was more serious than any of us knew. She was usually involved in missions that prevented catastrophic attacks on the GUP and the individual member planets.

"Lieutenant Commander Kavat, Lieutenant Kier'Ahn, you're with me to greet our mysterious visitors," Captain Drake had said. "Commander Velheim, you've got the bridge."

"Sir?" the ensign said, a deep frown on her dark brown face. "Um...the ship has requested that they are provided a secure meeting room and that Nurse Carter be present."

Unease prickled along my spine as Drake's frown became concerned.

"What would they want with Chloe?" Jax asked, popping out of his seat. "I don't like this. Not only are they diverting us without explanation but now they want to see Chlo – I mean Nurse Carter? This all stinks, Captain."

The tone of possessiveness in his voice made something dark and hot stir in my chest and I turned a fiery glare at him. To his credit, Jax held my eye steadily, arms folded across his chest. To the primal part of my mind, the part that I had let out during my rut, this was a challenge. The urge to lunge across the bridge and fling the arrogant Zorestran into the wall was so strong I had to clench my hands together.

He had no right to be so protective of Chloe. She was mine to guard. Mine to touch, to taste, to have.

Has he had her? Does he want her now? Is that why he's acting this way? He means to show himself a good mate, that he can defend her? I will not allow it.

Inside I was a seething, snarling mess, my instincts boiling as I scrambled to create barriers that would contain all of it.

Outside, the only proof that I felt any of this was how tight my fists were, and the narrowing of my eyes as I stared Lieutenant Vabaris down.

"Lieutenant Kier'Ahn?" Antony's voice drifted to me through the haze of anger I was attempting to control.

I jumped a little and turned back to him.

"Yes, sir?"

"Are you alright?" he asked.

"Of course."

"You were growling."

I glanced at Sonta, standing beside the captain as if she were ready to come between us if something should happen. Althea frowned at me with more concern than anything else, and Jax had the good sense to at least appear rattled.

I am more out of control that I first realized. This is not good.

"I apologize, sir," I said, making sure my voice was even. "A response to stress perhaps. I assure you, I am able to discharge my duties."

"Good, because I'm going to need you focused. Can I count on you?"

"Absolutely sir."

Unease stirred in the back of my mind regarding why Zephyr had requested Chloe and why she was here with an Atavarian but I quieted it. There was no advantage in expending energy with worry. I would wait to see what Zephyr had to say.

Chapter Eleven

CHLOE

I rubbed my forehead as my latest test with the nanites failed to produce results. It was the one thing that could distract me from the ever growing grief and anger at what had happened to my friendship with Kier.

He'd been successfully avoiding me for four days now and I suspected that it wasn't going to get any better. I'd practically lived in sick bay and my small lab, snapping at anyone who dared try to engage me in civil conversation. Even Eddie had started to avoid me and not much could usually make him scarce.

I wasn't sure how much longer this would go on, but I was pretty sure that I couldn't keep avoiding everyone and sulking forever. But whenever I thought about going back to my usual routines, Kier's absence was a big, gaping hole. He'd managed to work his way into so much of my life that everything just reminded me of what I was sure I had lost.

At first, I thought that maybe he just needed a little space to get over the intimacy of what we'd done. But then I'd seen him turning around the moment he spotted me in the officers lounge. I had tried to send him a coms message, but the computer said he'd put himself on Do Not Disturb. I'd even gone so far as to leave him a note with the chef, asking if we could talk.

Nothing.

No response.

Not even a polite brush off!

All of it added up to one horrible conclusion: He couldn't get over what had happened enough to remain friends.

Tears clouded my vision and I scrubbed my hand over my eyes. I'd cried way too much about this the last few days and I needed to stop. It wouldn't change anything or give me back my friend. I had to start building new habits, new memories with other people.

"Okay, what the hell is going on with you?" Thanh asked as she marched into my lab. "You didn't meet me for our usual lunch yesterday, you canceled classic movie night and this morning I had to eat my breakfast almost next to Jax. The male is lucky I didn't rip a horn off his stupid head."

"I've been busy," I groused as I began typing in a new data set for a new test.

I didn't have the patience to listen to her complain about Jax right now and tried to turn my back to her but the small pilot yanked my chair around to face her.

"Spill," she demanded.

"Nothing to say," I retorted and tried to spin back around.

"Liar."

"Menace."

"Just talk for fucks sake so you can stop sulking!" Eddie yelled from sick bay. "This med bay only has room for one grouch and you're not it."

"Thanks Eddie, feeling the love," I shot back.

Thanh rolled a nearby chair closer and folded her arms across her chest as she stared at me.

"I know something is going on with you and Kier," she announced.

"Oh really? News to me."

"They fucked," Eddie said from the doorway.

"Eddie!" I screamed.

"You what?!" Thanh said at the same time.

"I'm tired of the moping. You weren't gonna cut to the chase so I did, now I'm leaving. Be done with your girl talk in half an hour, we've got a staff meeting."

And with that Eddie closed the door, muttering to himself as he did so.

"Oh my god, seriously?" Thanh squealed. "I knew it! I knew you two were in to each other!"

"No we weren't it was just medical."

"Um...'kay?"

I pinched the bridge of my nose, silently plotting revenge against Eddie.

"He went into a rutting fever," I said after a moment. "It's fatal for Atavarians if there isn't a connection. So, since I'm the only he would trust I had to—"

"Treated his illness with your pussy?"

"God Thanh! Can you be any cruder?"

"Yes, and also that was mostly Tohm-Tohm's question, but that's the beside the point. How was it? Oh wait, was it bad? Is that why you've been hiding? Don't want to have to tell him that he couldn't find your clit?"

"No, I'm not the one hiding, he is!"

"Oh, ouch. Sorry Chloe. But wait, does that mean he *did* find your clit?"

The stupid organ actually quivered in response and I let out a groan of frustration.

"Yes, he did. It was amazing! I've never come so hard in my entire life. And I thought I kept it casual, you know, just 'hey I'm doing this to save your life, after let's get brunch', but..."

"Brunch, you guys get brunch?"

"Not the point Thanh."

"Right yeah, sorry, Tohm-Tohm again, he's just...okay, yeah let me talk buddy this is serious...."

I waited while the two of them had a quick internal conversation and then she nodded.

"Okay, I'm back, anyway," she said, "I'm just trying to wrap my head around Kier relaxing enough to actually get off. The guy is wound tighter than...well, I have nothing to compare it to actually."

"The fever kind of loosened him up, and he was..." I took in a deep breath, trying to steady myself. "He was different."

"Different how?"

"Like, unhinged, primal."

Thanh's brown eyes widened.

"Whoah, I bet that was intense."

"You have no idea."

I gave her the broad strokes regarding the mental sex in tandem with the physical and her eyes got even bigger.

"That sounds like it would be too much, scary even."

I shook my head.

"I wasn't scared. He was growly and his incisors were down and he held me by the throat a lot but he wasn't scary. He was...just more, different. But it was still Kier."

She shook her head and chuckled.

"You've got it bad."

"No I don't!" I scoffed. "I was there for a friend, that's it."

"You're not acting like that's it."

"Because I didn't expect it to end our friendship. I thought that everything was okay. We had breakfast and he was being a little nervous but not too bad. Now, he won't even be in the same room with me and I have no idea what to do."

"He's an Atavarian, they all have sticks up their asses when it comes to emotion. You'll just have to wait him out, he'll come back around after he's processed it I bet."

"But what if he doesn't? What if I pushed too much or...I don't know, what if...what if he saw something that made him run?"

"Like what?" she asked, her tone only a little playful now.

I cringed and let out another grunt.

"Okay, fine, I do like him a little bit more than a friend."

"I knew it!"

"Finally!" Eddie said from the other side of the door.

"What the— ? Eddie, what the hell?" I demanded, opening the door to find him lurking on the other side.

"You were never gonna tell me what was going on so you left me no choice," he said, crossing his arms. "And if that idiot is too chicken shit to see what a treasure you are that's his loss."

"Here, here!" Thanh said.

I wanted to be angry at both of them for making me talk about this, but I had to admit I did feel a little bit better. And Eddie's fatherly outrage was also kind of nice even though I was definitely going to get back him for telling Thanh what had happened and eaves dropping.

"That's really sweet of you two," I said, "but that doesn't solve anything. He was one of my best friends and now he's cut me out. I just feel like I did something or scared him off. And I tried to play it so casual."

"It's probably not you," Thanh said.

"You know how Kier is," Eddie added. "He's probably just all caught up in trying to figure out what happened logically. Emotions aren't his area of expertise."

I nodded though I didn't think either of them were right. There was a nagging suspicion that something was wrong, that I had scared him off.

"I just wish he'd talk to me," I whispered.

"I can't make him tell you but I bet we can help you feel better," Thanh offered.

"Oh yeah, how?"

"Well, traditionally," Eddie said, "there's ice cream and booze."

"And friends who will dump on the person while you cry."

"Yes to ice cream and booze, no to crying. I'm too angry still."

"Alright, tonight then, my quarters," Eddie offered.

"You gonna clean?" I asked.

"I'll pick up my underwear if that's what you're asking."

"What a relief."

"Nurse Carter, report to the Captain's quarters immediately," Sonta's voice came over the med bay coms.

"Copy that," I said and turned a frown to Thanh and Eddie. "What's going on?"

Thanh turned to a nearby computer terminal and typed in a few things.

"We've been diverted to a nearby asteroid field by...oh shit."

"What?" Eddie demanded.

"The Intelligence Branch of the GUP," Thanh said.

"What would they want with us?" I wondered.

"Or with you?" Eddie asked.

My heart kicked up several beats and I entered the security code on my nanite research.

"I better go find out."

"Be careful, and don't agree to anything without really thinking about it," Eddie cautioned.

"I'll be fine," I assured him with a smile.

But inside, anger and nerves began to ricochet, momentarily distracting me from the aching loss of Kier's friendship.

Chapter Twelve

KIER'AHN

We made it to the asteroid field quickly and the captain, Althea and I made our way to where the secure airlock bridge would be opening.

During the lift ride, my body was buzzing with a mixture of residual anger at Jax, and the dregs of the need to protect Chloe from whatever mysterious plots Zephyr was bringing with her. By the time we made it to the open air lock on our side, my body was a rigid mass of tension. I was controlling it so far, but if this continued it was only a matter of time before it broke free and I would have to do something.

The air lock on the other side of a very short bridge hissed and popped a few seconds before Zephyr stepped out of the ship, followed by a towering, broad Atavarian male.

Zephyr's silver mesh of cybernetics glinted in the light of the hallway as she stepped onto the Intrepid. Her dark brown hair was braided tightly on the side of her head with the cybernetics, with some of the plates extending past her temple and onto her skull above her ear. The braids were gathered on one side into a bun. Her light brown skin was lined with scars on the right side of her face from the same attack that had killed our mother. Her remaining eye sparkled with amusement when she looked at the guns drawn on her and I knew, even if others did not, that her left arm was almost completely cybernetic, the forearm contained an incredibly powerful weapon that was a cross between a proton rifle and a blaster. Even if that was disabled, I'd seen her take out a group of six men twice her size before. Zephyr may have been quite small, only just above five feet tall, but the alterations to her skeleton and muscles from the implants gave her the fighting power of a man twice her size.

"Captain Drake," she said, "thank you for allowing us aboard."

"We can use my quarters for the meeting, they're just over here."

The Atavarian gave me a cursory glance with his completely black eyes and then ignored me as he followed the captain at the head of the group. I lingered at the back and Zephyr fell into step next to me.

"Don't mind Vas'Rach," she whispered, "he's a good agent but an asshole."

I didn't acknowledge her words but the obvious displeasure she felt when he'd snubbed me gave me an oddly comforting sensation.

"Why do you need Chloe?" I whispered. "Nurse Carter, I mean."

"She's made a discovery recently that's brought her to our attention," she answered. "But the real question is, why did you call her Chloe?"

I arched an eyebrow as I glanced down at her. Zephyr gave me a knowing smirk before looking forward again.

"She is a friend," I answered.

"I see. A friend."

No one except me would notice the playful hint in her tone. It was both comforting to have her giving me a hard time and extremely annoying at the moment.

"Is this about the attack?" I asked as we neared the captain's quarters.

"Yes, but not exactly. There's a situation, and right now, the thing that will tip the scales in our favor is the research your 'friend' has been doing."

My head whipped down to her and back again before I could stop myself.

"She'll be safe."

"The fact that you would need to say that is not reassuring."

When we entered the captain's quarters, my heart gave a strange lurch in my chest at the sight of Chloe by the window. She was shaking out her hands, stretching her neck, all things she did when agitated. She turned toward me, eyes wide and our gazes locked instantly.

Anger slammed into my mind and I swore that I *felt* her panic mixed in behind it. That warm presence that I'd been fighting against for two days flared to life, enveloping me in a soothing pulse even as I scrambled to resist the feelings that awakened.

It was all so confusing, and so strong that I wasn't sure what to do, or how to act. I wanted to run out of the room and attempt to purge this, but was also driven to Chloe's side and make sure everyone knew that she was mine. That scared me more than anything else.

In spite of what my instincts demanded, I stayed still, mesmerized by Chloe's light eyes as they stared into mine.

"Lieutenant?" Captain Drake asked.

The connection between was broken and I looked around the room. Everyone was frowning at me in concern and confusion except for Chloe, who appeared quite miserable, now sitting near the fireplace.

"Forgive me, Captain. I believe I am having some difficulties from my previous illness. Nothing I cannot handle for the duration of our meeting however."

Captain Drake hesitated but I went to sit on a stool in the kitchen area, as far as possible from where Chloe sat. Everyone else gathered in the seating area near the fireplace, with the exception of Vas'Rach, who stood apart near the windows.

"The room is secured," Antony said. "Would you mind telling us what this all about now?"

Zephyr nodded.

"I am Agent Zephyr Vaughn, a specialist with the Intelligence branch of the GUP. I was dispatched to intercept your ship before you arrived at the Jump Station because we have a situation that requires your assistance. Or rather, the assistance of one member of your crew."

She turned to Chloe, who stared back with huge eyes.

"Nurse Carter, I believe that you wrote the thesis that eventually led to the creation of the vaccine for the Lavat virus."

"Yes," Chloe answered slowly, "though I was never named in the project."

"I know, a fact that we are currently working to remedy."

Chloe's eyes widened and she glanced over at me. Though I had to remain distant, I could not help but feel happy for her to at least receive the credit she was due.

"That is...well, unexpected and nice, but what does that have to do with the Intelligence branch?" she asked.

"The Lavat virus has mutated in the recent years," Vas'Rach said, "causing the leadership of Atavar to turn inward in an attempt to find a cure. This has created the perfect environment for isolationist tendencies to spread through the High Council."

"Combined with the increase in anti-Human fervor," Zephyr said, her voice slightly pinched, "it has created a situation where Atavar has been pulling back from joint GUP missions."

"That is regrettable," Antony said, "but what does that have to do with us, or Nurse Carter?"

Zephyr took a small disc out of her pocket and set it on the low table in the middle of the sitting area. She pressed a button and a 3D holo screen appeared. Images of devastation, burned out buildings, dead bodies and crying survivors floated across the screen.

"That's the colony on Polnite Three, what's left of it," she said, and swiped her hand across the image to reveal similar images. "Lafhar, and S'Dath as well. All three destroyed after the K'Tavi came into GUP space and fired upon them."

I slid from the stool and stood on shaky legs. The room became thick with tension, as all of us looked at each other. Althea was the only one who didn't look away from the screen, her face blank while her hand rested on her blaster at her hip.

"Steady, Kavat," Antony put a gentle hand on her arm.

"I'm fine," she shook him off and leaned against the wall next to the fireplace.

"It's difficult to look at," Zephyr agreed, "and it almost happened to the colony on Jahnus Five. If you hadn't been there, it would have."

"Why do this? What do they have to gain?" Antony asked.

"Testing boundaries is one theory," Vas'Rach replied. "Looking for weaknesses to invade. Thus far, they have only crossed over where there was little GUP supervision, we theorize so they can be undetected."

"It is what they do," Althea said, her voice razor sharp. "Poke at you until they find the weak spot and then they attack. Over and over until you're overwhelmed. They are patient, and have no qualms about sending their own to their deaths if it will wear us down. This carnage is just the start."

"Which is why we need to shore up our borders and prepare for war," Zephyr said. "Strengthening our weak spots is priority one at the moment, and we need all planets to work with us. Especially Atavar."

It clicked into place then, the reason why Zephyr was here and why she needed Chloe.

"You wish to send a Gex-Corps member to create the cure for the new mutation of the Lavat virus to engender good will with the High Council," I said.

"Along with easing the suffering of the Atavarian people," Vas'Rach shot back at me.

"Of course."

"You're both correct," Zephyr gave me a small smile. "If a Human is the one to create the new vaccine, it will also take some of the teeth out of the anti-Human sentiments, which will translate to fewer members of the High Council working against us. The isolationists will have two of their biggest arguments for withholding Atavar from the coming conflict taken away."

"What makes you think I can do this again?" Chloe asked. "I got lucky the first time. I don't have any records of the mutation, and all my attempts to get them have failed."

"First of all, you weren't lucky, you were creative and brilliant," Zephyr said.

My heart swelled unexpectedly to see my sister praise my...well, my friend...mate...Chloe.

"And second," Zephyr continued, "your theories about these new nanites have caught the attention of a scientist on Atavar who has been working on this new strain. He believes that working with you will enable him to create a new vaccine in a few weeks."

"How did you know...Never mind. You're with Intelligence. I get it, you're everywhere," Chloe said.

Zephyr chuckled as Vas'Rach cleared his throat and shifted uncomfortably.

"Yes, we are," Zephyr agreed, "but in this case, it was your inquiries and the recommendation of your Chief Medical Officer that brought your nanite work to our attention."

"Okay, so I assume you came here with the models and samples of the virus?" Chloe asked. "Even with that, I have to tell you, there is no guarantee that I can turn this around in weeks. Sometimes things you don't expect can go wrong."

"Her hesitancy indicates a lack of confidence," Vas'Rach said to Zephyr. "Are we sure she's up to the task?"

Chloe's jaw dropped, her disbelief and anger infiltrated my mind. Now that I knew what it was, I was able to control better how her feelings affected me. I sequestered them mentally, sending calm logic to Chloe to try and counter the way her mind was beginning to spin out of control.

Remember how smart you are. Remember your talents and gifts. You can do this, Chloe.

She swallowed, straightened her spine and looked Vas'Rach in the eye.

"Not lack of confidence. Lack of *arrogance*, a trait I would suggest you cultivate," she said to Vas'Rach, then to Zephyr, "I need access, unfettered, to all the research, and to the live samples or this will not work."

Zephyr glanced at Vas'Rach, whose face had gone a very dark shade of red.

"Done," Zephyr said. "But in order to get you what you're asking, you will need to be on Atavar. They won't let any information about the virus off planet for fear that someone will weaponize it, so you'll need to go there."

I frowned. Chloe was Human, Atavar did not allow Humans to access the archives. How was she supposed to...

"You'll need a cover," Zephyr continued. "And since all research will have to be done on site, I've arranged for you to get a special fellowship to the Science Institute as a research assistant to lead Scientist Char'Vahn, he's the one I mentioned that's been working on this."

"But, I'm Human," Chloe said with a wary look. "How did you overcome their prohibition on other species attending the Institute?"

"The mate of an Atavarian can attend," Vas'Rach said, his voice sour. "As such, I have agreed to take you as my mate for the duration of the mission."

Her shock and distaste exploded in my mind at the same time that feral possessiveness roared to life inside of me.

"No," I growled, my voice deeper than normal.

"Lieutenant Kier'Ahn, what are you doing?" Antony asked.

"He cannot have Chloe," my voice was far more forceful than respectful, but I did not care.

I stalked straight to Vas'Rach, meeting him toe-to-toe. He was taller than me by almost a foot, and broader, but I still let out a low growl of challenge from the center of my chest. Vas'Rach stared down at me with barely concealed loathing. I clenched my hands into fists as a fire I could not fully understand stirred to life within me, and all of my efforts to control it slipped through my fingers. The phantom taste of her blood was on my tongue, the smell of her fear thick in my nostrils as the sensation of her mind in mine beat in a fast rhythm.

I had to protect her from this male. He could not touch her, I would not allow it because...

"She is *mine*."

Chapter Thirteen

CHLOE

"What the hell was that?" I asked as I practically ran into my quarters. Kier and Zephyr followed me close behind.

"I assumed you did not want to be mated to Vas'Rach," Kier said, his voice far too calm for this situation. "Therefore I solved the situation by volunteering myself."

"*Volunteering*? Is that what you call that?" I scoffed as I mindlessly fixed myself a drink from my secret stash of whiskey. "If the captain hadn't stepped in, the two of you were going to perform ritual combat."

"It was—"

"What would I have done if you'd died? He's huge, Kier! He could've wiped the floor with you."

I got an impression of something, a feeling that he was touched by my concern but I was too damn angry to wonder where it was coming from.

"I would've had to pretend to be that asshole's wife, while devastated because you died defending my honor or some shit!"

"I believe I would have been in no real danger. He was fighting for his pride, not you. Whereas I—"

"Would've been working out your issues with Atavarians at the risk of your own damn life!"

I was so angry I couldn't see straight. Which, as I stopped and thought about it, was rare for me. Where was this extra rage coming from? Why did I want to rip Vas'Rach in half?

"I'll take one of those too," Zephyr said.

I poured her a glass and downed half of mine in one, scorching swallow.

"While the situation with the virus is serious, I do not believe this level of panic is necessary," Kier said.

The glass stopped half way to my mouth and I stared at him in disbelief. Beside me, Zephyr mumbled something that sounded suspiciously like "Oh boy," under her breath. Distantly I wondered why the agent had followed us, but that was not what was in the forefront of my mind at the moment.

I advanced on Kier, who backed up the closer I got until he was pressed against one of the walls in my room.

"I just sat in a meeting where I find out I'm expected to help create a miracle vaccine to help prevent an intergalactic war," I said, my voice strained and starting to rise, "where one Atavarian looked at me like I was shit on his shoe while deigning to pretend to be my mate, and another looked like he was going to beat him with a club because I'm supposedly 'his', after avoiding me for *four days* I might add! And all the while, I get no say in any of it! I think this level of panic is perfectly reasonable, Kier!"

"She's got ya there," Zephyr said behind me.

I spun around and glared at the agent.

"I'm sorry, but who are you? Why did you follow us?"

Kier made a sound behind me as if he were trying to answer when Zephyr walked up to me, extended her hand and said, "I'm his sister. Welcome to family, Chloe."

I gaped at her, my world tilting around me for a moment before righting itself.

"I...sister?" I turned to Kier. "You have a sister?"

"Zephyr is the daughter of my mother," Kier said. "But not my father."

"In other words, your sister."

He nodded.

"Look," Zephyr said, pounding her drink and setting the glass on my small side table, "I know all of this is a lot. It would be overwhelming even without what my brother just did, but this might actually work to our advantage."

"How so?" Kier asked.

I got the barest hint of apprehension from him, like I could *feel* it from him. It was unnerving and he glanced at me for a moment, his eyes full of worry and questions that I wished he'd ask even though it wasn't the time for it.

"Vas'Rach was never going to be able to sell being mated to Chloe," Zephyr said.

I snorted.

"No kidding."

She gave me an apologetic look.

"He's a very good agent, but not great at this sort of thing. It was the best we could do at short notice. But, after what you did, Kier, I think you will not only be able to sell the relationship, but you can help soothe the anti-Human sentiments there."

"How do you expect me to do that?" Kier asked, irritation coming off him in waves.

Or am I feeling that too? What is going on?

"You're part Human," Zephyr said, "and with having a Human mate, it's double the good will. Logically speaking, they can't deny that keeping and nurturing their connection with Humanity would be beneficial."

"You say that like they're thinking of leaving the GUP," I said.

Zephyr's lips pressed together.

"They have been for quite some time," she admitted. "It's only been by the slimmest of margins that they haven't. And if they leave, some species will follow. Not a lot, but enough to make defending our borders against a K'Tavi incursion costly and difficult. So you see, brother, this has to work."

"It would only be a matter of time before the K'Tavi targeted Atavar if they left the GUP and weakened the alliances," Kier said. "It is not logical to instigate such a thing."

Zephyr gave him a sad smile.

"Brother, you and I both know that sometimes a person's logic is influenced by fear. And I think that is the case here."

Pain, bone deep and all-consuming flashed in my mind and I winced. It had been so fast, there and gone before I could fully comprehend it, but the reverberation of the emotion still echoed in my mind.

"Chloe, are you alright?" Zephyr asked.

I looked up at Kier, whose eyes were closed, but I *knew* what he was feeling, as if I had a road map to his mysterious emotions.

Guilt, fear, pain. It was all there. How did I know what he was feeling?

"Kier, what is going on?" I asked.

He let out a long breath through his nose and finally met my gaze before diverting his attention to Zephyr.

"Sister, there is something I must discuss with Chloe in private. If you would give us some time, I would be most grateful."

Zephyr looked from him to me and back again, both her natural and cybernetic eyes wide.

"Kier, did you...you didn't...did you?"

"Zephyr, please, give us some privacy."

"Alright. I'll go to your quarters and wait for you because we still have things to discuss." She walked over to me and leaned close, whispering in my ear. "Go easy on him. I know he didn't mean to do this."

I wanted to reassure her that I would, but I couldn't. I didn't even know what 'this' was.

When the door closed behind Zephyr, Kier stood up straighter, hands clasped behind him as usual. He was all business, at least on the outside.

Inside, he was a ball of nerves that he was just barely controlling.

"I want you to know," he said, his voice low and a little unsure, "that I did not intend for this to happen. And that I am sorry."

"Okay, I believe you, but you haven't told me what *this* is. Why can I feel your feelings? Why do I know that you're scared?"

And why did you call me 'yours'?

"During our...time...together, when we shared our thoughts, that connection became a bond between us. It was not something I intended, nor could control. I realized what I had done when you were sleeping, and have been attempting to weaken the bond these past few days. I have not been successful."

"So…" I took a deep breath, trying to calm my racing heart, "that's why you've been avoiding me? Why didn't you tell me, at least let me know why you felt like you had to act like I didn't exist?"

"I assumed that it would be better if you did not know, that it would frighten you. I thought I could rectify the situation before you noticed anything unusual."

I didn't think my eyes could get any wider. My face was flushed and I wanted to scream at him. I had no idea if those were my feelings alone, or his as well. When a tiny cringe rippled across his features, I remembered that this went both ways and took a breath, though it did little to stem the tide of anger inside of me.

"What I *noticed*," my words came out measured, slow, "was that you acted as if you didn't want to be around me. I thought you regretted that night and were avoiding me because of it."

He stepped toward me, his gaze intensifying the closer he got, until I was breathless from the look on his face. Kier stopped a few inches from me, his hand twitching at his side, and I wanted him to touch so badly in that moment. But I had no idea what the rules were anymore, so I stood still, hands to my sides.

"I could never regret what we shared," his voice as rough and it sent chills down my body. "It was…incredible. I am sorry that my silence has hurt you. I was only trying to protect you."

"I believe you. But that's not how this works."

"What?"

"Whatever this is. It's more than a friendship, at least with this bond in place. And while I'm not saying it has to be an official relationship, things have changed between us."

Kier nodded, his eyes flitting down to my shoulder where he'd bit me and then back to my eyes.

"Yes," he agreed, "they have. So what do you require from me?"

I let out a shaky laugh and shook my head. This was how he spoke all the time, but right now, I wanted him to be as twisted up as I was inside.

Maybe he is and I just don't know it.

Right then I caught a glimpse of confusion, frustration, and knew it was him. Kier was having just as difficult a time with this as I was. But instead of letting it out, he held it back with an iron fist, and kept himself controlled more than usual. It helped to know that he could be as rocked by all of this as I was.

"I don't 'require' much," I said, rolling my eyes to act as air quotes, "just that you *talk* to me about these things. That you don't shut me out anymore. This bond obviously complicates things and now we're on a mission where we have to act like mates after...after having a very intensely emotional event with one another. It's messy, the whole thing. And the only way we'll survive it, and come out the other side still friends, is if we are honest with each other."

His brow furrowed and he let out a long breath.

"Yes, that is logical. It will be difficult for me. I have never had to be aware of and considerate of another's feelings in this way. I will know what you feel but I may not know how to respond. If you would give me guidance, I would very much appreciate it."

"Wait, back up," I swallowed as panic began to make my thoughts spin. "You can feel what I feel, and I can do the same? Is that all? Do you know what I'm thinking too?"

"We can sense one another's emotions. And as the bond strengthens, we will be able to speak to one another through it. Though, I will not be able to know your thoughts unless you intend for that to happen, I will only be able to sense them."

"So you can't read my mind then?"

"No, not as such."

At least I won't have to worry about that.

He cleared his throat and my eyes widened.

"Did you...?"

"I could sense your relief. It was profound."

I nodded.

"I trust you but I don't know if I want my private thoughts open to you all the time."

"I understand. Such things are intrusive. It is why I am covered constantly. It is considered a great sin to enter someone's thoughts and emotions without their consent. I never wanted to be that kind of person."

Self-loathing rolled off of him, followed by guilt. I couldn't take it, not when I also knew that he'd seen himself as so unworthy of the basic connection of touch, of sex. I wouldn't allow him to continue seeing himself this way, not when I knew in my soul that he was so much more than that.

Kier took in a sharp inhale, eyes widening as I purposely thought those things *toward* him.

"You're not that kind of person," I said out loud. "You've never been."

"I bonded you without your consent," his whisper was rough, tortured. "You trusted me and I—"

"Made a mistake."

"You are not angry with me?"

"I was angry at you for avoiding me. But this? I'm not thrilled that you know what I'm feeling. Though I'm not gonna lie, it's kind of nice to finally know what's going on inside that head of yours."

I grinned up at him and he gifted me with a grunt that was his version of a chuckle.

"And yes, I will be patient with you and I will be honest with you about what I need. If you will do the same with me."

His shoulders relaxed and he closed his eyes as a wave of relief hit me. I gasped at the impact of it and reeled back a bit.

"And now I'm a little overwhelmed. Is there any way to mitigate this?" I asked.

"Yes, I can teach you some meditative and visualization techniques to help you build a wall between yourself and the emotions. It will not keep you from experiencing them completely, but it will decrease their intensity."

"You think we'll have the time for that during our fake relationship ruse?"

I asked it playfully enough, but I couldn't hold back the trepidation and hint of frustration that all leaked through. I saw the moment Kier felt those things from me, and it hit me just how much this was going to take getting used to. I couldn't really hide anything from him, not even when I was trying to. Unease wormed its way through me and I turned away from him.

"You are experiencing a lot of emotions at once," his voice was a little strained. "It is confusing."

"Yeah, no kidding."

"If you would prefer I leave—"

"I didn't say that."

"Then what should I do? Your mind and behavior are not offering me any direction."

I couldn't help but laugh.

"Welcome to being in a relationship."

He stared at me and my stomach dropped.

"I mean...we're not in a relationship, not a real one. I know that but the situation it, um, it's kind of like one."

I cringed inside at how damn clumsy I was being and then tensed because Kier probably knew that.

I don't have any privacy, any way to keep my feelings private. What if he finds out...no, shut it down! Don't even think about it.

"You are panicking," he said.

"You think?" my chest tightened. "I can't hide anything from you. Everything is just out there for you to see...oh my god, this is going to be a disaster."

He opened his mouth and closed it.

I was taking huge gulps of air in but it still felt like I couldn't breathe. My heart was pounding hard enough to break out of my chest and my palms were sweating.

Calm down, I have to calm down. But what if he finds out how I feel? What if I let it slip and then...?

"I assure you that when we get to Atavar I will seek out a psychic healer to break the bond," he said.

"And until then you know everything. I-I need help to calm down."

"Chloe," he stepped closer. "Breathe. I am using my own mental shields to help shut out your emotions, but when you are like this, it is impossible."

I closed my eyes and forced myself to focus on my chest moving up and down, the air moving in and out of my nose. It took time but finally, the anxiety that had threatened to overwhelm me was abating, leaving a smaller worry in its wake. But nothing I couldn't handle. All these years wanting to know what was going on in Kier's head, and now that I had a front row seat, it wasn't what I thought it would be.

"I just need time to adjust to it," I said, as much to him as myself. "I'll be okay, promise."

"I know you will."

I startled, his voice was so close. When I opened my eyes, Kier was leaning toward me, much closer than before. His eyes were intense on my face, his concern wiggled in the back of my mind. It was odd, to be so frightened of this connection one minute, and mesmerized by it the next. His emotions were a gentle presence that I wanted to explore but didn't dare. He didn't want this bond any more than I did. And with all of his insistence on us being just friends, I knew that this must be particularly frustrating for him. He was getting all the stress of a girlfriend without actually wanting one.

But the way he was looking at me, it was full of mixed messages. There was heat in those green depths, but also fear, and hesitation. All the things I too felt with him, so was it his feelings or my own reflected back at me?

"Why did you do it?" I asked before I could stop myself. "Why did you tell Vas'Rach that I was yours?"

He let out a ragged breath and so very slowly, he raised his hand. The tips of his gloved fingers grazed my temple as he slipped a strand of hair behind my ear. My breath stalled as he cupped my cheek and I leaned into the touch, closing my eyes. It felt so good, and I realized that I'd been craving this for four days, walking around like I was missing a piece of myself.

"Because," his deep voice was soft, "that is what you are while we are bonded. You are mine, Chloe, in the deepest sense of the word. Atavarians do not believe the mind and soul are separate. We believe they are one and the same, two sides of what makes us who we are. So this bond between our minds is really a connection of two souls. It is why mental bonds like this are frowned upon in some circles. Because this, what I have with you, is the most intimate of connections."

It was exactly what I'd wanted and yet, also feared to hear. It awakened a longing in me that I'd been trying so hard to control. I wanted to belong to him, I realized. I wanted us to belong to one another. Longing flooded me, but was it his or mine? A sense of rightness warmed me, a comforting pulse that I wanted to cling to because somewhere in the midst of it was Kier, my dearest friend, the man I was starting to fall in love with. This bond was definitely unexpected and it was going to take a lot of adjusting. But the thought of losing it, of losing *him* made my chest hurt.

When Kier withdrew his hand, I almost whimpered at the loss of contact but I swallowed it. If all of this was a lot for me to process, when I'd lived my life feeling things fully and not suppressing them, what must it have been like for him? Still, it stung that he was retreating from me. Even if it was quite a bit to handle, I wanted him near. The intensity of that alone had me realizing just how strong this bond was.

This is going to break me when it's over if I'm not careful. I need to start protecting myself.

"I should let you rest," he said, taking several steps back and his emotions became dim in my mind. "And I must speak with Zephyr about the mission."

I nodded as I came back to myself.

Mission. Right. We had a mission. I had a vaccine to create and we had a relationship to fake.

But is it fake if we're bonded like he said we are? How can what I feel myself, what I get from him, make any of this not real?

I couldn't ask any of that though. Hell, I was afraid to even feel it for fear that he would know what was rocketing through my body right now. So I just nodded again and straightened my spine.

"Right. I need to pack and finish up a few things in sick bay, make sure my duties are being covered properly."

He lingered for a moment by my door, and I thought for sure that he was about to run back to me and kiss me. It was just a flash of feeling, there and gone so fast.

But he didn't. Kier simply nodded and then walked out the door.

Chapter Fourteen

KIER'AHN

My body was a mass of conflicting instincts and emotions as I walked back to my quarters. Our bond was getting stronger by the hour, there were moments when I could swear that I heard her voice whispering in my mind.

It was a relief that she was not angry with me, but that did not take away the complications of the situation. I was driven to protect her from every threat, and even the captain looking at her; being too close to her tonight had set me on edge. What would happen on this mission? Would I harm someone just for looking too long at her?

I may have reassured Chloe that she had nothing to worry about when I had been facing Vas'Rach, but the truth was I had been very close to losing control and driving my fist into his face just for suggesting that he could be her mate. The control I had relied on for so long felt fragile and yet I also had the sense of completeness when I was with Chloe just now. Was there a possible balance here I was not seeing, or was that simply my weakness where she was concerned coloring my logic?

If I gave in to the need to be with her, to touch her, would my primal nature be unleashed? If I became a monster who cared only for her blood and her body and nothing else...

I paused outside my door and attempted to calm myself. Now more than ever it was imperative that I not give in to my emotions, not when they could hurt Chloe. She might not have been able to recognize all of my feelings within the tumult of her own, but they had been there. And they had driven hers to a breaking point. Clearly, my usual methods of control would not be enough. She was sensitive to the bond, something that I should have expected. Chloe was one of the most empathetic people I had ever met. It had served her well in her career, but it would not do the same here.

When I entered my room, Zephyr was looking at the empty shelves in my room. I had managed to clean the majority of the broken furniture, glass and carpet away. But replacing the items I had destroyed would take longer and there was still the matter of the dents in the walls. One look at my sister and I knew that Zephyr must have figured out what had happened by now. She was smarter than nearly any person I had ever known, and her powers of observation had only become sharper in the years she had served in the Disavowed.

"You want a drink?" she asked.

"I do not keep alcohol here."

"Good thing I brought this then," she pulled a bottle of old Earth tequila out of her bag.

"Yes, then."

She found a few glasses that had not been broken, and pulled a knife out of her bag with a rather large lime.

"You keep a lime and bottle of tequila in your bag?"

She smirked up at me.

"No. But after what I saw in there? I may have raided the officer's lounge."

"I am grateful for your thievery."

"I thought you might be."

We clinked our glasses together and drank the shot down in one gulp. The tang of the lime was welcome after that, and Zephyr poured another.

"So," she said, leaning against a nearby wall since there was not much seating, "you bonded her."

I let out a long sigh.

"Yes. It was an accident."

"You don't need to justify it."

"Yes, I do."

Zephyr glanced around the room.

"Your suppressors stopped working, which meant you were going to die. She helped you with that and you didn't mean to bond her, but you did."

"Yes."

She examined me, a wrinkle appeared above her nose and then she drank down the tequila.

"You know," she began, "Prem'Ahn isn't always right."

It was not surprising that Zephyr said my aunt's name with venom. Aunt Prem'Ahn did not approve of my father mating my mother, and had ignored Zephyr's very existence. But she was the closest thing I had to a mother while growing up, and so I could not help but regard her guidance even now.

"It is not just Aunt Prem'Ahn. I was not deemed worthy by the House of 'Ahn's Council of Elders."

"Kier, you were expected to be more Atavarian than those that were full blooded. The elders' expectations were so high that no one could have been good enough."

"I still cannot control my telepathy!" It came out sharper than I would have liked. "It is dangerous to enter a person's mind without their permission, much less form a mating bond. If I do not control myself I could hurt Chloe's mind, I could drive her mad."

"And you believe that, because of your Human side, you won't be able to control yourself enough."

"Yes."

"I disagree."

"Zephyr, with all due respect, your judgment is clouded by your affection for me."

She snorted.

"Yes, that may be. But I would argue that my affection also gives me a perspective that you need right now."

"How so?"

"Because I love you, and I want you to be happy."

My pulse quickened and I looked away.

"How do you know Chloe makes me happy?"

"I don't exactly, but I know *you*. And I can tell by now when you are having feelings. And you, dear little brother, are absolutely *full* of feelings for her."

I slumped into one of the chairs at the table and stared at the floor, letting my guard down enough to be vulnerable with my sister.

"I do not know what to do," I admitted. "I do have feelings for her, but I do not think she returns them. And even if she did, would it not be better to retreat from her if I truly did care? Atavarians and Humans are not compatible."

"I know you're not speaking of procreation," Zephyr sat in the other chair, "you're talking about Mother and Father."

"Yes. I have no doubt that Father had affection for her, perhaps he did love her in his own way. But he did nothing to ease her way in Atavarian society. Our mother was shunned, treated as an outsider to be ignored at best. The opinion regarding Humans has not changed since her murder. Would I truly subject Chloe to such a thing?"

"You're both in the Gex-Corps, you wouldn't be living on Atavar."

"But I am not just speaking of the threats. Chloe is Human, she deserves a companion who would understand her emotions, supports her. I am...I am defective in every way that matters."

"You were made to feel that you were defective in every way that mattered to an *Atavarian*. But you have never allowed yourself to explore your Human side for fear that it would unleash the darker Atavarian side. You've had a lifetime to nurture and strengthen that side of you, what if now is the time to let your Human side grow? And what if she is the path toward that?"

I considered her logic and admitted that I could not find much at fault with it.

Except for one glaring issue that loomed over all else.

"And if what your suggestion *does* let my darker side out? What if that hurts Chloe?"

"I counter with, what if you are rejecting the very thing that will bring you what you have yearned for your entire life?"

"And what is that?"

She gave me a gentle smile.

"Connection. The kind of connection that is deep and true with someone who does not shun any part of you, but accepts all of you and loves you."

My heart lurched, and an ache begun to take root in my chest at the truth of her words.

Zephyr had been my closest companion growing up. So when she was sent away after Mother's death, loneliness was my reality. Few children would play with me, and those that did often could not admit our friendship to their peers or parents. No matter what I did, I was outcast. After a while, I found a way to accept this, to see it as better. If I was not around others, I could not expose myself or my family to shame by being unable to control my emotions or telepathic abilities.

My two years on the Intrepid showed me that I could have friends who were not put off by my mixed heritage. I could be accepted and welcomed as simply myself, Kier'Ahn. I had started to see how faulty my coping mechanism had been, and now this bond with Chloe was showing me just how much more there could be. My sister's words made me realize why I was so fearful of losing Chloe, why this bond was as wonderful as it was terrifying to me.

As if reading my thoughts, Zephyr continued, "I know you're afraid of the bond, but I think it has been misunderstood by the elders. Just because your ancestors used it to control and abuse, doesn't mean that it should be tossed out or feared."

"How do you know that?"

Her grin turned wry and she shrugged.

"I talk to Father more than you do."

I arched an eyebrow.

"And he expounded on Atavarian mating bonds?"

"In a way. He's been rocking a lot of boats on Atavar, between advising the Intelligence Branch on how best to reach the High Council and continuing his hobby of compiling the original writings of the Enlightened Ones. He's exposed a few modern beliefs that are actually contradicted by the Enlightened Ones and the High Council of Elders is not pleased by either activity."

I was more than a little surprised that my father was doing anything to challenge the traditions of our people, considering the education he allowed Aunt Prem'Ahn to put me through. He had said at the time that it was because it was the best education available, yet it still felt as if he was simply ensuring that his half Human son did not shame him, rather than it being due to a love for such things.

"You should ask him about that when you visit," Zephyr continued. "I think he's a little lonely."

My entire body froze at the thought of seeing my father after all this time.

"I did not know I would be seeing him."

"I may have notified him of the change while I was waiting for you and Chloe to finish."

"And?"

"He indicated that, due to your mixed heritage and Chloe being Human, adhering to some of the traditions around Atavarian mating rituals would be necessary to gain full access to the Science Institute. Starting with the family co-habitation part of the engagement. Since Chloe has no family, it will just be your family."

I stared at her for a long moment, my mind attempting to grasp what she was saying.

"You want Chloe and me," I started slowly, "to undergo the rigors of a traditional Atavarian mating ceremony?"

"I don't, no, but," she paused and downed her drink before continuing, "Prem'Ahn may have been on the holo call as well."

My eyes widened even as my heart lurched. I had not thought about telling my aunt, or subjecting Chloe to what I knew would be a very unpleasant visit with her. My aunt may have raised me, but she had no love for Humans.

"She said outright," Zephyr continued, "that in order to save the family honor, since you weren't supposed to enter into a mating of any kind, and to prove that Chloe could be trusted to have access to the Institute, that the two of you should undergo a kind of shortened version of the traditional Atavarian wedding ceremonies."

The engagement ceremonies were supposed to stretch out for six months and a traditional Atavarian wedding ceremony was a week long affair. All of our traditions were sacrosanct. Not deviating from them had made our society firmly rooted in the teachings of the Enlightened ones. I could see my aunt's reasoning, it was wise in many ways. But even though I understood this, I did not like it. I knew that Chloe and I could not remain bonded, for her sake at least.

"This was supposed to be a cover," I said, unable to hide my displeasure. "Now I will have to explain to Chloe that, according to Atavarian law, we are getting married?"

"According to their laws, you already are, Brother. Remember, mating bond and all that?"

I pinched the bridge of my nose and let out a long sigh. This was quickly getting out of control.

"This is to appease those pesky elders and High Council members. And probably Prem'Ahn. Chloe will understand," Zephyr said.

"Will she?" I asked, finally looking at her.

"She seemed to take the bond in stride, and she helped you with your rut. She also stood up to Vas'Rach like a champ. I like her, she'll do just fine on Atavar."

I grit my teeth at the mention of that male and took a breath.

"It is not her doing well that I am worried about."

Zephyr's expression softened and she nodded.

"Yeah, I know. It's not exactly safe for a Human there right now."

"And yet, you are sending her there."

"I am, because she's the only one that can do this and do it fast. There are billions of lives at stake, and having met her even just for a few minutes, I know she would choose to go there no matter the risk."

I jumped up from my seat and paced in my living space. Every instinct told me to take Chloe and run. This was too dangerous, she was going to get hurt. But I also knew that while my sister may have to be coldly strategic in her job, she was not without compassion for me and my feelings.

"She'll have you," Zephyr said. "You can keep her safe."

"Can I?" the words came out sharper than I intended.

"It wasn't your fault, Kier."

I stopped in my tracks, every muscle in my body contracting. I could smell smoke suddenly, feel the burn along my back. I almost touched my shoulder where the scaring was the worst, but I did not.

"If not for me—"

"Stop," Zephyr stalked toward me. "I have never blamed you for that and if she had lived, neither would Mother. You have to let go of this guilt, you have to trust yourself now more than ever. Chloe needs you."

I swallowed, knowing that she was correct about Chloe. I did not know if I could believe her about our past.

But she is right, it will cloud my judgment, hinder me from keeping Chloe safe. I must find a way past it.

"Thank you for your honesty," I said to her. "I have always appreciated your directness with me."

Zephyr grinned at me.

"That's what big sisters are for."

I paused, considering if I should ask her advice about the other thing that had been haunting me since the rut. I had thought to simply hope it would fade with the mating bond, but since I would be with Chloe in close quarters, pretending to be mated...

"There is another matter I would like to ask your advice about," I said.

She crossed her arms in front of her and cocked her head to the side. I knew that look, it was Zephyr sizing me up, seeing all my 'tells'.

"Go ahead," she said.

"I find myself...curious...to explore something with Chloe and—"

Zephyr held up her hand.

"Brother, if you're going to ask me about sex—"

"What? No!"

"Okay, because there are lines."

"I would not... that is, I do not believe Chloe would appreciate me doing that."

"Just making sure. Continue."

"I am surprised to discover that I like touching Chloe. That instead of feeling like an intrusion on my body and mind, it feels...natural. But I am unsure how to approach this with her, especially after how things between us have changed so rapidly. I worry this will only further blur the lines of our friendship."

Zephyrs lips curled up at the mention of 'friendship' and I could guess what she was thinking. I left that alone, however, not wishing to defend myself that at the moment.

"I would say," Zephyr said, "that Chloe strikes me as the direct type. She would listen if you told her the truth, and she'd probably help you find a way to do it that wouldn't be overwhelming. Just be honest with her, trust her."

I nodded. It was almost exactly what Chloe had requested of me tonight and it made sense. In spite of all the ways in which my world had suddenly been upended today, I felt a sense of peace about this plan. At least this I could have some control over, perhaps even find a way to enjoy, touch without fear.

"And you'll have plenty of time to do that," Zephyr continued, "because while the Intrepid waits here, you and Chloe will take my shuttle through Jump Gate Alpha and on to Atavar. The Intrepid will go to the station a day later with the cover of having engine core trouble from the attack. You will have two days on the shuttle to work out all of this and help Chloe come to terms with the Atavarian wedding torture Prem'Ahn has in store for her before getting to Atavar."

"I had thought that we would stay here on the ship to prepare."

"No one can know I was here, so this needs to look like you're just bringing your new bride home to introduce her to the culture and get her settled for her internship. If the Intrepid drops you two off, it will look official."

My initial instinct was to be uncomfortable, to shy away from such intimate contact with Chloe, considering how odd our circumstances were. But in reality, things could not get more complicated than they already were, so what was the harm?

"That makes sense," I said.

"Once Chloe has done her work, you will be the GUP representative to the High Council and it will be your job to convince them that working with us on the K'Tavi is in their best interest," she said. "I know this isn't a comfortable position for you either, but—"

"Being one of the Atavarians in the Gex-Corps and mated to the woman who discovered the cure, I am in a unique position to have influence."

"Exactly."

Zephyr hesitated, her lips twisted into a frown before she pinned me with a serious gaze.

"You have a chance at happiness, Kier," she whispered, "real happiness. Don't let our family, or your culture, take that away from you. Not many of us get what you could if you'd just trust yourself...and her."

It couldn't be as simple as trust, could it? I had no experience trusting myself, not when it came to feelings. But trusting Chloe? I had done that many times and she had never failed to embrace me.

Perhaps...perhaps I should consider this.

Chapter Fifteen

CHLOE

"You're sure about this?" Eddie asked me as we waited in the shuttle bay a few hours later. "Because I can find a way to get you out of it. I'll say you've got some disease or something."

I chuckled at his attempt to protect me.

"Wow, 'some disease' will sure terrify them."

"You know what I mean. You shouldn't have to do anything that makes you uncomfortable."

I glanced over my shoulder as Kier, Zephyr and the captain walked into the shuttle bay. Kier's gaze met mine like we were magnets, drawn to one another even across the span of the shuttle bay. I got a small brush of his mind against mine, a curious touch like a child testing the water with his toe before it was yanked away and he turned his back to me.

I let out a long breath and gave Eddie a shaky smile.

"I'll be fine."

"Don't let those Atavarians treat you like shit, okay? You're the most brilliant virologist I've ever worked with, and anyone, whatever their species, that doesn't see the same isn't worth your time. Hear me?"

"Got it, boss."

He yanked me into a hug, the raised floor platforms making it so that I my head was buried in his neck.

"Be safe," he said. "If anything happens to you, I'll kill Kier and make it look like a painful accident."

I choked out a laugh and nodded.

"You worry like an old woman."

"Reckless child," he retorted. "There are extra PPRs in the same case as Kier's synthetic blood packs, just in case."

Heat rushed to my face as Kier, Zephyr and Captain Drake came closer.

"I'm not going to need any of that. Not like he's going to get near enough to bite me."

"You're bonded."

"And first thing, he'll probably find someone to break it."

A hot pain hit me square in the chest at the thought and I swallowed the hurt down. Kier's determination to break the bond shouldn't affect me like this. I knew it was no strings attached when I jumped into that night with both feet. And it was my own fault that I let myself get attached when Kier didn't feel the same way.

Even if it sometimes feels like it through the bond. Just a little glimpse of something...maybe I'm imagining it.

"I may not like Atavarians as a rule," Eddie said, staring at his feet, "but that one? He's different with you, Chloe, and you're different with him. Maybe...maybe think about it."

I could only stare at Eddie as the group stepped up to us. He'd never, *ever* comment on my relationships, other than to tell me on occasion that I could do better. This was the first time I could remember him encouraging me toward anyone. And the fact that it was Kier? That had me more speechless than anything.

"Well, Doctor Goodman, are they all set?" Captain Drake asked.

"All supplies have been loaded. I also programed some protein dense foods into the printer on the shuttle, just in case your hosts don't feed you enough."

"I assure you, Doctor, there is no reason to fret. I will ensure that Nurse Carter is properly taken care of," Kier said.

A hint of something like frustration rolled into my mind and quickly dissipated. It was incredible to me how much was actually going on below Kier's stoic surface. I'd always wondered, but to have access to even a little of it made me admire his restraint more than ever.

"The navigation is all set for you," Zephyr said, her cybernetic eye spun as she interfaced with the shuttle. "And I've confirmed that Char'Vahn has just released some of the basic data regarding the new virus strain to you, Nurse Carter. You should be able to study on the way there. The cloaking device should guarantee that no one will bother you on the way, but just in case the shuttle is equipped with photons. The shuttle will automatically give the Atavarian orbital station the correct codes to ensure a smooth docking. Gav'Ahn should meet you at the station and take care of the rest. Good luck."

Kier and Zephyr exchanged a look that spoke volumes, the hint of his affection for her leaked through before he closed it off, and the captain gave us a stern nod.

"I've negotiated a 'routine' stop over on Atavar in two weeks to ensure that you both are alright. Until then, take care."

We nodded back at the captain and boarded the sleek, snug shuttle. I stowed my shoulder bag in one of the side compartments of what appeared to be a combined eating and lounging area. Ahead, through a doorway was the cockpit with two seats and control panel that looked like it had a lot more bells and whistles than a standard shuttle.

Not surprising considering this is the Intelligence bureau. They probably have tech we won't see for years.

Off to my left was another door that I assumed led to sleeping quarters and the bathroom, but that was the only other door.

One room.

One bed.

I glanced at Kier who was also staring at the door. He turned to look at me, a deep frown on his face, and a sharp sense of trepidation shot through the bond before it disappeared and his face relaxed into a tense but far more neutral expression.

Oh, this will be fun. Kier constantly censoring himself while we both try to ignore the elephant in the room.

"I will prepare the shuttle for departure," he said, walking up to the pilot's seat.

The lounge area had two seats that pulled away from the wall with restraints for turbulent flying or for when we went through the jump gate, which we would in a few hours. In the meantime, it wouldn't matter where I was, so I sat down on the shuttle equivalent of a couch, determined to make the most of this time.

"Computer, table with interface," I said.

"Recognized, Nurse Carter, GIB temporary clearance confirmed. 3D model or 2D interface?"

"2D please."

"Affirmative."

In front of me, a long rectangle on the floor began to glow and a moment later, it raised up. The rectangle was perched on a thick round pillar and it stopped at the level where a table would sit. I realized that this would probably be where we ate our meals when it wasn't being used as an information interface.

The glowing around the edges faded and a small screen in the center began to separate and raise up on two thin legs. It was a large holo tab, with a dozen or more files available to me, including several on Atavarian culture. I realized that I should probably read up on the basics, since my cover was that I was mated to one.

I glanced over at Kier, who was occupying himself with flying us out of the shuttle bay. He'd likely keep his distance even when the autopilot took over, partly to give me time to prep for the mission, but also because he didn't want to be around me. It stung, but I understood it. He needed to process this in his own way. And so did I.

Which is obsessing about it. And lucky me, Zephyr was thoughtful enough to give me just the thing to make me able to do that and still call it work.

I tapped on the first Atavarian file, which was essentially a breakdown of what Atavarian society was like, including family hierarchy, the Enlightened houses, and the Enlightened Council of Elders.

Were those the ones that had told Kier he wasn't worthy of having a mate or any connection with others?

I rather forcefully selected that option while I ground my teeth together and began to read.

The Enlightened Council was made up of elected representatives from each house, totaling ten, one for each house. A Minister was elected every five years and could not be from the same house for two consecutive terms in order to spread out the influence of each house. They tended to oversee the larger issues and decisions.

Whereas each of the Enlightened Houses themselves had their own council that ruled over everything from disputes on territory, marriage contracts and whether a child had passed their maturity tests. The Council of Elders for House 'Ahn would've been the ones to deem Kier unworthy, I realized. And while Atavarians could disagree with the decisions of the Council of Elders for their house, most did not when it came to personal rulings.

Like whether an Atavarian was worthy of having a mate or not.

It all felt overly complicated in my opinion, but I found myself unable to stop reading. I didn't know why, but I needed to understand the environment Kier was raised in. Maybe if I did, I would know how to help him with this bond between us. Or at the very least better grasp his anxiety around it and any connection to me.

On the surface it looked like the family was more egalitarian than I would've thought, with both parents seen as having equal rights on raising children. But then I dug down into marriage laws, because obviously I needed to know that for this mission and no other reason. Marriage was rather strictly regulated within family units. This was supposedly to make sure that marriages weren't solely based on emotion, but it seemed like a system that would be rife with abuse and heartbreak. While there was no prohibition on marriage across Houses, the parents had the final say on whether or not their children married. If one House didn't agree, then the children could still marry but they could forfeit their rights to their house names and Atavarian citizenship.

I wonder if Kier is nervous because our fake mating wasn't sanctioned by his father? How did his father even get permission to marry a Human without losing his place? Was it political something else? Maybe his father's parents weren't against it or they were dead so he didn't need their permission?

I became lost in article after article about Atavarians as we flew toward the jump gate. Every aspect of their lives was deeply rooted in traditions that stretched back to the Enlightenment. Then I came across the news about the virus strain and my heart broke.

It was spreading fast in the densely populated areas, too fast to track in some places. Quarantines were being enacted, with strict regulation of who could come into the city. Council meetings in person were forbidden at the moment. At the moment, it was hitting the Atavarian version of a middle class the hardest. Interstellar travel was cut back, and imports and exports were starting to be affected.

The planet is looking at a shutdown at this point. And they've rejected almost every attempt at help from the GUP. Why? Just because they don't like Humans? That seems oddly emotional and illogical for Atavarians.

"We will be arriving at the jump station within the hour," Kier said, startling me.

I looked up; he was standing over the table, his gaze intense. Was I projecting my questions down the bond? Maybe my confusion and nerves?

"Oh," was all I said, then, "I guess I got distracted with my studies."

He gave me a short nod and didn't move, his gaze shifting side to side as if he were considering something.

"Do you want to sit?" I asked.

"No, thank you. I would like to discuss something with you, however."

The seriousness of his tone combined with the nerves that were flowing down our bond set me on edge and started to fidget with the tablet.

"Sure, what's going on?" I asked, my voice a little too bright.

Kier cleared his throat, eventually taking the seat next to me.

"Chloe, I realize that this entire situation is fraught with difficulties and that there is a potential to be overwhelmed by it all. It is for that reason I regret what I have to tell you."

I swallowed, heart thudding against my ribs.

"You're making me nervous. Whatever it is, just say it."

"Yes, of course I...I can be loquacious when I am nervous."

I couldn't help a slight burst of laughter.

"Only you would use such a big word when you're worried about something."

Usually, I'd be concerned that he would misinterpret my laughter as making fun of him, and sometimes early in our friendship he did. But this time, his gaze softened, and there was the barest hint of a smile around the edges of his mouth. He knew I was joking, he knew it was meant with affection. I wished I could grab his hand, and thread my fingers through his. Instead, I put my hands in my lap and clenched them tight.

"What do you want to say?" I asked.

He cleared his throat again.

"My sister informed me that my father and my aunt know of our mating and due to my particular status—"

"Not being allowed to take a mate?"

"Yes, and because you are Human and I am half Human, my aunt is insisting, and my father is supporting her in the idea, that in order to be seen as Atavarian enough to gain access to the Institute without offending anyone, we must perform the wedding rituals."

He said it very fast, his voice firm but also louder than his norm.

At first I just stared, not sure I heard him correctly. But the longer I went without saying anything, the more strained his expression and the more anxiety came down the bond.

"I, uh...so, we have to get married?" I asked finally, my voice shaking.

"Essentially, yes."

I opened and closed my mouth several times while I tried to process this. I had feelings for him, and they were deeper than I thought at first, that was certain. But while the idea of pretending to be mates had a certain appeal, actually going through with it was another thing entirely.

"Why? I thought...I mean, we can just *say* we're mated, right? They'd have to let me in, right?"

"Theoretically, yes. But Atavarian society is built upon tradition. It would be an understatement to say that our traditions and rituals are important to us.

Therefore, going through with even a modified version of the wedding rituals would show that you can be trusted at the Institute. It would put many fears to rest, and while it does not solve the problem of others thinking less of you because you are Human, it would remove any barriers anyone may reference in letting you have access."

"It smooths the way, in other words."

"Precisely. It is a complication, I recognize that and I am sorry. I...I am not sure you would've had the same problems with Vas'Rach."

I didn't miss the way he growled the other Atavarian's name or the way his hands clenched on the table. He hated the idea of me with Vas'Rach more than I did. Did he hate the need for this marriage too?

"How do you feel about this?" I asked.

"It is not ideal."

"That's true, but how do you *feel* about it?"

He let out a long breath and frowned as he thought about my question.

"Conflicted," he finally answered. "On one hand, I see the logic of it, and I understand the need to satisfy tradition. On the other, I dislike, intensely, the idea of making you any more uncomfortable than you already are. I have already forced a mental bond onto you, and now you are being forced into an actual marriage. I have...guilt over the situation."

"You didn't force anything on me, I want to be clear about that. It was an accident," I said.

He tried to speak and, without thinking, I pressed my hand to his lips.

"Nope, not another word. Accident, not forced."

And then I realized what I'd done, how my fingers were against his soft mouth, the silky heat that was trickling down the bond and into my mind...and shining out of his eyes. I wanted to keep my hand there, to run my index finger around the fullness of his lips, let him nibble at the tip.

God, to be honest, I wanted him to nibble all of me, and the way his eyes suddenly widened, I knew that I must've telegraphed some of that to him. My face turned red and I wanted the floor to swallow me up.

"Sorry," I started to remove my hand when he caught it in his.

"I...did not mind."

That one sentence, said with a voice that was rough and almost needy, turned that trickle of heat into a full blown stream in an instant.

"Oh," was all that squeaked past my lips. "I...I didn't...I mean, you're alright with me touching you?"

He was staring at my hand where it now rested in the palm of his gloved one as he traced each of my fingers with one of his.

"This is not an ideal time to discuss this," he finally said, "but—"

A notification beeped in the cockpit and the moment was shattered.

Kier let go of my hand and stood so fast that he bumped into the table. The tablet almost fell onto the ground but I caught it.

"I did not realize the time," he said, his voice once again steady and calm. "We are nearing the station and I will need to pilot us through the gate."

If I'd thought that knowing his mind would help mitigate the emotional whiplash he seemed so good at producing, I was sorely mistaken. If anything, it made it worse since whatever he had been feeling was there and gone so fast that I was left reeling from the loss.

Kier was already sitting in his seat in the cockpit and had guided us to our place in line to go through the jump gate by the time I'd been able to get my own thoughts and feelings in order.

I walked to the front, knowing it would be more comfortable up here in a cushy captain's chair than one of the barely padded jump seats in the back. I stared in wonder at the strange beauty of the three concentric rings in front of me. They looked impossibly thin in some places and enormously thick in others. And the closer we got, the more it looked like some giant had etched runes all around them, but in reality, it was simply thousands of conduits and computers, hatches and tunnels that made the rings work and enabled engineers to keep them from breaking down.

Despite all the times I'd seen them, it still inspired awe in me that these were the constructs that channeled and balanced the energy needed to generate a stable worm hole for travel across great distances. The creativity and ingenuity that went into constructing them was a true wonder.

The GUP currently had five of these, tying all the quadrants together. The jumps through the worm hole could take anywhere between ten minutes to an hour depending on the size of the ship and the amount of space being traversed. Each gate could potentially connect to up to five different exit points. This one had three different exit points, all connected to this outpost, Space Station Alpha. Since this was the first jump gate the GUP ever made, the exit points were to the three main hubs that comprised the early days of the GUP: Earth, Atavar and the edge of what is now known as the Terran Quadrant. After we passed through the gate, it would only take us two days to reach Atavar.

I'd done more jumps than I could count, having spent more of my life on a space ship than a planet, and Kier had done his share, being part of the Gex-Corps, so neither of us really listened to the automated recording that went over safety protocols. I was used to the sensations of being pushed and pulled at the same time, of gravity being simultaneously heavy and light. It would last a few seconds, until we were over the threshold of the gate, and inside the stable part of the worm hole. Then ten minutes or so of zero gravity, which could be fun if you're a kid and have a bet about how many globs of juice you can drink in that amount of time without throwing them up. And then we'd be out the other side, in a different corner of space.

Larger ships, like the Intrepid, had sophisticated inertial dampners and environmental controls that were powerful enough to adjust the environment automatically so most of the crew wouldn't even feel the effects of the jump. But smaller ships, like the one I'd grown up on and like this one, usually didn't have that capability.

Station Alpha was a hub for commerce and there was a completely separate area for trade ships to be inspected before and after a jump. The station was considered neutral ground, and disputes were often settled at a jump station rather than a planet for that reason. As I stared out our front view screen, small ships flew by on their way out of the gate on this side or to dock at the station or one of its three biodomes. Large ships waited in a holding area for their turn to jump, their mass too great to jump with other ships. As we got into position, it looked like we were jumping with five other smaller shuttles, not surprising since this was quite a compact cruiser.

I strapped in as we were given the green light to enter and took a deep breath as we breached the gate. In spite of my experience, this part never got easier and I realized that I might've gotten a bit soft after so long on a Command ship.

Just breathe, it's okay.

We were over the threshold before the sensations could wreak too much havoc on my system and soon our shuttle was enveloped in a sleeve of bright lights of silver, pink and blue. Auto navigation took over and all we had to do was sit back and watch as our bodies experienced the weightlessness of the wormhole. Though we were strapped in, I still felt as if I were about to levitate up to the ceiling. My hair creeped up around me, and my arms rose at my sides. I'd always found this rather fun and wondered what Kier thought about it. I was about to ask when I noticed how he was looking at the lights around us. Pure awe and delight shone in his eyes, like a child on holiday.

"Have you ever seen it like this before?" I asked.

"No. I did not experience many jumps before joining the Gex-Corps. And those that I did, were in larger ships."

"It's so beautiful."

His sharp gaze fell on me, holding me in a soft warmth.

"Yes, it is."

I should've broken away from his stare, remembered that everything was going to end and I absolutely should not get attached. But I was never very good at doing what I *should* do.

Our seats weren't close enough for me to reach out and touch him, so I tried something and made myself picture taking his hand. I created each detail as clearly as possible. The feel of his glove on my palm, the strength of his fingers winding around mine, the emotion I would feel. It was all so very real to me as I imagined it. I had no idea if I was sending him these images, if I was making a fool of myself or stepping out of bounds. I just missed him in a way I hadn't before. He'd been closed off to me for four days, and it was too long. I needed to feel close to him again, though I couldn't put it into words.

Just when I was starting to wonder if my thoughts had penetrated Kier's mental barriers, he flexed his hand, eyes flicking between his fingers and me. His pupils were dilated, lips parted on a sharp breath and I knew that he had seen it all, felt it all.

Then, gently, almost imperceptibly, an answering picture appeared in my mind.

Kier bringing my hand to his mouth, kissing the tip of each finger down to my palm, to the veins of my wrist.

"Before the jump gate," my voice was a little shaky, "you were starting to tell me something, about touch?"

"I am...curious to explore touch with you," he confessed.

Those words, simply spoken were like a shot of whiskey to my system and even if I hadn't been in zero gravity, I would have felt on fire and weightless, all at once.

"I would like that."

"I have been very nervous to tell you that. I did not want to overwhelm you with everything happening. The wedding is...well, *unexpected* is an understatement."

I barked out a laugh.

"Yes, it is!"

The edges of his lips quirked up.

"Zephyr suggested that I be direct with you, to ask for what I wanted and so, if it would not impose too much upon you, could we explore touching?"

"It isn't an imposition, at all. I do have to ask though, um, considering what we've already done, what do you mean by exploring?"

His gaze heated and I knew I wasn't imagining the sudden burst of arousal from him. I kept my own reactions as locked down as possible because I really didn't want anything to stop us from having this conversation. If Kier wanted touching, no matter how little, I would give it to him gladly. But I also didn't want to make assumptions and cross any boundaries, so I had to get this out of him before he clammed up again.

"You're asking if I would like to have sex with you again?"

I nearly choked at his directness, but instead I just nodded.

"I," he looked down, "I do not know. The rutting fever allowed my usual inhibitions to be lowered. I was not as aware of things as I would be now without the fog on my logical mind. Therefore, I could become overwhelmed by too much touch after so long of not having it."

"That makes sense."

"And, I do not want others to touch me, only you. I feel I must make that clear. Perhaps it is the bond or what we shared, but you are the only one I will be exploring this with. Is that also too much pressure?"

I smiled at his concern because it was utterly unnecessary. I had been slightly afraid that I'd be easing him into being comfortable with touching other people, only to have him go around gloveless with everyone else. And, to my shock, I was a bit jealous of Kier's touches.

"That's just fine," I said.

His shoulders relaxed a bit, affection warmed my mind and my smile widened as I looked at him.

"Asking me to help you with this isn't a burden. It's actually the least stressful part of all this and it makes me happy that you asked. I like it."

He almost smiled at that, and it wasn't the lack of gravity that was making me feel light and airy. It was him, and my feelings for him. His request had put rocket fuel into them and now they were running out of control within me. There would be no way to contain them now, and a reckless part of me that was growing by the minute didn't want to.

Maybe, just maybe, Kier was worth a little heartbreak.

Chapter Sixteen

KIER'AHN

Chloe liked what I had requested.

A lot.

Which should have soothed any anxiety I was experiencing around this, but for some reason, it only made it worse. I could tell that she wanted to begin after we had completed our jump, but I wanted to be sure I would not cross more lines with her and for that, I needed to be centered.

"You must be tired," I said to her before she could suggest anything. "Would you like me to prepare dinner?"

"Um...sure."

It was a very simple thing to program the printers appropriately, but I took my time, focusing on each step. Cooking was a meditative act for many, and prior to my rut, the captain had been teaching me a few simple techniques. I had found it pleasant, if sometimes tedious.

By the time the printers had finished the meals, I was calmer. I turned with the bowls of rice and vegetables, one with chicken for Chloe, and saw her pacing the small living area, mouthing something she sias reading from the holo tablet in her hand. I indulged in a moment to simply look at her, the way she bit her bottom lip between her two crooked front teeth when something perplexed her. The way she fidgeted with a strand of hair, and the sway of her hips as she walked.

Hips I had gripped hard many times during the rut. I knew because flashes of those moments had invaded my dreams the last two nights. She liked it when I held her tight. She liked it when I had clasped her throat particularly. I remembered that quite viscerally, the sensation of her pulse against my thumb, how excited I became when it raced.

My body grew hot and my phallus started to stir at the thought. All of the calm I had achieved was gone, leaving me with a deficit now.

"Is it ready?" she asked, breaking me out of the moment.

"Um, yes. It is."

"Great, I'm starving."

We sat across from one another, as we usually did, and Chloe began to eat as I attempted to quell the surprising burst of arousal inside of me. This was one reason I was reluctant to begin touching her; what if I became lustful with her? What if she saw my phallus hard, the nodes pulsing, and became afraid?

Would she become afraid though? She had liked the rutting and I knew that she was attracted to me, I could feel it.

What would she do? Would she *touch* it? Would she grip it in her small hands, press her thumbs to the nodes and...

"So, this wedding," she said, yanking me from where those thoughts would inevitably lead.

While it wasn't a desirable subject, it was preferable to becoming hard at the table with her at that moment. Especially since the more aroused I became, the less I was able to hide it behind my mental barriers and Chloe would start to sense it.

"Yes?" I asked. "What would you like to know?"

"I just read that it's a multi-day affair? And that it can take up to six months to prepare for. There are rituals I have to perform and seven different dresses I have to be fitted for."

"You read quite fast."

"I skimmed the introduction of the *five-hundred-page* book on 'the enlightened path of mating'."

"Yes, Atavarians can be quite...verbose when it comes to rituals. But I believe my aunt has said she will expect us to perform a rather shortened version of the usual rituals. She and my father know you are there for a fellowship, though they are not privy to the details."

Chloe let out a relieved breath.

"Good because I really do want to get started on this vaccine as soon as possible. Did you know that it's spreading faster? That they believe the rate at which it propagates with in a host has doubled, that's why it's so severe this time."

"I had not heard that. I confess I do not keep up on news from Atavar."

She paused, chewing thoughtfully on her dinner.

"Is it going to be difficult, returning after all this time?"

"Yes. I did not leave on the best of terms with my aunt and father."

"Why not?"

"They both had wanted me to attend the Science Institute but I chose to leave for the Academy instead."

"Getting a place at the Institute is prestigious, and I imagine not easy for you since you're half Human. Why didn't you want it?"

I frowned and set down my utensil as I tried to find a way to answer her. This was something that I often skirted answering, or came up with a simple half-truth that revealed very little, but conveyed that I did not wish to elaborate. But with Chloe, the things I had once hidden in shame were becoming the very things I longed to show her. I was not sure why, it made no sense to me that one night of rutting would change so much. But the evidence was very clear: it had. And I had tried to fight it, and failed. The thought of continuing to shut her out seemed foolish and was quite distasteful to me.

So, very slowly I found the words to tell her about a moment I had not spoken about with anyone, ever.

"At that time, I had attempted a very difficult rite of passage and failed. If I had succeeded, I believed that it would have settled the question once and for all if I were Atavarian enough or not. But my Human physiology was a hindrance to completing the rite and I nearly died. I knew that no matter what my accomplishments were in the future, this one failure would cast a shadow over all I would do as proof that I was only half of an Atavarian. And I did not want to live like that."

Chloe's face twisted in remorse for me and she began to reach across for my hand, but stopped, unsure about whether I would want such comfort. And prior to my rut, I would not have. Now, I had a sudden craving for it.

So I took off my gloves, set them aside and slowly reached across to her. My heart was pounding in my chest with anticipation and nerves at, once again, feeling her skin against mine. When I brushed her fingertips, Chloe turned her hand palm side up, as she had in the observatory and I placed my hand, soft at first, in hers.

The moment I pressed my palm to hers, peace coursed through my body, wrapping my mind in gold ribbons of light. I let out a long breath, muscles unwinding that I had not been aware were tight. My fingers rested against her wrist as hers did against mine, and I traced one of the veins. Her thumb ran along the outside of my hand, slow and soft, sending tingles through my wrist and up my arm. It was perfect.

"It was brave of you to choose something different," she whispered after a few moments. "To choose what you needed instead of what your family wanted for you. Not everyone has that strength."

I frowned at that and tilted my head to the side as I took in her words.

"I had never considered it brave in that way," I replied thoughtfully. "But I must confess, I am nervous for you, for the treatment you will receive and..."

I swallowed, the words refusing to come. I could not speak of this to her yet, nor could I bear to think of it in connection to her.

The smoke...the smell of burned flesh in my nose...

Chloe's hand came to my face, startling me out of the visceral memories. When I looked up, her brows were drawn low over her eyes, which were roaming over my face as if she were looking for something.

"Are you alright?" she asked. "I got a feeling from you that was very strong."

"I am fine," I said, raising up my mental shields fast and firmly.

I took my hand from her and stood up, my food only half consumed but my appetite gone. I did not know if the touch had brought on these strong feelings, or if they were there, lurking under the surface and waiting for me to be weak.

Whatever the reason, I needed space to gather my defenses. This was one thing I could not think about, not when Chloe needed me to be at my best, my most vigilant.

"Forgive me, I need to meditate," I said. "Do you mind if I take the room for an hour?"

"No, of course not," she said, with confusion and turmoil in her eyes. "I will, um, I'll just knock in an hour? We should probably get some rest."

"Yes," I glanced at the room, at the one bed. "I...Yes."

I stalked to the room quickly and as I was closing the door she said, "Let me know if you need anything."

I pressed my forehead to the cool metal and breathed through the hammering of my heart.

I was not in that building now. Chloe was not in that building.

She would be safe. I would make sure of it.

But not if I couldn't get my mind and emotions under control.

So I found my meditation cushion and dimmed the lights.

"Computer, play Octoforgen Monks, chant one, confine to this room."

"Affirmative."

The resonate tones of the monks chanting washed over me and I let out a breath of relief. I should have been doing this all along, but meditation had been so fraught with difficulties the last two days that I had not wanted to risk letting something out. Now, as my mind fell into the rhythms of the chanting, a peace fell over my mind and I allowed myself to relax.

When I came to the end of the chant, my mind and spirit were balanced, my thoughts calm and orderly. I needed to forge new paths to control these feelings, discover new tactics. It could be done, and Chloe's safety, as well as the rest of the galaxy, was at stake. I would find a way toward balance, there was no other option.

And perhaps, balance must start at accepting what has happened instead of fighting it. We are bonded. We will be wed. I want her to touch me, and she wants me to touch her. Expending energy fighting all of this takes it from places where it is needed.

I nodded to myself. This was logical.

The clock we had synced with the Intrepid's told me I had meditated for longer than I had planned and I hoped Chloe was not angry with my monopolization of the room.

I quickly changed into a pair of loose sleep pants and opened the door to find Chloe curled up on the small couch in the main room. She had a cookie in one hand and the tablet in the other, a deep frown of concentration on her face as she read. Somehow, she hadn't realized I was there.

Chloe had the lights low, her body wrapped in a soft blanket as she nibbled on the cookie. Her hair was in loose, soft waves around her face and I wondered if she would like me running my fingers through it. She had always been beautiful, but now I could admit that, to me, Chloe was the most stunning woman I'd ever seen. Especially when she was lost in reading. Her nose wrinkled suddenly and she snorted in disbelief. It was quite adorable.

"I hope I have not kept you up too late," I said, wanting her attention on me now.

She jumped at my voice, her eyes wide when she turned to look at me. I was not wearing a shirt and I realized that this would be the first time since the rut that we had been in the same room with so much of my skin showing. It was not an unpleasant thought, though it was shocking that I felt that way.

Her eyes skated down my torso in obvious appreciation and I could not deny the pride invading my emotions. She liked my body, it was not too alien to her.

"I, um, no, you didn't," she said, placing the tablet back into the small space inside the table and getting to her feet. "I was just reading up on...things."

"I see."

We stared at one another, the space between us filled with things that I had run from all my life.

Longing.

Desire.

I almost raised a mental barrier against them; a lifetime of training had created a reflex that would be challenging to break. But I managed to stop myself and simply took in how it felt to have these emotions at the surface, alive and unfettered.

It was...tantalizing.

And as she walked closer to me, slowly, her skin flushed and her chest rising and falling fast, those emotions became hotter under my skin. My heart beat faster, and for a second, I was afraid.

Then there was that golden ribbon in my mind. Liquid sunshine that grounded me and told me I was safe.

I let out the breath I had been holding and swallowed. Chloe stopped a few inches from me, the top of her head reaching only my collar bone, and I had the urge to wrap my arms around her, to keep her safe.

She had changed into a pair of soft pink shorts and a tank top for sleeping. It showed off her muscular thighs and the beautiful curve of her shoulders. I glanced at the spot where I had bitten her, an odd sort of disappointment lanced through me to see that the marks were gone.

I had assumed that the urge to mark and bite would be gone with the rutting fever, but perhaps it is a byproduct of the bond?

"I was thinking," she said, gesturing to herself and me, and then the bed, "and I feel like we need to be adult about this."

"I agree."

"Our mission is important and difficult, we need to make sure we are focused, sharp."

"Absolutely."

"And it's because of this that I think we should share the bed."

"Yes."

"Don't argue with me and hear me out. I know that you...wait, what?"

She frowned up at me and I smirked at her surprise.

"I agree," I said. "It would be foolish to expect one of us to not rest properly."

"Oh, well...I guess I expected more of a fight. I had a whole speech planned."

"Would you like to give it anyway? I promise to interject the appropriate arguments so you may feel properly challenged."

She huffed out a laugh and playfully smacked my arm. Then her eyes stuck to the spot where she'd touched me and her cheeks became even pinker. When she took her bottom lip between her front teeth, I had the oddest urge to run my thumb across that part of her mouth. I had a vague memory of drawing blood there...

When she straightened her shoulders and looked me square in the eye, there was a playful gleam that I had missed very much in her eyes.

"That won't be necessary," she informed me. "I'll save my brilliant arguments for a time when they are needed because I have a feeling you're going to be stubborn at some point in all this."

"Very logical."

"Why, thank you."

"Please," I stepped aside and gestured to the small room, "I'm sure you have things to do in order to prepare for sleep. I am going to warm some synthetic blood and I will be in shortly."

She gave me a nervous smile and walked past me. I did not linger, but took my time with getting the blood out of the cooling unit and warming it up. The taste had become a little strange to me since my rut and I wondered if it was because I had tasted actual blood for the first time. Not that it mattered, I should not do that again. Touching Chloe was one thing, biting her like an animal was another. No matter how much my incisors ached at the thought.

When I had sated my cravings and cleaned up, I double checked the navigation to ensure we were still on the correct trajectory. The auto pilot confirmed it and long range scans showed no signs of other ships. Our cloaking device was holding and everything appeared safe, normal.

I no longer had any excuse to remain outside the room and while I had indeed accepted the logic of Chloe's proposal, I found myself nervous.

What if I touched her in the night?

What if I entered her mind in sleep?

It was a risk, one that I would be faced with every night on this mission, as it would appear strange if I did not sleep beside my mate as other Atavarians did.

I suppose it is best to test this while we are alone instead of when we are staying with my father and aunt.

So I walked to the room, where I found Chloe already snug under the covers, her back to the door, with the lights nearly out. It was far darker than I usually liked it, but I did not say anything. Perhaps Chloe needed it this dark to sleep and I did not want to deprive her of rest. I would be fine for one night.

I slid in beside her, a wide space between us as we both seemed to cling to the outer edges of the bed.

"Are you comfortable?" I asked.

"Yes."

"Are you certain? There is quite a lot of room."

She glanced behind her and gave me a grin.

"I'm alright, promise."

For a moment I considered reaching out to her, and pulling her to me. I remembered holding her after each of the ruttings very clearly, likely because the hormones were not clogging my mind. I had liked the feel of her body against mine very much. She was soft in all the right places, and her hip fit perfectly in my hand.

But in the end, I refrained. Even though I had reconciled myself to the logic of accepting everything, that did not mean I was without trepidation.

"Good night, Chloe." My voice was husky, soft.

"Good night, Kier."

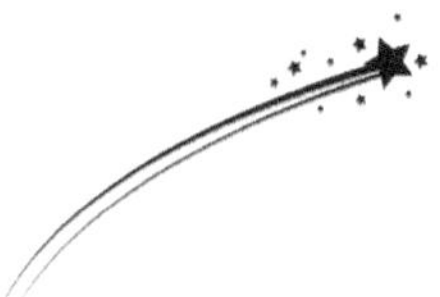

#

The smoking rubble of our home in the city of Ruval on Atavar. The place where my mother had died. Where Zephyr had been maimed.

"Help! Help us!"

My tiny voice was powerless to find the salvation I craved. Darkness was everywhere, stone and glass hard and cutting under my hands and torso. Burning pain was rocketing through my back and arm, constant and terrifying.

"Mommy! Mommy, where are you?"

I screamed in the dark, the smoke thick in my mouth as I did, trying to silence me as it drifted down my throat. Tears fell down my face, stinging the cuts there but I could not stop them. Was I alone? Were they dead? Was I going to die?

We were buried, I knew that much. The explosion had decimated our home and I'd been thrown away from my mother and sister. Where were they now? Had they escaped? Were they searching for me?

I reached around me, wondering if they were close and something viscous met my fingers. It smelled coppery, and wrong.

"Kier...Kier..."

My mother's voice was so very weak and I crawled over more things that slashed the skin of my palms and legs, desperate to get to her. I knew what I'd find, even as I hoped that she'd be alright. I knew how this ended but I couldn't convince the child version of myself to stop before I reached her body.

In the way of dreams, a light appeared from somewhere and I was no longer a child. I was myself as I was now, full grown but weeping. And the broken woman before me, was not my mother. It was Chloe.

Her blond hair was red with blood, her skin gray as her sightless eyes stared up at me.

"No...no! It's all my fault...all my fault...I'm sorry...I'm sorry...I'm sorry."

I screamed and screamed, my broken apologies became the cries of a dying creature whose heart was being torn from its flesh. I wept over her corpse, surrounded by the rubble of my home and knowing that this would be my tomb too. I could not leave her here, I did not want to live in a galaxy where she did not exist.

"Kier..."

The call came from a distance.

"Kier, stop!"

Chloe's voice, but she was dead, I was holding her destroyed body...wasn't I?

"Wake up, you're dreaming. Kier, wake up, please!"

I was ripped from the nightmare and my eyes flew open in panic. I took a gasping breath and raised up my hands, grabbing hold of flesh. The room was dark, like the tomb that my childhood home had become, and I screamed.

"Lights! Lights!"

"Computer, lights up fifty percent," Chloe said.

Light blinded me at first and I cringed against it. My fingers dug into soft skin and I heard a whimper. That began to snap me out of the fugue left over from the dream, and I slowly became aware of my surroundings.

I was holding onto Chloe, and my fingers were biting into her arms. I didn't want to let her go so I simply loosened my grip and took in deep, shaking breaths. The present came back to me in small ways.

The gentle brush of Chloe's fingers against my face.

The tears down her own cheeks.

The way her legs straddled me.

"Y-you were dreaming and it...I felt it," her voice trembled. "Kier...your mother. That's how she died?"

Horror rocked me as I realized that I'd been so out of control with my telepathy that I'd sent all of it down through the bond to Chloe. She had experienced the dream with me, all the fear, the pain, the memories. I pushed her off me as gently as I could before sitting on the edge of the bed. I buried my face in my hands, desperate to make sure that I was controlling my telepathy now so I didn't traumatize her any more than I already had.

"Stop!" Her voice, steely and firm broke through my concentration. "Stop shutting me out."

"I have *hurt* you," I could barely get the words past the loathing that was choking me. "I knew I would do something like this."

"It was an *accident.*"

"It was recklessness on my part. Weakness of the worst kind."

"Stop beating yourself up. Kier, please look at me."

She dragged my hands from my face, forcing me to meet her gaze. I was afraid to at first; afraid I would see pain, fear, revulsion in her eyes, even if she was trying to hide it.

But that was not the case.

Instead, Chloe was kneeling in front of me, her face so open, and concern shone in the remnants of tears in her eyes. I was not at all sure how to respond to this, so I said nothing.

"I'm alright," she said, her thumbs running along the backs of my hands, soothing me. "I promise you didn't hurt me. It was just...shocking to see your dream, painful yes, but only because I was sharing *your* pain. Something I *want* to do by the way."

"This has been my burden for my whole life." I could barely get the words out. "It is not yours."

"It is now."

I flinched at that.

"No, that's not what I meant," she said quickly. "I mean that after seeing it, feeling it, I want to help you carry this. It's what friends do, we help each other with our baggage."

I didn't miss the way she stumbled over the word 'friends', and I was glad. I was beginning to hate that word in connection with us.

"I won't make you," she continued. "But it might help us with the mission if we are honest with one another about our worries, about our past. This seems like a big part of your past on Atavar, shouldn't I know about it if I'm supposed to be your mate?"

Once again, I could not find fault with her logic, so I nodded. My voice was low, the words sticking in my throat but I pushed on anyway.

"During the time of year that I was not in school, we lived at our country estate, far from the prying eyes of others who judged us. I loved it there, as did my sister and my mother. But my school was in the city of Ruval, and we had an apartment there where I lived with my father during the school year. My mother and my sister lived almost exclusively on the estate and I always hated leaving them. I did not know it then, but one of the reasons they lived out there was because my mother had received threats against her life and my father feared she would not be safe in the city. This particular year, he had been on his final trip to Earth as ambassador before his retirement to ensure his replacement was up to the task, but the trip went longer than anticipated and he was not home in time to take me to Ruval for the beginning of the school year."

I gulped in a breath as guilt seared my heart and tears fell down my cheeks.

Chloe did not say anything, only cupped my face and wiped my tears away. I was too weak to resist the bloom of her presence in my mind, a beautiful golden flower full of warmth and sweet acceptance, so I fell into it, let it hold me.

"It's okay...I've got you."

We both gasped as her words floated up to me psychically. I stared at her in wonder and trepidation. Would she retreat from me? Would this be too much for her?

She swallowed, took a shaky breath and nodded.

"Go on, I'm okay."

"I-I do not know if I have words...I have never spoken of it to anyone."

"Alright well...how about this? If you want to tell me, why don't you say it mentally? Send me the words and images if that would be easier."

"That will not be too much for you?"

A look of beautiful determination crossed her face and she shook her head.

"Go for it. Use your 'other' words, the mental ones."

I hesitated; not only was I unsure if she was truly ready for this level of communication, but it would further deepen our bond, making it that much more difficult to break.

But the temptation to share the weight I'd carried my entire life, to share myself with someone on such an intimate level when I had always thought I'd be alone, separate from others, it was too much to resist.

"If it becomes too much, picture a door between us and close it."

"Got it," she whispered.

I took a deep breath, grasping Chloe's hands in my trembling ones, as I found the words within me to tell her about my greatest shame.

"I was angry at my father for not being home to take me to school. I had turned eight that year and there was a ceremony I had worked hard to take part in, a rite of passage at the beginning of the school term. I was very proud of it, believing this would make others accept me as Atavarian. I was going to miss it because my mother refused at first to take me. But when she saw how important it was, she went against my father's orders and took my sister and me to Ruval."

Memories flooded my mind, though I tried to keep them back. The strange man who had been at the apartment, the argument my father and mother had over holo coms, and the anger from believing that he did not care about things that were important to me.

"It was the night before school, before the ceremony. A servant had awakened my mother to inform her that there was a strange man lurking around the

apartment. She woke Zephyr and me, telling us to pack up. I was furious, and refused, marching back to my room. She and Zephyr chased after me when...when everything exploded around us."

A broken sob escaped my lips as the memories flew fast and viciously through my mind.

My mother's broken body, crushed under a block of stone as she died saying my name.

Zephyr laying near her, arm crushed and half of her face burned.

The hours I'd spent curled up next to my mother's dead body, telling her I'd be good if only she would wake up.

"Oh, Kier," Chloe's arms wrapped around me.

I buried my face in her neck and drew her body to mine. I'd been trained to shun this, to fear it, and yet her touch on my body and mind was the only thing I wanted right now. It soothed the rough edges of the grief I'd never been able to let go of, and told me it was alright to *feel* this, even if it was not my fault.

And that was what Chloe was saying to me, over and over in her mind.

"It's not your fault. You were just a child. You are not responsible for the actions of that man, or anyone that hurt your family."

She used those words to drip a balm I did not know I needed onto the wound left behind from the guilt of my mother's murder.

"It is not easy to accept that. If I had not insisted on being there, she would not have died. Zephyr would not have been forced to leave Atavar...leave me."

Instead of words this time, there were the same colors I had seen during the rut, when our minds touched, and now I knew that it was Chloe's presence. She was wrapping herself around me, holding my soul as well as my body, in a tender embrace that I could not resist.

There was so much feeling that beat against the barriers I'd constructed over a lifetime of training and fear. I longed to let them out, but trepidation stopped me from opening the flood gates.

It did not, however, prevent me from letting a trickle of the emotion out, a tiny sampling to taste and explore the bright miasma that Chloe had awakened within me. I had been afraid that such a thing might cause me to lose control.

But instead, it soothed me. The longer I allowed myself to accept her presence in my mind and her skin against me, the calmer I became.

It was illogical.

It was against everything I had been taught.

And yet, the evidence was irrefutable.

She did not cause me to lose control. Chloe, helped me to find it.

Chapter Seventeen

CHLOE

Kier had let me hold him long enough that my legs had started to cramp, bent like they were on the hard floor of the shuttle. When he realized that I was uncomfortable he pulled back and my heart sank. I hated that he had carried so much guilt and sorrow for so long, but I had loved hugging him and didn't want it to be over.

"If it would not be too inconvenient," he said, "may I hold your hand while I fall asleep?"

He said it with such vulnerability and shyness that it made me want to bundle him up and hold him all night long. I would've loved more but recognized this was not the time.

"Yes," I said quickly, "absolutely."

I dimmed the lights and slipped back into bed with him. But now, instead of being all the way over on the other side, we met in the middle and faced one another. I held my hand out palm up and he placed his much bigger one in mine. His grip swallowed my fingers and I loved the sensation of being so tiny next to him.

"Will you be able to sleep or do you want me to stay up with you?" I asked.

"I believe I will sleep after…after unburdening myself to you. Thank you, Chloe."

"You never have to thank me for that. I'm here for you, always."

Kier scooted toward to me until our faces were close together. We stared at one another for a while longer until sleep dragged me into a very deep rest.

When I awakened it was slow, my body unwilling to come to consciousness fully. As I did, I felt warmth all around me, something firm and hot behind me that I realized was a very strong body.

And not just any body, it was Kier's.

When I opened my eyes fully, I realized that at some point in the night, he had pulled me against him and my back was to his front, with one of his very strong, red arms slung around my hips, and his hand precariously close to my breast.

Small puffs of breath ruffled my hair and I was suddenly very aware of his phallus, half erect poking me in the back. Very carefully so I didn't wake him, I put my hand on his forearm, which was smooth and firm. It was a heady thing to know that no one else had ever awakened with him, that I was the only one who had that privilege.

I ran my hand up his forearm to his elbow and back down, reveling in my ability to touch him finally. Kier's arm pulled me tighter against him and his phallus was starting to pulse against me. I remembered what those nodes did, how they felt inside of me and heat flooded my sex. I moved to see if I could get a little distance between myself and his erection when Kier groaned behind me. His hips bumped against mine and I flushed deeply.

I'd only aroused him more and if I wasn't mistaken, he was asleep and dreaming of having sex.

Usually, I would've awakened a partner with my mouth on his dick, but Kier was different. Not only was he inexperienced, touching was a new experience for him. It felt like a severe breach of trust to do that when I had no idea if he wanted intimacies right now.

Kier's hand suddenly moved and he cupped my breast. I bit my bottom lip at how *good* it felt. His fingers massaged my breast and then he found my nipple, pert and sensitive. How was he playing with it so well in his sleep?

A low moan escaped my mouth and I was grinding myself against him before I could stop myself.

Behind me, Kier growled, low and ragged in his chest as he had during the rut and I could see the things he wanted to do to me, just like I had then. Flashes of his mouth on my breasts, suckling and taking me deep as his fangs scraped against my nipples. My head fell back on his shoulder and I reached back to sink my fingers into his hair.

This was getting out of control fast, and I needed to wake him up before I let myself go and did something he might not actually want outside of his dreams.

"Kier," I panted as his other hand began to stray lower. "Kier, wake up."

His mouth fell on the skin by my ear, then lower and I could feel his fangs.

I tried to turn and he held me firm, but I managed to turn my head just enough to see his face.

"*Priash*," he murmured against my skin.

There was that word again, the one he mentally kept blocking from the universal translators. What did it mean?

"Kier, wake up. I-I don't want us to do anything you don't want to."

He stilled behind me, his hands stopping their exploration. A part of me was furious with myself because I was in serious need of release by now, wound up by what his hands had been doing to me along with the flashes of what his mind was doing to me.

"Chloe," he breathed against my skin, ragged. "I...I am sorry. I thought it was a dream and I..."

"I'm alright. I just wanted you to be awake, to be sure that you wanted to do something before we did."

He ran his nose along my jaw, breathing deep and his phallus gave another pulse.

"You are excited by me," he said.

"Yes."

"I am excited by you as well."

I gave him a breathy laugh.

"I hadn't noticed."

His eyes blazed as he held mine, a deep well of feeling that I'd never seen before shone there and I was mesmerized. I reached up and brushed my fingers against his cheek, savoring the way he leaned into it. In my mind, I sensed him, like a shy ghost popping in and out of my consciousness. He was nervous, unsure how to proceed, or if he should.

"Can I kiss you?" I whispered, dragging my index finger along his bottom lip.

Kier swallowed and then nodded.

"I would like that."

I turned in his arms, slow and careful so I didn't graze his very hard phallus. He wanted to take this slow, I could feel that and I agreed with it. The rut had been one thing, a primal moment that had been full of desperation and physiological need. It had been passionate, and I had glimpsed parts of him in it, but it hadn't been this. The threshold we were about to cross was another level entirely. This was a choice and it would change everything between us.

Once we were facing each another, our bodies were close but no longer flush. Kier's eyes were on my mouth, and the knuckles of his clenched hand slowly caressed my cheek, and I nuzzled him. When his fingers unfolded, cupping my cheek, he leaned forward, hovering just above my mouth, as my hand slid up his chest and a shuddering breath skated across my skin.

"Chloe," he murmured my name in disbelief and longing.

I closed the sliver of space between us, skating my mouth across his, feather light and soft. We'd kissed in his rut, but this felt like a first kiss with all the anxious anticipation it was supposed to hold. After the first moment of breathless shock, Kier pressed his lips against mine more firmly, as his fingers threaded in my hair, sending hot tingles through my body. He held me in place as his mouth danced with mine, slow and thorough. A sense of wonder came down the bond to me, an innocent awakening to what he had been missing.

When I grazed his lips with my tongue, asking for entry he opened eagerly to me, sliding his tongue against mine in a tentative exploration. He wanted to know all of this with me, to know how to please me.

Hold me close to you, I told him through the bond.

A soft moan rolled up from him, and he tilted my head with one hand while he gathered my body against his with his other, as if he'd been waiting for permission. My mind began to go hazy as his mouth devoured mine, burning away the inhibitions that had held me back.

I whimpered as his hand ran down the side of my body to my hips and held me tight. His phallus pressed into my belly and I rolled my hips out of instinct and need to feel him.

He groaned against me and trailed his mouth along my jaw, his fangs longer than before.

"What...what do you want?" I breathed, my fingers curling around one of his sets horns.

"I am unsure," he nibbled on my throat while his fingers skimmed across my collar bone. "I...I know we have done this before..."

"We haven't though, not really."

He looked up at me and there was such perfect understanding there that I saw why this kind of bond was dangerous. In this moment, we could know one another so completely that if one of us wanted to, we could easily manipulate the other.

"No," he whispered, dragging the tip of one finger around my mouth, "we have not done this before. This is no rut. This is..."

"Special."

"Yes."

I licked my lips and he watched with a voracious glint in his eyes that sent a shock of heat to my sex.

"We can take it slow if you want," I said, even though I was aching and wet for him.

"What if...what if I was not sure I wanted to be inside of you, but I wanted to keep touching?"

I nodded, probably a little too enthusiastically.

"Yes, I would like that."

"Would you tell me how you liked to be touched on your breasts?"

I smiled at him. The question was so erotic but also innocent.

"I can definitely do that."

I sat up enough to take my top off and then took his hand and placed it on one of my breasts. His eyes widened and he immediately began to knead it, not hard, but firmly as if he were in awe of them. My nipple was hard and when he dragged his thumb across it I hissed in pleasure and nodded.

"You can pinch it, kiss it," I said, practically begging him with my tone of voice.

A feral sound poured from him just before he brought his mouth down to me and drew my stiff peak into his mouth, just like he'd been dreaming about. I wound my fingers into his hair and held on tight while he absolutely destroyed me. Kier went from one breast to the other, pushing me onto my back in the process. This might be his first time exploring someone's breasts outside of his rut, but Kier was a damn artist at it. Soft and hard at just the right time, he licked and laved before sucking on them again, while his hand played with the other. I almost wondered how the hell he knew the exact time to stop and start, the exact pressure to apply when I realized that I was probably shouting such things down the bond at him.

"I think you're ruining me for anyone else."

I hadn't meant to think it but it was out before I could stop it. I would've been mortified if not for his response that rolled through me like molten steel, and I almost came from one word.

"Good."

My core ached so much, I needed to be filled, to be touched but I wasn't sure Kier wanted to go that far. So I slid my fingers into my shorts and found my clit, the hood pulled back to expose the sensitive pearl. Suddenly Kier stopped kissing my breasts and I opened my eyes to find him staring at what I was doing to myself. When he looked back at me, his gaze was ravenous.

"You want to watch me or touch me?" I asked, my voice husky with need.

I pictured what I would do, how it would feel and how much I wanted him to watch me come to an orgasm.

He swallowed, his jaw tensing as the images aroused him. After a moment, he slipped his pants down just enough for his phallus to spring free. I remembered it well, but it still took my breath away.

So thick, the dark red tip weeping with arousal. The nodes on either side pulsed as his knot swelled at the base. Then I was seeing *him* in my mind, fisting his cock as I played with my clit. Him watching me, as I watched him. I felt everything he felt when he asked a silent question, did I want this?

"Yes," I panted.

He fell down toward me, his free hand catching himself, holding his phallus in the other as he pleasured himself above me. He crushed his lips to mine, sucking on my bottom lip and plundering my mouth with his tongue as if I were air and he were drowning. And I suppose we both were. Drowning in the sensations of one another.

I felt my fingers plunging inside of me as my other hand worked my clit in hard circles, but I also felt Kier's hand pumping himself, the way he pressed on those sensitive nodes sent little sparks of lightning through his body and mine.

My entire being was a tight, hot coil. But it was also an inferno of want.

"Kier," I cried out as my orgasm built and built inside of me but never crested.

He mumbled harsh words in Atavarian against my throat, between biting and sucking on my sensitive skin. His motions were getting harder, faster, or was that me? Our emotions were entwined so tightly that I couldn't tell anymore if what I was feeling was my hands on me or Kier's hands on himself. The rut had been intense and erotic beyond belief, there was no doubt about that.

But this was so different. This was intimate in so many different ways beyond our bodies. There was no frenzied fucking, no sense of danger, but there was a connection that was quickly becoming addictive. I never believed in souls connecting in sex, not really. It always sounded so romantically naive. Yet as this connection with him simultaneously scorched me to nothing and built me back up again, there was no other way to look at it.

My soul was coiled with his, for better or worse.

When everything finally shattered inside of me, I screamed, my toes curled and back arched as my orgasm, and Kier's, utterly wrecked me. Warm ropes of cum hit my stomach and thighs as a flood of wetness poured out of me.

It kept rolling over and through me, and I babbled incoherent syllables. I think I might've begged him to make it stop at one point, but either he was too far gone or I was or both, because it didn't stop. When it began to abate, and the blinding pleasure started to fade, I was aware of Kier's mouth on my temple, gentle, as he crooned soft words to me. I reached up and clung to the back of his neck as I touched my lips to his, a semblance of the soft kiss that had started all of this. Only instead of it being shyness that kept it so light, it was exhaustion. I was wrung out but I didn't want him to stop touching me, not yet. There was still so much sensation that I feared if his hands weren't on me, I would simply float away.

"It is alright...I am here."

"Me too...Kier, I'm here too."

I didn't know which of us had needed to hear that and perhaps it didn't matter. Soon our bodies began to come down from the orgasms, our minds separate until I was no longer wound around his consciousness like a vine, nor he around mine. I could still sense him, sweet and patient, but no longer were every one of his physical sensations invading my awareness.

I could breathe again and my muscles began to relax until I could finally think clearly.

"I would ask if you liked that but..." I said and started to laugh.

He gave me a tiny smirk and shook his head.

"I have no words, Chloe," he said, and placed one last, gentle kiss on my lips. "Stay here, I will be back momentarily."

He tucked himself back into his pants, even though the front was wet with his release, and was back in a minute with a wet washcloth. Kier cleaned the cum off of me, and I shook my head in wonder.

"What?" he asked.

"For never having done this, you are very considerate."

"It is basic, but thank you. Would you like to shower first? The bathroom is too small for the both of us."

"No, you go, I want to imagine you in there all wet and soapy."

His eyes flared for a moment and I knew he was picturing it, even if he didn't let me into his mind just then.

"You are very wicked," he chided as he gave me another kiss.

"And you like it."

"Quite a lot."

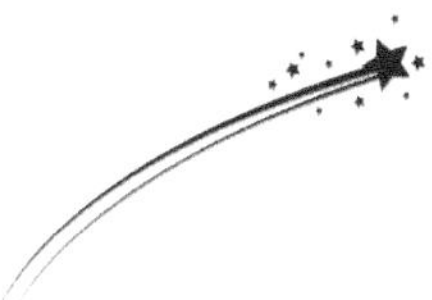

When I had showered and dressed, I came out into the main area and found Kier arranging food on the table.

"Is this going to be an every morning occurrence?" I asked.

He turned with the barest hint of a smile on his lips.

"I do hope so."

Mischievous warmth filtered down our bond and I was delighted to realize that this was Kier chuckling in my head. He rarely laughed outwardly, so to be the only one to experience this was indescribable.

"I like seeing you in the morning," his resonant voice sent tingles through my skin. "And I like doing things for you as well."

I wanted to reach out and kiss him, to twine my fingers through his, but I had no idea what the new rules were. He wasn't wearing his gloves so that could mean hands were okay. But he was new to this, and we had done quite a lot this morning.

Best not to push it too fast.

The table was set with mostly printed food, with the exception of his synthetic blood and...

"Are those Bean Fruits?" I pointed to a small bowl of the bright small fruit.

"I requested them from the kitchens for you. I thought you might like some fresh fruit on the way."

I stared up at him with my lips parted. I wasn't sure why I was surprised at the thoughtful gesture; Kier was actually quite observant of those around him. But for some reason it touched me deeply that once again, he'd thought of such a small detail.

"Was I not correct?"

"No, you were, I just...it's very sweet of you. Thank you."

He inclined his head and we sat at the small table.

The meal was very simple, and while the printed eggs benedict was good, it wasn't as flavorful as the real thing and my coffee was a bit bland. All of that was secondary, however, to the distraction of Kier's presence in my mind. He was currently grousing about the need to stay at his father's house during our visit because that was what engagement traditions dictated. It wasn't the tradition that was really bothering him, but his father specifically.

"What do you have against him?" I finally asked after a while.

Kier quirked an eyebrow at me, clearly surprised at the question and then his eyes widened.

"I had no idea you were privy to...I apologize. I will have to work on strengthening my barriers."

"I don't mind knowing what you're thinking, or what's bothering you. I like helping you but you seem awfully determined not to stay at his house, why?"

He carefully wiped his mouth and straightened in the chair. This was Kier making a safe space for himself, and while it grated on my nerves after all we'd shared, I understood that it didn't mean that he was suddenly going to throw open the doors of his heart and mind. Nor did he have to. Hell, there were things I wanted to keep private too,

So I waited patiently for him to find the right words while he sipped his chamomile tea.

"The relationship between my father and myself is complicated," he finally said.

"You blame him for your mother's death."

His eyes flew up to meet mine and I leaned my elbows on the table, waiting for him to think of an answer.

"I suppose I do. Though, not completely."

I nodded. After what we shared, mind to mind last night, I knew exactly what he wasn't saying, though I disagreed with it. That kind of guilt would not be shed easily, or just forgotten after an epically good orgasm.

He coughed on the last of his tea and my jaw dropped.

"Did you hear that?"

"I see that we will have to teach you some cognitive barriers as well."

I cocked my head and narrowed my eyes as an idea bloomed.

Kier's eyes widened.

"Chloe—"

"Not up for the challenge?"

"I did not say that."

I raised my eyebrows in silent challenge, to which Kier answered with a sharp exhale through his nose.

"You will do it anyway, I am guessing."

"No, I would respect your boundaries on this. But," I leaned closer, a wicked smile on my face, "it would make things interesting while on the shuttle."

He leaned forward as well, a thoughtful frown on his face.

"I propose a combination of our ideas," he finally said. "As a way to practice your cognitive exercises, and for me to strengthen mine, we will imagine...salacious things throughout the day and see what gets through and what does not."

"Alright, but only if it's a game, with a winner and a loser. And no manual stimulation."

"If you wish. What does the winner receive?"

I studied him, liking the subtle way he squirmed under my gaze. He was a little nervous about this, but also excited. Kier liked competition, though he'd never admit it.

"A prize to be determined?" I asked.

"Hmm...If I did not trust in my abilities to win, I would not agree to such a thing. But I admit that the thought of you owing me a prize of my choosing is very appealing."

"You're so sure you're going to be the winner?"

His lips quirked up.

"I have spent a lifetime honing my cognitive skills."

"That's true but..."

I got up from my seat and his gaze heated as I ambled toward him. When I leaned down, I made sure that my hand slid up his arm slowly and my lips hovered close to his ear.

"I've had more practice handling unfulfilled sexual desires. So I'm looking forward to that prize."

He took in a sharp breath, and clenched his hands into fists under the table as a spike of arousal hit me from him.

I grinned and place a soft kiss right next to his ear.

"Now are you going to teach me those exercises, or have you already lost?"

Chapter Eighteen

KIER'AHN

I may have severely underestimated both my ability to resist sexual advances and Chloe's mental strength.

While I was teaching her some of the basics of cognitive blocking, she was reserved, focused. When she had successfully blocked three of my simple thoughts, I sent something more complex to her.

Specifically, an image of me stimulating her the way she had done to herself this morning. I wanted to try it, to see if I could find that small little protrusion that was so sensitive. Her body fascinated me in every way and, while I was inexperienced with sex, I could easily fantasize about things I would like to try.

Her pupils had dilated and she had let out a gasp of excitement. Inside, I was preening with delight. Not only had I thought I would surely win, but she had clearly liked the image. Therefore, I was going to be able to try that with her.

But then she had countered with an image of her mouth around the head of my phallus, her hands gliding over my nodes. I had no idea she would want to do something like that and I was so aroused so quickly that I let out a long growl as my phallus started to harden.

"Well, that was a very enlightening lesson," she'd smirked before flouncing away.

That had been several hours ago and since, I had just barely hung onto my resolve against a barrage of images and feelings from her. While I was attempting to give as good as I got, Chloe's experience meant that she was able to get far more creative, and I worried that I would, in fact, lose this little game. Especially since she showed no signs of giving in as she sat in the common room, sipping a glass of water and continuing to study the few notes on the new Lavat viral strain that Zephyr had supplied.

Whereas my phallus was aching from the back and forth of becoming full and decreasing when I forced my mind to refuse Chloe's advances. Her tactics were quite clever. Since she realized that she might not be able to breach my mental barriers head on, she began to lull me into a false sense of ease, waiting long periods of time between attacks. It had worked until I recognized what she was doing and began to anticipate when she might attempt an onslaught.

It was at the noon meal that I decided to view all the erotic images Chloe had sent me through the bond as learning opportunities.

I may not have ever imagined the things she had, but now I had them in my memory, the things that Chloe obviously wanted to do with me. And while I did not know if I would be comfortable enough to explore such things physically today, I had no doubt that she was wearing my fears down with this newly awakened craving for physical passion.

This morning had been...incredible.

Even if we did not touch with our bodies extensively, letting her touch my mind in such a way was the most intimate thing I'd ever done, the rut excluded. I was fully present for this, lost in every sensation of hers and mine. It was frightening in some ways, but also exhilarating. I had no idea that sharing such a thing with someone could be so fulfilling.

And so now, when Chloe sent me images of things she wanted us to do, that small fire that had been stoked within me this morning was fast becoming an inferno. One that I was wanting to sate.

However, I also wanted to win.

Attempting to get under her skin with assaults to her mental barriers that were spaced out had not yielded the desired outcome. So I endeavored to try a different tactic after lunch.

I had retreated to the cock pit to firm up my strategy, and checked in with her mind over the next hour. She was quite occupied by the mission, making notes about possible applications of not only her nanite research but a host of other discoveries as well. I temporarily forgot what we were supposed to be doing and simply observed the workings of her beautiful, complex mind. She was fascinating in so many ways, but none more so than her intelligence. I could, and had, sat for hours listening to her expound on complex scientific theories, medical discoveries, quantum physics and a multitude of other things that fascinated her. She may have been a nurse and therefore mainly concerned with medicine, but Chloe possessed an endlessly inquisitive mind that fascinated me.

What would it be like to spend a life time with her, seeing all the curves and dips of her mind play out? To see what she discovers, what she creates?

I had never been one to hunger for companionship in this way because I had been forced to give it up. But could Zephyr be right? Could Chloe give me that one thing I thought to never have? Would she be the one person who I would not have to surrender in my life?

I became so lost in watching her mind that I forgot that I was supposed to be thinking of how to win, and Chloe took advantage.

In a second, her mind shifted from the mechanics of medically programmed nanites, and she pictured herself pinned to a wall as I plunged into her again and again.

I gasped in shock at first, the change so startling that I had not the chance to censor my reaction. When I heard a snort from the common room, I decided it was time to employ my strategy.

Instead of creating a whole new scenario, I took hers and embellished on it.

If she wanted me to rut her against a wall, I would do that. But I would also nip and suck at her beautiful breasts, drawing one nipple into my mouth until it was a stiff peak then going to the other. All the while merely holding myself barely outside of her, letting her writhe and beg me for more as I took my time with the rest of her body.

Something fell in the common room and Chloe swore.

I let myself make the error of celebrating too soon.

The next thing I knew, I saw her reach between us and take my phallus in hand, dragging the sensitive tip through her wetness as she massaged the nodes.

I hissed as my phallus physically began to swell, the nodes reacting as if she were actually touching them. Out of pure instinct, my hips bucked just a little.

And that's what I sent to her. Me aroused from what she did, my fangs scrapping along her neck just before I bit down into her shoulder.

I was not sure if the cry from her was in my head or in the common room, but at that point it did not matter. I was so hard and full that my pants were pressing painfully onto my phallus and I had to breathe through the urge to take myself in hand.

Chloe sent me the image of me thrusting hard up into her as my teeth were latched onto her shoulder, one of her hands clasped tight onto one set of my horns.

So I sent her me, stimulating her clit in hard little circles.

My breath was coming in harsh puffs of air, my hands so tight on the arm rests of the chair that I swear I heard a rip in the leather as Chloe came in my mind, the sensation of her milking me was so real that I let out a rough groan.

And then, I allowed myself to come in my thoughts, filling her to overflowing as my knot breached her, sealing us tight.

"Fuck!" Chloe moaned from the common room.

I did not have the strength to wonder if I'd won or lost, since my pants were now full of cum.

A few moments later, Chloe called from the other room, "That's a draw."

I actually laughed at that, and replied, "Agreed."

I cleaned up quickly and waited for Chloe to finish in the bathroom. The moment she was out, I pulled her to me for a rough kiss that left us both breathless. I decided that I liked kissing, very much and I wanted to do it more.

A lot more.

"It did not feel right to have that with you and not touch you," I said when I finally stopped.

"I feel the same way."

She reached up and threaded her fingers through my hair, a feat considering our height difference. I greedily drank in more of her kisses.

"Do you wish to go back to your studies?" I asked, my lips hungrily devouring her jaw.

"Hell, no," she gasped, "you?"

"This morning was very intense, and I am uncertain I am ready for what intercourse would feel like with you but," I slid my hand under her shirt, a little uncertain at first, "I would very much like to touch you more."

She was nodding emphatically, her eyes lit up and lips swollen from my kisses. I liked the way she looked when I had aroused her. Wild and flushed, it called to that primal part of me, the one that I had just begun to accept and not fear.

My hands skated up her sides under her shirt until I was at her breasts. Chloe was so expressive, everything written on her face and I adored watching her arousal bloom like a flower. So I took my time and teased the underside of her soft mounds with my thumbs, running them just under her erect nipples. Her breath caught, her cheeks flushing more, as her fingers tightened on my arms.

"Kier," she panted.

"Is this what you want?" I asked, letting my thumbs at last dance across those sensitive peaks.

She bit her bottom lip and nodded fast.

I bit and sucked my way down her throat and back up until I was at her mouth, devouring the sighs and whimpers as I pinched those stiff peaks. My phallus was hard again, the nodes pulsing. Chloe did this to me, even without our minds completely enmeshed. The thought that I was giving her pleasure, the way she responded, so openly without shame. It was intoxicating.

"Tell me how to please you," I asked. "I want to make you come."

"There is...something, but not everyone likes it."

"Tell me," a growl punctuating those words, and I knew my primal side was more at the fore more than I had anticipated.

Suddenly the only thing that I could think of was making Chloe feel good, having her scent in my nose.

"Alright."

She tried to step out of my arms and I pulled her back. She chuckled and pressed on my chest.

"Hold on, big guy. I need to get out of these clothes."

"Oh...Yes, I...apologies."

I released her and Chloe stepped back. But instead of ripping off her clothes quickly, she bit her lip and gave me a heated stare.

"Would you like a little show?"

My eyes widened at the question. She was being playful and seductive, and it was all for *me*.

"Yes, very much."

Then, slowly, she drew her shirt over her head. Those beautiful, soft breasts with their pale pink tips bounced a little when the shirt released them and I reached for her.

"Not yet," she chided, backing away.

"Chloe," I growled.

Her smile widened. Oh, she liked that and so did I.

Keeping eye contact with me, she untied the laces of her lounge pants and just as slowly as she had the shirt, slid them over her hips and thighs, kicking them off her feet. Her panties must have been included because Chloe now stood before me completely naked.

I had seen her before, and remembered her from those lucid moments of my rut, but now I could savor the sight of her body on display. The dip of her waist, the swell of her hips down to her thighs, the thatch of trimmed, blond curls at the apex.

I was about to step forward when Chloe laid on the bed with her legs dangling off the end. Her eyes never leaving me as her hand glided down from one of her breasts, to her stomach and to her sex, parting herself for me and exposing a tiny nub at the top of her folds that was pink and swollen.

"That's my clitoris, it's where I want you to kiss me. Use your tongue, your lips, your fingers if you want to."

For a moment, all I could do was stare in wonder. Her most intimate part was beautiful and so very tempting. She was offering it up to me to drink from. Of all the things she wanted me to do, Chloe wanted me to taste her and I was curious to know what it was like. Her scent made a possessive fervor stir deep in my bones. When I had drawn her blood during the rut, it had been a claiming of sorts, likely one of the things that had led to our bond. This was different, but no less intimate.

A wild need began to pulse in my body as I knelt between her legs. One word beat through me as I ran my hands up her calves and to her inner thighs, the scent of her arousal a siren call.

Mine...mine...mine.

I recognized this from my rut, this drive to mate and claim. But I did not allow it to take over this time. I would use it, not the other way around. And so I was still able to think, to ponder as I stared at her sex and ran my knuckle through those wet, pink folds, so soft, so perfect. She let out a harsh breath and I glanced up at her.

"It looks delicate," I said, and licked my lips. "I do not want to do it wrong."

She chuckled at that.

"Follow your instincts, Kier, and you'll do just fine. I'll guide you if I need to."

She removed her fingers and I seized them before she moved too far away. They were coated in her wetness, and I wanted to taste her. I sucked her fingers into my mouth, letting my fangs, which I had just stopped from descending, scrape against her flesh as I devoured her arousal. Her taste was like fine wine, and made all the better knowing that I had done this to her. The thought of me touching her had Chloe dripping.

I licked my way down her fingers to her palm and then to the sensitive skin on her wrist before changing to her inner thighs, which shimmered with more of her wetness.

I bit and sucked her skin, consuming all of this as my own and not fighting the ferocious instincts building me to claim her at the source.

With a growl, I parted her with my thumbs and dove in, running my tongue from her opening to the tiny bud at the top. Chloe gasped out a swear word, and grabbed hold of one set of my horns.

"Yes...more at the top...please," she drew out the last word.

And, oddly enough, I found that I liked her begging.

"Here?" I asked, knowing it was not the spot. "Or maybe, here?"

All around it, I peppered her labia with my kisses and nips but never on the precious spot she was yearning for. Finally, she gave my horn a yank and I huffed out a laugh against the junction of her thigh.

"Patience," I said. "I am exploring."

"Kier...you...please."

"Say it again."

In her mind, I knew my voice was darker, thunderous and I stared up at her from between her legs as I said it.

Her breath caught, lips parted in shocked delight.

"Please."

I skated my thumbs almost to the place.

"Beg me, Chloe. Beg your priash for what you want."

I had a vague memory of calling her that during the rut and had thought it was just an impulse born out of that moment. But here, and now, I was lucid, I was choosing this. It felt right to call her such a precious thing, and that scared me. I had to be careful here, even though I craved this new connection with her and I saw no reason to keep myself from exploring with her, I knew that to become too lost in all of this was dangerous. She and I could never have more than this, for her own safety.

I put those thoughts aside for later and focused on the stunning woman in front of me. When I did, those golden ribbons of Chloe's consciousness in my mind went hot and red. They pulsed and sang around my own consciousness, which had become a feral predator, waiting to strike but held back. My logic controlled it, balancing those profane instincts of my rut. I realized, in this moment, that I could be passionate with her, ferociously so, while also retaining control.

When she finally spoke, her voice was breathy, on the edge of becoming lost with me.

"Please, my *priash*, please touch my clit."

I did not expect the burning lash of need upon hearing her call me that produced. My incisors lowered, though only slightly, and I wanted to drink more than her cum, though I held back. Instead, I dipped my head to that treasure between her folds and pressed my tongue to it.

I grinned against her as Chloe's hips jumped and she let out that sound I coveted, half way between a cry and grunt. So I stayed there, running my tongue hard in circles around it. I could not get enough of her taste and the more I used my tongue on her, the more arousal she produced and the brighter her colors became in my mind. I couldn't help but press my mouth once again to her opening, my tongue lapped at her while my finger pressed tiny circles to her clit.

"Yes...just...just like that," she panted.

I saw in my mind what she wanted next and I growled with delight. Chloe was so bold, so trusting to let me do this.

When I plunged my tongue into her core, both of Chloe's hands found my horns, which she grasped hard as she started to pulse her hips in time to my tongue, now thrusting inside of her. Deep down, in places that I had been taught to fear, was a possessive pride that began to roar, demanding that I give her so much pleasure that she would never think of abandoning me.

But I knew from the feelings she was sending me, the unspoken directions, that while this was deeply pleasurable, it would not get her to a release. And I wanted to give her that, more than anything.

I moved up to her clitoris once again, and knowing the exact right pressure to use, I sucked it between my lips. At the same time, I plunged two fingers into her and curled them as I pumped. Her thighs clamped around my head as her back bowed, and a rolling cry echoed through the room.

The rush of endorphins from her flooded me, and I gasped in shock. I felt her orgasm in a smaller measure, not nearly as shattering as this morning when it had been impossible to tell our sensations apart, but it still caused my nodes to expel obscene amounts of precum.

The sensations from her were a blissful explosion that I wanted to keep going as long as possible. But when I went to take her again between my lips, when I started to pump my fingers again, she pulled on my horns to stop me.

"N-no... no more...too much."

I pulled back, sucking her off my fingers as she watched.

"Good god almighty, Kier," she breathed and reached for me.

I climbed onto the bed and gathered her in my arms. Chloe curled against me and unzipped my uniform jacket.

"I just need to be closer to you, is that okay?" she asked.

"Yes."

She burrowed against my chest and I closed my eyes as I held her against me. I was fully clothed and she was naked. Somehow, that felt more elicit than before. And I liked it.

I liked many things I had not ever considered before Chloe had awakened a side of me that I had suppressed and feared for so long. My arms tightened around her and I pressed a delicate kiss to the top of her hair. We both smelled like sex, like her cum, and I liked that too.

"What about you?" she asked after the trembling in her body had ceased.

"I just want this," I said. "Is that acceptable?"

"Of course. We can cuddle as long as you want."

Forever.

The thought startled me and I hoped I had not let her know of it. This would not last forever, it could not. Could it?

She was Human.

I was Atavarian.

There was no outcome that did not result in blood and tears.

But where is the logic in worry? I must choose now, even if later it hurts.

Chapter Nineteen

CHLOE

I must've fallen asleep against Kier's chest because the next thing I knew, I was stretching under a blanket by myself. I should've been soaked in the afterglow of that orgasm. Instead, as I laid there for a moment, I was worried.

Though I was somewhat relieved that this time wasn't as intense as our morning romp, I also didn't like the way he'd shut me out of his mind during. It wasn't definitive, I could still reach him, but it wasn't as intimate as before. There were parts of himself that weren't accessible and it made me worry that I was the only one falling here.

Maybe this is just exploration of sex for him, with someone he trusts. I did introduce the idea to him before the rut, friends who fuck and all that but...

I bit my lip as I realized I didn't want that. I didn't want to get him comfortable with this side of himself only for someone else to become his forever lover. I wanted to be the one he chose forever with.

I covered my face with my hands and let out a long sigh.

We have a mission that affects billions, and I'm getting all soggy about falling in love with a man who only wants friends with benefits. Priorities, Chloe!

I got up and dressed, my stomach growling a bit when I saw the clock we'd synced with the Intrepid. It was almost dinner time but I had a mountain of reading left to do. I'd tried to focus today but half of my brain was occupied with either defending those weak mental barriers Kier had taught me about, or trying to breach his. I smiled at the thought. It had been fun tempting him and seeing what things he liked.

It had also been arousing as hell and I was glad he'd taken the edge off it for me.

I found Kier on the couch with a holo tablet. His uniform jacket was zipped up only half way, his gloves off and he was barefoot, which for him was downright casual. It loosened a worry in my chest, and I was happy that he was comfortable enough around me to relax like this outside of sex.

"What'cha reading?" I asked as I went to the food printer and made some tea.

His eyes snapped up to mine and I felt a flicker of heat before it faded away. I was wearing another pair of lounge pants and a loose shirt; not exactly lingerie but it seemed that Kier liked it.

"My father has sent us a list of the things we can expect for the...wedding."

"Oh," the air left my lungs in a rush. "Right...okay."

I had tried to sort through how I felt about this wrinkle in the mission and I was realizing that it was *a lot*. It wasn't just the unexpected nature of it, but the way it further blurred things between us. I was already falling for him, if not all the way lost, and marrying him would make me even more attached. But also, and perhaps more importantly, it delayed my ability to create the anti-viral and vaccine.

"So," I said as I sat next to him, "what is the situation?"

"My aunt has taken it upon herself to shorten the usual wedding to three days and planned everything on our behalf. She has streamlined the traditions down to the necessities."

"We're still going to have to do three days of this? With their own people dying, they're going to drag it out for three days?"

His forehead wrinkled and I got the distinct impression of irritation from him. But was it because of what I said or the situation?

"There is a reason the ceremony lasts over several days," his voice took on an imperious tone.

Well, that answers that. He's frustrated with me. Lovely.

I took a long sip of my tea and tried to calm down. It was only natural that Kier would defend his culture, especially one that put such a high value on traditions. It was just unexpected; I would've thought that logically, they would put lives above such things.

I asked him to talk to me honestly on the Intrepid, and I should offer him the same courtesy. I need to help him understand where I'm coming from.

"I'm not happy about the delay," I explained, "and it's making me snappy. I hope you can understand that I mean no disrespect, but I'm stunned that this is the priority."

Kier studied me for a moment before giving me a short nod.

"I understand your vexation and to some extent, I share it. But I also understand why this is important, and why we must perform these rituals. It is the path toward the very thing we both want. Saving my people from the virus and defending the galaxy from the K'Tavi."

"That's true, I wasn't thinking of it like that. All I'm seeing is a delay and it will be hard for me to see it as anything else, but I will try."

The muscles in his face relaxed.

"Thank you. I will try to keep all of that in mind. Would you like to hear what we can expect?"

"Yes, the more I know, the better."

"That is precisely how I feel as well."

He handed me the tablet and I scrolled...kept scrolling...and finally reached the end.

"This is streamlined?" I asked as I took it all in.

"Yes. Normally, the rituals are from sun up to sun down for a week, but my aunt has thoughtfully done away with the need for that. Also, you will only have five dresses. She has been sent your sizes and the dresses are already in the process of being made for you. All that is required is a final fitting when we arrive."

I gulped down more tea.

Five dresses instead of seven...

"There are usually five main rituals but she has chosen three for us to perform and spread them out one per day, so you do not have as much to memorize.

Also, since you have no family and finding a proxy would take time, she has volunteered to be your proxy."

I was reminded of the overbearing mother in all the old Earth holo videos I'd seen. The one who took over and ran rough shod over everyone to the detriment of the couple.

Except we aren't a couple, not in that sense. And maybe letting his aunt take over will give me time to do a little work. When Char'Vahn sends me all his data, I might have enough to come up with some models I can test on a computer, even if I won't know final numbers and outcomes without actually having the virus in front of me. This could actually be alright.

"Okay," I scrolled to the section of the list where the rituals were. "But this has five, so I'm confused."

"Ah yes, the entry and the exit of the bride, that is a simple enough ritual. You will walk up a gravel path in a blood red gown, expressing all the things you feel as a symbol of our time before enlightenment. This begins the wedding. Then, at the end of the three days, you walk back down the same path, barefoot in a gown of gold without expressing emotion to symbolize the enlightenment of our people."

Barefoot over rocks...

Wow, they've actually incorporated literal torture into their wedding traditions.

It almost made me want to laugh. Or scream. Fifty-fifty.

"Okay," I drained my tea. "What about the other three?"

He nodded and I sensed that he was pleased that I was taking such an interest in this. For some reason, that just frustrated me more. How could he be so calm about this? How could he sit there and look over this ridiculous list of hoops we had to jump through?

I'm going to need alcohol for this.

I went to the printer and found the only alcoholic beverage available was tequila with lime. I hated tequila but I printed a double.

"After your entry," Kier said, as I waited for the drink to print, "will be the ritual of mutual sacrifice. We both will fast from sun up to sun down and then exchange glasses of synthetic blood."

I spun around to stare at him.

"Your aunt does know that I can't do that right? I cannot drink blood, it will make me violently ill."

"Yes, I believe yours will be a red wine instead."

I let out a breath of relief and snagged the tequila. Instead of sipping it, which I probably should've done, I shot it and then sucked on the lime as the liquid burned down my body.

Kier just frowned at me, and even if I hadn't been feeling worry from him through the bond, I would've seen it.

"This is a lot, I needed that," I said maybe with a little too much snappiness in my tone. "So that was day one? I walk on gravel, expressing emotion, don't eat all day and then have a glass of wine on an empty stomach."

What could go wrong?

"What's next?" I asked out loud instead.

He cleared his throat and looked back down at the list.

"On the second day, I will go with my father to visit..."

His frown deepened and then his expression turned stormy. I started to ask what was wrong when he continued.

"This is the ritual of reconciliation." He bit out the word. "We each serve tea to someone we dislike."

"I don't know anyone though, who will I serve tea to?"

"My aunt has also volunteered for this task as well. I will be serving tea to...someone else."

"Someone you dislike."

"Vehemently. But the ritual is meant as a reminder that in marriage, one must sometimes humble oneself for the sake of reconciliation."

I wanted to say that we didn't have to do this, that he didn't have to put himself through all of this, and see people who had likely treated him like shit just to satisfy a stupid ritual. That we'd find another way to get me inside the Institute. But I knew better. Atavarians could be stubborn to a fault, and I had a feeling this was one of those times if we didn't dot every 'I' and cross every 'T'.

"I'll be there for you," I said, "if you want to talk after."

"Thank you."

I could see him compartmentalizing his feelings around this person before continuing, and I wondered how this could get any worse.

"The third and final day of the wedding, is the ritual of trust. The bride will prepare a dish that is special to the groom's family without a recipe. Instead, the groom's mother recites the recipe and directions to her and the bride trusts the direction she receives. My aunt will, obviously, be proxy for my mother."

If I'd been drinking something, I'd have spit it out.

"I have to...*cook*?"

I couldn't even cook *with* a recipe in front of me, how the hell was I supposed to cook trusting Kier's aunt, who I was starting suspect was not doing this out of the generosity of her heart?

"Yes," he said as if it were nothing. "There is only one possible dish and my father has sent the recipe so that you may commit it to memory. It is an audio file so that you will be able to memorize it in Atavarian since you will have to turn off your subdermal translator for this."

"Why?" I almost yelled it.

He looked at me in utter confusion.

"Because that is the tradition."

I paced away from him and back. Suddenly all of this was just too much. I could handle being dressed up like a doll; I actually did like fancy clothes on occasion. And walking? I could do that even over gravel. Drinking tea with someone I didn't like? Okay, that wasn't ideal but I could probably handle it. But for some reason this was the last straw and I felt my body heating up with anger and nerves. My mind started grasping at anything it could to find a reason why I shouldn't have to do this.

"What about your mother, did she have to make a dish without a translator?" I asked.

"She and my father did not have a traditional wedding. It is one of the reasons she was never accepted into Atavarian society."

"Okay, well...how about any other non Atavarians? Did they have to do this ritual without translation too?"

He frowned in thought before shaking his head.

"I am unaware of other non Atavarians performing any wedding rituals."

"So this is just to punish us then?"

"Punish? No. It is—"

"*Tradition*. Yeah, I know."

"Chloe, I realize that this is not ideal. But you are one of the most intelligent women I have ever met. You will be able to do this without a problem."

I bit back the words I wanted to say, because they were without any kind of filter, and the last thing I wanted was to fight with Kier right now. Still, I couldn't stop the rush of anxious tears rising to my eyes. If I didn't get all of this exactly right, they could deny me entry into the Institute and what then? Zephyr had made it sound like I was the only one that could do this and do it fast. I'd felt a mountain of pressure just with that, and now *this*?

"I need to...I need to just be alone for a little while, okay?"

"Of course," his voice was steady but there was a hint of worry there. "Would you like the tablet so you can begin to study the rituals? It may help your anxiety if you see that they are nothing to fear."

My eyes snapped up to him, a spike of anger heating my face. Was he seriously suggesting that studying our fake marriage rituals was what I needed right now?

I stormed up to him, snatched the tablet from his hands and then took off to the bedroom.

"Computer, lock door," I said.

"*Affirmative.*"

I didn't need to see Kier's face to know that he was also angry and confused. Those feelings were rushing through our bond and then, just as suddenly as they'd appeared, they were gone.

He'd closed himself off to me. Again.

And yet everything I felt was wide open to him, if he wanted it. I could try the cognitive barriers he'd taught me that morning, but just thinking about that made me angrier for some reason. I tossed the holo tablet onto the bed; the thought of looking at that list was just making me more furious.

I needed to move, to get all of this out. But there was no running track on this shuttle like there was on the Intrepid. Instead I paced at the foot of the bed. At first very fast, and then, as the physical exercise started to leach some of the stew of emotion from me, I slowed down until finally, hot and sweaty, I was able to think clearly.

This was a complication. And when I faced complications or roadblocks in research I just had to step away and think before coming back and finding a solution. Sometimes it took a while, but I did it.

There was really only one solution for this problem and that was, as Kier had said, to go through it. Perhaps, as I thought before, within this mess of a wedding there might also a way to still do my job. Hearing about the rituals, I might not have as much time as I'd thought to do research and experiment, but maybe I could do some interactive chats with Char'Vahn in the evenings, since it looked like there were no rituals during that time. If we could run through some of the models like that, then maybe this wouldn't be a complete waste of time. But if he were as much of a stickler for these traditions as everyone else seemed to be, he might not allow me to do anything until I had completed them. I'd just have to take that chance and hope for the best.

I plopped down onto the bed on my back, and let out a long breath. It wasn't a satisfying solution, not even close. But it was the only one presenting itself just now and it would have to do.

The holo tablet slid toward me on the bed and knocked into my head. I snatched it up, still frustrated but less angry at least, and opened the tab for the second ritual where Kier's father had helpfully left instructions for me. The moment I saw what it was, I let out a long sigh, sat up, and squared my shoulders.

"If I can perform delicate surgeries while a starship is under attack, I can make a stupid dinner."

I nodded to myself and turned on the audio file.

I got the gist of the recipe from the audio file, which was in Atavarian but my subdermal translator helped me follow. Once I got tired of hearing it over and over, I went over the ritual of reconciliation, which had me humbling myself on my knees to Kier's aunt. I already didn't like the woman very much and I highly doubted from her snide notes for the wedding, that my opinion was going to improve.

Now, I was hungry and tired, and knew that it was time to go out and face Kier.

When I opened the door, he wasn't in the sitting area, not that I had expected him to wait around for me. But there was a covered dish on the table, and the faint scent of beef from the food printer.

Even though we had fought, he had made me dinner.

I'm not sure he needs that whole humility ritual. He's got that down.

I set the holo tablet on the table and glanced into the cockpit, where he turned to look at me over his shoulder.

"Can we talk?" I asked.

He gave me a short nod and walked into the room, hands clasped behind his back. His expression was one I'd seen thousands of times throughout our friendship; stoic and almost blank, revealing nothing. But it was clear to me that he wasn't wearing it because it was just normal. He wore it with me right now to protect himself, to hide the truth of his emotions, which I could barely sense.

He was frustrated, confused and a little angry, all of which I could understand. And there was an odd relief that he felt that way. It meant that this situation wasn't nothing to him. I could work with that.

"I'm sorry for the way I stormed away from you," I began. "I was overwhelmed and worried about not getting any of this right and failing at our mission."

"An understandable concern. Were my reassurances not sufficient?"

A flash of irritation, confusion came from him.

"You're frustrated because you don't know how to handle me like this, do you?"

He pressed his lips together and let out a sharp exhale through his nose.

"You are perceptive."

"No, actually you've just let me see it from you."

"Apologies."

"No, I don't want apologies for it. I want to know that you're having feelings about this. I want to know that it scares you, that it frustrates you. That you're not happy about it. I don't want you to hide those things from me, I want you to let me *share* them with you."

"What purpose would that serve? You are already having anxiety regarding this roadblock. If I were to allow my emotions entry, would it not overwhelm you, as it did in your quarters when I first alerted you to the bond?"

"Maybe," I admitted. "But I'd rather risk that than feel like I'm the only one struggling with all of this."

His eyes darted away, a frown creased his forehead. I felt that he was thinking this through so I let him process it for a moment.

"It would be a comfort to you," he said slowly, "to know that I shared your feelings on this matter?"

"Yes," I let out a breath of relief with the word. "It would help a lot."

"Commiseration is what you require?"

"Yes."

"In that case, yes, I am angry at my aunt's insistence regarding this. I am annoyed that she chose rituals that gave you far more work than I, who was raised in this culture and would have been able to understand and perform the rituals without extra effort. I have, in fact, sent a message ahead of us to my aunt and father informing them that it there is no reason you should have to turn off your subdermal translator, or prepare a dish you have no culture frame of reference for, without at least having the chance to become familiar with the basics of the recipe. I focused on that ritual specifically because it seemed the most...frightening to you."

I bit my bottom lip as a smile emerged across my face, and warmth spread through my chest.

Kier had listened and observed and done even more than I hoped he would. He'd stuck up for me with his family, he'd advocated for what was reasonable for me.

"That's...that's more than I would've asked for, thank you," I whispered.

His expression softened and I felt his relief.

"I am sorry," he said, "that I gave you the impression that this was not a source of negative emotions for me. I had thought that I should be reassuring and steady in order to balance you. These emotions are all very new and confusing to me, and I am sure to make mistakes."

I took a few steps toward him, my shoulders relaxing.

"I know, but I hadn't really thought about that at the time. I was emotional, and I needed you to be there with me in a way. It's a relief to know that you're not just blindly going along with this."

"Far from it. In fact, I am beginning to suspect that my aunt may have ulterior motives for all of her helpful input."

I couldn't suppress a grin because she *definitely* did.

"In any case," he continued, "I do not want you to feel alone. Please know that while I may not always show it, especially while we are on Atavar, I share your feelings on this matter. You are not alone, in this or anything else on this mission."

"I believe you."

My tone must've given something away, or maybe he was letting my emotions through instead of closing them off, but he frowned at me and stepped closer.

"You are not satisfied with that answer, why?"

I took a breath and considered my words carefully before looking up at him.

"I know that our bond can be just as overwhelming for you as it is for me, and that to handle that you close your emotions away and even block mine at times."

"I block yours to give you privacy. Though sometimes, such as before you went into the room, I did let them through as I attempted to understand you."

"But see, I don't have that luxury. While you get to decide whether or not to let my emotions through, I don't get to do that with you. And because of that, I don't know what's going on with you the same way you can with me."

"I see, that is...a problem. You would like me to open my mind to you more often, let you know what I am feeling?"

"If it wouldn't be a breach of privacy, yes. Not all the time but maybe more often than just during sex?"

If he could've flushed, I think Kier would have. He shifted on his feet and swallowed convulsively.

"Yes, I, ah, I see. That does make sense. I will endeavor to be more open with you. But knowing does not necessarily translate to understanding. I knew your feelings but clearly did not understand how to respond to them."

I chuckled and nodded.

"That's true, you did kind of stick your foot in it back there."

For a second his expression hardened, and then I could see the moment he let down his barriers and saw how I was feeling. His face relaxed and there was a playful glint in his eyes.

"Human females are notoriously mercurial, I am at a disadvantage."

I let my jaw drop in feigned offense.

"Are you saying that I'm irrational?"

"No more than is normal for your species and gender."

I smacked him on the arm and he seized my hand, pulling me to him. Slowly, his hands came to my hips and then around to the small of my back. I let mine rest on his shoulders as I looked up into his eyes. Not that long ago, I was ready to scream at him, and now, all I wanted was to curl against him, let his strength and warmth soothe away all my worries.

"I would not have you any other way," he whispered to me. "You are perfect as you are."

"How can you be so bad at parts of this, and so damn good at others?" The words slipped out before I could stop them.

He cocked his head to the side, the corners of his mouth just barely tilting up.

"I thought that was obvious. I have a very good teacher."

Chapter Twenty

KIER'AHN

It should not have surprised me that Chloe would need more openness from me with my emotions, but it did frighten me. I did not want to reveal too much and I worried that, in moments when I allowed my guard down, when I let her see what I was feeling, she would discern things I could not reveal.

Such as, I believed my feelings for her were deepening very quickly.

I watched her sleep, our hands clasped between us as they had been last night, and there was a peace behind all the anxiety that I had never known before. A completeness I could not quite understand.

How could one person, one Human female, make me feel as if a missing piece of myself had been found? I had been around other species enough to know that many believed in such things. Even Atavarians had a belief about soul mates, though such a teaching had been seen as suspect for a long time now. The word still remained in our tongue: *Priash*. Soul mate. Lover. Best friend. The word encapsulated many things and was often translated to mean the second half of one's mind.

I had uttered it to her several times without thinking; during the rut, and when I had been pleasuring her with my tongue.

Just the thought of that moment had my phallus stirring and I wondered if Chloe would like to be awakened in such a way. Perhaps, if we have time prior to docking at the orbital station tomorrow morning, she would let me do it again. I had no idea how much privacy we would have at my father's estate.

As I stared at Chloe, and brushed a strand of hair from her face, letting my fingers trace the curve of her cheek, I realized that I wanted to call her *priash* all the time. Never had I felt so close to someone, so accepted. Never had there been a person in my life who held such an impossible image of me in their mind. The image of someone perfect as they were, of someone intriguing, funny, kind. Someone who was worthy of love.

And she was making me believe these things about myself, purely because *she* believed them.

I drifted off to sleep and was awakened by the shuttles communications alarm. I went to move and realized that, just like yesterday morning, Chloe was pressed against me.

We stared at one another for a moment and she gave me a sleepy grin that made me wish I could keep her in bed all morning. There were parts of her I wanted to explore further, and I was quite intrigued at the idea of her exploring me as well.

"I must see who that is," I whispered.

"Yeah," she agreed.

"Stay here."

Her grin turned playful.

"Yes, sir."

The submissiveness in her tone, joking though it might have been, caused me to wish her to do that more. Especially when we were intimate.

"You better go get that," she said when I did not move.

"And you better stay in bed and wait for me."

She took in a sharp inhale, cheeks flushed and eyes bright with a sudden excitement. It pleased me very much that she liked that and I wondered if there was a way to experiment with such things without crossing any lines of consent.

I will have to do some research.

I slipped on a shirt as I walked to the cockpit and switched off the alarm.

"Computer, what is the communication?"

"Arrival at Atavarian orbital station in less than one hour. Prepare for docking and disembarkment."

We had both slept longer than anticipated.

"Computer, show exact time to docking."

Thirty-five minutes and forty seconds showed on the screen. I sighed. There would be no time for anything between Chloe and me.

Perhaps I can convince father and aunt Prem'Ahn to allow us to share quarters. It is not as if we had not been mated for a week now...or rather, in the timeline of this cover.

I ran a hand over my face and shut away how natural it had felt to say I was mated, in truth, to Chloe. There were many other things that required my focus at the moment.

"You have one prerecorded message from former Earth Ambassador Gav"Ahn of House Ahn. Shall I play it for you?"

My shoulders stiffened at the mention of my father's name and I straightened my spine out of pure habit.

"Yes, play message."

When his face appeared on the screen, I was shocked at the age that showed there. His pitch black hair had gray at the temples, and there were lines appearing around his black eyes as well. His two sets of horns, which had always been a very dark gray that was almost black, were turning white at the tips. He also looked thinner than usual; his cheek bones stood out too much in his face and I wondered if he'd been ill. But, the stiff set to his posture, the deep timbre of his voice, and the sense that he was displeased with me, even over a recording, were all still there.

"Kier'Ahn, your aunt and I have been informed of your estimated time of arrival and we will be meeting you and your mate at the station. If the timing is true, then your mate can perform the entry ritual as soon as we land at the estate and the wedding can be expedited. Your aunt has her garment and will be preparing her in the shuttle."

The message cut off after that and I was startled at first, having forgotten that most Atavarians do not extend a salutation upon leaving a conversation. Still, his manner was as abrupt as ever and his message was frustrating.

Not only would we have no time for more intimacies, Chloe would have no time to acclimate to landing on a new planet.

But at least we will not have to waste a day waiting for the ceremonies to begin.

When I walked back into the bedroom, I found Chloe grinning at me from the bed, the covers tossed off to reveal her long legs, in the sleep shorts she favored, open and waiting for me. For a moment, I imagined what it would be like to make my family wait while I took her small bud into my mouth again, but that would open us both up for derision and only make things more difficult. Chloe took one look at my face and her smile faded.

"What is it?" she asked, sitting up.

I told her in as brief a manner as possible and braced for her panic. It hit me in short bursts as she closed her eyes and breathed. I swallowed and opened my own barriers just enough to let her know that I too felt a bit overwhelmed and not at all happy about this.

When she opened her eyes, her face relaxed and she crawled over to the end of the bed toward me. I caught her around the hips, loving the way they filled my hands and she looked her arms around my neck.

"Thank you," she whispered and danced her lips softly across mine.

I groaned into her mouth and slid my tongue languidly against hers. So many things I wanted to experience with her, so many things I wanted to feel. When this was over, would she still want to, or was this precious pocket of time all I would have of her?

"You should eat something," I whispered as my lips brushed against her jaw. "It will be a long day."

"What about...the whole fasting thing?" she breathed as her hands slid under my shirt.

My jaw clenched on a moan as the sensation of her hands on me sent bolts of heat through my body.

"It is not sun up...not technically," I said, holding back every impulse in me to throw her to the bed.

"I wish we had more time. I was going to show you something else this morning."

The only response I could manage was letting out a breath against her throat as I tried to get a hold of myself.

"I will insist that we share a room," I promised as I drew back from her. "But there will still not be much privacy."

"Well, then," she grinned up at me, her fingers running circles along the small of my back, "I guess I'll just have to be quiet then."

I huffed out a laugh and shook my head.

"I like you loud, and am tempted to risk their displeasure. Though I would not wish to embarrass you."

"I'm not embarrassed by my feelings..." There seemed to be something else she was going to add to the end of that and stopped herself. I wished I could know what it was, but would not dip into her mind to find out.

"Come," I said instead. "You take a shower and I will prepare a breakfast for us. Something fast."

"You're going to spoil me. What am I going to do when this is over and you're not making my breakfast for me?"

Her voice was bright, but there was an edge to it. It made me reckless, which is the only explanation for what I responded with.

"I will always take care of you, Chloe. Always."

She swallowed and there was a hint of hope from her along with...something else. Something gentle and bright, there and gone again as quickly. The urge to hunt it down was strong, but she was turning away from me and heading toward the shower.

Yes, Chloe has the right idea...we must prepare for Atavar.

We had just finished our simple breakfast, when the computer alerted us to our arrival at the orbital station. We quickly placed our dishes into the cleaning unit and strapped into the seats in the cockpit for our arrival.

Chloe took in a sharp breath as the orbital station came in to view. I had seen it many times, but even I had to admit that it was quite stunning.

It was constructed of three, huge, bronze colored spheres, connected by thin bronze pillars. The bottom of the station was a circular red disc and along the sides of the middle sphere were spike-like protrusions that connected to a dozen or so smaller red spheres. Ships came and went at dizzying speeds to escort those who were leaving and arriving.

We were contacted by a drone and guided toward one of the smaller docking areas at the top sphere; I frowned at that. The upper levels were for Atavarians only, was this an oversight? Chloe would not be welcome in that part of the station and I hoped we would not linger there long. From the urgency of my father's message I thought it unlikely, but I was still concerned.

As we climbed toward that tier, Atavar rose in front of me, a beautiful bright green, blue and red surface. The planet had once been mostly desert, with a large population of animals but not much in the way of plant based foods. But then the Enlightenment happened, and Atavarians swore off any food sources from living creatures. We terra formed most of the planet slowly, creating vast forests, farms and entirely new eco systems full of edible plant matter. The only place where this had gone wrong was the upper most part of the planet, where a swirling mass of pink and red clouds revealed a storm that never stopped.

Instead of seeing this only as a failure, however, one of our scientists had discovered how to turn the violent electric storms into renewable energy, inventing technology that harvested the power without doing damage to the environment. It was said that one hour of energy collected could power an entire continent.

The sun shone to the left, sending blinding reflections of light off the orbital station and the inordinately shiny escort shuttles.

"It's beautiful," Chloe breathed.

"Yes," I murmured, "it is."

But it was also dangerous for her. And under all the beauty of my home, laid a xenophobia and bigotry that had colored my entire life. Chloe was strong, she could endure it for the time it would take to create the vaccine Atavarians needed. Yet I still loathed the idea that she should have to encounter it at all.

I must have allowed some of this past my barriers because Chloe reached out and took my now gloved hand in hers. I hated the separation of our skin, but also knew that I must wear them on the planet.

"It's going to be alright. I'm here, you're not alone, remember?" she said.

I nodded, her words of reassurance at once comforting and unnerving. I did not want my emotions to be on display to my father and aunt, both of whom had an uncanny way of knowing what I was feeling.

Coming home was not something I had thought about very much these past five years.

It had been understood that when I left to join the Gex-Corps Academy, I was turning my back on the path my aunt and father had wanted for me. I had disappointed them, and when neither had come to my graduation from the Academy, I knew that the break between us was complete. There had never been a reason to return and so I had never sought to heal those wounds. Now, they ached as if fresh, awakened with the sight of my home and all the memories it produced.

The hours I had spent riding Shel'mok's through the fields around the estate. Learning to fight with Leigth Blades from the instructors at the Institute that my aunt had procured for me. Meditating in the moss covered clearings by the hot springs. I passed many a night in the gardens reading everything I could about Atavarian culture, about Enlightened One Ahn, trying so very hard to know what was missing inside of me in order to fit in.

Until I had found Chloe, and all her bright joy, her warmth.

Her fingers tightened around mine and I endeavored to center myself in these last few moments we would have, just the two of us.

When we docked, I took care locking down the ship as Zephyr had instructed, while Chloe double checked that all of our belongings had been stowed in our bags. All too soon, it was time to depart.

I took a deep breath, strengthened my mental barriers and stepped beside Chloe as our ramp was lowered.

"I will not be as open with you around my family," I said, "and I apologize in advance for any hurt I may cause. Being home I find myself at odds with a lifetime of training in order to protect myself and who I have become on the Intrepid, and with you."

Chloe leaned over and planted a kiss to my bicep, both our hands occupied at the moment.

"I understand," she said. "Thank you for telling me."

"I want to be open with you. I will be in private. You are...you are a safe space."

She bit her lower lip and looked down. At first I thought perhaps I had offended her but when she looked back up at me, there were tears shining in her eyes.

"As are you to me," she whispered.

There were volumes in those words that I did not have the opportunity to discover; our ramp was fully lowered, and two very large guards waited for us at the bottom. But I did not care that they could see me, or that I was keeping them and my family waiting. I drew in my fill of her in that moment, letting her feel my affection for her, before I had to hide it away.

I led the way down the ramp, the two guards much taller than I, and they dwarfed Chloe. Their black uniforms with gold piping indicated a ceremonial guard reserved only for family members of high ranking officials. My father had never cared for such things. My aunt, however, did care and would have been the one to assign them to us.

"This way," one of them said, eyeing Chloe with thinly veiled disgust.

I bit back a growl and reached out to Chloe with my mind as we followed them.

"Stay close to me, look ahead and attempt to remain expressionless. We are in a section of the station that is usually reserved for Atavarians only. Some may not respond well to your presence."

"Great."

"Do not worry. You are with me. I will not let anything happen to you."

I said it in my mind with far more ferocity than I had intended and I caught a brief smile crossing Chloe's face.

"I know you won't."

Her trust made pride swell within me, though I was very careful not to show it.

"Your father is currently waiting for you in the lounge," one of them said. "He has taken care of all the necessary security questions and you both have clearance to continue on to the planet immediately."

I nodded and we followed him down a wide walkway that was enclosed on all sides, but with open views of space all around us. The floor was bronze colored and polished to reflect our images as we walked, our footsteps the only sound as we made our way to the doorway in front of us.

At last we came to the end, which let us out into a wide room with exceptionally comfortable looking chairs scattered around a thick black carpet. Waitstaff walked with unnerving grace between the Atavarians waiting for their shuttles, serving drinks and small plates of food. The air was scented with *vanra* spice, an expensive luxury that was usually added to synthetic blood to give it the ability to inebriate.

To my left was a floor to ceiling window with a stunning view of a portion of the planet and the stars behind it. Small vessels zoomed around the windows, down to the planet and away from it. I realized the moment our feet touched the carpet that my aunt had also arranged for us to walk through a lounge for high ranking families, who valued tradition perhaps more than most. Every person in the room turned to stare at us, and more specifically, Chloe.

I glanced down at her out of the corner of my eye and saw that her head was high, shoulders back. She wasn't being cowed by all the Atavarians who were starting to talk about her, loudly.

"What is the meaning of this?" one of them said.

"A Human, here? This is highly improper."

All of this and more was said without emotion as other species recognized it, but to me, I heard the subtly as loudly as I would have from a Human. They were furious, offended and did not care if it made Chloe uncomfortable. The further we walked into the lounge, the more my anger began to boil. This was my mate, whether or not it was a cover, Chloe was the most important person in the galaxy to me. And to see her treated this way had my control slipping by the time we reached a private dock on the other side of the station.

We went through a wide, arched doorway and into a comfortable private waiting room where two people I had not seen in many years stood waiting for us.

My father was taller than me, and his posture was ram rod straight in his black and red robes. He looked at me, staring for a bit longer than I would have expected, though I was unsure as to why. Then, his gaze flitted over to Chloe and he took his time there as well. When he was done examining her, he looked at me again and I swore there was an odd hint of a smile in his eyes before my aunt stepped forward, diverting all the attention to herself, though she spoke not a word.

Short for an Atavarian female, she was only half a foot taller than Chloe; a fact I believe she attempted to use to full advantage when she stopped a few feet from us. Her dark hair was pulled back into the same bun it had always been, though streaks of white now accented it. Her expression was, as usual, hard, though others might describe it as more admirably stoic. Today, the slight twist of her lips as her dark eyes quickly took in Chloe beside me said that she was displeased and saw no reason to hide it. When her eyes landed on me, my instinct was to divert my gaze to the floor, as I had throughout my entire childhood. But I was not a child anymore, nor was I a youth desperate to prove myself.

I was a decorated officer, admired by my peers, and no longer beholden to her approval.

So I held her gaze, staring her down until one of her eyebrows arched in surprise and she looked away.

"The Human is shorter than anticipated," Aunt Prem'Ahn said in Atavarian to my father, "and the traditional colors of the gowns will make her pale complexion sickly, a consequence that will be unavoidable."

"That's alright," Chloe said next to me. "I know this was all last minute and I appreciate your help."

My aunt turned slowly back toward her, eyes narrowed. I could feel Chloe trying not to shrink beside me.

"Do not fear her. You are her equal in every way."

Chloe took in a breath and sent me a flash of warmth through the bond.

"You speak Atavarian?" Aunt Prem'Ahn asked.

"Yes."

Chloe did not. At least, not without her subdermal translator, a fact that I was unsure if my aunt did not know or had simply forgotten. I, however, was not going to correct the situation.

"If we are to begin the rituals today," my father's voice was calm, "then we must leave immediately. The sun will rise in a few hours at the estate."

Aunt Prem'Ahn exhaled sharply through her nose and gave him a short nod.

"Come with me," she instructed, as she turned and walked toward the shuttle with a sweep of her red and blue robes.

Chloe gave me small smile and handed me her bags.

"If you don't hear from me in an hour, call for help. It may have come to fisticuffs and your aunt looks scrappy."

I managed to hide my laugh, but did not succeed in keeping the smallest smirk off my face as I watched her follow my aunt into the shuttle.

My father stepped up beside me and we both watched them go. When I turned to look at him, there was the most peculiar expression on his face. I could not describe it as anything but bittersweet. It shocked me into silence and I stared at him.

"She reminds me of...your mother," he murmured after a moment.

My eyebrows raised and it took several seconds to find a reply.

"Chloe is a kind, intelligent and supportive mate. I am fortunate to have found her."

Father nodded.

"Yes," was all he said.

An awkward silence descended upon us, reminding me that my father and I never had much in the way of meaningful conversations. Or, really, any kind of conversations.

"Captain Drake sends his greetings," I offered after a moment.

"Your Captain is an...interesting Human. I have followed his career with great interest."

A spike of red, hot jealousy hit me so fast that I could not hide it. My jaw clenched and I looked away from him.

"You follow the career of a man you barely know, but make no inquiries as to the success of your only son. That is quite telling."

And with that, I proceeded down the hall toward the shuttle, not bothering to see what father's response may or may not have been.

Chapter Twenty-One

CHLOE

It turned out that the dress for the first ritual was a plain, dark red, high waisted sack made out of scratchy material that hung on my frame. The edges of the skirt were ragged, as was the long sleeves, the ends of which dragged on the ground. Apparently that was exactly as it was supposed to be, helping to further symbolize how unenlightened they had been. My face was smudged with dirt the second we arrived on the small landing platform on the outskirts of the grounds, and Prem'Ahn took an unmistakable delight in roughly tangling my hair. The woman hardly spoke to me the entire shuttle ride, and wouldn't let Kier see me at all until I had successfully walked up the incline to where he and his father waited at the top.

I had no trouble letting the pain of the gravel and the utter discomfort of the dress show as I made my way to the top.

"Well done," he said when I arrived.

"This was the easiest one. Wanna help me get out of this monstrosity and clean up?"

I sent him an image of the two of us in a bathtub for good measure and his eyes flared.

"Something wrong?" Prem'Ahn asked.

"Not at all," Kier said, clearing his throat and clasping his hands in front of his body, instead of in the back.

I didn't bother to hide my smirk at all as I took a moment to look around the estate. The back room of the shuttle, where Prem'Ahn and I had been hidden away, had no windows and I was disappointed to have missed our approach.

The landing platform was at the bottom of the hill I'd just climbed and nestled in a clearing surrounded by tall trees with silvery trunks and purple and silver leaves, all of them evenly spaced, and the blue grasses between them well-manicured. Up here, I could see a vast field of trees to my right and on the left were dozens of large raised beds where vegetables were grown, four beds to one square, all laid out on a grid. Beyond that, far away, was what looked like a plain of more blue grass with maybe pink flowers. Directly ahead was a round courtyard divided into four sections. Two of the others on the right and left led to what looked like gardens, while the fourth led to the house with a metallic sculpture of some kind in the middle.

And then I saw the house.

"When you said country estate I did not picture this," I said as Kier and his family led me through the courtyard.

"Too small or too large?"

"Enormous! This looks like one of those palatial houses I've seen in history books when they're talking about nineteenth century England. How many rooms does it have?"

"I have never bothered to count them."

I swallowed and tried not to fidget with the loose strings hanging off the ends of the sleeves of the dress. I knew that Kier's family were diplomats and were part of the higher ranking families of Atavar, but I had no idea they were wealthy.

"We do not really have wealth on Atavar," Kier said, probably hearing my very loud thoughts. *"We do have tiers, I suppose you would call them. But the goal is equality. We share our surplus with the town nearby and employ many of their residents. No one is hungry or wanting. Everyone has access to what we have. When the river near the town has flooded, or the woods have caught fire, we shelter as many as we can accommodate."*

As we approached the house, I realized it's not quite as large as I'd thought. The outside was metallic, like the sculpture, with a rounded roof that was covered in solar panels. There was what looked like three floors to the house, with a wide window facing out and an extremely wide door that looked like it folded into thirds on each side to open.

But it was the ends of the house which fascinated me the most. On the left and right of the structure were black, rectangular protrusions, which I had thought were more rooms at first glance. But on closer inspection, I realized they were actually huge repositories for rain water, with more solar panels running along the tops.

"Is the house completely self-sufficient, energy wise?" I asked.

"Yes," Kier's father, Gav'Ahn answered. "We also have a wind farm a few miles away on top of the tallest hill on the property, and another solar farm near that, to power the town and store surplus."

"One of the few places I stayed for longer than a few months growing up was Velsav Seven. Half of their surface is covered in wind farms. It was incredible. Your home is so unique."

We were right up to the house now and my mind was momentarily distracted from the itchiness of the dress and the ache in my feet by the wondrous building in front of me. I stepped away from Kier to get a closer look at the water tanks, forgetting my bare feet as I accidentally stepped in mud.

"Oh, crap," I said, holding my foot up. "I'm sorry, I wasn't thinking. I've just never seen solar construction like this before and— oh my goodness! The sides of the house, that's nonabsorbent solar siding!"

I ran my hand up the smooth surface and marveled at it. Nonabsorbent solar siding was an idea that Humans created during the climate crises of the late twenty-first century. The idea was that solar heat could be bounced back in such way that it wouldn't be absorbed on earth, thus helping cool homes and the planet. Wars prevented wide spread implementation of it until the peace accords preceding first contact. Earth had many buildings made out of the material now, but I'd never seen any that looked like this.

"It's completely smooth, and there are no seams anywhere. That's extraordinary!" I said with a laugh.

Then I heard someone clear their throat behind me and I knew before I turned around who it was. My stomach sank and I wondered if I'd literally, and figuratively, stepped in it already.

I turned around with a sheepish smile on my face to find Prem'Ahn glaring at me, and Kier not bothering to hide the tiny upturn of his lips, both of which I'd expected. But it was Gav'Ahn that surprised me. He was staring at me in such a curious way, as if he'd seen a ghost, but also like someone observing a specimen.

"Should we go into the house?" Kier asked.

"Her feet are filthy," Prem'Ahn spat.

Kier didn't miss a beat; he stepped forward and picked me up bridal style.

"What are you doing?" she demanded.

"Her feet are dirty, as you helpfully pointed out, and I am sure they hurt," Kier answered evenly.

"We do have cleaning drones," she answered. "But if you must show such…affection, so be it. One more moment of shame to add to the list."

She turned on her heel and marched toward the door.

"It's okay, I can just wipe the mud on the dress, it's filthy enough, one more mud stain won't matter," I said, even though being held in his arms was the best part of all of this.

His gaze softened though his expression remained emotionless.

"I do not mind."

Kier carried me inside and I gave him a mischievous grin.

"You do know that there's an old earth tradition about carrying brides across thresholds right?" I teased him.

"Of course."

And then he added, *"But what does it say about carrying them to the suite and helping to wash every part of them clean in a warm bath?"*

"It says that you absolutely should do that right now."

"Her bath has been prepared in the guest quarters up the stairs to the right," Prem'Ahn said in the wide entry way.

Kier came to an abrupt halt and all the flirty, sexy thoughts and feelings evaporated in the presence of her sour glare.

"She must wash and make herself available so that the seamstresses may fit the remaining gowns," she continued. "Kier, you will try on your attire. I have laid it out in your room."

"We will be sharing a room," he said to his aunt.

Between his tone and the look he was giving her, whatever she was going to say died a swift death on her tongue.

"Very well. This...union is not traditional, so I see no logical reason to uphold the traditions of separate living quarters. But remember that you are not the only ones here. Keep your...*Human* proclivities quiet. No one wants to see or hear them."

My face flushed hot and I instantly wanted to die. There was absolutely no misinterpreting what she had been implying, and while Atavarians weren't prudes, I imagined their idea of sex did not include being very verbose about it.

"Can you take me to the room please?"

Without commenting, Kier stalked up the curving staircase to our left. What I saw of the entry way and the hall at the top of the stairs was a simple home in dark browns, blacks, oranges and reds. Nothing ostentatious or too bright, but surprisingly not dull and dreary either. There were more windows than I'd seen from the outside, letting in an abundance of natural light as the sun made its way further into the sky. The lighting fixtures were plentiful and there were bouquets of bright flowers on side tables at even intervals. Kier stopped and stared at one of these for a moment before proceeding down the hall and to the right.

"What is it?"

"My mother, she...she was the one who insisted on having fresh flowers in the house. My aunt had thought it wasteful and ceased it after her death. I...I did not realize that my father had started doing it again."

"It's nice, it brightens up the place."

"That is precisely what she had said," his voice faded and he swallowed. "I did not expect to be reminded of her so much. After her death, my aunt seemed to scrub the house clean of any remnants of her. But now...for some reason, my father seems to have brought some of those things back."

"Maybe he misses her and wants to be reminded of her."

His jaw clenched as he ran his hand over the sensor to open the door and stepped through.

"That would be a change indeed," he muttered.

He set me down onto the bed and I let my eyes explore his room. The floor was covered in more black carpet and the walls were a dark gray, accented with paintings of orange flowers and landscapes. His Atavarian-sized bed was covered in a soft coverlet of orange and red, and behind me, he pressed a button to raise the thick shades covering floor to ceiling windows, revealing that they were actually doors that led out onto a balcony. Beyond was a perfect view of the valley that I'd glimpsed at the top of the hill where the house sat. Miles of blue grasses stretched out until they hit a town in the distance. The morning sun shone onto a mountain in the distance that sparkled like diamonds. At the base of it was the Science Institute; the very building where, with any luck, I'd be working soon.

"That's beautiful," I said.

Kier stood in front of the glass doors, hands clasped behind his back and nodded. He'd closed himself off to me once again, and I wondered if it was because returning here had dredged up memories of his mother and a life that had been painful, to say the least.

I wanted to go to him, but in addition to the mud on my feet, I discovered that I was also bleeding and didn't want to get that on the rug. I was about to dab the cut with a shockingly clean part of the dress when Kier stopped me.

"I apologize, I should be helping you to the bathroom."

"It's alright, just tell me where—"

He scooped me up again and carried me through an automatic door on the other side of the room. Lights turned on the moment we stepped through and illuminated one of the largest bathrooms I'd ever seen. It was almost the size of his bedroom, with an oversized standing shower in orange and black tiles, a soaking tub that looked like it was carved out red stone of some kind and was deep enough for both of us to sit easily, as well as a double sink carved out of red and black stone. The floors were the same orange and black tile as in the shower, and tucked into a corner, was a private toilet stall.

"Our family colors are orange and red," Kier explained as he set me on the edge of the soaking tub.

"I hadn't noticed," I said with a smirk.

When he didn't react, I reached down where he knelt, now cleaning the dirt from my feet and skated my fingers along his cheek.

"This is hard for you, isn't it?"

He nodded.

"More than I anticipated."

"What can I do for you?"

For a moment I thought he'd say 'nothing', but then he leaned his forehead against my knees and let out a long, shuddering breath. I ran my fingers through his thick, dark curls, light and soothing. Little by little, his mind opened to me and I felt a modicum of his grief, his anger and his fear. It spun and boiled inside of him as he tried so hard to confine it behind his cognitive barriers.

"You don't have to do that with me," I whispered. "I won't run or judge you."

"You do not understand," he looked up at me, and the tortured look on his face took my breath away. "Our emotions are more volatile than Human ones. They can easily run away with us, rule us. They are dangerous. I cannot simply let them out, but the longer I am with you, the less I want to hide them."

"There might be a middle ground, a way to do both perhaps?"

"Yes, I have considered this. But it is new, uncharted territory. This is not something that is taught on Atavar, our beliefs are absolute on this matter."

"But you are Human as well as Atavarian, so maybe there should be room for a gray area, an in between. Maybe there *needs* to be."

He frowned at that, taking it in. Eventually, he slowly nodded.

"Yes. That is sound logic. I must give it some thought, meditate on it."

A hard knock invaded our cozy moment and I jumped.

"The seamstresses will be here in ten minutes. It would be preferable if you were ready for them," said Prem'Ahn from the other side of the bedroom door.

Kier glared at the door and clenched his jaw.

"I do not remember her being so...rude," he said. "I apologize."

"You do not need to apologize for her, she does," I said. "Especially since she blocked our bath time."

He huffed out a laugh and shook his head.

"You are a constant surprise, Chloe."

"I'll take that as a compliment."

"I do not hear a bath being run," said Prem'Ahn from where she was obviously waiting outside of Kier's door.

I bit back a retort that she was being a bit of an overbearing bitch, and got to my feet.

"I'll take a quick shower, if you could just let her know?"

"Of course. I will also have a conversation regarding proper boundaries."

Boy did I wish I could be in the room for *that* talk.

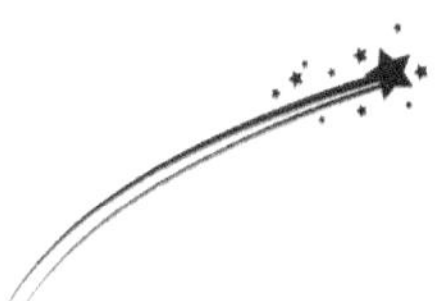

The rest of the day was filled with fittings by multiple seamstresses who expected me to stand completely still for hours on end, while they pinned and hemmed mountains of fabric. Where the first dress had been plain to the point of ugly, these were layered monstrosities of ornate fabrics in various shades of orange and red. One of them was so full that I wasn't sure I'd be able to fit between furniture. Another was heavy enough that I wondered if Prem'Ahn had sewn in weights.

By the time we were done, I was exhausted and starving. There were still three hours until sundown and I was told that the rest of the day should be spent in quiet meditation. Which, I was relieved to discover, meant that she would leave me alone in the room.

I wrapped myself in a soft robe that I found in the bathroom, and fell onto the bed. Although I really wanted a nap, I knew I'd get precious little time to do work over the next three days. I put in a request to Char'Vahn for his research notes and any up to date real time data he had, and hoped he'd be as anxious as I was to get this resolved.

Unable to do much else until I heard back, I decided to try and memorize the audio file for the damn recipe I would be making in a few days. In no time, however, I'd fallen asleep and was being roused by loud knocking on the door.

Kier had programed it to only open if he or I gave the command, and from the way Prem'Ahn was talking through the door, I bet she hadn't been aware of that.

"This is unacceptable," she fumed. "I must be able to come in and dress you for these rituals since you are incapable of doing it yourself!"

I indulged in a satisfied grin before schooling my features and sliding my hand over the sensor to open the door.

"Prem'Ahn," I said with an even tone, "it's so kind of you to come help me. Apologies for not answering right away, I was finishing my meditation."

Her lips pressed together and her dark eyes narrowed.

"The formal breaking of the fast is happening shortly," she snapped as she swept into the room, "I will barely be able to make you presentable in time."

"Well, let's get to it then."

She paused, her eyes scanning down and back up my body.

"You know," she said slowly, "I raised Kier to be a flawless Atavarian, in spite of his tainted parentage. He was on the path to becoming as great as his father should have been. But I did not account for his Human weakness to so thoroughly destroy all my work. First the failed climbing of Mount Chal'teth, then his enrollment in the Galactic Academy. And now...*you*. It seems his Human weakness is more like a disease than I thought."

Oh, how my hands itched to smack her across the face, to scream all the things that crossed my mind in that moment and let her know, in no uncertain terms, that she was the weak one. Instead, I tempered all of that, knowing I would only hurt Kier if I unleashed on his aunt. Still, I couldn't just let her get away with insulting Kier so savagely.

"He's not weak," I bit out. "He is stronger than you or anyone here ever gave him credit for, to have survived all of you and still have compassion and kindness."

She sniffed.

"Yes, I expect that is what a Human would say. Gav is correct, you are much like Christine."

The way she said it, Prem'Ahn was not giving me a compliment when comparing me to Kier's mother. But I wasn't about to let her think she was insulting me.

"Thank you," I replied. "I'm honored. Now, we don't want to be late to the ritual, do we?"

Chapter Twenty-Two

KIER'AHN

The next day, the tea ritual had started as well as could be expected, considering the male my father had chosen for me to humble myself before was none other than the head master of the school I had attended.

Revel'Vahn had made my life a living hell at the school. Siding with every bully that I came across, calling all of my exceptional test scores into question, not giving me the graduate honors I had more than earned, and so many more injustices that I cringed to consider them.

He had always terrified me, made me feel small, unworthy.

Of all the males my father could have chosen, this was the absolute worst one.

And I suppose that is the point.

The tea room in the nearby city of Ruval was a small establishment, old and very traditional, with its red and black decor. There was quiet music coming from a hidden quartet and the light gurgling of several well placed fountains around the room. The cakes and elaborate pot of tea before me were all things I could not partake of since they were made with synthetic blood that lacked the enzyme I needed to digest them. As such, I had been forced to order a smaller pot of tea without blood, making myself even less of an Atavarian in the eyes of Revel'Vahn, if that was possible. The room was deserted, as was a large portion of the city, due to the quarantine in effect in some areas. I was shocked my father had set up the ritual in the city instead of the country, where the virus did not seem to be spreading as quickly. But then I suppose Revel'Vahn would not have dirtied himself to come out to our country town.

"I had considered the Ahn family council's ruling to deny you the honor of a mate a very wise decision. But it seems," he said, staring down his hawkish nose at me, "you found a way around it. Although I suppose mating a *Human* is not truly breaking the ruling. After all, it is not as if you had any options here. What full blooded Atavarian female would lower herself to mate someone with such tainted blood?"

I clenched my hands in my lap, but otherwise kept my features neutral. I had not been in a position to need these skills in a long time and I found myself struggling to fall into those habits with the ease I once had.

"You are correct that I was forbidden an Atavarian mate," I replied. "But I am fortunate that an honorable female has agreed to be my mate."

"I was most pleased that you chose me for this ritual," he said, sipping his blood tea. "It showed an unusual wisdom."

"My son has always been wise," Gav'Ahn said, "though perhaps he has not shown it very often."

A compliment, and then an insult to nullify it. How very familiar.

"Hmmm…" Revel'Vahn said. "Quite. I was not surprised at hearing he took a Human female as mate, after your questionable example, Gav'Ahn."

My father showed absolutely no reaction to this slight against my mother, as usual. Instead, he inclined his head in acquiescence and my blood began to boil.

"My mother was also an honorable female," I said, careful to control my voice.

Revel'Vahn simply glared at me and returned to the tea.

The rest of the hour and half long ritual consisted of Revel'Vahn insulting me and my mother, even my father at times, and me finding a way to be humble about it. By the time the end of the tea approached, I was writhing with unspent anger. I needed to get away, to calm myself. I needed Chloe and her way of soothing me so quickly. Just her presence accomplished this, though I had no idea why.

I took a deep breath and determined that for her, for the mission we were on and for myself, I would get through this next part.

I knelt on the carpeted floor beside Revel'Vahn's chair, bowed my head and recited the ritual words, though they were ash on my tongue.

"I humble myself to you, honorable and wise Revel'Vahn, and seek reconciliation for the ways in which I have offended you through the years."

I waited, knowing that part of ritual was to make the supplicant linger for a time on his knees. I did not expect it to feel so humiliating, however, or so infuriating.

Finally, the horrid male sneered, "I accept your humility and offer reconciliation for the ways in which you offend me."

I noticed the difference in his response, how could I not? He did not forgive me for the things I had once *done* to offend him, but instead, forgave me for existing at all.

I clenched my jaw and stood, the ritual now completed, and I saw no reason to hide the hatred I had for him. When I looked down into his neutral, yet somehow still smug face, his dark eyes widened and know he saw my abhorrence plain as day.

"Thank you, Revel'Vahn, for your participation in this ritual," my father said.

I did not stay to hear the rest of the pleasantries. I turned my back on them both and marched out of the tea room. I stood outside, our vehicle waiting for us a few feet away. My father had driven this morning, seeing no reason to involve one of the towns people he employed to take him places. We had taken a simple, solar powered vehicle that some called a Sled for its long, simple design. It had four seats, two in front and two in back, the engines were very soft, almost imperceptible. In my youth, I had enjoyed driving them through the deserted valleys around the estate.

Ever since my mother's death, I loathed the underground pedestrian tunnels, which is what we would have had to take if we flew anything larger. It was a small consideration, and I had been grateful for it. Now, I was just angry.

Angry at my father for choosing this male when he had to have known the ways in which he'd tortured me as a child.

Angry at Revel'Vahn for treating me like that.

Angry at Prem'Ahn for insisting on all of this.

And finally, I was angry at this place. I hated Ruval, I hated the bigotry and xenophobia of my people. And that hate dragged at me, ate away at the confidence I had built up for myself all these years. It made it difficult to believe that anything would ever change the minds of my people.

"Would you like to visit any of the shops?" my father asked behind me.

"I would like to leave now," I said, and walked quickly to the Sled.

He followed me, getting in and navigating us through the city without a word. We flew like that for a long while as I attempted to control my emotions.

"You did well," my father said.

I wanted to snort, to dismiss his compliment. But I gave him the bare minimum and nodded.

"I do not believe Prem knew how vile he was when she chose him."

I turned to look at my father, hiding my surprise.

"You did not select him?" I asked.

"No, I would not have chosen to spend a minute with the odious man, much less an hour and half."

"Odious? You sent me to his school for seven years."

"Yes, because it was the best training and only true sons of Atavar went there."

"And if I went there, then I would be a true son."

"You *are* a true son."

"I am half Human."

"Yes," he said, the word almost tender. "And half Atavarian. You are a child of both worlds."

I struggled to understand what he said, to believe he was saying this at all. In the years since Mother had died, he had never acknowledged my Human side, except to tell me that I had to control it, hide it away so that I could be accepted. And now he was telling me to live in both worlds?

"I do not understand," I finally said.

He let out a long sigh and nodded.

"Yes, I know."

We did not speak during the remainder of the hour-long drive to the estate. When we pulled the Sled into the garage, I could not get out of the vehicle fast enough. I needed to escape to Chloe, to find out how her ritual was progressing, when my father blocked my way.

"Come, we will have a Shel'mok ride and we will talk."

I did love riding the beasts, with their shaggy hair and long, powerful legs. But I did not want to ride with my father. It was on the tip of my tongue to refuse when he added, "Please, son."

I could not remember the last time my father had pleaded with me.

"Very well," I said. "I will send a com to Chloe to explain my absence."

"Of course. I will prepare the mounts."

I stood still for a moment, gathering my thoughts, trying to find equilibrium. The day had been too full of turmoil, and now this. The house was just around a bend in the dirt road. I could almost make out the solar water tanks along the side. The tanks that had fascinated Chloe so much. The memory brought a warmth with it and I closed my eyes imagining her smile, her laugh and pure delight at discovering something new. Even something as simple as a water tank.

"...Kier?...Is that you?"

The question was from far away, watery and weak, but it was still enough to shock me. The mental bond, the one I should have been tempering, weakening by disuse, had become strong enough that we could now communicate over a short distance. I had indulged in its intimacy because the temptation of being with her in that way was too much to resist. I was not sure if I simply thought it would not grow this strong this fast, or if I did not want to even consider the possibility. Whatever the reason, it would do no good to berate myself, to let regret poison this beautiful connection.

And right now, I needed her in the very deepest parts of my marrow. If that was weakness, so be it.

"Yes, it's me. I am sorry to frighten you."

It took a moment but she answered.

"Not frightened...shocked."

"Pleasantly?"

"Yes. It's nice to have you here in a way."

"Has it been very difficult?"

"Yes. But I'm alright. Almost done if this dress would stop slowing me down...."

Her voice faded away and I wondered if my aunt had interrupted her or if something had happened. I sent a soothing image of me standing right beside her and hoped it was enough. I could have told her about the delay getting back to her mentally, but chose to send her a com so that I would not distract her.

That brief interaction soothed me enough so that by the time I had changed from my long, flowing robes that I had worn for the ritual into light riding gear, I was calm, controlled. The shirt was sleeveless so I could feel the warm sunlight on me, and I still wore gloves, light synthetic leather that protected my hands while handling the reigns of the animal. It was pleasant in an unexpected way to slip back into clothes that I had once worn nearly every day on holidays from school and it strengthened my mental barriers even more so that, by the time my father brought the two mounts around, I was prepared for whatever he may need to say.

We rode out down a small incline that led us past the vegetable gardens and toward the fields of wild grass that my aunt had not convinced him to cut back. This had been our same route since I was a child and I gave the animal lead, urging him to ride side by side with my father. Like this, with the wind and sunshine on my body, the vast field of wild grasses and flowers, I could forget that I was different, unacceptable. The small town of Felk was not that far away and if we kept going we would enter its borders. I loved that place as much as it was also filled with difficult memories. Some of those living and working there had always treated me with respect, if not full acceptance, while others had simply ignored me which was preferable to being treated as if I were nothing.

The dirt road that would have taken us to the town was to the left but my father signaled that he wanted to go to the right and I followed him. It wasn't until we began to head for a very familiar hill that I realized where he was taking me.

The site of my mother's old observatory.

He'd built it on one of the hills surrounding the house, the only one that had an unobstructed view of the sky and was far enough away from buildings so that any nighttime light would not interfere with her instruments. There had been a hidden path, one that she had cut through for her own convenience, that did not require her to go around the hills and down through the plain. It was that secret route that I had taken as a child after she had died. I hadn't bothered to look for it when we arrived yesterday; in part because I assumed it was gone, and also because I could not bring myself to. And now, at the foot of the hill, I wanted to balk, to run away. But something drew me forward, in spite of these feelings, and I followed my father.

The known path, which I had assumed would have been over grown, was well kept, the grass on either side trimmed. When we crested the hill, I braced for the grief that hit me like a Leigth blade. The grass here was taller than around the house, but trimmed enough not to be wild. And where the observatory once stood, there was now a Blood Moon tree, called so because once a year, on the harvest blood moon, the red blossoms on its drooping branches glowed exceptionally bright.

We tied off the mounts to a nearby post, and without a word, he walked up to the tree and placed his hand on the curving, black trunk. It was tall enough that it would have been planted a few years after the observatory had been torn down. The way the sunlight filtered through the leaves, it made the sharp bones of his face stand out even more, and once again, I wondered if he had been ill.

"I come here often," he said, looking out over the valley, "to think. To be near to her."

His words stunned me speechless. I had never heard him this vulnerable, ever.

"I believe," he went on, "that she would have liked Chloe."

I swallowed back the bereavement that tried to suffocate me.

"I do as well," my voice was hoarse. "Zephyr approved of Chloe."

My father grunted.

"I am not surprised."

"What does that mean?"

"Nothing cruel, I assure you."

Those words, this trip up the hill, his actions all snapped my restraint and I walked up to him, my voice shaking with anger and hurt.

"You sent her away after Mother died. You acted as if they both never existed. And now you perform for me, as if you have grieved them this entire time."

He turned quickly to me, dark eyes blazing and lips trembling. It was staggering to see such emotion on my father's face.

"I do not perform," he snapped. "I do grieve them both. I lost a daughter the day I sent your sister away. I feel the pain no less than if it had been...had been you that had died. I sent her away because it was not safe for her here. I let everyone believe she had died to protect her."

I wanted to ask him so many questions. Why did he do the same to me? Why had he refused to see me for a year after her death? Why had he hardly spent an hour in my presence after that? Why did he now act as if he were sorry, but did not say the words?

All of this was on my tongue, aching to spill out. But I could not get the words past the fear that I would not hear what I wanted.

"You tore down her observatory," I said instead.

He looked into my eyes with a firm determination, as if he wanted to make very sure that I heard him, and said, "I could not bear the constant reminder of her."

I knew then what he wanted, knew that he was trying to explain why he'd abandoned me in that despair. He wanted forgiveness, understanding. And logically, I should have accepted his olive branch.

But logic was hard to follow when a lifetime's worth of agony and rejection was screaming at me. So I said nothing, made no acknowledgment of it because I simply could not speak without yelling at him. But I did not look away, nor did I step back. I remained open to anything else he needed to say, and he saw it.

"I have kept abreast of your career," he continued. "Through your captain, I receive updates on your progress."

My eyebrows rose sharply and my hands tightened.

"Why have you never asked *me*? Why hide this and keep me believing that you were ashamed of me?" I demanded.

"Because I did not believe you would have welcomed my inquiries, or my presence, in your new life. You left without a word to me."

"You told me that rejecting the Institute was rejecting the House of Ahn."

"And it was because it was the House Council's sponsorship of you."

"No," I growled out, my eyes flashing, "do *not* hide behind the council. Every reason to shut me out of Atavarian society has been hidden behind the excuse that it was due to the council. I will not have it from you, I will have the truth."

His lips twisted and he walked a few feet away from me to once again look at the fields of long grass below the hill. For a moment, I wondered if I had asked for too much.

"I was angry with you for leaving," he said with his back to me. "I had finally come to terms with how I had pushed you away and was ready to attempt reconciliation. I thought your time at the Institute would afford us something in common with which to create a relationship. And when you decided against it, to leave Atavar entirely, I became...irrational."

"You believed it a rejection of you."

"Precisely. Prem will tell you that this has always been my weakness. I am prone to illogical decisions where those I love are concerned."

"Love?"

He gave me a short nod and that was all for several, very long minutes.

"I did the pilgrimage of Bat'var for your mother," he said.

Again, he shocked me into silence. That pilgrimage was rarely done at all due to its focus on expressing the emotions around grief in the fullest way possible. It was considered so uncomfortable to witness, that it was performed underground, through a series of caves and tunnels that, if fully traversed, took three months to complete. The mourner was expected to expel their emotions over the loss of the loved one the entire time and at the end, to burn something that belonged the one that died as a way to fully release the grief so they might move on.

"Did it help?" I asked once I had found my voice.

He tilted his head to the side, back still to me, and I knew he was considering my question.

"In a way," he said. "I suppose it leached the worst of it out of me. But it also left me hollow and uncertain how to live after."

I did not know how to respond to such honesty from him. If this had been Captain Drake, or Lieutenant Commander Althea, or Chloe, I would have known what to say or do. But my father was a mystery to me. He was wholly Atavarian, logical and strong. And yet, he was telling me how he *felt*. The dichotomy was unsettling, even as it also began to create an odd sort of connection between us.

"I do not expect you to accept all I have said," father said after a while. "I suppose I had hoped that you might at least listen and know that I am...proud of you. Proud of your accomplishments, of the courage you displayed in starting a life away from all you had known."

"I...I do not know what to say to that."

"That is understandable."

I attempted to absorb his words, things that I had longed to hear for my entire life. And now, he had laid them before me, but I did not know how to accept them.

"Why have you decided to say all of this to me now?" I asked after a moment.

He gave a long sigh and turned around.

"I have wanted to say these things for many years, and it has been my own failing not to seek out an opportunity to do so. Your arrival provided me with an easy one."

"I understand," I said, though I did not truly. "And, I have listened, but I will need to process before responding further."

"That is wise and I appreciate your consideration. I will leave you to do so without me. I find myself in need of sustenance."

I nodded at him in farewell, my mind reeling.

"Incidentally," he called out to me, "I very much approve of your mate. She is quite...extraordinary."

Warmth and pride swelled in my chest, and I found myself quite touched that my father liked Chloe.

"She is, very."

Father looked at the tree and then back at me before turning toward his mount and riding off, leaving me with much to think over.

Chapter Twenty-Three

KIER'AHN

I stayed long enough for the stars to shine above me, as they once had for my mother. I stood near the tree, attempting to find the constellations she and I and Zephyr had given silly names to when I was a child. And I tried, so very hard to see if I could feel her here. Not since I was eight years old had I allowed myself to seek her out like this, to conjure the memory of her. It reopened the wound of losing her, but it also eased some of it too. Perhaps my aunt had been incorrect in denying me an expression for my grief. Perhaps if I had been allowed to expel it, as my father had, I would not have carried it around inside of me for so long.

By the time I found my way back to the estate, the evening meal was finished. I had a quick snack of my recipe of synthetic blood, which I noticed was in abundant supply for tomorrow's dinner.

Ah yes, the ritual. I wonder how Chloe did today. I should not have abandoned her to my aunt. Or maybe, I should not have abandoned my aunt to Chloe.

The thought made the corners of my mouth turn up and I knew that while this was difficult and confusing, Chloe really could handle herself. That did not mean, of course, that she might not desire to vent her frustrations to someone.

Although...that is not the only reason I want to see her.

A sudden, hot hunger hit me and all I could think of was holding her, and wrapping my mind around hers. I quickly finished the blood and ran up the stairs two at a time. The need for her was all consuming and by the time I barged into my room, my incisors were fully extended and my entire body ached to feel her against me.

Not since the rut had I been so over powered by a physical desire as I was in that moment.

But when I looked over to the bed, Chloe was asleep, her tablet on her chest. The lights made the gold in her hair stand out and cast her skin in a warm glow. She was serene, beautiful and I was incapable of staying away.

I laid down beside her and put her tablet on the bedside table. The moment the weight was off her, Chloe stirred, her eyes drifting open. When they settled on me, a sleepy smile graced her lips.

"There you are," she murmured. "I tried to wait for you…but I got sleepy."

"I apologize for waking you," I ran the backs of my knuckles across her cheek.

The sensation of her skin against mine was acute, sending a thousand sparks through my body. I was ravenous for her, craving her very soul in a way that scared me as much as it drove me. There was no going back after this, no saying that I did not want to keep her with every fiber of my being.

And I did not care.

"I need you," I rasped out. "I need you so much."

Her eyes widened just before my mouth descended on hers. I could not be gentle or slow, something was driving me to make it clear to Chloe, with every crush of my lips, that she was mine.

Not for a mission.

Not because of a mistake.

But always. Forever. Indisputably *mine*.

I tore away the sheet that covered her as our hands and mouths grappled with one another. Her hands pulled the shirt from my pants even as mine tore her sleep tank down the center. My hands skated across her breasts as I shoved the fabric aside and I dove down to them, drawing one pink bud into my mouth with a savage suck.

Chloe let out a shocked yelp and her hands pulled at my hair as her back arched. Her consciousness spun bright pink around mine, sharing the sensation with me and the nodes on my phallus pulsed hard.

As I darted back and forth between her breasts, following the leads that Chloe's body and mind were giving me, I slid her shorts down her thighs with her tiny blue panties. The scent of her arousal hit me hard and I growled against the valley of her breasts.

"You're wearing too many clothes," she complained and yanked on my shirt.

I helped her take it off me and she tackled me back onto the bed. My feral passions were now driving her too, I could feel it twining around her mind.

"This is me," I gasped as she bit her way down my throat to my chest. "I am…I am losing control, Chloe, and you will too."

"Good…I want that. I want to get lost with you."

Our hands were everywhere on one another. Hers on my torso following the path of her little blunt teeth, mine on her arms her back, her head, desperate to brand myself into every pore.

When her hands came to my pants, I helped her with the laces and we both threw them off as if the very sight of clothing offended us. This would be the first time I was with her, skin to skin, no physical barriers between us since my rut fever, the first time I'd ever had so much contact with another being where my consciousness was not cloaked in rutting hormones.

I had always thought it would scare me, the potential for a barrage of sensations and thoughts. But Chloe was now a part of my thoughts, my soul, my very marrow. My body was as much hers as mine. My thoughts belonged to her, as hers did to me.

I did not fear her.

I craved her.

She knelt between my legs and stared at me in wonder as I did her. Slowly, she ran her palms up my calves, to my thighs and hips. My eyes devoured her naked body, the curves and dips of her, the sway of her breasts as she leaned over me, the long column of her throat.

"Is this alright?" she breathed. "How I'm touching you, is it too much?"

"It is perfect, do not stop," I captured one of her hands and brought it to my phallus. "Here...touch me here...please."

She bit her bottom lip, cheeks and chest flushed pink as the same color flared in my mind. This excited her, she wanted to do this to me. And that made me all the more aroused, all the more possessive of her.

I wrapped my hand around hers and took her down to my quickly swelling knot, then slowly, firmly I brought her hand along the nodes and up to the tip where a bead of fluid spilled.

To my utter amazement, Chloe leaned down and licked the moisture off with her little pink tongue. It sent fire through my phallus and into my stomach. I hissed and bucked my hips out of pure instinct and drive.

"What...? Chloe, what are you doing?"

"It's called oral sex and it's the same as what you did to me only reversed. But if you don't want it—"

"I did not say that. It just shocked me. This is not something that I was taught about."

"Do you want me to teach you about it? Show you what I like?"

"Yes."

"Tell me if it becomes too much," she said.

And then she took the head between her lips and I let out a rumbling cry. My fingers released her hand on my phallus and tangled in her hair as she bobbed slowly down and back up. I was far too big for her to take all the way, but that did not matter. Her tongue flicked against the underside, and her clever fingers worked the nodes along the side. When one of them released before I could stop it, she let out a moan that I felt down to my root and my fingers tightened on her hair.

"You liked tasting me."

"So much...it's sweet and it's you. I love making you feel good."

She sent an image of me rutting into her mouth and I let out a shocked gasp.

"I will come like that...I cannot hold on much longer."

She gave me a wicked grin around my phallus.

"Good."

She was getting so wet doing this to me, I could feel it as our minds entwined ever tighter. Her channel quivered and she wanted to touch herself as she took me deeper.

"Do not touch yourself. That is for me. That is mine tonight."

Her eyes glittered as she looked up at me, cheeks hollowed and my phallus between her lips. It was erotic and profane and I'd never seen anything more beautiful in my life.

"Rut my mouth, Kier, please."

A feral growl rumbled in my chest, my fingers tightened on her hair. It was such a sweet request, and I could not refuse her.

"Do not look away from me."

And then I bucked up into her mouth as I held her still, just like the image she sent me. I was using her in the most illicit way and with every second that passed, the more she ached for me to make her come. But if she kept letting me do this, I was the one that would come. And tonight, I wanted to do that inside of her. I wanted to knot her, fill her. I wanted to fully experience what being inside of her felt like when I was not in a rut fever.

So I pulled her off me, her eyes widening as I sent her exactly what I was about to do to her.

"Yes or no?" I panted.

"Yes!"

My hands gripped her waist. I lifted her up so she straddled my hips and then brought her down to meet me as I thrust up into her. We both let out a long cry as we felt the twin sensations of being filled and filling.

In that moment, I was utterly lost, with her as my only anchor. We drowned together, breathed together. Our eyes never left one another as we moved in tandem, rolling our bodies to separate and meet again and again.

An image rose up in my mind, of my large, red hand grasping her long, pale neck. Which of us thought it I could not say, but we both groaned for it.

I ran my hand greedily up her body, over her breasts until I came to her throat and I closed my fingers around it. Her eyes rolled back and her fingers dug into my chest. I felt her heart pound, her sex drenched, the moment I put pressure into the grip.

The sight of her like this, riding me with my hand around her throat made me feral. My teeth ached and sweet venom dripped off my fangs. I needed to bite her, but not yet. Not until I had seen her come apart above me.

My other hand found that bud in her cleft and I pressed my thumb to it as I bucked up hard into her. Chloe's mouth gaped on a silent cry, her hands going to her breasts as she pinched her nipples. I rutted her hard as I worked her, the flame of her presence in my mind wild as it spun until all at once, it burst as she did. Her sex clenched around my phallus and I expelled half my nodes as we both cried out release.

I had barely let her come down from the orgasm before I was pulling her off me and laying her on her front. I was driven by pure instinct now; the beast in me was controlled, but loose. I needed to bite her, to rut her, mark and own her. And because of the bond, Chloe knew that. When she presented herself to me on all fours, legs spread exposing her glistening, pink sex I was overcome. The only thing that I could think of was the blinding need to bury myself there.

With one hand on her hip, and the other curled around to grip her throat once again, I buried myself in one brutal thrust.

"Yes...yes, more!"

The slap of our bodies was punctuated by my snarls and her cries. I would mark her insides first and knot her. Then I would mark her outside with my bite.

"Yes, please, Kier...I want that."

"Chloe...my priash...priash veltosh..."

The rest of my nodes emptied inside of her and I could not wait any longer. With one powerful thrust, I bent over her and latched my teeth onto her shoulder as I also sealed my knot inside of her.

Ribbons of fire and ice danced and collided, broke apart and was sealed back together as our bodies convulsed around and in one another. Tears wet my lashes and hers and I knew what it was to be whole, bathed in sunlight after a lifetime in the dark.

"Kier...Kier...," she sobbed in my mind.

"I am here priash...my perfect, beautiful priash."

Slowly, like coming through clouds, I was aware of my own body again. Her sweet blood filled my mouth, and I slowly withdrew my fangs, licking the wound to close it. I had not realized that her hand had come up and was gripping one set of my horns tightly. I liked that she did that, that she liked to touch them.

My hand around her throat loosened and I fell onto my side, taking her with me and tucking her in close. I could not stop touching her in lazy strokes along her outer leg and hip, to her breasts, which I idly played with.

"I could become obsessed with these."

She gave me a breathy chuckle and planted a kiss on my bicep, which was under her head. She threaded her fingers between mine and held on tight.

There was fear under the honeyed afterglow of her release and I worried it was because of me.

"It's not," she said, reading my thoughts.

"Do you want to tell me?"

I could see her thoughts retreating from me as she attempted to close off whatever this was. I now understood perhaps a bit of her frustration when I did that. It was indeed unpleasant.

"I don't know."

"I will not push you."

"I felt..." she bit her lip. "I felt as if this time was different for you, is that true?"

"Yes," I whispered, planting little kisses to her shoulder. "I cannot explain it, but I needed you. To be inside of you, to hold you, to let my mind sing with yours. I *want* to feel all these things for you and with you. Chloe, you are...you are everything I never knew I wanted in this life."

The last part came out hoarse, unsure. I did not know what Chloe might think of that. Was this too fast? Was this a breach of boundaries, her belief that friends can do this and still only be friends? I did not know, but I also could not hold it back any longer.

Her breath came out ragged, I felt her tears in my mind a few seconds before they appeared on her cheeks.

"What is wrong? Are you hurt? Was I too rough?"

"No," she looked back at me, her fingers against my face. "It's different for me too, and I've been so scared that you wouldn't feel that way. I don't want to go back to just friends, Kier. I want...I want to be with you like this, I want to be yours after the mission, for as long as you want me."

I wanted to say 'forever', but the words stalled in the back of my throat. I saw that tree where my mother's observatory had been. I smelled the smoke from the rubble that had buried her body and the tiniest kernel of fear wormed its way in to this moment. I could not say forever to Chloe until we were off this planet. If I had to give her up to keep her safe I would, and therefore, I could not allow myself to be a liar. When we were done, when Atavar was behind us, then I would declare to her all that was in my soul.

And so for now, the only answer I gave her was a long, slow kiss and a night of passion.

Chapter Twenty-Four

CHLOE

I woke up the next day with Kier's head between my legs moments before he gave me an orgasm that made me see the beginning of the galaxy. Just when I thought I may be able to form coherent sentences again, he'd plunged into me with even, slow strokes that made my toes curl and my body go up in flames.

He didn't last long, in spite of how hard he was trying to. And before I knew it he was spilling himself inside of me as he whispered raspy Atavarian words against my throat. I didn't care what had happened to make him so passionate, I just knew that I wanted more. I wanted all of it, all of *him*.

"No knot?" I panted, as he fell onto his back.

"No time," he gasped.

In response, I trailed kisses up his torso, savoring every inch of his skin. He really did have a magnificent body, not lean but not bulky, it was all hard planes of muscle I wanted to memorize with my hands and mouth.

"At the end of all this, do we get a honeymoon?" I asked.

He frowned at me in slight confusion as he played with a strand of my hair.

"You know, a whole week to do nothing but eat, sleep and play?"

I waggled my eyebrows at him and he let out that huffing laugh I'd come to adore.

"Atavarians do not have such a thing, and I assumed you'd want to go straight to the Institute. But," he flipped me onto my back, his weight pinning me down wonderfully, "I suppose I could arrange for a private house near the Institute, where you could come home to me at the end of the day, and I could make you dinner, then take you to bed where you could teach me all the wonderful things you dream about."

I gasped.

"Is that why you woke me up like that?"

He nodded just before planting a tiny kiss on the tip of my nose.

"You were dreaming of me waking you that way and I found myself unable to resist. It is...delectable."

"Is it now?"

"Mmm...."

He kissed me with languid strokes of is tongue against mine as our hands lazily explored the landscape of one another's bodies. I wanted to stay like this forever, frozen in this moment when everything I wanted was possible, when there was no virus, no mission. Where we could see if this was the kind of connection we could build a life on.

But a very firm, very annoyed knock interrupted us, and we both let out a long sigh.

"If we are to make the dish correctly, we must begin after breakfast," Prem'Ahn's pinched voice filtered through the door. "And the morning meal is being served as we speak. If I have to, I will find a security override for this door."

I heard her robes rustle as she walked away.

"I wish your culture had elopement," I said.

He gave me a tiny grin and kissed me.

"It is one more day, and then we are free of her."

"I'll be counting the hours."

Kier gave me the first shower, even though the stall was more than big enough for the two of us.

"If I join you, my aunt will be quite vexed because you will not come out for many hours."

I didn't really see a down side to that but Kier, ever the rule follower, insisted.

Breakfast was a rushed affair, with Kier and his father setting out right after to place some quarantine drones around a section of the town where the Lavat virus had been detected. The news put a sour taste in my mouth, and Kier tried to reassure me, through our bond, that all would be well, that tomorrow I would be doing the work and soon the virus would be under control. But all I could think was, if I hadn't been doing all these stupid rituals for the past three days, maybe I could help.

I had made the mistake last night of just 'peeking' at the test results of some of the models I'd run with Char'Vahn's research and ended up spending the entire time from the end of the tea ritual until I'd fallen asleep running through the data, making adjustments, cursing at the new data and making more adjustments.

Char'Vahn had been gracious enough to chat with me about my theories, and through the holo tablet's visual interface we had been able to do some actual work. He was going to test some of my suggestions today and I was dying to find out if they'd worked.

But as Prem'Ahn pulled my hair viciously into a traditional Atavarian braid right before forcing me into the heaviest of the dresses, I knew that I would have no time to look over anything.

I also realized, as she marched me into the spacious kitchen, that I probably should've gone through the audio file of the recipe a few more times last night.

The ingredients, all fifty of them, were laid out along the black stone island in the middle of the kitchen and also on the counter. There was a pestle and mortar, a collection of large knives and cutting boards, six pans and a large covered dish that reminded me of a casserole dish from old earth vids. There was also a collection of spices, herbs and synthetic blood laid out. I checked the blood first to make sure it was the kind Kier could consume with the added enzymes and was pleased that at least his aunt had done that.

Prem'Ahn stood off to the side, hands folded in front of her, not a speck of anything on her orange and red gown. After a small bell went off nearby, she began directing me in Atavarian on how to prepare the dish. My subdermal translator took care of the language barrier, but there was no getting around the fact that I didn't know what half these ingredients were. I knew I'd get no help from her, but I really did not expect her to stack the deck so far against me. It didn't take me long to realize that she had placed the ingredients out of order, so I had an even harder time figuring out what item to do what with next.

I muddled my way through the first two hours, ignoring Prem'Ahn's very loud and distracting breaths of disapproval and one outright grunt.

Finally, four hours later, sweating, my arms tired, my back killing me, I had the dish in the outrageously hot oven. Now, it had to cook for two hours, with me stirring in the spiced blood mixture every half hour until it was done.

I fell into a chair in the nearby dining room and gulped down a large glass of water. I had hated this dress when it was just a heavy, voluminous concoction of red and black. Now, I loathed it since the undergarments were damp and I was pretty sure I had pit stains that went all the way down the side of my body.

"That was barely acceptable," Prem'Ahn announced from the doorway. "You often confused the ingredients and did not follow my instructions on how best to grind the blood root seeds. Your stubbornness does not bode well for your future here."

I knew it was the fact that I was starving, hot, in pain and in serious need of a bath that made me stand to my feet slowly, brace my hands on the black stone table top and pin her with a glare.

"I have been nothing but compliant to your every direction," I snapped. "I have let you squeeze and stuff me into these dresses that I can barely move in, while you call me ugly and short. I've listened to you tell your friend that I'm deficient as Human, much less as a mate for Kier, and that was one of the nicer things you said. I have smiled, and bitten my tongue, and all you've done is be downright hostile, in an Atavarian way, of course. Actually, you are *very* Atavarian. But what I do not understand, and what makes me the angriest, is your obvious desire to cause Kier unhappiness. He has chosen *me*, I make him happy. And you hate that."

"So, it is honesty you seek. Very well. Yes, I do despise you," she hissed at me. "I hate everything about you, from your sickly skin, to the smell of your sweat, to the immature need to show every single emotion you have. You are beneath the House of Ahn in every way. Our proud traditions, the unbroken lineage of direct ancestry from Enlightened One Ahn has been weakened and sullied time and again. I alone have born the burden of attempting to cleanse our family line, while my brother and my nephew revel in their weaknesses."

She walked slowly toward me and a chill raced down my spine at the dead, cold look in her eyes.

"But make no mistake, I will ensure that the stain of you, of another *Human*, is expunged from this house, just like I did last time."

I sucked in a shocked breath at the confession she'd just spoke as if it were nothing. My stomach twisted and cold sweat broke out on my palms.

"You...You...?"

"You were so verbose a moment ago, where are your bold words now?" she leaned closer. "Do not underestimate me. You may have endured my little trials the last few days, but this is just the beginning."

And with that, Prem'Ahn turned and walked out, leaving her threats hanging in the air like a guillotine over my head.

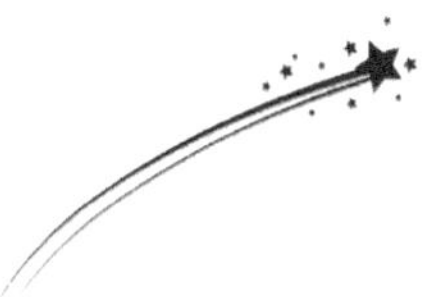

I didn't see her the rest of the day, though I did finish the dish as she would have instructed. It looked somewhat like a beef bourguignon, but without the meat, when it was done. It had to sit covered for a while before serving, so I left it on the stove and walked out of the still stifling kitchen.

I had hoped to have a moment alone with Kier in between those half hours of pouring the blood into the dish, but he and his father were gone all day. I doubted I'd see him before dinner, which he couldn't skip tonight.

Some of the staff were setting a table out on the wide patio just off the dining room and I let the breeze float over me as I looked out onto the grassy plains in the distance. It was a beautiful planet, even if half the population were xenophobic assholes.

I wanted to laugh at that, but I couldn't. Prem'Ahn's secret weighed on me. The threats she'd left had me looking at the two women setting out the utensils and wondering if one of them would stab me if I turned my back.

Come on, Chloe, this is silly. You just need to clean this sweat off you and toss this damn dress.

When I got up to the room, I indulged in a bath, letting the hot water unwind my muscles as I tried to get a handle on these new revelations. When I was done, my body was clean and my mind was a little clearer, if not peaceful.

I glanced at the dress I had worn all day, at the still-wet sweat stains, and shook my head. I didn't care if I was supposed to wear this monstrosity to dinner. Now that I knew what I did about Prem'Ahn, she could stuff these dresses right up her ass.

Except for the gold one, I actually do like that one so I'll wear that because this whole thing is ending tonight. I don't care if she swallows her tongue in rage.

As I slipped the beautiful gown on and went to work on my hair, I had to admit to myself that all of this had been a thin distraction from the way my stomach was twisting into knots; I would have to tell Kier that his aunt, the woman that had raised him, was the one that had orchestrated the murder of his mother.

I had no proof other than her confession, which I was sure she would deny. And while I knew Kier trusted me, that it was nearly impossible to lie to one another with this bond, I didn't know if he'd *believe* me.

I know I would have a hard time if the situation was reversed.

I'll come up with something. He deserves to know what really happened, maybe then he can heal and not blame himself for it.

Prem'Ahn struck me as the type of person who wouldn't have been deterred, no matter how many precautions Gav'Ahn took to keep his wife safe. My heart hurt at the thought of all this family had gone through just because of Prem'Ahn's prejudice and hate. I had no illusions that revealing her treachery would change hearts and minds. I wasn't at all sure what actually would. It seemed that this belief had been entrenched in Atavarian society for a very long time. One Human, one tragic murder, wasn't going to affect that very much.

I rubbed my forehead and tried to banish the headache taking root there. This was something I couldn't do anything about, not on a planetary scale anyway. But the virus, saving lives, that I could help with. I just had to get through tonight.

The holo tablet on the bed trilled and I snatched it up, longing for a distraction. It was a message from Char'Vahn letting me know that my theories had helped him discover that the virus was first targeting specific enzymes in the Atavarian's blood stream that enabled them to absorb nutrients. This weakened the host and allowed the virus to propagate at an accelerated rate. The anti-viral I had created with his data showed promise, but the attack on the enzymes were too fast, weakening the host to the point that the virus was over powering the anti-viral.

We have to solve the enzyme problem first...

I needed time to think, but a bell went off in the room, signaling dinner.

"Damn it."

I sent Char'Vahn a quick message, letting him know I would be arriving at the Institute in the morning to begin solving this issue.

It wasn't until I was downstairs that I realized that Prem'Ahn hadn't come to get me. Was she gone? Had she simply moved on in whatever 'plan' she had to get rid of me?

The last time she got rid of someone, they died.

I swallowed down the oily fear that thought produced and tried to smile for Kier and his father, who were waiting on the patio.

"What is wrong? I can sense your fear."

"I'll tell you later."

Gav'Ahn was looking tired, with dark circles under his eyes, and his hands trembled when he raised his glass of wine to me. I wondered if the day had just been that stressful, or if something else was wrong.

She wouldn't kill her own brother just because he approved of me, would she?

Had she done something to Gav'Ahn? Or maybe she was planning on blaming something on me. She could've made me poison the dish and because I wasn't familiar with the ingredients I wouldn't even know it. I suddenly felt like there were hundreds of invisible threats nipping at my heels and I wouldn't know they were there until I was in the thick of it. My breath began to quicken and palms sweat. I had to tell Kier, I had to have him on the lookout. He knew this planet, its customs and people ten times better than I did. He'd be able to spot something wrong.

"You are beginning to concern me," Kier said in my mind as he led me to the table.

"I need to tell you something about—"

Prem'Ahn swept into the room, this time in a gown of pure black with tiny red crystals sewn into the hem and bodice. Her dark red skin was dusted with a powder that made her glow and her dark eyes were lined with black, while her hair was fashioned in a dozen loops on the top of her head. She looked like the evil queen in old Earth fairy tales.

Without a word she sat in the place by her brother, face as impassable as always but once again, there was a cold glint in her eyes that made my mouth go dry.

The dish I'd prepared was in the center of the table, and I knew I was supposed to serve it to everyone, but it was the last thing I wanted to do.

Although, if I can get her to eat it first, that would help me know it was safe for Kier and his father.

Kier took a seat on the other side of his father and I began to serve. It smelled decent enough but I wouldn't be eating any of it, so at least I knew she wasn't planning on poisoning *me*.

Gav'Ahn coughed into his napkin when I set his plate in front of him. My worry that it might be disgusting must've shown on my face because he waved away my concern.

"It is not your cooking," he assured me. "I am just tired. It was a long day."

I glanced at Kier, who wore a small frown at his father's words, but continued to serve dinner. Once everyone but me had food on their plates, I sat back down and we all raised black glasses of wine.

"I am pleased to welcome Chloe Carter to the House of Ahn," Gav'Ahn said, coughing again into his napkin. "Excuse me, I am...just a small..."

He coughed again, this time harder and when he pulled the napkin away, there was blood on his mouth.

"Father?" Kier asked.

"I...do not know...I am not feeling well."

He stood up and immediately fell to the ground. I knew with a terrible certainty what this was even before I got to him.

"Kier, go to our room, I've got a med kit there, bring it to me."

He nodded and ran into the house.

"Get the physician," Prem'Ahn ordered to one of the staff who had rushed to the patio.

"No," I said. "Evacuate the house and get everyone to the stables so I can run a scan on them."

"You have no right to order— "

I stood and faced her, unflinching. "I have every right! I am a medical professional and unless you want to catch the virus, you should listen to me. Get everyone to the stables, *now.*"

I was in my element, and nothing, not the stony look she sent my way, not the prickle of unease down my spine, would deter me from doing what I could to help Kier's father.

The fact that we didn't have an anti-viral yet rolled in the back of my mind, but I refused to let it make me panic. I slipped into that space of calm that had always served me in a crisis, and focused on what was right in front of me, what I could control.

Kier set the med kit down beside me and I tucked my skirt underneath me so it would be out of the way.

"Come here," I said to him, as I calibrated my med scanner.

I ran it over him, looking for the telltale signs of decreased enzymes and the start of malnourishment that Char'Vahn had alerted me to. To my profound relief, Kier was fine. Next, I ran it over Gav'Ahn and my stomach sank when I saw the numbers.

"I need to take a blood sample and send it to Char'Vahn for analysis," I explained. "Your father can't consent to that but as his closest relation— ."

"Do it," Kier replied, his voice soft.

I looked up into his eyes and saw the pain, the worry there in spite of how stoic he was. There was nothing I could say to reassure him, nothing that wouldn't be a lie and he knew it. So I simply cupped his cheek and gave him a soft kiss.

"I need to get out of this dress and then we need to get your father to a more comfortable room," I said. "I've got your aunt evacuating all the staff to the stables so I can scan them."

"His study is on this floor and he has a wide couch there."

Kier and I managed to pick up Gav'Ahn and carry him to the study. He began to come back to consciousness, but his temperature was rising fast. I gave him a hypo spray to bring the fever down, but I knew it was only a matter of time before that would be useless. I took out a small collector needle from my kit and inserted the diagnostic end into my med scanner. Gav'Ahn flinched at the poke in his wrist and I sprayed a coagulant on it to stop the bleeding. Once the scanner beeped, I took the needle out and stored it in a secure vial for further use.

"What is...where am I?" he asked, eyes glassy.

"You're in your study," I said, pulling a blanket that Kier found over him. "I need you to stay here, and sleep if you can. I'm going to find someone to take you to your bed soon. But for now, stay here."

He nodded and then seized my wrist.

"I know what is wrong with me. I had thought that I was sick a few days before you arrived, but then I felt a bit better. Today, however, it has come back, but I hoped I could weather it through tonight. I am sorry to have ruined your wedding," he whispered, "and I need you to know...I am glad my son has found you."

I knelt down and gave him a smile.

"You haven't ruined anything. Kier and I are joined with or without these rituals. But if you want to make it up to me, you'll rest."

His mouth twisted into a half smile.

"So much like Christine. I wonder if this is a Human female trait, or if my son simply is as lucky as I was."

"Little bit of both probably."

He let me go and closed his eyes. A pit was opening up in my stomach. There was very little chance that I could save Kier's father, but I'd give it everything I had.

When I stood up, I found Kier leaning against the wall in the hallway, anguish seared across his face.

"He is dying and I do not know what to do," he said.

I put my arms around him and Kier nestled his head in the crook of my neck. We stood like that for a few moments, and I wished I could make it all better, and take away his pain.

"I need you to meet me at the stables," I said pulling away so I could look at him. "We need to do what we can right now. That's what your father would want, right?"

He nodded.

"Yes, that is logical. Do not sacrifice those who can be saved worrying over those who...cannot."

"Hey, look at me," I caught his eye and bracketed his face with my hands, "as soon as I'm done examining your staff, I'm taking the fastest transport I can find to the Institute and Char'Vahn and I will find a way to save him. I will work all night and day if I have to, understand? I'm not giving up, so you don't either."

"I will try."

"Good. Now, I need to change and get my other gear."

"I should as well, these robes are uncomfortable."

We raced to the room and threw off the ceremonial clothing. Kier dressed in his uniform while I slipped into the civilian clothes I'd brought for working at the Institute. All of my gear was still packed in the satchel so I slung the strap over my shoulder and quickly sent the blood and other med scans to Char'Vahn with a quick note about who the sample belonged to and that I'd be arriving there shortly. I was just out of the house when my wrist com beeped with a response, stating that he'd start to analyze the scans and looked forward to my arrival.

Well, at least he's happy to have me here.

We ran to the stables, which weren't all that far from the house, to find that a few of the staff had collapsed. Prem'Ahn was directing them to take the sick into the loft of the stables, which was clean and unoccupied. It was the first thing she'd done that I actually agreed with.

"Kier, have those who don't have symptoms line up so I can run the scans on them."

"What are you looking for? The doctors here have been perplexed as to what to look for prior to symptoms occurring," he asked.

"I'm looking for low metabolic enzyme count, a specific kind that enables them to turn blood into nutrients in their system. Full blooded Atavarians have this occurring naturally in their systems as ....as you know."

The revelation zinged through my mind in a second, shocking me into silence as my mind connected pieces of data and information that had seemed unrelated before. It wasn't linear, or coherent, and it was beyond speech, but I could see what my mind was constructing, the theory that had eluded Char'Vahn was at my fingertips. Just a little more...

"Chloe, are you—?"

"Shh!"

I held up my hand as the theory coalesced, not complete but there was enough there that I could see how it would work. I knew in my gut that this was what we'd been looking for. Kier's 'deficiency' as others had called it, would be the key to saving his people.

I ran up to one of the kitchen staff waiting outside.

"When did you start using Kier'Ahn's synthetic blood packs in the food?"

He paused at my odd question.

"As soon as we were informed he was visiting so few days prior to his arrival. The taste is different and I endeavored to acclimate Gav'Ahn and Prem'Ahn to the flavor."

I let out a long breath and grinned.

"That's great news, thank you."

I ran back to Kier, not caring that everyone was stunned and likely uncomfortable with my exuberant emotional show.

"Oh my god, Kier! I've got it, a solution!" I jumped into the air and let out a shout. "Go back to the house, grab about half a dozen of your synthetic blood packs and bring them back."

Kier didn't question me, he didn't look at me like I was nuts, he just sent me a kiss through our mental bond and raced off to do what I asked. My mind was only half focused on the scans I was taking of the staff as I ran through some of the data points that may present a problem with my theory. There were things I needed to test and I would do it on the live samples and blood work that Char'Vahn had. Which meant I needed to go to the Institute as quickly as I could.

When I finished scanning, I sent three more staff to the sick rooms in the loft because they were starting to show enzyme deficiencies. The others were fine, so after they put on masks and gloves, I had them go back to the house to move Gav'Ahn to a more comfortable place and told them to try and get him to eat some of Kier's blood packets specifically. They looked at me quizzically, but went without question.

When Kier got back, he was carrying a large container of his blood packs.

"Your synthetic blood has a lab created enzyme in it, which means it's slightly different than the one that occurs naturally in Atavarians," I said, as I led him into the stable, "and your father has been consuming that blood for the past several days. Which means he might've contracted the about a week ago, and the virus might have been attacking his metabolic enzymes, making him symptomatic. *But* consuming your blood with the synthetic enzymes helped his body fight it off until now. It bought him some time."

"So if those who are just starting to become ill consume blood with the enzymes in it, they may survive longer."

"Exactly. It might be enough to get them to hold on while Char'Vahn and I come up with a treatment. It's a long shot but I think it will work. I need you to get everyone in the loft to drink some of those blood packs and then make sure the staff gives some to your father."

He nodded and wove his fingers between mine.

"This gives me hope," he whispered.

I smiled and sent him a hug and long, lingering kiss through our bond.

"I ordered the shuttle prepped for you. It should be ready to take you to the Institute. I will meet you there when I can."

"Stay with your father, I'll be alright and I'll send any updates or medicines straight to you. But first, can I get a blood sample? You may not be fully Atavarian, but you've been consuming the synthetic enzymes and—"

"You do not need to explain," he bared his wrist.

I took two different samples, my mind creating a list of things to test. If I could do this, I could save Gav'Ahn and everyone else in the early stages.

Kier was silent as we ran to the shuttle and just before I was about to walk up the ramp, he pulled me to the side. Before I could say anything, he crushed his mouth to mine, giving me a long, hard kiss that temporarily distracted me from the science that had been my focus.

"Be careful," he whispered, holding me tight. "Do not go anywhere outside of the lab complex until I get there."

"Kier, I'll—"

"Promise me."

His voice was hard, a tinge of unease around the edges.

"I promise."

His body relaxed a little and he nodded.

"I am sending one of the uninfected staff with you as a bodyguard—"

I opened my mouth to protest when he stopped me with another kiss.

"Please do not fight me on this," the thought came as his tongue plundered me. *"I must know you are protected."*

And then I understood. He could do nothing to protect his mother, but he *needed* to protect me.

"I understand."

It wasn't until we were lifting off that I realized in all the panic, I hadn't been able to tell him about Prem'Ahn.

Chapter Twenty-Five

KIER'AHN

I watched the shuttle until it was a tiny speck on the horizon. And then I looked toward the towering, black and purple mountain where the Institute was built. The sun would set in a few hours and I indulged in a moment of disappointment that Chloe and I would not have the 'honeymoon' night she had wanted.

I turned back to the house where my father was laying in his bed by now, dying.

I cannot think like that. Chloe was so sure she would have a cure, or at least something to keep him alive. I have to believe, that is what she would do. What Mother would do too.

I had not thought of what my mother might do in any circumstance in so long that I was caught by surprise when tears stung my eyes. Just letting myself remember her view of the world made it seem as if she stood next to me. I closed my eyes and soaked that in, even though it was not something an Atavarian would ever do.

But I am not just Atavarian. I am Human too. I am Christine'Ahn's son too.

I squared my shoulders, knowing that my mother would want me to focus on helping those that I could, on being brave. So that's what I would do, I would channel her courage in this moment and help the people here.

The stables were in disarray when I returned, my aunt having disappeared on a mysterious errand. I settled the situation soon enough and organized a way for those in the loft to get the blood packs Chloe had left. Blankets and more comfortable mats were brought from the house for the sick, as well as holo tablets and com devices so they could communicate with their loved ones. By the time all was in order, the sun had set and the remaining staff looked tired and hungry.

It may serve to have all of us partake of my synthetic blood, as a precaution.

"I need two volunteers to stay and watch over the sick," I said, "the rest, come with me."

Once we were back at the house, I warmed enough blood for the staff and ordered them to drink it. Most hated the taste but they did not complain. I thought of the town, the sick that we had been forced to move into a small section that was now quarantined from the rest. We had ensured they had enough blood for a month at least, along with any other amenities they could want. But now I wondered if we should not make them drink this instead.

"How much of this do we have?" I asked the cook.

"I ordered enough for you for the next two months," he answered with twist of his lips as he swallowed the last bit. "Why?"

"Pack it up, as much as we need for the quarantined population in the town. If Chloe is correct, and I believe she is, then this may keep them alive long enough to receive whatever cure she and Char'Vahn are creating."

The cook nodded and organized some of the remaining staff into helping him get the blood out of cold storage. Meanwhile, I sent word to the pilot of the shuttle to return immediately so we could transport the staff and blood to the town.

With all the help, we loaded the blood so fast that the shuttle had barely been on the pad longer than ten minutes before it lifted off again. I volunteered to go with the group and ensured that my father had someone to watch over him.

"Give him the blood as often as you can," I instructed the man and woman staying with him.

The flight was short, but we had to land outside the town in order not to damage buildings. I radioed the town elders, asking them to meet us at the landing zone and to bring hand carts. I gave them instructions on what to do, though they eyed me with some suspicion.

"Where is your father?" one of them asked.

"He has been struck with the virus," I said, working hard to keep my emotions out of my voice. "My mate has gone to the Institute to work with Scientist Char'Vahn on an anti-viral. In the meantime, she has recommended that the sick drink this specific synthetic blood to help counter act the early effects of the virus and prolong the lives of the patients."

He eyed me suspiciously, and a few of the elders shook their heads.

"We are to trust a Human?" one of them at the back questioned.

"Yes," was my simple answer. "Is it not wise to listen to sound advice, no matter the source? Especially when lives are at stake?"

"He is correct," said a younger female member of the council. "This is Gav'Ahn's son. He was here just today, working alongside us. Do we accept his labor, but not his wisdom?"

The elders, one by one, reluctantly agreed.

"We will try your solution," the first one said.

I inclined my head and helped the staff offload the cases of blood packs onto the hand carts. Many of them still doubted me, and the instructions. In the past, this would have been cause to control anger and hurt. Although both feelings surfaced, they were not as potent as before. I easily managed those feelings, not allowing them to spill past my barriers. It was an odd but welcome change.

"I will confirm this treatment plan with Char'Vahn at my earliest convenience," said one of the head doctors. "Just to ensure that you are not mistaken."

"You may do as you wish, of course. But it seems highly illogical to disrupt his work to save our people simply to satisfy your own prejudice."

The doctor's spine straightened and his mouth tensed.

"I...had not considered that before," he admitted after a moment and turned on his heel.

"You are not at all what I had anticipated," said the female elder from earlier. "I am greatly impressed by your control and wisdom. I would be most honored to have you and your mate in my home when circumstances are more stable."

This was unexpected to say the least, but it warmed my very soul to hear her willingness to accept us both. It gave me a spark of hope that perhaps Chloe and I could make a life together that would not end in tragedy.

"That is most kind," I responded. "I will speak with her once her work is completed."

She nodded and turned to assist the unloading of the last cases of blood.

The short shuttle ride back to the estate was quiet as everyone was fatigued from the emotion and activity of the night. When I glanced at the clock in the cock pit, I realized it was actually quite late. I wondered what Chloe was doing, if she and Char'Vahn had made any progress.

I worried about her safety, and I missed her in the way I would imagine someone who has lost a limb might miss that part of themselves. Her presence still warmed my consciousness, and I could see her there, though her emotions were harder to discern over this distance, and I could not communicate with her. Perhaps in a year, our bond would be strong enough for that, but at the moment, it was still too new; I wished I had done more to cultivate it so I could at least see that she was alright.

I sent her a quick message on my com, updating her about the town and requesting a confirmation that she was well.

I got a message back almost immediately and it soothed the anxious knot in my chest.

"Good thinking about the town! We've hit a road block but we're working on it. The solution is close, I can feel it. Will update you soon. I miss you."

I closed my hand over the com device, holding it as if it were her and took a moment to control my urge to fly over there and stay with her. There was still work to be done here, though not tonight. I wanted to see my father, and ensure that he was being taken care of according to my instructions.

But I also needed to be by his side. Should the worst happen, there was something I needed to say, something I should have said on that hill. I was ready to admit how my own anger and hurt had contributed to our estrangement, and forgive him for the things he'd done. He had to know that before he died.

When we landed, I instructed the cook to order more blood. The rest of the staff went to guest quarters while I finished the post flight checks on the shuttle. I was mildly surprised to see my aunt at the foot of the ramp when I was finished.

"There you are, I have been looking for you." Displeasure was thick in her voice, though her face showed nothing.

She stood in front of me, her extravagant gown gone. Instead she was curiously wearing what looked like her dueling leathers, a set of tight fitting pants and jacket in the orange and black, her Leigth blade at her hip.

"Why are you dressed like that?"

"Follow me," was her only answer.

My aunt often gave little information and expected me to simply comply; it was our baseline really. But something about this order caused my skin to prickle with unease. Especially when she led me to the secret path to my mother's old observatory.

"How do you know about this?" I asked.

"I have always known about this. Since the day I found you, shaming your family with your display of emotion."

I clenched my jaw as I followed her. The path was well kept, with fresh gravel that had just been laid, and there were wild roses all along the path. My mother's favorite flower. The trees that grew in an arch over the path were trimmed recently, the scent of it was pungent when mixed with the perfume of the roses. I concluded that my father must have kept this path maintained and planted these here, as he had the tree; more evidence that I had misjudged him when it came to Mother.

When we finally emerged from the arching trees to climb the hill, I was confident that something was amiss. My aunt had never, to my knowledge, come here again after finding me that day. This place was sentimental and that was something my aunt definitely was not.

Cresting the hill, the first thing I saw was my Leigth blade against the trunk of the tree, polished and waiting for me. I glanced over at my aunt, who had drawn her sword.

"What is this?" I asked.

"Pick it up, Kier."

I did, knowing there would not be another warning. The moment my hand clasped the hilt I heard her feet on the grasses. I had just enough time to turn and block her strike to my side.

"You should have been so much more," she hissed in my face. "I tried, as a kindness to my brother, as a kindness to you. I tried to make you into an Atavarian, but your weakness was too great an obstacle."

I pushed her back, breaking the connection of our blades, and took attack position before delivering a series of fast strikes. I lunged toward her, and she pivoted to the side, just missing my blade, and attempted to strike my flank. I spun and blocked her. From the way she was fighting, how she delivered basic blows and expecting me to fall to them, I realized that my aunt had assumed I would be out of practice during my time on the Intrepid.

But sparing with Lieutenant Commander Althea had not only kept my skills sharp, it had taught me a thing or two as well.

"I am not a child anymore," I said. "I have learned much away from here."

"But nothing of value."

"We will see."

Our blades flicked and parried in quick succession against one another. I pressed her then she pressed me, back and forth until we were both breathing heavy. She swung to attack my side again, and I blocked her, though scarcely, and pushed her back. Her strikes became more ruthless, harder, clearly intending to kill me.

I did not want to take her life, she was my family, but I would defend myself.

"Why are you doing this?" I asked as I blocked her. "Is it because of Chloe? This situation does not make sense."

"I had thought you would seek me out," she stepped back and we circled each other. "After what I had said to your mate, I expected you to react emotionally, seeking revenge. But you surprise me and instead, acted logically."

"What are you talking about? What did you tell Chloe?"

Her eyebrows raised and she lowered her blade.

"She truly did not tell you? I had thought it would be the first thing she did when I was gone."

"Chloe was concerned with saving lives, there was no time for personal revelations."

Prem'Ahn nodded slowly.

"Then perhaps I will tell you. Perhaps it is time for all to be known and understood before I cleanse our House once and for all."

An sick sensation coursed through me at her words, and I suspected that I would not like what I heard. Yet I had to know, so I nodded at her to proceed.

"It was no secret that I despised your mother," she began. "My brother was betrothed to a respectable female, but he canceled it and brought home a Human. What was worse, he procreated with her."

The burn of her hatred scorched me and I understood that this was not new. This had been her way since the day she found me here. Loathing cloaked in love, her every action meant to tear me down.

"I had planned to dispose of your mother and her offspring soon after she arrived. But her pregnancy with you created a complication. I wanted to see what you would become, if you could be trained to make up for the failings of your father, the stain of your maternal line. But I waited too long. Your mother's humanity had infected your Atavarian side, and I knew that the three of you must be dealt with."

My heart dropped as her words struck me like blows from her blade.

"You...you killed her?" I choked out.

"Yes," she said it so simply, though I did not know why I expected any emotion from her. "Terrorists had their uses then, just as they do now. I do not agree with how emotional they are, but that does not mean they cannot be effective when applied properly. I had the house in Ruval under observation for months, waiting for the return of the three of you. I had almost given up, your father was so...protective of his Human. But then the three of you arrived, and I knew I had to act quickly. I authorized the bomb, told the man where to place it. But you lived, an unexpected outcome that I chose to make the most of."

"Murderer," I spat at her.

"It was necessary then as it is now."

I couldn't breath as what she was saying hit me full force. "Now...Chloe. What have you done?"

"Calm yourself. Remember what happened the last time you became emotional when it concerned a Human you loved? You caused her death."

My guilt over that had been the one emotion Prem'Ahn had not bothered to excise from me. She had nurtured it, used it as an example of what happened when I did not utilize my Atavarian side. I may have healed from this many years ago, found balance, if not for her.

The sun was starting to rise, glinting off the silver and blue of our blades. It was a new day, I had a chance at a new life, a new beginning with Chloe. And I would begin it now.

"It was not my fault," I said through gritted teeth. "I was a *child*."

"A child who used emotion to coerce his mother and sister into my trap. You did beautifully, Kier, truly. I only wish the lesson had taken more fully in you. Then perhaps I would not have to kill you now."

Her overhead blow came fast, like a viper striking. But the cold hatred of my fury was well stoked and I viciously batted it away.

"You destroyed my life," I said, savagely striking at her with my blade. "You destroyed my family." Again, she parried as I backed her into the tree. "You tried to destroy me, piece by piece!" I growled, while delivering a series of fast, slashing strikes. One hit her thigh, the other her arm, scoring the dueling armor through to her skin. "I will not allow you to do anything to my *priash*."

Her eyebrows raised at that and she went from defense to offense in the blink of an eye. Her strikes were as fast as mine but I blocked and parried every single one.

"*Priash*," her slash slipped past my defenses and sliced my upper arm, "are emotional fairy tales. You were tainted from your very birth." I lunged, she batted it away and countered with a swipe to my side that I barely blocked. "I should have done what I planned and killed your mother when she landed." Her blade came around and sliced into my side, but I spun before she could cut me too deeply. "Or tainted the blood you drank in your crib. Better infanticide than the shame you have wrought!"

Her venomous words hung in the air as the sun broke over the mountains in the distance, and I saw it all so clearly then. She was filled with bitterness, fear had become hatred inside of her and twisted her into this. Perhaps, if she had allowed herself to love me, as she had made me believe she had, then the poison in her soul would have been drawn out over time. But this woman before me was not capable of reconciliation, or seeing past her own prejudices.

If I had stayed, would she have twisted me into another version of herself? Would I be consumed with self-loathing that manifested in hating others to this degree? Deluding myself into taking lives and calling it logic?

I had worried that my time away would make me less Atavarian, but it had not. It had shown me a possible existance, it had begun to leach her poison from me. And being with Chloe, knowing her love and acceptance, had accelerated that. I did not have a full view of the path toward embracing both of my halves, but I knew it was under my feet. I knew that I would find a fulfilling life.

"What a terrible path you have chosen for yourself," I said, shoving her away from me with my blade.

"The path of logic—"

"Is not what you have chosen." I lowered my sword and shook my head at her. "I am proud that I am not like you. I do not practice cruelty and call it kindness. I do not destroy and call it logic."

She lowered her blade as well and stepped toward me. For several moments, Prem'Ahn said nothing, merely staring at me as if taking my measure.

"You are a fool to lower your defenses."

I could not block the blade completely, but I altered its course away from my heart, though it did pierce my shoulder. I grunted at the pain, compartmental-izing it, as I'd been taught by her, and punched her across the face.

She stumbled back, clearly shocked. Hand to hand was not part of Leigth blade fighting, but it was part of how I spared with Lieutenant Commander Althea. I slashed with the blade, then hooked her ankle with my foot as she parried the strike. She landed on her back and I pressed the tip of my blade to her throat. Undeterred, Prem'Ahn struck out and sliced deeply across my upper thigh. I winced and jumped back as she climbed to her feet, her bleeding mouth twisted in disgust.

Her eyes blazed and I knew that she was losing her hold on her emotions. If I could press her more, draw that out of her, I would have the advantage.

I let her get in close, spun behind her and shoved her. She lost her balance and fell to the ground. I took the opportunity to kick her in the stomach and roll her again onto her back.

"Yield!" I demanded, my blade once again at her throat.

"Never."

She batted it away and staggered onto her feet. I parried and blocked a dozen of her strikes, all of them far too hard and out of control. In a flick of my blade I sliced her wrist and she dropped her weapon. I kicked it aside and with the tip of my own sword, backed her to the tree.

"I do not wish to kill you," I said, "so yield."

It was then an explosion pierced the morning air and I looked toward the mountains where the Institute was nestled in horror. Black plumes of smoke rose into the sky, another explosion following the first. My heart stopped beating, my entire body freezing with shock.

Only the grunting approval of my aunt could tear my attention away from the smoke rising from the base of the mountains.

"As I said, terrorists have their uses."

Smoke.

Rubble.

Glass.

Blood.

The memory of it all assaulted my senses, and I stumbled back from her. I had to go to Chloe, I had to know if she was alright. I turned to run down the path when Prem'Ahn tackled me from behind. My sword dropped to the ground and I rolled. Her body fell on top of mine and a curved dagger gleamed in the sunlight.

She was about to plunge it into my chest when I seized her wrist and twisted it violently. The blade sliced into her sternum, shock lighting up her eyes as she stared at me, and for a moment I wondered if she regretted her decisions this day.

"It matters not...she is dead," she gasped.

I pushed her off me and lurched up onto my feet. The blood on my uniform and the sting of the wounds were distant. All I could hear was a pulsing terror in my blood as I limped down the path. I had to get to the shuttle, I had to get to Chloe. It was not too late.

I can...I cannot be too late.

Chapter Twenty-Six

CHLOE

Flying in the shuttle, over the Institute, I was struck by the beauty of the place. It was built at the very base of the black and purple mountains I'd seen in the distance from Kier's home. The purple moss, which covered much of the mountains' tops and sides, sparkled like diamonds in the sunlight, a breathtaking contrast to the black stone the mountains were made out of. The Institute itself was a series of towers divided by large courtyards, including a main courtyard in the very center with a sculpture celebrating the Enlightened ones. I expected us to land at one of the main landing pads, but we circled around to the very back where a smaller pad was tucked into the shadow of the peaks.

Char'Vahn met me when I arrived and escorted me through a series of small tunnels to a room at the very back of the west wing on the main floor of the Institute.

It looked as if it were a new lab; all the equipment was rather haphazardly positioned and some things were still in boxes.

"The main lab was vandalized two days ago," he explained, "and I have received multiple threats regarding my willingness to work with you. The High Council thought it best to move me to a secluded section of the Institute."

I nodded as I glanced around. It was well lit and spacious. A small room to the left had a couch and food printer. And to my right was a small patio with a garden.

"This will do nicely, though I'm sorry you've been driven out of your regular lab," I said.

He brushed it away.

"I will not mourn what is not necessary. Here is the most recent data on what you have sent me and your theories."

And that was that.

We'd been working ever since.

"The model has failed again," Char'Vahn said beside me. "The virus overpowers the artificial enzymes too quickly."

"And we can't give any more of the artificial enzymes to a patient?"

"No, it would not be a safe level."

I ran a hand over my face and plopped down into a chair.

I stared out the large, tinted window that looked out onto the private courtyard and saw that it was almost morning. I could see the barest hint of light on the horizon. We'd worked through the night and had come no closer to using my theory to solve the enzyme problem.

Char'Vahn agreed that it was a good stop gap and could help save lives. But only if we could find a way to stop the virus from gobbling up the enzymes so fast.

The older Atavarian shuffled around the lab, rolling his bottom lip between his thumb and forefinger as he thought through the problem. His horns were nearly white as was his hair, and there were deep wrinkles in his dark red skin. I had liked him the second I'd met him over the holo tablet. He was gruff, emotionless like all Atavarians, but he didn't look down on me because I was Human. In fact, he seemed to have a respect for my work and intelligence that my species did not diminish.

"I believe," Char'Vahn's thunderous voice jarred me from my musings, "that when a roadblock like this is met, it is perhaps time to change our perspective."

"How so?"

He nodded toward the courtyard.

"Get out of this lab and go for a walk Chloe'Ahn."

The name startled me and I was far too tired to hide the fact.

"Why did you...?"

"Are you not mated to Kier, of the House of Ahn?"

"Yes."

"Then you are now Chloe'Ahn."

I didn't know why but the fact that he accepted me as Kier's mate, had seen us both as worthy of recognizing at all, made a lump rise in my throat.

"Thank you for that. I haven't received much acceptance here."

"I should think not. Atavarians are slow to change, but eventually we do arrive. Now, please leave this lab and get some sunlight and fresh air. I will bring you back some food and drink from the lounge."

I got to my feet, wearier that I'd realized before, and walked out of the double doors to the beautiful courtyard. The guard Kier had selected for me followed at a respectable distance but it still rankled a bit that I had a shadow.

The yellow stepping stones had purple moss growing between them, sparkling in the dim light of dozens of short lamps. I made my way over to the small garden at the back of the courtyard where a tiny fountain gurgled away. There were yellow and blue flowers scattered among pink ones, none of which I recognized. I was exhausted but my mind refused to shut down. We were close to a solution, I could feel it, but I couldn't *find* it.

This was the most frustrating part of any project; the knowing but not knowing at the same time. The knowledge was in my mind, tucked away, waiting for a light to shine on it, but I couldn't make it happen. I could only let my mind follow along the winding path of discovery.

Maybe I should just take a short nap, get refreshed that way. I'm exhausted and sore from that damn dress.

I was staring off into the flower bed, half watching a flying bug, that looked a little like a bee, flit to the yellow flower and then the blue. But when it landed on the blue one it became stuck and I watched in strange fascination as the petals of the flower slowly closed over it.

Something sparked in my mind, information on the tip of my brain.

The blue flower somehow made the bee think it was safe...why are the blue and yellow flowers side by side, all throughout the garden?

There was something there that connected to a piece of information I'd learned a long time ago...what was it?

"Hey, could you come here for a sec?" I asked the guard.

He walked over, and I couldn't tell if he was annoyed or he always looked like that but it didn't really matter in the moment.

"Those two flowers, are they the same?"

A small wrinkle appeared on his forehead.

"No."

"Okay, um...well, humor me if you will. The insect went to the yellow flower and was fine, then it went to the blue one and became stuck and is now being consumed."

He glanced at the flower and back at me.

"The blue flower," his tone was definitely annoyed, "has the same scent and pollen type as the yellow. It tricks the insect so it can lure it in."

And suddenly, I remembered.

"Oh my god, that's it! Thank you!"

I ran back into the lab, leaving the stunned guard outside while I pounded way at the computer interface. It took me a few tries before I could pull up what I was looking for, and I wasn't at all surprised that archeological medicine, specifically from Earth, was not prevalent in their databases.

"Back so soon?" Char'Vahn asked as he stepped back into the lab.

"I think I figured it out!"

He walked up behind me and read over my shoulder.

"Decoys...huh," he muttered.

"So, I took a class in archeological medicine at the Academy and one of the things it talked about was how early nanite tech was used to create decoy cells for viruses to attack so that it wouldn't be able to propagate, effectively stopping it before it really begins."

"And you theorize that we could use the nanites as decoy metabolic enzymes?"

"Which would trick the virus into attacking them, instead of the real ones—"

"Giving our anti-viral time to build up in the system and destroy the virus."

"Yes!"

"How does this solve the problem of the virus eating the enzymes too quickly? Will it not consume these just as fast and then our problem is still present?"

"We make it a tougher meal."

He frowned and I pointed at the model I'd hastily constructed. I gave him time to look it over while I bounced on the balls of my feet, nerves and excitement making it impossible to stand still.

"This could very well work," he finally said. "Let us begin."

It took a number of hours to create the nanite that we needed and then run the necessary tests to ensure it would work and was safe. I fell asleep somewhere between the second to last and last test, and woke to the beeping of the machines.

"Did it work?" I yawned as I stumbled off the low couch in an adjacent room.

The sun was now up past the horizon, flooding the courtyard and the lab with bright golden light.

"Indeed," Char'Vahn said, his eyes sparkling. "I believe we can administer this safely. The only issue is that the nanites still degrade rather fast when placed in the solution."

"What about the test to deliver them via blood consumption?"

"The only one that did not have too quick of a decay was the synthetic formula that Kier'Ahn consumes. I believe the enzymes that are already in that formula play a key part in this distinction and may still be able to strengthen the patient even further against the viral strain in the future, but that will require more tests."

I couldn't help chuckling as I looked over the data. Kier had been ostracized for so many things, his special diet included. Now, that very thing would help save his people.

"They're safe for actual Atavarian testing then?"

"Yes, all the risk factors are within acceptable parameters."

I breathed a sigh of relief. I would send Kier a com once we had the first batch, and have him pick them up for his father and the staff. My relief was short lived when a loud boom shook the facility, followed by the blaring klaxon of alarms.

"What's that?"

Char'Vahn's eyes widened and he ran to the door just before another explosion sounded and the sounds of loud voices reached us.

"Hide," he commanded me. "I believe that the ones who have threatened me might be the ones attacking. I cannot ensure that they will spare you."

"Are there injured out there?"

Another explosion rocked the ground under us, followed by the horrific sound of something large falling.

"Most certainly," Char'Vahn answered.

"Then I need to help, risk or not, that's what I do."

He pressed his lips together and let out a sigh.

"What if I could bring you patients?"

"Char'Vahn—"

"Listen to me. You are the best hope my planet has to stop this virus from decimating us. If you die, millions, maybe billions, will follow. Sacrificing you is not logical."

"You have what you need," I replied, "you said it would work. You don't need me anymore."

He opened his mouth to argue.

"I am one person. One. How many are in this Institute?"

"Hundreds."

"And any one of them can help you produce this, can take our notes and help you with any issues. I've done my part and I'm not going to let others die for me."

He looked down and then back up at me.

"You may not have to. They do not know about this lab. If you can get to one of the landing pads, you can take a shuttle out of here. They might not stay if you are gone."

"Might?"

Char'Vahn opened a cabinet that I had assumed was full of equipment, just as my bodyguard rushed into the lab. Inside the cabinet were pulse rifles. He handed one to the guard who began to check it over and power up the cells, and one to me.

"Do you know how to use one of these?" Char'Vahn asked.

"Unfortunately yes."

Pulse rifles were technically non-lethal, but most beings would experience death from crushed rib cages or vertebrae, and a pulse blast on too high of a setting could definitely produce that.

Char'Vahn rushed to the computer.

"If you or I are killed, our work must be preserved. I am backing it up to the external servers. Do you have a data stick?"

I rummaged in my satchel, as I heard shouting from somewhere, some were calling for help.

I handed him my data stick and he began transferring the data. "If I do not survive, take this to the High Council and present them with our findings. They can authorize an emergency planetary wide creation and distribution project."

I swallowed as the sound of blaster fire reached us. If there were wounded and I just ran away...

"There are many medics here," Char'Vahn said, as if he could read my thoughts, "some of them are helping. This is not your responsibility."

"I don't agree, but thank you for trying to make me feel better."

"We need to go," the guard said. "If they went to the lab and didn't find either of you, they will start searching."

Char'Vahn nodded and grabbed his own pulse rifle. I slung my satchel on and made sure I had my med kit before following the guard out. I ended up being between the two Atavarians as we made our way through the tunnels that had brought me here. The lights flickered as another explosion rocked the ground beneath us and dust fell from the roof. The lights dimmed but continued to glow, and I realized that the Institute may be on reserve power.

If they blew the power, does that mean no one knows we're under attack?

I checked my wrist com for a signal, but we must've been too deep underground; there was no way to contact Kier. Above us, there were screams, the echoes of shouting and the boom something heavy falling.

"Keep going," Char'Vahn said.

The guard led us up a small incline and out onto the landing pad, but all that met us was rubble. Whoever they were, they'd blown up one of the shuttles.

"There's another one this way," Char'Vahn said.

We double backed and were just about to round a corner when the pounding of footsteps reached us. The guard slammed me against the wall and peeked around the corner. A blaster round took a chunk off the wall but missed the guard. Two more rounds flew past us and the guard stepped out, firing his rifle. The assailants shouted and I heard the sound of bodies crumpling.

"Down here!" someone shouted.

"They are coming from the other landing pad," the guard said.

"If they've already searched the lab maybe going that way would make sense."

"Unless they left someone there to find us," the guard said.

"It is our best option," Char'Vahn replied, "and from there, you can get her to the underground maintenance tunnels. They lead into the mountain and out through a cave. It's a hike, but you should be able to escape that way."

"Let's go."

The guard took point and led us back to a maintenance hatch we'd passed before. It was a snug fit but we managed to squeeze inside and crawl to a small room just outside the lab. The guard opened the door and confirmed it was safe before motioning for us to follow him out into a broad hallway.

This was the most exposed we'd been since leaving the makeshift lab and the hair on the back of my neck rose. I was nervous about every single sound, and there were a lot of them here. Atavarians screamed or cried for help, and the smell of blood was thick in the air the closer we got to the lab.

This had obviously been the place that had taken the most damage.

We began to see bodies under rubble and some with blaster burns in their chest. There was a hole in a wall to my right, the debris still smoking. We were almost to the first section of labs before we saw anyone who was alive. They were huddled in groups, with several Atavarians, themselves wounded, attempting to help them, as others dug through stone and wood looking for survivors or equipment.

I ran to one that was bleeding from the head, their eyes half closing.

"Chloe'Ahn –" Char'Vahn began to say.

"I know," I snapped, "but I took an oath and I refuse to walk on by when I can do something."

"I will scout ahead and make sure the maintenance hatch is unobstructed," said the guard.

Considering the amount of damage here, I thought it was an even chance that it was. I scanned the wounded woman, who showed signs of a severe concussion and head laceration. I gave her a hypo spray for the pain, and then put sealing gel on the head wound.

"What can I do?" asked Char'Vahn.

"Can you get her to a more comfortable position, some place she can rest?"

He nodded and gently picked her up.

"You are the one they are looking for." An Atavarian male stalked up to me. "This is your fault."

"No," I said. "I didn't do this. I was working to save all of you. If you want to be mad at someone, blame the ones who bombed you, and are killing you. Not me."

I brushed past him to examine the next person, who had internal bleeding and two broken ribs, one perilously close to his lung.

"Do you have a working surgery bay?" I asked the male who'd accused me of all this.

"No, it was destroyed."

I swallowed down my guilt; I knew this wasn't my fault, I wasn't going to take responsibility for this. But still, it was hard not to.

"The maintenance hatch is completely blocked," the guard said. "And I think the radicals are circling back around. We should move."

I looked around at the frightened faces of the wounded and those trying to help. Most didn't have any medical equipment and I wondered if it had been destroyed in the blast.

"How long before someone comes to help?" I asked.

"The emergency signal is still transmitting," one of the Atavarians nearby said, "so we should see some of the planetary guard shortly."

I nodded.

"Then I'll stay."

"I cannot guarantee your safety, and I gave Kier'Ahn my word," the guard said.

"I know that, and I don't mean for you to break it, but I'm not leaving these people."

"But they are after you," said an Atavarian woman. "And you are Human, your species is emotional, irrational. Why would you stay?"

"Because you all need my help, and yes, I am emotional. And right now, I'm pissed as hell."

The guard stepped back the way we came, and looked down the hall.

"This could be a choke point," he said. "If we had at least four of us with weapons..."

I handed him my weapon, and Char'Vahn did the same.

"I am more use as a medic."

I nodded and the two of us began to sort through the wounded. I'd only treated two others when the firing began. My guard ended up recruiting the two Atavarians who had spoken to me and one other that scrounged up a blaster pistol, and they were holding the choke point for the moment. It wouldn't last long though, and I hoped that whoever was coming would get here fast.

"There is movement down this way!" someone yelled and pointed down a hall that was half obstructed with fallen stone.

"They are outflanking us," Char'Vahn glanced up at me.

I pressed my lips together and finished the makeshift splint. Fear began to choke me as I faced the very real possibility that I would not live through this.

I closed my eyes, breathed and decided that I'd fight like hell right to the end, but I wasn't going to betray my morals and run away. Even if the thought of not seeing Kier again left me with a jagged hole in my chest.

So I wiped the tears away, blew out a long breath and said, "Next patient."

I was barely done sealing the wound on this patient's thigh when one of the Atavarians firing down the hall screamed and fell back, sightless eyes staring up at the ceiling, a smoking hole in their chest.

"They are starting to overwhelm us!" the guard shouted. "They've got laser and pulse weapons!"

My fingers trembled as I administered the hypo spray and a tear fell down my cheeks, but I brushed it away. I could do this, I could be brave. Then I heard something that yanked away the cloud of fear that had started to envelope me.

"Chloe!" Kier's voice was ragged, desperate.

I gasped and jumped to my feet.

"Kier!"

The movement down the partially blocked hall hadn't been more attackers, it had been him.

He stumbled through fallen planks and wiring. Bood soaked one pant leg and sleeve, obviously making him a bit weak. What happened to him? Had he fought his way here and been wounded?

It didn't matter, I'd take care of him. And while he was one person, I had an insane moment of hope that I'd get through this now that he was here.

I'd just taken a step toward him when his look of relief turned to horror.

"No!" he screamed like it was being ripped from him, and I turned half way to look behind me, just in time to see the pulse blast before it forced all the air from my lungs, and threw me into darkness.

Chapter Twenty-Seven

KIER'AHN

I fell over debris, smoke hung in the air and glass cut my hands as I half crawled half stumbled to where she'd fallen. Blaster bolts landed around me, one singing my arm but I didn't care. I barely noticed when the fire fight ceased and the sound of shuttles and other kinds of blasters echoed in the distance.

I was reliving my nightmare and my greatest fear, all meshed into one.

Blood soaked Chloe's hair on one side from a gash on her forehead. I touched her chest, no movement.

An old Atavarian male ran a med scanner over her as I gripped her hands.

"Don't die...please don't die...don't leave me alone..." the sobs shook me, tearing at my heart.

I was too late...how could I be too late?

"Her ribs are miraculously not broken," the old Atavarian said, pulling something out of the med kit.

Her presence in my mind, that warmth and light, I couldn't see it, couldn't feel it. I was cold, alone and in the dark once again.

"Please come back..."

I couldn't breathe without her. A yawning darkness began to open up inside of me, swallowing me piece by piece each second that she was gone.

The older male ripped her shirt down the center, exposing her chest to everyone. I snarled at him and seized his hands.

"What are you doing?"

"These have to go on her skin!" He pulled himself free of me. "If you want to save her, help me."

I took the nodes he held out to me and my brain suddenly focused. These led to a defibrillator.

I took the small box as the older Atavarian placed the nodes on her chest. The unit was charging but every second stretched into years, how long could she go like this?

The green light went off and I hit the button. Her body arched and went still. No heartbeat.

"Again," he said.

I waited, then hit the button.

Again her body seized up, but there was no heartbeat.

Agonizing fear choked me as I hit the button for a third time.

"Please...priash fight...come back to me!"

Through the darkness I saw a glimmer in my consciousness, a spark.

"...Kier..."

"I do not think she is coming back," the old Atavarian said.

I didn't listen, and hit the green button again. Her eyes fluttered, a spike of a heartbeat then nothing.

"Come back to me...do not leave me alone in the dark...please priash."

"...Kier...Kier..."

"Cease this. She is gone," the old male said solemnly.

I leveled a cold stare at him and hit the button again and her eyes flew open. She shuddered, taking in a jagged breath before coughing and stirring on the ground.

"Chloe..."

I gathered her in my arms and held her gently as I sobbed into her hair.

"I...I'm here...you're here..."

My mind was filled with the contradictions of profound relief and soul wrenching terror. I could not form words physically or mentally; all I could do was hold her, relishing each rise and fall of her chest, the way her hand curled into the front of my uniform. My wounds ached and I was weak from blood loss but I could not let her go. Not when the medics came in to take care of the wounded, not when they wanted to transport her out of there.

I snarled and growled at them, a purely instinctive response to almost losing the other half of my very soul.

"Kier," her voice was hoarse and she cupped my cheek, "it's alright. You need help too."

"We go together," I said, and tried to stand up.

My wounded leg was too weak, however, and I feared dropping her more than I did letting her go. I watched every single movement of the two medics that placed her on a stretcher and accepted the help of another to get to my feet. Though I would not allow them to treat me until I was sitting beside her in the emergency transport.

I held her hand as they tended to both of us, checking her vitals and closing her head wound, while they attached me to a PPR and closed my own wounds. They put an oxygen mask on her face, and told her to rest as we departed from the Institute. I could not take my eyes off her.

"We have given her a sedative," said one of the medics. "She must rest to recover her strength."

"Of course, thank you."

I was memorizing every inch of her beautiful face, the gold flecks in her blue eyes, the feel of her hand in mine. Though I had been worried for her safety since we landed on Atavar, actually experiencing the loss of her had been brutally visceral. The echo of it lingered inside of me, and I could not seem to shake it.

What if she was attacked again at the hospital? What if she died another time?

With Chloe, I had just brushed the surface of allowing emotions past my cognitive barriers after a lifetime of suppressing and controlling them. Passion, joy, the closeness of a mating bond, all of these emotions were strong and overwhelming in their own way. But none had prepared me for feeling her die. I was horribly unskilled in navigating the harsh, overpowering experiences that accompanied her death.

I did not know how to process such mind numbing terror or how to move on from it. I wanted to never leave her side to ensure she would be safe, at the same time I wanted to flee so that I would not experience this again.

I was afraid, irrational. And I did not know what to do.

Chloe squeezed my hand and pulled the oxygen mask down.

"You saved my life."

I shook my head.

"Yes...you did. If you hadn't been so distraught...then I wouldn't have felt you."

"You felt me?" I asked, forehead wrinkling as I frowned.

"I knew I was dead...I was slipping away but...I felt a tug right here," she tapped her heart. "It was you, calling to me, not letting me go. You saved me."

I could not speak past the way my throat tightened. Those same emotions that I thought had cost the life of my mother had saved the woman I loved.

And now, they were drowning me.

I pressed a soft kiss to her lips and replaced the oxygen mask on her face.

"Sleep, *priash*."

She gave me a drowsy smile and closed her eyes.

It did not take long for us to arrive at the medical facility. Chloe was asleep by then and I refused to leave her side, even walking quite slowly due to my injuries. The healers balked at first when they saw that Chloe was Human and I was about to order them to treat her or else, when the same older male from the tunnel marched through the door. His white and red robes were smudged in dirt and blood from the attack, but he swept regally into the waiting room all the same.

"I am Char'Vahn, Lead Scientist of the Virology Department of the Institute, you will treat this female as an honored member of my department."

Their eyes widened and they nodded in assent before wheeling her away.

"Thank you," I said, and went to follow when Char'Vahn's voice stopped me.

"She is remarkable, your mate. I have never met anyone like her among Humans. Tell me, is she an anomaly or are there others like her?"

I bristled at Chloe being referred to as if she were some specimen but knew that this man was not being rude, merely curious in the way of most Atavarian Scientists.

"In my experience, Humans are far more surprising than we assumed. Chloe, is not unique in the way you implied, and yet she is."

He nodded.

"Fascinating. You know, I would not have been able to create the anti-viral without her. I will personally see that her care is of the utmost quality and put our findings into action immediately."

"My father and some of our staff have been struck with the virus. I know I have no right to ask, it is illogical to prioritize my own family over all else but—"

"It is understandable," Char'Vahn cut in. "And, seeing as how Chloe'Ahn was one of the lead scientists on it, perhaps it is only right that her family be one of the first to receive it."

His words struck me silent.

Her family.

My family was now *her* family.

I had not thought of such a thing, and yet it was true.

"Thank you," I said, my mind reeling as I walked toward the room where Chloe had been taken.

I lingered in the doorway as the healers worked with the 3D holo read out of her vitals. She looked so small on an Atavarian healing bed, her hair still matted with blood and her face paler than usual. I could have gone into the room; as her mate, no one would have questioned it. But my feet were frozen, and I was unable to make them move forward. I kept looking at her chest, making sure it was moving, wondering if it was too fast or too slow. Was she sleeping too deeply? Would they know if she had a head injury in enough time?

I rubbed my head.

The conflict inside of me was too much.

When the healers were done, the lead, a woman with short black hair and long, curving horns walked up to me.

"Your mate is stable, though we will monitor her heart rate for the next day to ensure everything has returned to normal. There is some bruising around her chest and in various parts of her body, likely from a fall or a pulse weapon."

I nodded.

"Both."

"I see. We will administer healing gels over those to expedite recovery. Would you like to stay with her? We can have a cot brought in."

"No," the word stuck in my throat and my feet were already moving backwards. "I must return home, my father is ill."

"Very well. We will keep you apprised as to her recovery."

"Thank you."

Though I could not step into the room, my feet seemed to have no trouble moving me to the exit and toward a taxi. It wasn't until I was in the transport and headed toward the public shuttle that would take me back to the estate, that I realized I should have also seen a healer. My wounds were closed but I ached all over, especially in my chest.

I rubbed the spot as it throbbed uncomfortably.

"Kier? Where are you?"

I cringed at her voice in my head. There was a tug where the ache was beginning to grow and I knew that this was no injury, at least not one that could be healed by anything other than turning the taxi around. But the thought sent a bolt of fear through me. I could not face her, could not see her weak and wounded. These emotions were too much, too powerful. I needed time to sort through them.

Yes. I just needed some time.

"Rest," I said to her. *"I must return to my father and you must rest."*

She accepted this and the warmth of her presence shifted into something quiet. Then, the more distance between us, the more it was muted; there but not as strong. And I realized that the further from her I became, the more I could suppress and compartmentalize these emotions. When I boarded the transport shuttle and the hospital complex was in the distance behind me, I began to feel as if I could think clearly again, though that ache still persisted. I breathed through it, attempted to ignore it, until eventually I could pretend it was not clamoring for my attention.

It was the bond, I knew that. And the bond was demanding that I stay by her side. Having lost her and now having her back, it had strengthened, but also made it more in need of Chloe's presence. It was causing a war inside of me, between my instincts.

Something inside had told me to run, so I had.

But there was also something, that twinge in my chest that pressed upon me to return to her.

And the need to run was winning.

A few days, that is all I need. A few days to find my equilibrium again.

But then what?

Ask her to remain with me? We were not done with our mission here. I would need to stay as the GUP representative on Atavar and convince the High Council to support the GUP in defending our borders against the K'Tavi. The anti-viral was only the first step, an important one to be sure since it was removing one of the High Council's excuses for isolation, but it was not the whole mission.

My job could take months. Would I risk keeping Chloe on this planet to be attacked again?

The thought made all the air leave my lungs and I could not take a full breath. Once again, I was at war with myself.

She would not leave me if we were mated.

And I could not imagine breaking the bond. When she'd died, I thought I would perish too.

Yet, would I risk her life simply to avoid pain?

I could not think in my present state. I needed space, time to consider all of this. And she would be with Char'Vahn helping to ensure the medicine was created correctly and solve any problems. The hospital complex was well guarded, and it would only be for a few days. Once I had settled things with Prem'Ahn's death and knew my father's fate, then I would be able to see the path forward.

A small part of me knew that I was hiding behind all of this, using it as an excuse not to face what my heart and soul were telling me to do. But I ignored it, all of it in favor of feeling safe behind my cognitive barriers.

Chapter Twenty-Eight

CHLOE

I stared at my wrist com for the hundredth time today, as if I could will a response from Kier.

It had been a week and half since he saved me at the Institute and I hadn't seen him since. I'd messaged him only to receive the most curt responses, if I got anything at all. I tried to reach out through the bond, but the distance was too great and all I got back was a vague impression of his presence.

His father had been one of the first to receive the anti-viral and while I would have thought that I would be the most 'logical' person to monitor the effects, it had been Char'Vahn who had been requested to come to the estate. When I asked Kier if he wanted me to accompany the scientist, I got a "No thank you" and that was all.

I knew that Kier had been dealing with a lot since that day at the Institute. He had been accused of murder and released from jail almost immediately when his father had told the council it was a duel of retribution. It had been touch and go whether or not anyone would accept that when her part in helping the terrorists who had attacked the Institute came out as well. The High Council was in an uproar, for Atavarians, about the conspiracy and the attack, and they'd ordered Kier to appear before them to explain everything. I was sure that had to be stressful and I asked if I could help, but got no response. I sent him messages asking how he was, telling him I was worried. And finally, after what must've been the tenth one, he finally replied with "I am well, thank you."

His appearance before the High Council had been all over the holo network here and I'd watched with my heart in my throat as he calmly told them about his aunt's treachery, their duel and his murder of her in self-defense and as retribution for his mothers' murder. He'd been exonerated quickly after that and I wondered how much of that was both Gav'Ahn and Char'Vahn's influence weighing in Kier's favor.

A few days later, Kier once again appeared before the High Council to report on the new medicine for the Lavat virus. I hungrily looked for any hint of what he was feeling while talking about me. But there was nothing I could see. Just the same cool, distant expression that all Atavarians wore.

Between the silence and Kier's emotionless face, I was almost certain that I had misread everything between us. It seemed that all of it had been merely for the sake of our cover and his exploration of emotion and touch. I had been a safe space for him, and now that our need for our fake mating was done, he was cutting me out of his life.

But I couldn't quite bring myself to fully accept that.

Sometimes flashes of memory or emotion would hit me and I just couldn't believe that it wasn't as meaningful for him as it had been for me. Something else had to be going on, but he wouldn't tell me what it was.

"You could simply go see him," Char'Vahn said.

I jumped and looked up to see the old Atavarian studying me. We'd grown quite close in the last week and half, as we worked out any issues with producing the anti-viral, and analyzed the data from the first round of doses. It had been good, fulfilling work and I was so proud of what we'd accomplished. But it hadn't been enough to banish this empty feeling inside of me.

"I don't want to impose," I said, turning my attention back to the data set in front of me.

"You are his mate. Going to see him is not imposing."

"You don't know him like I do. He wants space for some reason and I...I think I need to give it to him."

Char'Vahn let out a long sigh.

"Sometimes," he said slowly, "space only gives us the opportunity to lie to ourselves. Do not wait too long and allow him to plant those lies too deeply."

An hour later, my wrist com beeped and I tapped it excitedly only to be disappointed when it was from the Intrepid. They'd arrived yesterday but no one had contacted me directly until now. I dismissed the message at first, thinking that it could wait. But then another message came up. A notification that my reservation for the shuttle to the orbital station was ready for tomorrow afternoon.

I tapped through to the previous message and everything around me stopped, my heart suddenly turning cold.

"Looking forward to having you back aboard. The shuttle Octavia will meet you tomorrow at the orbital station."

It was from Captain Drake specifically, and since I had not sent them a request to leave Atavar and return to the ship, I could only surmise that Kier had. He wanted me gone.

That was it. I couldn't stand around anymore waiting for him to talk to me. I had to look him in the eye and know for certain that I was either wrong or right.

"I need to go see Kier," I said to Char'Vahn.

"I just received the message that you would be returning to your ship tomorrow?" he asked.

"I-I don't know. Maybe."

"It is alright if you wish to do so. We have plenty of help and the interim lab facility at the Institute should be up and running next week. I know this was a temporary assignment for you."

I nodded, forcing back tears.

"I appreciate your understanding. I don't...I don't know what's going on, but yes, I may need to leave. I've loved every second working with you."

He nodded.

"As have I with you. I am recommending an honorary position in my department for you. As such, you will always have a place with me at the Institute, Chloe'Ahn."

That name almost made me burst into tears and I simply smiled at him in thanks as I rushed out of the room. The hospital had given us six different labs and break rooms to work with. They'd even given us both temporary housing on site, but there wasn't anything of mine that I needed to get. I had my satchel with me, and all I could think of was getting to the estate and finding out what the hell was going on.

I was able to get a transport shuttle to the town just outside of Kier's estate and from there I took a Sled to the house. It took almost two hours but I still didn't know what I was going to say when I saw him. When I knocked on the door, Gav'Ahn opened. He still looked a little too thin, but he had begun to gain weight and the data from his blood samples was extremely promising.

"Chloe," he said. "Kier told me you had returned to your ship."

"No, not until tomorrow. Is Kier around? I really need to speak with him."

"Of course, come in."

He stepped back and let me inside. The house smelled of food and I had an unpleasant memory of that last wedding ritual.

"I believe he is upstairs in his room, please feel free to go up."

"Thank you." I could hardly get the words out as nerves ricocheted inside of me.

My hands clenched around the strap of my satchel, and my heart felt like it was going to jump out of my chest as I climbed the stairs to his room. I tried to reach out through the bond, and almost cried with relief to finally find him there. He felt startled, afraid, relieved and tempted. But then he was simply gone.

He'd shut me out.

But a second later, Kier came rushing out of his room and down the hall toward me. His face was impassable, body covered as always but the outfit looked rumpled, as if he'd slept in it. His usually perfectly combed hair was disheveled, and dark circles surrounded his eyes. Whatever had been happening, Kier was not handling it well. I wondered briefly if it was the strain of his father being sick, but that only explained a few days. Gav'Ahn had rallied quickly with the anti-viral. Was it the High Council? Or was it missing me?

I wanted it to be that last one, and tried not to hope. Instinct told me that he would pull away from me if I hit him with a flood of words right off. So I defaulted to giving him a smile, and attempting to act like this hadn't hurt like hell.

"Hi, stranger." The levity I was attempting in my voice came out forced and hollow. "I've been worried about you. And I'm fine by the way, thanks to you and Char'Vahn, just in case you were wondering."

"What are you doing here?" his voice was rough but also distant, cold.

His brusque response was like a kick in the stomach. Painful, sudden, but also a very good wake up call. Suddenly, that anger and hurt that had been brewing for a week and half came to the fore and my cheeks flooded with heat.

"Saying good-bye apparently. I just got a message from the Intrepid. Captain Drake is under the impression that I'm leaving tomorrow. Know anything about that?"

"I had assumed since your work here was done that you would wish to return to your duties."

"And what about you?"

"My work here is merely beginning. I must ensure that the High Council changes their isolationist stance."

"And having your mate here wouldn't help that?"

"Our ruse has served its purpose," he said. A flicker of something like regret came through the bond but was gone too fast for me to examine. "It is not needed for the High Council to hear me."

"I see." The words choked me and I hated that tears stung my eyes. "And... and everything we shared, that was part of the 'ruse' as well?"

His jaw clenched and I felt something from him, a ghost of an impression. He was holding himself back because he didn't want me seeing what was going on inside of him. Would it contradict what he was saying and showing me? Would it only hurt me more and he was trying to spare me?

"Well?" I demanded. "What is going on? You're tender and open with me, you run into danger to save me and then after all of that, after everything we've been through you shut me out! I deserve— no, I *need* to know what has happened. You don't get to just decide that whatever this was is now over without having a conversation with me. I need to hear it from your mouth."

"What do you need to hear?" he whispered.

"If any of it meant anything to you at all!" I furiously scrubbed the tears from my cheeks. "And I know this will probably end our friendship but if this is it, if you're sending me away like this, then I've got nothing left to lose, so here goes. I have fallen in love with you. So every single thing we shared wasn't fake for me. I gave myself to you because I *love you*."

My voice broke on the last few words, my cheeks drenched in tears by now.

"So I'm asking you, do you love me?"

He stared at me in silence so long that I thought he wasn't going to answer, and that ripped me up inside far more than anything he could've told me. Or so I thought.

"No," he breathed it out as if it were dragged from him. "I...care for you as a friend and colleague, but I do not love you."

I gasped down a sob and turned away from him, desperate for a shred of dignity that I could leave with. It wasn't the first time I'd put myself out there only to be told my feelings weren't returned. But it was the first time it felt like I was dying inside from it.

"What about the bond?" I asked, my back still to him.

"With time and distance, it will fade."

"Time and distance," I was straining hard to hold back my crying. "That's what you want?"

Again he didn't answer at first, and when he did I almost didn't hear it, his voice was so low and harsh.

"Yes."

"Okay. Thank you for being honest, good-bye." The words tumbled out of me, ending on a broken sob before I bolted down the stairs.

I think Gav'Ahn might've tried to catch me, but I couldn't hear anything above the pounding of my heart in my ears.

Anger boiled in my blood as I marched to the shuttle that would take me back to the small town and then to the hospital. I understood needing to get a handle on things, on taking care of his father. But I didn't understand his cold indifference; it wasn't *him*. This wasn't even the Kier I met two years ago when he'd still been trying to be a good Atavarian.

I wanted to believe that he was lying to me, that he was simply pushing me away and there was something else going on. But what if that was just wishful thinking? What if it was only what I wanted to see?

Whatever the truth, Kier was not going to tell it to me. And I didn't have the heart to humiliate myself any further.

Maybe...maybe he is just telling me the truth. He doesn't love me.

My heart lurched and I swore it was being shredded with hot knives. This hurt a hell of a lot more than any other break up I'd ever gone through, but I knew that pain had been a risk. I knew and I'd jumped anyway, and now here I was.

I took several deep breaths as the shuttle prepared to leave the estate.

Insanely, part of me had hoped he'd stop me before it took off. I stared out the window, hung on every sound, praying it was him running toward me. That he'd rip the seat belts off me and swear to never hurt me again.

But he didn't. And I knew that was it. We were done.

"Time to go back to reality," I whispered to myself.

Chapter Twenty-Nine

KIER'AHN

"Do you love me?

Her words echoed in my mind all night, torturing me, and I did not try to escape it. I deserved this for hurting her, for lying to her. I had time to think it through over the last many days, and knew that forcing her to leave would ensure that she was never at risk for dying as she had been at the Institute. It was the only thing I could think to do in the midst of the blinding fear that hit me any time I thought of losing her again. I had to keep her safe, whatever the cost. Even if it that cost was both our hearts.

But as I went through the long night and morning with this encounter in a loop in my mind, I realized that maybe the cost was more than I had anticipated. I had been empty without her before, but now it was worse.

The look on her face, the pain in her voice hit my mind like punches. I had thought that protecting her would justify the awful thing I would have to do, and comfort me.

But it was the opposite.

Logic was failing me.

Emotion was tormenting me.

I wanted her with an anguish that bordered on insanity and I hated myself for lying to her.

"Do you love me?"

"Yes," I whispered, bent over in half, on my floor, "yes, I love you. I have only ever loved you."

My fingers curled in the carpet fibers and I ripped them from the floor as I cried. This had seemed logical, to sacrifice what I wanted to keep her safe. And perhaps I would have been able to weather this, if I had not allowed my cognitive barriers to weaken this past month.

But if I had not opened myself, I would not have known what it was to love her. And that is unthinkable.

I cried and screamed into the floor until I was hoarse, until my body cramped and large swaths of carpet had been ripped to shreds under my hands. Even then, all I felt was exhausted, and more desolate than before.

I fell asleep like that and woke to the household com trilling in my room. My eyes were dry and my body sore from the awkward position as I stood and tapped the button on the wall.

"Yes?" I asked.

"I need to speak with you," my father said. "Come to my study."

"I will be there shortly."

I took the time to change and shower quickly before descending the stairs in an attempt to hide what was happening to me. Perhaps if I tried to look as if all was well, one day it would be true.

Since his recovery, my father and I had been in an odd kind of space with one another. Not quite reconciled, but not the cold distance from before. I was unsure what to make of it, but didn't have the energy to analyze it. As it was, separating myself from Chloe had made me ill-tempered and unwilling to examine my feelings. Now that I had firmly ended things with her, I had no desire to feel anything at the moment.

My father sat at his desk, looking through his holo tablet and motioned for me to enter. I closed the door behind me and stood with my hands behind my back, waiting for him to speak.

"I saw Chloe yesterday. She did not stay?" he asked, looking up.

"No. She did not."

"I see," he stood and moved slowly around to the front of his desk. "You have ended things with her then?"

I pushed past the pain of the answer and nodded.

"I have."

He paused, thinking.

"Son, I have never known you to be a coward. It is most distressing."

It was a most unexpected response and it startled me out of my self-pity. I stared at him, not sure what I was hearing.

"Chloe almost died because of me, because of Atavarians. Our efforts have barely begun to put a patch on the problem. This will happen again. If she is away from Atavar, she is safe."

"And that is all you are concerned with, her safety? This has nothing to do with how the small amount of time she was dead affected you?"

I shifted uncomfortably and clenched my jaw, but I did not answer. What could I say? His pointed question told me that he somehow knew exactly how this had affected me, so what was the point in lying?

"You know," he said, slowly, "I once told your mother something similar. I told her that logically, it was foolish to put her life at risk. I even attempted to stop speaking to her for a few days, to break things off."

"What did she do?" I asked, unable to stop myself.

The tiniest of smiles turned the corners of his mouth for a moment before his expression once again became calm and stoic.

"She refused to let me simply pretend as if I did not know her. She marched over to my quarters and told me that she loved me. She said that bravery was logical as well, it forged new paths, which were not safe. We would do that, we would show future generations tolerance, bravery, love."

"Mother was very brave."

"No," he shook his head, "she was not the brave one here. Bravery requires fear to be overcome. That was me. I was afraid of losing her, of..." his voice broke, and when he finally recovered it, I saw the sheen of tears in his eyes. "Of losing my *priash*, the one who saw me and helped me see."

I started at his use of that word. I had thought that my Human weakness made me sentimental and that was why I had used that word with Chloe. But here was my father, a respected Atavarian, known for his logic and wisdom, using it to describe my mother.

"Christine was everything I was not," he continued. "So it was I who needed bravery. Your mother only ever needed love. It was her true north, her guiding principle, always. Just like your Chloe."

I could not speak; grief and longing choked me, made me incapable of rational thought. I could not show that to my father, so I looked away, let it all coalesce into a ball in my throat.

"Son," his harsh voice cut through, but still I did not look at him. "This fear of yours, it is my fault. I shut you out, closed off the memory of your mother because I was not brave. I did not want to lose you, as I lost her. So I allowed Prem to teach you. I thought that making you an Atavarian without fault would protect you. But all I did was make you loathe the part that came from your mother. I have regretted it for many years, but when I saw Chloe with you, I saw the balance you should have always had. She brought out the best in you. Human and Atavarian, as Christine brought out a balance in me. Do not shut yourself off out of fear as I did. Do not be like me. Be like your mother and choose love."

"I need bravery too. I am both of you, Father," I whispered. "Chloe did show me that. But I do not know *how* to balance these parts of myself. When I was with her, I could sense the possibility. But now, I am adrift. Logic does not provide the answers to this. And my emotions are frightening. I thought I was doing the correct thing but..."

"Logic cannot be applied to love, my son. Perhaps that is why we arrange marriage and seek to control that part so sternly through all our rituals. Love is necessary for survival, it is powerful. It is also frightening for all its wildness. No matter how many rules we make, we cannot control it. Perhaps we should not try."

I closed my eyes as I tried to let all of this simply *be* inside of me instead of attempting to put it behind a barrier. His words were permission to choose what was simultaneously illogical and what my soul cried out for. I swallowed convulsively, restraining the urge to run from the room and intercept Chloe's transport to the orbital station. There was one question only he could answer, and before I acted, I had to know what he would say.

"Did you ever regret it?" I asked. "After losing mother like that, did you regret your decision?"

"No. The loss was...profound. But I have never regretted one day I spent with Christine."

I turned to face him and saw the evidence of tears down his face, though he showed no other emotion.

"Then Father, I must request your help."

"I had hoped you might."

Chapter Thirty

CHLOE

I replayed the conversation with Kier over and over. I'd cried all night, until I couldn't any more. When I was unable to find a single food printer that knew how to make bourbon or chocolate, I fell into a restless sleep that I woke from only a few hours later. Making sure there were no lingering tasks for the lab was a nice distraction from the way my whole body ached, but it didn't last long.

Now, I was standing in the mixed species lounge of the orbital station, waiting for the shuttle from the Intrepid to dock and take me back to the star ship and away from Kier.

It was pure masochism, but I stared out at the planet anyway and wondered how I could have gotten it all so wrong. I stopped myself from reaching out to touch the bond between Kier and me, as I'd been doing all night. It had become habit very quickly to reach out to him like this, to get support or comfort, or just to talk. Now, I would watch it fade and eventually break. I didn't want a constant reminder of what I'd almost had, but the thought of it going away made me want to curl into a ball and cry.

I had been schooling my expression since I stepped into the lab that morning, and still was here in the lounge, because the last thing I needed was to scandalize

Atavarians. There weren't as many here as on the Atavarian-only side, but this was an Atavarian station so they were around. Everyone was a bit subdued and I wondered if I wasn't the only one who felt the need not to offend with any obvious displays of emotion.

My wrist com beeped with a message from the Intrepid, asking me if everything was alright. They'd been told that the shuttle couldn't dock.

I frowned and looked around until I found an Atavarian official.

"Excuse me, my shuttle isn't being given permission to dock."

"Shuttle name and designation?"

"Octavia, 3991-Int"

He tapped the information into his holo tablet.

"There was a notification that you were needed...hmmm."

"What?"

"This is highly irregular, but you are needed at the upper level lounge. Follow me."

"But that's the Atavarian-only side."

"I am aware. Follow me."

I sent the ship a quick message while I trotted after the Atavarian, who was walking fast enough that I had to run at the last minute to catch the lift with him. We zoomed up to the top deck and, once again, had to walk double time to keep up with him.

"Please wait here for the official," the Atavarian instructed and turned to walk away.

"Wait, who is it?"

He didn't turn back around or answer me. I looked at the Atavarians who were staring at me as I stood in the middle of the lounge, waiting for someone to show up and explain all of this. Some of them glared, others simply got up and walked out. But there were a few who shocked me by nodding, as if they were giving me acknowledgement of some kind.

I returned it and resisted rubbing my palms on my pants leg as I waited.

"Chloe," said a voice behind me.

I froze. Kier's voice hit me like a knife while simultaneously giving me hope I didn't want. I turned slowly, unsure if I wanted it to be him or not.

There he was, standing in the middle of the walkway on the edge of the main lounge, his clothes less rumpled this time. There was a desperate glint in his eyes, an almost nervous way about him, like if I didn't acknowledge him, he would die right there. Every Atavarian in the place was staring now, some whispered to one another but most just looked on in curious silence.

"What are you doing here?" I asked, a hoarse echo of his question from yesterday.

"I came to apologize," he said, "and to...to tell you the truth."

I could barely breathe. I wanted to believe that he was here to tell me what I'd needed to hear yesterday. But I was also still bleeding from the words he'd said, the way he'd shut me out for almost two weeks. I didn't know if I wanted to hear him out or scream at him, but I opted for the former and nodded.

"Go on then."

He glanced side to side and very carefully removed the gloves on his hands. Murmurs sounded around us at the action, and I wondered if he wasn't supposed to remove them at all, another stupid Atavarian rule imposed on him.

"I have lived my life believing that my Human side was an irredeemable weakness," he began, moving toward me. "I never felt accepted or comfortable in my own skin, until I met you. From the moment you became my friend, I felt at peace with myself, for the first time in my entire life. Every moment with you has shown me who I could be, who I wanted to be. I thought it was because we were friends, but when your mind touched mine, I finally knew why you affected me that way."

I blinked back tears only to have more fill my eyes. He was so close to me now, our bodies mere inches apart. He lifted his hand slowly to my face, his thumb gently brushing away a stray tear.

"You are the other half of my soul," he whispered. "Best friend, lover, soul mate. You are my *priash*."

The word I'd been scared to know the definition of was what broke me and a sob escaped my lips. I shook my head and tried to step back, but he held my hand in his.

"You told me you didn't love me," I started, "you told me—"

"I lied."

"Why? I was standing there, giving myself to you and—"

"I was afraid," his voice broke. "I felt you die, Chloe. My soul was ripped in half and I...I was terrified of feeling that again. I told myself it was logical to send you away, to keep you safe. That only one of us needed to risk their lives securing the help of the High Council, but really, I was just afraid of losing you."

"You hurt me so much," I whispered. "And just saying this...it doesn't make it go away."

"I know that. I can only say that I am still learning how to feel, how to process these emotions. I have not learned balance yet so that when I was faced with such an overwhelming sense of terror and loss, I reverted back to what I had known. Distance, control. But that is not who I want to be with you. That is not who I have to be anymore."

Without breaking eye contact, Kier knelt in front of me, and the Atavarians around us started to talk louder. There were gasps of shock, some marched away, while others stared, open mouthed. I had no idea why this was such a big deal, but Kier was obviously taking a bit of a risk here. It touched me to know that, melting the thin resistance I was trying to hold onto.

He held my hands in his, our palms touching, and gazed up at me. As I watched, his mask of cool, unsentimental control slipped and the love I'd longed to see stared up at me. Then, the tiniest brush of his mind against mine, asking permission to speak to me and I sobbed with relief to find him there.

"I will say this all out loud too if you want," he said, *"but for this moment, it is for us alone."*

I nodded, unable to stop the tears from falling. I was coming apart at the seams in the most wonderful way and I was starting to not give a damn if I made everyone in this room so uncomfortable that they fled.

"I beg your forgiveness for hurting you. If you will let me, I will spend the rest of my life loving you, soothing your hurts, protecting you and never leaving your side. I want a life with you, Chloe, a future that we can build together for however long that is. Five years or fifty, I will cherish every second with you. I cannot say that I will always be perfect with emotions, but I will try, all my days, to learn how to love you the way you need. Please, give me another chance, priash?"

Every word mended the cracks in my heart and when his mind opened to mine, I knew that this was real, that he would never run from me again. I saw the scarred landscape of his life, the broken parts becoming whole because of my love for him. It wasn't perfect, but it was beautiful because it was *him*. He'd never opened to me so fully before, and more than what he said, this proved to me that I could trust him, that this was real.

Some might say that I forgave him too easily, that it wasn't 'logical', but we both knew something now; love was not logical but it was worth it.

A loud sob flew out of my mouth as I nodded.

I couldn't speak, and my thoughts were all a mess of feelings, but that must've been enough for Kier because he gave me his beautiful grin just before I took his face in my hands and kissed him.

"I love you," he breathed, his arms wound around my torso. "My *priash*."

He kissed me deeper, long, scintillating strokes of his tongue that made my knees week.

"I love you too," I whispered.

"I will never let you go again. Never."

He was still kneeling, so when he pulled our bodies flush, his head landed square between my breasts. My arms went around him and I cried happy tears as we held onto one another, not caring one bit that we were causing a scandal. Most of the Atavarians were now fleeing the area, as if our public display was an infection of some kind.

"I think we broke your fellow Atavarians."

"I cannot bring myself to be concerned."

"Should we take this some place more private?"

"Why Chloe, are you trying to seduce me?"

He grinned up at me and I kissed him again.

"Damn right, I am."

Chapter Thirty-One

KIER'AHN

"Where are we going?" Chloe asked as I led her to the small side path by the house.

"It is special, you will see."

She gave me an indulgent grin and took my outstretched hand.

It had taken us a bit of time to leave the orbital station and get back to the estate. Between the scene we had caused with our emotional reunion, explaining what had happened to Captain Drake so he did not cause more trouble, and then formally introducing Chloe as my mate to the town, we did not arrive until sun down.

My father had wanted to greet Chloe and had prepared a meal to celebrate her return. It was a very kind gesture but I bristled at the block to getting Chloe alone. Now, the meal was done and my father announced that he would be departing for business in town that would last at least a week.

We both saw through the lie. He was simply giving us much needed time alone, for which we were grateful.

Now I was leading her along the secret path to the hill where the observatory had sat. She took in a sharp breath and gazed with wide eyes at the overarching trees, their blue-green leaves full of bioluminescent bugs that glowed magenta. The roses were very potent as we took our time walking, our fingers entwined.

"I did not think I would like holding hands so much," I said, gazing down, "but I find myself finally understanding the appeal."

"I like that you're not wearing your gloves."

"I do as well."

She stood in front of me with a wide smile that made my heart feel like it was stretching in the best kind of way. One of my hands came up to cup her cheek and I marveled at how the magenta light made her skin glow pink. She was otherworldly, so small and so bright.

"I love you" I whispered, half to myself.

The awe of this would surely never wear thin. I had found *love*, and it was not destructive. It did not require me to turn my back on my Atavarian side.

"I love you too," she brought my hand up and pressed soft kisses to my knuckles. "I missed you, so much."

"It was torture, being away from you."

"Hmmm...you do know that it's very tempting to require you to make it up to me, right?"

"*Priash*, I do believe that I would willingly spend my life making it up to you. Especially if it meant..."

I sent her an image of me on my knees, her legs over my shoulders as I ran my tongue through her folds, and sucked on her clit.

Chloe's cheeks flushed and her lips parted. I could see her nipples tighten beneath her shirt and I longed to draw them into my mouth.

"Maybe we should take a walk later and go back to the house?" she breathed.

"I know why you wish that, but as I said, I have a surprise for you."

"Is it a naked surprise?" she asked as I pulled her along.

"I suppose it could be."

"Well then, come on, I can look at fireflies any old night."

She pulled on my hand as she barreled ahead and I could not help a small smile. How had I lived without her brightness, her warmth for so many days? I now understood why some risked so much for those they loved. It was worth any price, any danger, to have Chloe in my life.

When we reached the base of the hill, Chloe stopped and stared up at the Blood Moon tree. The flowers were glowing faintly, nothing like they would in a few months, but it was still a sight to behold, it's long branches drooped down like a curtain under the twin full moons above us.

"It's beautiful," she sighed.

"It is where my mother's observatory once stood," I said as I led her up the hill. "I wanted to share it with you."

When we reached the top, Chloe gazed up at the stars above us with pure delight shining in her eyes.

"It's almost like our special place on the ship."

"But without the vibration of the engines under us."

"Oh, I think we can make our own vibrations," she said, wiggling her eyebrows.

I huffed out a laugh and led her over the tree. We parted the branches and stepped under the short dome they created before letting them close around us. Chloe knelt down and gasped, reaching up and brushing her fingers along the faintly glowing blossoms.

"It's like sitting among stars," she whispered.

I could not take my eyes off of her. Chloe glowed in shades of gold and red, the sparkling joy in her eyes even more breathtaking than anything I had seen before. Perhaps because I had done something to put it there. Perhaps it was this place. I reached out and ran the tips of my fingers across her cheek, to her chin and then down the slender column of her throat.

Touching her was like being able to breathe again after being underwater. I discovered that I was starved for the sensation as much as I hungered for her mind to touch mine.

When I reached the collar of her top, I wanted to strip the shirt from her body so I might continue to caress her unobstructed. But we were outside and I did not know if—

"Do it," she said to my mind. *"There's no one but us, in our little pocket of the galaxy. Make love to me among the stars, Kier."*

Now it was my turn to stare in awe.

"Are you certain?"

Chloe gave me a wicked little grin and drew her shirt slowly up her body and tossed it to the side. Only a thin, pink bra hid the rest of her torso from me and this she unhooked and dropped with her shirt. Her nipples pebbled with the cold but also because she was aroused, I could feel the heat begin to build inside of her.

I skated my hand up her side, taking my time to savor every inch until I came to her beautiful breasts. A perfect handful each, I cupped them as I feathered kisses from her throat, down to her collarbone and to the valley between her breasts.

Gold and pink ribbons danced around my thoughts, flirtatious and more free than ever before.

Chloe's cool fingers found one set of my horns and she ran her fingers up and down the short stub while her other hand tangled in my hair.

"I love it when you do that." I nipped around one of her pert peaks.

"It feels...naughty, I like it."

When I moved away from her nipple she whimpered. I knew she wanted me to suckle it, letting my teeth give her the edge of pain she so loved. But I wanted to savor this, and perhaps tease her as well.

"I do so love to make you beg."

"A touch of domination?"

"If that means I like you at my mercy, then yes."

I laid her back onto the soft grasses, her thighs parted to welcome me between them and I knelt, drinking her in with my eyes before pulling my shirt off. I needed her hands on me, her mouth, her body against mine. I still loathed touch from others, but with her I craved it like an addict. And I had been deprived of her for far too long.

Chloe reached for me at the same time I lunged over her. Our lips met with a crash of teeth and tongues. The fear we'd both experienced in nearly losing one another mixed into a heady concoction with the lust that drove me. It wasn't just that she had almost gone back to the Intrepid, she had died. I had nearly lost her forever twice within a few weeks.

Suddenly, I could not touch her enough, kiss her enough. I ground my pelvis against her, desperate for the sensation of being joined to her but our clothing was in the way.

I sat up and yanked her pants down as she fumbled with the fastenings on mine. The moment they were undone, I pushed them down as she reached for my aching phallus. My nodes were swollen and pulsing, so the moment she took the head of me into her hot mouth, two of them burst, sending pre-spend down her throat.

I curled my fingers through her golden tresses and held on tight, guiding her down my shaft as I'd seen her imagine before. She moaned and reached down to touch herself. This time I did not stop her; I wanted to watch, wanted to feel her clit caressed as I also felt her pleasuring my phallus.

My hips bucked a little and she moaned, sending vibrations through me.

"I love you...I love you, priash..."

"I love you too, so much. I missed this, missed you."

I imagined that it was my fingers touching her clit instead of hers, and to Chloe it was. My mouth tonguing her opening as hers flicked against the underside of my phallus. When Chloe erupted, a rush of wetness ran down her thighs and she cried out around me so beautifully that the rest of my nodes nearly went off.

"I need...I need to be inside of you...Chloe, please."

Her mouth slid off me, saliva and pre-spend dripping off her chin, even as her cum coated her thighs. I ran my thumb over her bottom lip roughly, only to have her dip her head and take my thumb beneath her teeth and bite.

A growl rolled up from my chest, my incisors starting to drop.

Her eyes shone and a sultry smile tilted her mouth up.

"I love it when you do that," she pressed me back until I was sitting on my bottom. "I love the way you growl, like you can't help it."

"With you I cannot. Maybe I was lost from the moment I met you."

She climbed on top of me and notched the head of my phallus to her opening. My hands kneaded into the soft flesh of her hips, her hands on my shoulders as she balanced, not descending, just holding us both in terrible, delicious suspense.

"Do you remember the end of the wedding rituals?" she asked, her voice breathy like she'd been running.

My mind could not quite understand the question at first, until she began to recite them in her mind and then I understood.

"Until the sun sets on our lives," she said, slowly lowering herself onto me. *"I freely give to you my bonded promise to stand by your side, to forgive your faults..."*

Her breath caught as she reached my knot and rolled her hips against me. I dove to her throat, licking and sucking the sensitive skin there as her tight, wet channel held me so perfectly. But being still was not what we needed.

Our bodies retreated and crashed into one another, and our minds spun higher, wound tighter together, hurtling toward the savage release we both coveted.

"...to trust you," I continued as we fell into a rhythm that only we knew, *"to give you of my mind, and of my body."*

Each undulated slap of our bodies against one another strengthened that bond into something everlasting, stronger than it had been. Our souls entwined with each shared breath, each thought. The slide of her breasts against my chest sent sparks of fire cascading over my skin that I knew were partly hers. There was no hesitation tonight. I did not fear losing myself this time. Instead, I yielded to her fire with abandon.

"I am yours," Chloe said, her fingernails dug into my skin.

"I am yours," I bit into her shoulder and drank of her just as my knot slipped into her opening.

And the coiled heat burst, consuming us both in an inferno that we did not want to escape. Chloe cried out my name as I spilled myself inside of her, branding her inside and out.

She pulled my head up and seared my mouth with hers, her legs wrapped around me tightly. She was sobbing and clinging to me, the crashing wave of her orgasm pummeling her, as it also did me. We clung to one another until it receded, and even then, my arms held her flush against me as her limbs did the same.

"I will never leave again," I said, kissing away her tears, "I swear it to you. I am yours."

Her mind was a flood of conflicting emotions. Relief, spent arousal, joy and the dregs of grief from our separation. I poured my own thoughts gradually into those spaces, shared my own memories of those days with her and the feelings that led to our reunion. Little by little, the commiseration soothed her, and she relaxed, though she did not let me go and I was glad of it.

I ran my fingers up and down the beautiful skin on her back and soon she did the same to me. I adored this calm exploration and let my hands wander in wide arcs to her hips and thighs, then back up to her shoulders. When my fingers ran over the now closed bite marks, a low purr of approval escaped my mouth.

"I like you wearing my bite," I said.

"I like it too," she nipped my collar bone, "makes me wish I could mark you."

"If you look at my back, I think you have."

She grinned at me.

"Good."

Our kisses became languid, and soon my knot receded. I shifted and brought her to the trunk of the tree where I leaned back and settled her on my lap. Our hands touched in lazy curves and spirals, each of us drinking the other in under the glow of the tree.

"Do you have the PPR at the house?" I asked.

She nodded against my chest.

"We'll have to think of something else for more regular use though. Maybe an herb I could take?"

"I will ask the healers at the concubine temple."

She looked up at me in surprise.

"They bite there?"

"Sometimes. They help young Atavarians to control their urges as much as they also assist those in a rut fever."

"Speaking of," she sat up a little, "when is your next one?"

I frowned as I thought of the answer.

"I do not know. I have not had regular ruts ever. I suppose we shall have to wait and see."

She bit her bottom lip and gazed up through her lashes.

"I'm looking forward to helping you through them."

A thrill shot through me, but if it was from her or myself, I could not tell.

"I am as well," I admitted, my incisors aching at the thought. "Perhaps I could have better memory of them with a bonded mate."

"Maybe we could try something with it. Something like…"

I received an image of her arms tied above her head, a blindfold covered her eyes as I rutted her.

My phallus stirred at the illicit nature of it and I growled.

"I believe something like that," I said, "may require practice in order to do correctly during a rut fever."

"Oh, really?" she arched an eyebrow.

"Oh, yes," I leaned her back until she was laying on the grass.

I seized her wrists and pinned them over her head.

"We will forgo the blindfold for the moment," I whispered into her ear, "but I quite like the idea of holding you down."

"Me too. Almost as much as your hand around my throat."

"Then I suppose," I started to trail kisses down her throat, "we will have to do much rutting," now to her chest, "in order to give you a proper balance of each."

"I guess we will…." Her breath caught as I captured her nipple in my mouth. "Kier…"

We did not leave the hill for many more hours.

Read the bonus epilogue, Sinful Honeymoon by subscribing to my website and receive access to the exclusive Gex-Corps reader hub! You'll find artwork, bonus short stories, and tons more content from the Infinite Unions series. Click here or copy and paste this into your browser: https://trishheinrich.com/secrets/sinful-mate-bonus-content-sign-up/ Or, if reading in print, go to trishheinrich.com for more information.

Now read on for a sneak peek at the next book, Corrupted Mate.

Epilogue

ALTHEA-THREE WEEKS AGO

I screamed as I sat up in my bed, drenched in sweat and tears. My heart was breaking in two all over again, the pain of my past never fading no matter how many times I dreamed of it.

"Computer, lights,"

"Affirmative."

The lights went up twenty-five percent and I tore out of my bed. I needed movement so I paced, my feet slapping against the bare floors of my quarters.

I had been unable to sleep since the K'Tavi attack on the colony, though I did everything I could to hide that fact from Captain Drake. He was already keeping an eye on me, looking for any signs that the PTSD was making me unfit for duty.

I was using my treatment tools, taking my medication and not drinking to try and sleep.

And still, I had the nightmares.

And still, I saw seven foot black and blue armored K'Tavi out of the corner of my eye when there weren't any.

The briefing from Zephyr Vaughn did not help matters.

I had worked hard to heal my mind and body in the seven years since the K'Tavi destroyed my planet and scattered what remained of my people through the universe. It had taken every bit of strength left in me to create a new life with Gex-Corps, to open myself up to build new relationships.

And now, the same threat that had ravaged my former life, was seeking to do the same to my new life.

I rubbed my fingers across my forehead and tried to banish the memories. Since Kier'Ahn had left for Atavar with Chloe, I had few that could keep up with me in a sparring match, so I'd been fighting against the training droids. I'd already broken two and Rex, the engineer who maintained the droids had been giving me the stink eye, as Humans called it.

The GUP is not Boethelia. They are starting to prepare. They aren't going to welcome the K'Tavi in with open arms.

I flinched, my stomach roiling as the old guilt tore through me. I just managed to make it to the bathroom before I vomited the meager dinner I'd managed to choke down.

When I was done, I rinsed my mouth and stared at myself in the mirror. Some of my sacred markings were beginning to fade; I would have to seek out one of the few sanctified markers that remained from my people to refresh them. But that was just a distraction from the thing that I was trying not to look at, namely the thin scars that marked my face and chest. The scars from debris that had flown at me when the House of Amouna was attacked.

Echoes of that day pierced my ears and I cringed.

"It is in the past, it is not now. I am safe...I am safe."

It was not enough.

"Aim for my heart."

I flinched and stumbled back.

I always heard *his* voice. Every dream, every hallucination. It was always *him.*

I used to think it was a punishment from Amouna, one I well deserved. My therapist had insisted that was not a healthy way to view my traumatic memories. But he did not know what it was like to be responsible for the death of your people and your home, for the destruction of the sacred city, and the secrets of the great Goddess.

While death was no longer the remedy I sought for my transgression, neither could I accept forgiveness. Not when my people were scattered throughout the galaxy, either free but completely dependent on the GUP, or enslaved to the K'Tavi. I may not have initiated the destruct sequencing, but I had welcomed in the one who had.

"Aim for my heart."

I had failed in that too and let the murderer of my people live to continue his devastation across the galaxy. Perhaps one day, I would have a chance to correct that mistake at least.

But today, I needed to get a hold of myself and there was one thing that always worked, always helped me find my center.

I dressed quickly and went to my small spot in the hydroponics lab. Most of the space was taken up with food for the ship and experiments. But the captain had arranged for a small area for me as part of my PTSD accommodations. The doors slid open and I was enveloped in the slightly humid, warm air. I closed my eyes and breathed in the pungent scent of earth and plants before shedding my jacket, putting on my apron and grabbing my tools.

The cool earth and the delicate plants soon captured my attention and the nightmares were far away. There was nothing but the simplicity of the task at hand, the repetitive nature that soothed me.

My Tears of Amouna were flourishing in the artificial Boethelian environment, along with several medicinal plants that had taken a long time to bloom again. I didn't know how long I stayed, there was no clock in here. I imagined I could've stayed quite a while longer if I hadn't received the com.

"Lieutenant-Commander Kavat report to the captain's ready room," said Commander Velheim.

"Copy that, on my way."

I cleaned my hands and brushed any residual dirt off my shirt before slipping back into my uniform jacket. While I would've preferred to remain in my lab, work would also help to distract me.

Since we'd arrived at jump station Alpha it had been in short supply. Captain Drake had given half the crew shore leave and there was next to nothing for me to do as security chief since the jump stations were heavily guarded. The engineering team was busy with finishing the repairs from our encounter with the K'Tavi, most of the senior crew were catching up on reports and other minutiae that I had taken care of days ago.

I arrived just as Commander Sonta and Zephyr Vaughn were rounding the corner toward me. While I appreciated the Intelligence branch and their need for secrecy, as the security officer, I did not like unknown quantities on my ship. And Zephyr, was an unknown quantity. She was hiding more than her mission, I could feel it, but I had no idea if it would affect the Intrepid and put us in danger. I tended to assume the worst, so I was prepared.

"Lieutenant-Commander Kavat," Zephyr said, her expression serious. "I was assured you would not cause any trouble at this meeting. I hope Captain Drake is correct."

I frowned at her and glanced up at Commander Sonta.

"I'm not sure what you mean."

"You will," she cryptically replied before stepping inside.

Tension crawled up my back and I found myself checking my peripherals for a threat.

"Sonta, what the hell is going on?"

"Antony didn't talk to you?" she asked, her eyes wide.

"No."

She pinched the bridge of her nose and swore. Obviously her friendship with Dr. Goodman was teaching her a wide vocabulary.

"Look," she said, "I was against bringing you in to this and so was Antony, but the decision was made far above our heads."

"Decision about what?" I asked through gritted teeth.

Sonta opened her mouth to tell me, when movement behind me caught her eye.

"Shit, I thought it was going to be a holo meeting."

My hand automatically went to the blaster on my hip, ready to draw. That tension turned into white hot adrenaline when I turned around. The bottom dropped out of my stomach as the air was filled with the stench of blood and ash. I could feel the heat of the flames around me, the sting of the debris in my wounds. I tasted blood and tears on my tongue.

But Boethelia was gone, that day was in my past. So why were *they* standing in front of me?

Three K'Tavi were walking straight toward me in an apex formation, with two behind and to the side of the lead figure. All three were dressed in black and gold battle breast plates and scaled kilts that hit their knees. The two in the back had their faces covered with menacing face plates that left their spiked green and blue crests exposed at the top of their heads. Over each shoulder peeked the blue and gold hilt of a Scyltine blade and phase pistols hung from the belts around their waists. Their massive hands were uncovered, obsidian claws shorn but still glinting in the bright light of the corridor. Around their forearms were golden plates with the royal crest etched into them and accented with bits of black jewels that caught the light. The one sign that was encouraging was that neither of them had covered the ends of their tails with the spiked armor that K'Tavi wore in battle, and their backs were clad only in the same loose, scaled armor of their kilts. If this had been an attack, there would've been a chitin-like plate of armor covering the soft scales of their back, much like the one they currently wore on their chest.

The K'Tavi in the front did not wear a face plate, however. While the rest of his armor was exactly like his guards, his spiked crest at the top of his head was golden, tipped in red and taller, a sign of his royal heritage. His face was covered in beautiful, iridescent black scales that I knew were as soft as butter to the touch. A jagged scar ran from the bridge of his noble, broad nose to his full lips and down to a square chin. His features were oddly humanoid for a species that shared much in common with Earth lizards. I knew that, behind those lips, was a long, forked tongue, and sharp incisors. A chill raced through me, a sense memory of what his mouth had felt like on my flesh.

His sinuous black and gold tail, which came to his knees, twitched from side to side, sensing the area around him, seeking danger. The edge of a jagged, ugly scar peeked up from the left side of his chest piece.

The place where I'd shot him the day my entire world had been decimated.

I have to be seeing things. He can't be here.

They stopped a few feet from me and someone was saying my name, but I could not stop staring at the K'Tavi male in front of me. He stared me down with cold, multifaceted golden eyes with narrowed vertical slits.

"Hello, Althea."

His voice was the same deep rumble, like distant thunder, resonant and rich.

I had not realized I'd drawn my weapon until the two K'Tavi behind him, drew their pistols.

"Lieutenant-Commander, stand down," Captain Drake ordered.

The heft of the blaster was comforting, the pummel digging into my palm as I gripped it tight, like a child with a blanket.

"Aim for my heart" he'd said.

"What heart?" I'd replied.

I wanted to run.

I wanted to shoot.

I wanted to scream.

I did none of these things.

Instead, I found that coal of burning hatred that I'd never fully extinguished, the one I'd told my therapist I'd been 'working on', and I breathed on it.

I remembered the fullness of who I was.

Sister of the Broklan Gate.

Mistress of the Cleave.

Boethelian.

I would not be pushed back by him again. I would not allow him to empty me of all the resilience I'd wrought.

I pushed forward all the hatred I had nurtured over the years, all the parts I'd kept for myself if I ever again had the chance to face one of his kind. And I let it radiate from my eyes. His head raised just a little and he glared down at me through a narrowed gaze.

He understood.

I was not the naive priestess I'd been before. The one who had believed his pretty lies, who had embraced him, loved him.

That girl was dead. Buried under the smoldering remnants of our temple.

I was new.

And he best remember it.

"Lieutenant-Commander," the captain continued, with more force, "Prince Zireth is as a guest of the Galactic Union. You will stand down."

I shoved my blaster into Sonta's hand.

"Aye, Captain." I almost didn't recognize my voice. "I understand."

I turned on my heel, and marched into the ready room.

Whatever brought him here, it wasn't peace, nor was it straightforward. I knew how he thought, the dark twists of his mind. And this time, I would be sure to protect my home, even if I was the only one.

The tension in the room was so thick, it pressed on my chest like a weight. Everyone could feel it. I saw it in every look my way, every fidget. The only ones who weren't showing it was myself and *him*.

He met my gaze, that gold fire I remembered so well searing me, and I turned away. He was a ghost, a thin reminder of the naive girl I'd been. If he thought to find me the same, he would be sorely disappointed.

Zephyr Vaughn stepped forward and activated a 3D interface on the table. A star navigation chart came up, showing a system I knew well. The one where Boethelia used to be and where the K'Tavi had conquered every single planet.

"Prince Zireth is here as a secret envoy," Agent Vaughn said, the light catching on her cybernetic eye. "His government, led by his uncle, King Rexian, is not aware of his presence in GUP space. This meeting is classified and sealed. Any disclosure of what we discuss here, including Prince Zireth's presence, is grounds for immediate imprisonment under GUP Espionage, codes seventeen through twenty."

Which means no trial, no means of appeal. Life imprisonment and all records of our existence wiped clean.

I clenched my teeth, forcing myself to remain outwardly controlled and unaffected. But inside I seethed. How could they do this? How could the GUP be so stupid as to allow any K'Tavi to be within their borders and see any of our territory? This was a ploy, a deep cover effort to find our weaknesses and exploit them. It's what they did.

It's what *he* does.

Agent Vaughn stepped aside and gestured for Zireth to step forward. He towered over the agent, but she didn't seem at all put off by the size difference. In fact, there was a hint of a smile around her mouth.

Did she arrange this? Was this somehow her doing? I had thought she was smart.

"I know that my people have been destroying your colonies," he began, "and I know that we have been threatening your borders. But that is not what all of us desire. My uncle has the throne of the K'Tavi, taken by force from my father when I was a boy. He has always been aggressive, and has coveted your space for a long time. He has recently decided on a course of action that would pit us against every planet in your Union. But that is not what I, and other K'Tavi, want."

"What do you want then?" Captain Drake asked.

"Peace. A planet to call home."

I gripped the arm rests tight enough to hurt. I remembered how persuasive he was, how pretty his lies were. As Zephyr and the captain glanced at each other, I could see that Zireth had lost none of his potency.

"And how are we to help you?" Agent Vaughn asked.

"My uncle holds the throne by a slim measure of power," Zireth continued. "Many of my people long for an end to constant war, and more join that side every day, but they are afraid. I have slowly been amassing power in quiet, but my uncle has one advantage. A planet killer, a weapon that could annihilate an entire world in minutes. No one is willing to settle on a planet, or defect openly into a rival faction with me while he holds it."

My eyes narrowed. This was all far too familiar.

"And you want us to help you get it?" Captain Drake concluded.

"Yes."

"How do we know you won't use it against the GUP?"

"You don't," he replied, "but you can either help me do this and diffuse the war brewing on your doorstep. Or turn me away and see if you can survive the onslaught of our forces."

"Our starship survived quite well against yours," the captain replied. "And we are already analyzing your tactics, your technologies. We could have guns at the ready that would easily puncture the hulls of your ships before your uncle reaches our borders."

I may not have had classified security clearance, but I knew we weren't doing any of that. The captain was bluffing to see how Zireth would react.

"You've done well against our scout ships," Zireth replied smoothly. "You haven't seen our new technologies, our new fighters or command ships. We could rip through your fleet like a child's toy, and take your core planets in weeks."

"You ask for help and then threaten us?" I said, my soft voice lethal.

"I am being honest with you," he waved his hand over the interface and stats came up, lists of ship, warriors. "And I'm giving you all you need to bring my uncle down and prevent a war. But it will mean nothing if he has that weapon."

"And if we help you," Zephyr interjected, "what do you want, besides your throne?"

"The right to build a home for my people on an uninhabited planet outside of GUP space and a promise to work toward inclusion in your Union of Planets."

"Tell me," I said, somehow managing to keep my voice steady, "this planet killer weapon. What's it called?"

His gaze finally swung back to me and I detected a mere hint of trepidation before he answered.

"Mariah Two."

I was not sure what he expected from me. That name still haunted my dreams as much as his face did. Mariah One had destroyed my world. It had been the beating heart of our greatest city, of our Goddesses strength and myth. And he had detonated it, burning Boethelia.

The air around me pressed tight to my body, and everything narrowed to the two of us in this stifling room. A toxic soup of memories thickened between us until I could barely breathe.

"So," I said after a moment, "you didn't keep it out of his hands after all."

His lips pressed together, and his back straightened.

"No, I didn't."

I nodded and stood up. My ears rang, and I was aware that something was wrong with me. I was too calm while my heart was pounding in my chest. The next thing I knew, I had lunged for him, drawn the Plethtach blade I knew he kept hidden in his kilt, and had it to his throat. His guards drew their swords and Captain Drake ordered the security personnel in the room to hold their fire.

"Stand down," Zireth said to his guards.

"I won't let you destroy this home like you did the last one," I said through gritted teeth. "I will stop you, and this time, I'll make sure my aim is true."

"I can't change the past," he whispered, "but I can save your new home, if you'll help me, Althea."

"Like you had me help you last time?"

"No. This will be different. This will end it, end him."

I pressed the blade tighter and saw a trickle of green on the blade. One of his guards hissed out something in his language and he responded. I vaguely remembered the words meaning something like "I've got this under control."

"Give me one reason why I shouldn't paint my skin with your blood right here," I demanded.

"Captain Drake, I strongly suggest you control your security officer before I do," Agent Vaughn said behind me.

"Holster your weapon, Agent."

"Captain—"

"I am in charge on my ship and I say stand down Agent Vaughn. Althea..." His tone changed, less hard but no less concerned, "I'm asking you to lower that weapon and step back."

"Not until he answers."

Zireth's golden gaze pinned me in place as he said, "A thousand labors can build a world, or destroy it. Which will you choose?"

I growled at him in fury and pressed the blade one more second onto his skin before stepping away.

He'd quoted the sacred text of Amouna's Passion to me, knowing that I would not be able to refuse him. I was still honor bound by my sacred oaths to aid those who invoked the labors of Amouna, even if Her temple and city no longer existed.

"You bastard," I hissed. "You unforgivable bastard."

He didn't speak or even bother to wipe away the blood that was trickling down his throat. Zireth just stared at me, waiting for my capitulation, knowing I had no choice.

"By my oath as priestess of Amouna, I vow to aid you in your time of need, I choose to build," the words tasted bitter on my tongue before I added, "but if you betray us, I will burn you and your entire species, just as you burned mine. This I swear on the name of Amouna."

I tossed the blade at his feet and stormed from the room, not bothering to see if I was about to be arrested or if the meeting was going to continue. None of that mattered. Even if they locked me up, I'd find a way to keep my eyes on Zireth.

"You are extremely lucky," fumed Agent Vaughn when the doors were closed and we were in the hallway. "If Prince Zireth hadn't made your involvement in the mission a condition of his cooperation, I'd be escorting you to the brig."

"He did what?" I asked.

"Ease off, Agent," Drake said as he came out of the room to join us.

He gave me a stern look that was far more like a worried big brother than my captain. It was strange sometimes to see this tall blue, horned male be concerned; it was almost sweet.

"Are you alright?" he asked.

"Yes, as much as I can be."

He nodded.

"You don't have to do this."

Agent Vaughn opened her mouth and he shot her a look that made her snap her lips shut.

"Oh, I'm doing it," I said. "He can't be trusted, not after..."

"I figured you must have known each other once," the captain said. "If you want to talk to your therapist before you go, I'll make the necessary delays."

"No, I want to get this over with."

"What a vote of confidence," Agent Vaughn said. "Look, I understand your animosity. Hell, I share some of it after what I've seen the K'Tavi do first hand. But this is our best chance to stop an intergalactic war that could kill billions."

"I thought that's what we'd sent Kier'Ahn and Chloe off to do," I snapped.

"Their mission is still vital for a number reasons, only one of which are the K'Tavi," Zephyr said. "They are ensuring that we have the allies we need in the event of a war. But this could stop a war before it even starts."

"I won't jeopardize keeping the peace," I said, "but I won't trust him either."

"You don't have to. You just have to be willing to work with him long enough to neutralize the weapon and his uncle."

"And then?"

Agent Vaughn's cybernetic eye whirred as her natural one hardened.

"He'll be on the throne, and hopefully our new ally."

I couldn't say what I was thinking. I already suspected that Agent Vaughn would probably have someone accompany us that had orders to kill me if I so much as twitched wrong around Zireth. But that wouldn't stop me from finishing what I started with that laser bolt to his chest.

"Do you understand that, Lieutenant-Commander?" Agent Vaughn asked me. "Is your mission, and its parameters, clear?"

"Crystal," I answered before turning on my heel and heading for my quarters. I had gear to pack.

COMING 2024: CORRUPTED MATE: AN ENEMIES TO LOVERS ALIEN ROMANCE. ORDER YOUR COPY HERE, OR COPY AND PASTE THIS INTO YOUR BROWSER: https://www.amazon.com/ dp/B0CJWZJN69 IF READING IN PRINT, GO TO TRISHHEINRI CH.COM FOR MORE INFORMATION

Acknowledgements

Though we are estranged, I would like to first thank my father for introducing me to Star Trek and giving me a love for all things space. I will never forget watching TOS with you, and will forever be grateful that you spent that time with me as a kid. It changed my life and helped me to dream.

For countless hours of hand holding, comforting, and finally telling me that I needed to just trust myself, thank you to my husband, Dan. You have always believed in me, encouraged me and saw in me the person I have always wanted to be. I love you.

For being my editor, best friend and general kick in the ass, Raechelle I could not have done this without you. You are my Suzy, the one who will always give it to me straight and I can never buy you enough whiskey to repay you for all the times you've made me face things I didn't want to but needed to. Thank you!

To my kids, who make me laugh, remind me to keep dreaming and that my best is always good enough, I love you both so much and hope that watching me follow my dreams gives you the courage to do the same.

To my other best friend and cover designer, Remy Flagg, thank you for putting up with my panicked last minute overhaul to the cover. And for always being there for me when I need someone to pull me out of my spiral or 'drink tea with'.

And to my readers, how can I ever say 'thank you' for coming on this journey with me? Knowing that you've read this and (hopefully) loved it as much as I do means the world (or galaxy) to me. Thank you for supporting me and being a fan.

Also By

Craving more books by me? You can find all of my books on Amazon and read free with your Kindle Unlimited subscription! Check out my backlist below!

Infinite Unions

Sinful Mate: A Friends to Lovers Alien Romance

Corrupted Mate: An Enemy to Lovers Alien Romance (Coming 2024)

Monsters & Artifacts

Feral: A Werewolf Monster Romance

Bound: An MMF Gargoyle Romance

Abandon: An Orc Monster Romance

Sinner: An Orc Bodyguard Romance (Coming 2024)

Monsters & Artifacts: The MacDonald Werewolf Clan

Broken: A Second Chance Monster Romance

Hunger: A Haters to Lovers Monster Romance (Coming 2024)

The Silver City Celestials

Devil's Temptation

Devil's Desire

Angel's Awakening

Angel's Agony

About the Author

Even as a little girl, Trish always believed that any story could be made better with some kissing...or a lot of kissing. Deciding to take the plunge into romance was like rediscovering a part of herself that she'd not seen in years. And once that genie was out of the bottle, Trish embraced it with a no holds barred kind of passion. Experimenting with angelic-human hybrids in her Silver City Series, diving head first into Monster Romance and soon to be going where many a smutty author has gone before, Sci Fi Romance, Trish has rarely met a trope she didn't like! Mixing her love of strong women, adventure, and all things geeky with an unapologetic excitement for the naughtier side of steamy romance, Trish is constantly pushing herself in her writing.

When she's not chained to her laptop creating the smutty worlds we all adore, she can be found curled up with a good book, playing a board game with her kids or binge watching Lucifer...Again.

Connect with Trish by signing up for her newsletter on her website (trishheinrich.com) or following her on Instagram @trishheinrich